15

"What a novel . . .
[Robinson] builds a cast of eclectic,
sometimes pathetic characters . . .
[His] plots are ingeniously created in true
police procedural fashion, narratives
expertly honed. All in all, the author is
not just a master storyteller,
he's a literary magician."
Montreal Gazette

"One bleak day last month,
I picked up Robinson's new Banks novel,
Playing with Fire . . . I've had five encounters with
Banks since and, well, I don't want to jinx it, but we've
become almost inseparable . . .
[Robinson] gives us in Banks a human being who is
prey, like most of us, to all the slings and arrows
of just being alive . . . Fascinating.
He's not just anyone; he is everyone."
Raleigh News & Observer

"Believable and affecting . . .
energetic and original . . .
Robinson expertly weaves a thread of
betrayal and fraud throughout."
Fort Lauderdale Sun-Sentinel

"It's good to see Peter Robinson's books . . .
beginning to get the critical attention they deserve.
Playing with Fire . . . has a loud ring of truth and
a good deal of suspense."
Chicago Tribune

Books by Peter Robinson

The Inspector Banks Novels

STRANGE AFFAIR
PLAYING WITH FIRE
CLOSE TO HOME
AFTERMATH
COLD IS THE GRAVE
IN A DRY SEASON
BLOOD AT THE ROOT
INNOCENT GRAVES
FINAL ACCOUNT
WEDNESDAY'S CHILD
PAST REASON HATED
THE HANGING VALLEY
A NECESSARY END
A DEDICATED MAN
GALLOWS VIEW

And Also

THE FIRST CUT

PLAYING
WITH
FIRE

PETER
ROBINSON

AVON BOOKS
An Imprint of HarperCollinsPublishers

This is a work of fiction. Names, characters, places, and incidents are products of the author's imagination or are used fictitiously and are not to be construed as real. Any resemblance to actual events, locales, organizations, or persons, living or dead, is entirely coincidental.

AVON BOOKS
An Imprint of HarperCollins*Publishers*
10 East 53rd Street
New York, New York 10022-5299

First Avon Books paperback printing: February 2005
First William Morrow hardcover printing: February 2004

Avon Trademark Reg. U.S. Pat. Off. and in Other Countries, Marca Registrada, Hecho en U.S.A.
HarperCollins® is a registered trademark of HarperCollins Publishers Inc.

Printed in the U.S.A.

10 9 8 7 6 5 4 3 2 1

For Sheila

PLAYING
WITH
FIRE

19th JULY

I was on my third sleeping pill and my second glass of whiskey when he knocked on my door. Why I bothered to answer it, I don't know. I had resigned myself to my fate and arranged matters so that I would leave the world as peacefully and comfortably as possible, and nobody would mourn my passing.

Beethoven's *Pastorale* symphony was playing on the stereo, mostly because I had once seen a film about a futuristic society in which a man goes to be put to sleep in a hospital, and there are projections of brooks, waterfalls and forests on the walls, and the *Pastorale* is playing. I can't say it was doing much for me, but it was nice to have something to go along with the incessant tapping of rain on my flimsy roof.

I suppose answering the door was an instinctive reaction, like a nervous tic. When the phone rings, you answer it. When someone knocks at your door—especially as it was such a rare occurrence in my isolated world—you go and see who it is. Anyway, I did.

And there he stood, immaculate as ever in his Hugo Boss suit, under a black umbrella, a bottle in his free hand. Though I hadn't seen him for twenty years, and the light was dim, I recognized him immediately.

"Can I come in?" he said, with that characteristic, sheepish smile of his. "It's raining fit to start the second flood out here."

I think I just stood aside dumbfounded as he folded his umbrella. I might have swayed a little. Of all the people I never expected to see again, if indeed I ever expected to see anyone, it was him.

He stooped and walked in, and I could see his eyes register everything immediately, the way they always did. It was another characteristic of his I remembered, that instant absorption and interpretation. The minute he saw you, his eyes were everywhere, even in your very soul, and within seconds he had you completely pegged. It used to scare the hell out of me, while it fascinated me at the same time.

Of course, I hadn't bothered hiding the whiskey and the pills—everything happened too quickly—but he didn't say anything. Not then. He propped his umbrella against the wall, where it dripped on the threadbare carpet, and sat down. I sat opposite him, but my brain was already fogging up, and I couldn't think of anything to say. It was a hot summer evening, and the heavy shower only served to increase the humidity in the air. I felt sweat prickling in my pores and nausea churning in my stomach. But he looked as cool and relaxed as ever. Not a bead of sweat on him.

"You look like hell," he said. "Fallen on hard times?"

"Something like that," I mumbled. He was going in and out of focus now, and the room was swirling, the floor undulating like a stormy ocean.

"Well, it's your lucky day," he went on. "I've got a little job for you, and it should be a profitable one. Low risk, high yield. I think you'll like it, but I can see you're in no shape to talk about it right now. It can wait awhile."

I think I nodded. Mistake. The room was spinning out of control, and I felt the contents of my stomach starting to heave up into my throat. I saw him lurching across the room to me. How he could even stand when the floor was tilting and throbbing so much, I had no idea. Then the waves of nausea and oblivion engulfed me at last, and I felt his strong grasp on my arm as I started to keel out of my chair.

He stayed for two days, and I spilled out my guts to him. He listened to it all patiently, without comment. In the meantime, he took care of my every need with the uncomplaining competence of a trained nurse. When I could eat, he fed me; when I was sick, he cleaned up after me; when I slept, I am sure he watched over me.

And then he told me what he wanted me to do.

Chapter 1

"*The* barge she sat in, like a burnish'd throne, burn'd on the water," Banks whispered. As he spoke, his breath formed plumes of mist in the chill January air.

Detective Inspector Annie Cabbot, standing beside him, must have heard, because she said, "You what? Come again."

"A quotation," said Banks. "From *Antony and Cleopatra*."

"You don't usually go around quoting Shakespeare like a copper in a book," Annie commented.

"Just something I remember from school. It seemed appropriate."

They were standing on a canal bank close to dawn watching two barges smolder. Not usually the sort of job for a detective chief inspector like Banks, especially so early on a Friday morning, but as soon as it had been safe enough for the firefighters to board the barges, they had done so and found one body on each. One of the firefighters had recently completed a course on fire investigation, and he had noticed possible evidence of accelerant use when he boarded the barge. He had called the local constable, who in turn had called Western Area Police Headquarters, Major Crimes, so here was Banks, quoting Shakespeare and waiting for the fire investigation officer to arrive.

"Were you in it, then?" Annie asked.

"In what?"

"Antony and Cleopatra."

"Good Lord, no. Third spear-carrier in *Julius Caesar* was the triumph of my school acting career. We did it for O-Level English, and I had to memorize the speech."

Banks held the lapels of his overcoat over his throat. Even with the Leeds United scarf his son Brian had bought him for his birthday, he still felt the chill. Annie sneezed, and Banks felt guilty for dragging her out in the early hours. The poor lass had been battling with a cold for the last few days. But his sergeant, Jim Hatchley, was even worse; he had been off sick with flu most of the week.

They had just arrived at the dead-end branch of the canal, which lay three miles south of Eastvale, linking the River Swain to the Leeds-Liverpool Canal, and hence to the whole network of waterways that crisscrossed the country. The canal ran through some beautiful countryside, and tonight the usually quiet rural area was floodlit and buzzing with activity, noisy with the shouts of firefighters and the crackle of personal radios. The smell of burned wood, plastic and rubber hung in the air and scratched at the back of Banks's throat when he breathed in. All around the lit-up area, the darkness of a pre-dawn winter night pressed in, starless and cold. The media had already arrived, mostly TV crews, because fires made for good visuals, even after they had gone out, but the firefighters and police officers kept them well at bay, and the scene was secure.

As far as Banks had been able to ascertain, the branch ran straight north for about a hundred yards before it ended in a tangle of shrubbery that eventually became dry land. Nobody at the scene remembered whether it had ever led anywhere or had simply been used as a mooring, or for easier access to the local limestone for which the region was famous. It was possible, someone suggested, that the branch had been started as a link to the center of Eastvale itself, then abandoned due to lack of funds or the steepness of the gradient.

"Christ, it's cold," moaned Annie, stamping from foot to foot. She was mostly obscured by an old army greatcoat she had thrown on over her jeans and polo-neck sweater. She was also wearing a matching maroon woolly hat, scarf and gloves, along with black knee-high leather boots. Her nose was red.

"You'd better go and talk to the firefighters," Banks said. "Get their stories while events are still fresh in their minds. You never know, maybe one of them will warm you up a bit."

"Cheeky bastard." Annie sneezed, blew her nose and wandered off, reaching in her deep pocket for her notebook. Banks watched her go and wondered again whether his suspicions were correct. It was nothing concrete, just a slight change in her manner and appearance, but he couldn't help feeling that she was seeing someone, and had been for the past while. Not that it was any of his business. Annie had broken off their relationship ages ago, but—he didn't like to admit this—he was feeling pangs of jealousy. Stupid, really, as he had been seeing DI Michelle Hart on and off since the previous summer. But he couldn't deny the feeling.

The young constable, who had been talking to the leading firefighter, walked over to Banks and introduced himself: PC Smythe, from the nearest village, Molesby.

"So you're the one responsible for waking me up at this ungodly hour in the morning," said Banks.

PC Smythe paled. "Well, sir, it seemed . . . I . . ."

"It's okay. You did the right thing. Can you fill me in?"

"There's not much to add, really, sir." Smythe looked tired and drawn, as well he might. He hardly seemed older than twelve, and this was probably his first major incident.

"Who called it in?" Banks asked.

"Bloke called Hurst. Andrew Hurst. Lives in the old lock-keeper's house about a mile away. He says he was just going to bed shortly after one o'clock, and he saw the fire from his bedroom window. He knew roughly where it was coming from, so he rode over to check it out."

"Rode?"

"Bicycle, sir."

"Okay. Go on."

"That's about it. When he saw the fire, he phoned it in on his mobile, and the fire brigade arrived. They had a bit of trouble gaining access, as you can see. They had to run long hoses."

Banks could see the fire engines parked about a hundred yards away, through the woods, where a narrow lane turned sharply right as it neared the canal. "Anyone get out alive?" he asked.

"We don't know, sir. If they did, they didn't hang around. We don't even know how many people live there, or what their names are. All we know is there are two casualties."

"Wonderful," said Banks. It wasn't anywhere near enough information. Arson was often used to cover up other crimes, to destroy evidence, or to hide the identity of a victim, and if that was the case here, Banks needed to know as much about the people who lived on the barges as possible. That would be difficult if they were all dead. "This lockkeeper, is he still around?"

"He's not actually a lockkeeper, sir," said PC Smythe. "We don't use them anymore. The boat crews operate the locks themselves. He just lived in the old lockkeeper's house. I took a brief statement and sent him home. Did I do wrong?"

"It's all right," Banks said. "We'll talk to him later." But it wasn't all right. PC Smythe was clearly too inexperienced to know that arsonists often delight in reporting their own fires and enjoy being involved in the fire fighting. Hurst would now have had plenty of time to get rid of any evidence if he had been involved. "Heard anything from Geoff Hamilton yet?" Banks asked.

"He's on his way, sir."

Banks had worked with Hamilton once before on a warehouse fire in Eastvale, which turned out to have been an insurance fraud. Though he hadn't warmed to the man's gruff, taciturn personality, he respected Hamilton's expertise and the quiet, painstaking way in which he worked. You didn't rush things with Geoff Hamilton; nor did you jump to conclusions. And if you had any sense, you never used the words "arson" or "malicious" around him. He had been browbeaten too many times in court.

Annie Cabbot joined Banks and Smythe. "The station received the call at one thirty-one A.M.," she said, "and the firefighters arrived here at one forty-four."

"That sounds about right."

"It's actually a very good rural response time," Annie said. "We're lucky the station wasn't staffed by retained men."

Many rural stations, Banks knew, used "retained" men, or trained part-timers, and that would have meant a longer wait—at least five minutes for them to respond to their personal alerters and get to the station. "We're lucky they weren't on strike tonight, too," he said, "or we'd probably still be waiting for the army to come and piss on the flames."

They watched the firefighters pack up their gear in silence as the darkness brightened to gray, and a morning mist appeared seemingly from nowhere, swirling on the murky water and shrouding the spindly trees. In spite of the smoke stinging his lungs, Banks felt an intense craving for a cigarette rush through his system. He thrust his hands deeper into his pockets. It had been nearly six months since he had smoked a cigarette, and he was damned if he was going to give in now.

As he fought off the desire, he caught a movement in the trees out of the corner of his eye. Someone was standing there, watching them. Banks whispered to Annie and Smythe, who walked along the bank in opposite directions to circle around and cut the interloper off. Banks edged back toward the trees. When he thought he was within decent range, he turned and ran toward the intruder. As he felt the cold, bare twigs whipping and scratching his face, he saw someone running about twenty yards ahead of him. Smythe and Annie were flanking the figure, crashing through the dark undergrowth, catching up quickly.

Smythe and Annie were by far the fittest of the three pursuers, and even though he'd stopped smoking, Banks soon felt out of breath. When he saw Smythe closing the gap and Annie nearing from the north, he slowed down and arrived panting in time to see the two wrestle a young man to the ground. In seconds he was handcuffed and pulled struggling to his feet.

They all stood still for a few moments to catch their breath, and Banks looked at the youth. He was in his early twenties, about Banks's height, five foot nine, wiry as a pipe-cleaner, with a shaved head and hollow cheeks. He was wearing jeans and a scuffed leather jacket over a black T-shirt. He struggled with PC Smythe but was no match for the burly constable.

"Right," said Banks. "Who the hell are you, and what are you doing here?"

The boy struggled. "Nothing. Let me go! I haven't done anything. Let me go!"

"Name!"

"Mark. Now let me go."

"You're not going anywhere until you give me a reasonable explanation why you were hiding in the woods watching the fire."

"I wasn't watching the fire. I was . . ."

"You were what?"

"Nothing. Let me go." He wriggled again, but Smythe kept a firm grasp.

"Shall I take him to the station, sir?" Smythe asked.

"Not yet. I want to talk to him first," said Banks. "Come on, let's go back to the canal."

The four of them made their way through the woods back

to the smoldering barges. Smythe kept a firm grasp on Mark, who was shivering now.

"See if you can scrounge up some tea or coffee, would you?" Banks said to Smythe. "One of the fire crew's bound to have a flask." Then he turned to Mark, who was staring at the ground shaking his head. Mark looked up. He had pale, acned skin, and the fear showed in his eyes, fear mixed with defiance. "Why won't you let me go?"

"Because I want to know what you're doing here."

"I'm not doing anything."

"Why don't I believe you?"

"I don't know. That's your problem."

Banks sighed and rubbed his hands together. As usual, he had forgotten his gloves. The firefighters were resting now, most of them in silence, sipping tea or coffee, smoking and contemplating the wreckage before them, perhaps offering a silent prayer of thanks that none of them had perished. The smell of damp ash was starting to predominate, and steam drifted from the ruined barges, mingling with the early-morning mist.

As soon as Geoff Hamilton arrived, Banks would accompany him in his investigation of the scene, just as he had done on that previous occasion. The fire service had no statutory powers to investigate the *cause* of a fire, so Hamilton was used to working closely with the police and their scene-of-crime officers. It was his job to produce a report for the coroner. There had been no one hurt in the warehouse fire, but this was different. Banks didn't relish the sight of burned bodies; he had seen enough of them before, enough to make fire one of the things he feared and respected more than anything. If he had to choose a floater over a fire victim, he'd probably choose the bloated misshapen bulk of the former rather than the charred and flaking remains of the latter. But it was a tough choice. Fire or water?

And there was another reason to feel miserable. It was now

early on Friday morning, and Banks could see his planned weekend with Michelle Hart quickly slipping away. If, indeed, the fire had been deliberately set, and if two people had been killed, then it would mean canceled leave and overtime all around. He'd have to ring Michelle. At least she would understand. She was used to the vagaries of the police life, being a DI with the Cambridgeshire Constabulary, still living and working in Peterborough despite the controversial outcome of the case she and Banks had worked on there the previous summer.

PC Smythe came back with a vacuum flask and four plastic cups. It was instant coffee, and weak at that, but at least it was still hot, and the steam that rose when Smythe poured it helped dispel some of the dawn's chill. Banks took a silver hip flask from his pocket—a birthday present from his father—and offered it around. Only he and Annie indulged. The flask was full of Laphroaig, and although Banks knew what a terrible waste of fine single malt it was to tip it into a plastic cup of watery Nescafé, the occasion seemed to demand it. As it happened, the wee nip improved the coffee enough to make the sacrifice worthwhile.

"Take the cuffs off him, would you?" Banks asked Smythe.

"But sir . . ."

"Just do it. He's not going anywhere, are you, Mark?"

Mark said nothing. After Smythe had removed the handcuffs, Mark rubbed his wrists and clasped both hands around the cup of coffee, as if its warmth were sustaining him.

"How old are you, Mark?" Banks asked.

"Twenty-one." Mark pulled a dented packet of Embassy Regal out of his pocket and lit one with a disposable lighter, sucking the smoke in deeply. Seeing him do that made Banks realize they would have to have the boy's hands and clothing checked for any signs of accelerant as soon as possible. Such traces didn't last forever.

"Now, look, Mark," said Banks, "what you have to realize

first of all is that you're the closest we have to a suspect for this fire. You were hanging about the scene like a textbook arsonist. You're going to have to give us some explanation of what you're doing here, and why you ran when we approached you. You can either do it here and now, without the handcuffs, or you can do it in a formal interview at Eastvale nick and spend the night in a cell. Your choice."

"At least a cell would be warm," Mark said. "I've nowhere else to go."

"Where do you live?"

Mark paused for a moment, tears in his eyes, then pointed a shaking hand toward the northernmost barge. "There," he said.

Banks looked at the smoking remains. "You lived on that barge?"

Mark nodded, then whispered something Banks couldn't catch.

"What?" Banks asked, remembering that the firefighters had found a body on that barge. "What is it? Do you know something?"

"Tina . . . Did she get off? I haven't seen her."

"Is that why you were hiding?"

"I was watching for Tina. That's what I was doing. Did they get her off?"

"Did Tina live with you on the barge?"

"Yes."

"Was there anyone else?"

Mark's eyes burned with shame. "Yes," he said. "That's where I was. A girl. In Eastvale. Tina and I had a row."

That wasn't what Banks had meant, but he absorbed the unsolicited information about Mark's infidelity. That would be a tough one to live with; you're screwing another woman and your wife, or girlfriend, burns to death in a fire. If, that is, Mark hadn't set it himself before he left. Banks knew that Tina's was probably one of the two bodies the firefighters had found, but he couldn't be certain, and he was damned if he was going to tell Mark that Tina was dead before finding out what he'd been doing when the fire broke out, and before verifying the identity of the bodies.

"I meant, was there anyone else living with you on the barge?"

"Just me and Tina."

"And you haven't see her?"

Mark shook his head and rubbed his nose with the back of his hand.

"How long had you lived there?"

"About three months."

"Where were you tonight, Mark?"

"I told you. I was with someone else."

"We'll need her name and address."

"Mandy. I don't know her last name. She lives in East-vale." He gave an address and Annie wrote it down.

"What time did you get there?"

"I got to the pub where she works—the George and Dragon, near the college—a bit before closing time. About quarter to eleven. Then we went back to her flat."

"How did you get to Eastvale? Do you have a car?"

"You must be joking. There's a late bus you can catch up on the road. It leaves at half past ten."

If Mark was telling the truth—and his alibi would have to be carefully checked with the bus driver and the girlfriend—then he couldn't possibly have started the fire. If it had been set before half past ten, there would have been nothing left of the barges by half past one, when Andrew Hurst reported the blaze. "When did you get back here?" Banks asked.

"I don't know. I don't have a watch."

Banks glanced at his wrist. He was telling the truth. "How late? Twelve? One? Two?"

"Later. I left Mandy's place at about three o'clock, by her alarm clock."

"How did you get back? Surely there are no buses running that late?"

"I walked."

"Why didn't you stay the night?"

"I got worried. About Tina. Afterward, you know, sometimes things start to go around in your mind, not always good things. I couldn't sleep. I felt bad. Guilty. I should never have left her."

"How long did it take you to get back here?"

"Maybe an hour or so. A bit less. I couldn't believe the scene. All those people. I hid in the woods and watched until you found me."

"That was a long time."

"I wasn't keeping track."

"Did you see anyone else in the woods?"

"Only the firemen."

"Mark, I know this is hard for you right now," Banks went on, "but do you know anything about the people on the other barge? We need all the information we can get."

"There's just the one bloke."

"What's his name?"

"Tom."

"Tom what?"

"Just Tom."

"How long has he been living there?"

"Dunno. He was there when me and Tina came."

"What does he do?"

"No idea. He doesn't go out much, keeps himself to himself."

"Do you know if he was home last night?"

"I don't know. It's likely, though. Like I said, he hardly ever went out."

"Seen any strangers hanging about?"

"No."

"Any threats made?"

"Only by British Waterways."

"Come again?"

Mark gave Banks a defiant look. "You must have worked out that we're not your typical middle-class folk." He gestured to the burned boats. "Those were clapped-out hulks, hadn't been anywhere in years, just sitting there, rotting away. Nobody knows who owns them, so we just moved in." Mark glanced at the barge again. Tears came to his eyes and he gave his head a little shake.

Banks allowed him a moment to collect himself before continuing. "Are you saying you're squatters?"

Mark wiped his eyes with the backs of his hands. "That's right. And British Waterways have been trying to get rid of us for weeks."

"Was Tom squatting, too?"

"Dunno. I suppose so."

"Was there any electricity on the boats?"

"That's a laugh."

"What did you do for heat and light?"

"Candles. And we had an old woodstove for heat. It was in pretty bad shape, but I managed to get it working."

"What about Tom?"

"Same, I suppose. They were both the same kind of barge, anyway, even if he had done his up a bit, slap of paint here and there."

Banks looked back at the burned-out barges. An accident with the stove was certainly one possible explanation of the fire. Or Tom might have been using a dangerous heating fuel—paraffin, diesel or Coleman fuel, for example. But all that was mere speculation until Geoff Hamilton and the pathologist had done their jobs. *Patience,* Banks told himself.

Were there any motives immediately apparent? Mark and Tina had had a row, and maybe he had lashed out and run off after starting the fire. Certainly possible, if his alibi was false. Banks turned to PC Smythe. "Constable, would you put the cuffs back on and take Mark here up to headquarters. Turn him over to the custody officer."

Mark jerked his eyes toward Banks, scared. "You can't do that."

"As a matter of fact, we can. For twenty-four hours, at least. You're still a suspect and you've got no fixed abode. Look at it this way," he added. "You'll be well treated, warm and well fed. And if everything you've told me is true, then you've nothing to be afraid of. Do you have a criminal record?"

"No."

"Never got caught, eh?" Banks turned to Smythe. "See that his hands and clothing are checked for any signs of accelerant. Just mention it to the custody officer. He'll know what to do."

"But you can't believe I did this!" Mark protested. "What about Tina? I love her. I would never hurt her."

"It's routine," said Banks. "For purposes of elimination. This way we find out you're innocent, so we don't have to waste our time and yours asking pointless questions." Or we find out you're guilty, Banks thought, which is another kettle of fish entirely.

"Come on, lad."

Mark hung his head and Smythe put the handcuffs on again, took his arm and led him to the patrol car. Banks sighed. It had already been a long night and he had a feeling it was going to be an even longer day as he saw Geoff Hamilton walking along the canal bank toward him.

Mist clung to the blackened ruins of the two barges as Banks, crime scene photographer Peter Darby, SOCO Terry Bradford, and FIO Geoff Hamilton climbed into their protective clothing, having been given the green light to inspect the scene by the station officer, who was officially in charge. Annie stood watching them, wrapped tightly in her greatcoat.

"This isn't too difficult or dangerous a scene," Hamilton said. "There's no ceiling left to fall on us, and we're not likely to sink or fall in. Watch how you go, though. The floor is wooden boards over a steel shell, and the wood may have burned through in places. It's not a closed space, so there should be no problem with air quality, but you'll still have to wear particle masks. There's nasty stuff in that ash. We'll be stirring some of it up, and you don't want it in your lungs." Banks thought about all the tobacco smoke he'd put in his lungs over the years and reached for the mask.

"Got a film in your camera?" Hamilton asked Peter Darby.

Darby managed a smile. "Thirty-five-mill color. Okay?"

"Fine. And remember, keep the video running and take photos from all angles. The bodies will probably be covered with debris, and I want photos taken before and after I remove it. Also, photograph all possible exits, and I want you to pay particular attention to any hot spots or possible sources when I tell you."

"Basically every square foot, at least twice, while videotaping the entire search."

"You've got it. Let's go."

Darby shouldered his equipment.

"And I don't want any of you under my feet," Hamilton grumbled. "There's already too many of us going over this scene."

Banks had heard the complaint before. The fire investigation officer wanted as few people as possible on the boats to lessen the chance of destroying evidence already in a fragile state, but he needed police and SOCO presence, someone to bag the evidence. Not to mention the photographer.

Banks adjusted his particle mask. Terry Bradford picked up his bulky accessory bag, and they entered the scene, starting with Tom's barge. Banks felt a surge of absolute fear as he stepped onto the charred wood. One thing he had never told anyone was that he was terrified of fire. Ever since one particular scene back when he was on the Met, he'd had recurring nightmares about being trapped on a high floor of a burning building. This time it wasn't so bad, he told himself, as there were no flames, only soggy debris, but even so, the mere thought of the flames licking up the walls and crackling as they burned everything in their way still frightened him.

"Go carefully," Hamilton said. "It's easy to destroy evidence at a fire scene because you can't see that it *is* evidence. Fortunately, most of the water the fire hoses sprayed has drained over the side, so you won't be ankle-deep in cold water."

All Banks knew, as he forced himself to be detached and concentrate on the job at hand, was that a fire scene was unique and presented a number of problems he simply didn't encounter at other crime scenes. Not only was fire itself incredibly destructive, but the act of putting out a fire was destructive, too. Before Banks and Hamilton could examine the barges, the firefighters had been there first and had probably trampled valuable evidence in their attempts to save lives. The damage might have been minimized this time because the firefighter who spotted possible signs of arson had some knowledge of fire-investigation techniques, and he knew they had to preserve the scene as best they could.

But of everything, Banks thought, it was probably the sheer level of destruction caused by fire that was the most disturbing and problematic. Fire totally destroys many things and renders others unrecognizable. Banks remembered from the warehouse fire how burned and twisted objects, which looked like nothing he had ever seen before—like those old contests where you're supposed to identify an everyday object photographed from an unusual angle—had definite shape and identity to Hamilton, who could pick up a black shapeless object, like something from a Dalí painting, and identify it as an empty tin, a cigarette lighter or even a melted wineglass.

The barge was about thirty or thirty-five feet long. Most of the wooden roof and sides were burned away now, exposing the innards as a maze of blackened and distorted debris—sofas, shelving, bed, chest of drawers, ceiling—all charred by the flames and waterlogged from the firefighters' hoses. One part of the room looked as if it had been dominated by a bookcase, and Banks could see soggy volumes lying on the floor. He couldn't smell the place now, through his mask, but he'd smelled it from the canal side, and the acrid odor of burned plastic, rubber and cloth still stuck in his memory. As most of the windows had exploded, and the stairs and doors had burned away, it was impossible to tell if anyone had forced access.

Banks walked carefully behind Hamilton, who would stop every now and then to make a quick sketch or examine something, instructing Terry Bradford to pop it into one of his evidence bags. The three of them moved slowly through the ruins. Banks could hear the whir of the camcorder, which he held while Peter Darby took still photographs on Hamilton's instructions.

"This looks to be where it started," said Hamilton as soon as they got to the center of the living quarters.

Banks could see that the fire damage here was greater and the charring went deeper in certain areas than anywhere else they had seen yet, in places gathering in pools. They had to go slowly to make their way through all the debris littering the floor. Hamilton's voice was muffled by his mask, but Banks could make out the words clearly enough. "This is the main seat. You can see that the burning on the floor is more severe than that on the underside of this piece of roofing." He held up a piece of partially burned wood. "Fire moves upward, so the odds are that it started at the lowest point with the worst degree of burning. This is it." Hamilton took off his mask and instructed Banks to do the same. Banks did so.

"Smell anything?" Hamilton asked.

Amid the mingled odors of ash and rubber, Banks thought he could smell something familiar. "Turps," he said.

Hamilton took a small gadget from his accessory bag, bent and pointed a tube at the floor. "It's a hydrocarbon detector, technically known as a sniffer," he explained. "It should tell us whether accelerant has been used and . . ." He flicked a switch. "Indeed it has."

Hamilton instructed Terry Bradford to use his trowel and shovel two or three liters of debris into a doubled nylon bag and seal it tight. "For the gas chromatograph," he said, sending Bradford to other parts of the room to do the same thing. "It looks as if it's multi-seated," he explained. "If you look at the pattern of burning closely, you can see more than one fire occurred in this room, linked by those deeply charred narrow channels, or streamers, as they're called."

Banks knew that a multi-seated fire was an indication of arson, but he also knew he wouldn't get Hamilton to admit it yet. Peter Darby handed him the camcorder and clicked away with his Pentax. "Hasn't the water the firefighters used got rid of any traces of accelerant?" Darby asked.

"Contrary to what you might imagine," said Hamilton, "water cools and slows the process down. It actually preserves traces of accelerant. Believe me, if any was used, and the sniffer indicates that it was, then it'll be present in these bits of carpet and floorboards."

Terry Bradford bent to remove some debris and uncovered the mostly blackened human shape that lay twisted on its stomach on the floor. It was impossible to tell whether it was a man or a woman at first, but Banks assumed it was most likely the man known to Mark only as Tom. Though he looked quite short in stature, Banks knew that fires did strange and unpredictable things to the human body. A few tufts of reddish hair still clung to the cracked skull, and in some places the fire had burned away all the flesh, leaving the bone exposed. It was still possible to make out patches of a blue denim shirt on the victim's back, and he was clearly wearing jeans. Banks felt slightly sick behind his particle mask. "That's odd," said Hamilton, stooping to look at the body more closely.

"What?" said Banks.

"People usually fall on their backs when they're overcome by flames or smoke inhalation," Hamilton explained. "That's why you often see the knees and fists raised in the 'pugilistic' attitude. It's caused by the contraction of the muscles in the sudden heat of the blaze. Look, you can see the pooling where the accelerant trickled into the cracks of the floor around the body. Probably under it, too. The charring's much deeper around there and there's far more general destruction."

"Tell me something," said Banks. "Would he have had time to escape if he'd been conscious and alert when the fire started?"

"Hard to say," said Hamilton. "He's on his stomach, and his head is pointing toward the source of the fire. If he'd been trying to escape, he'd most likely have been running or crawling *away,* toward the exit."

"But *could* he have got out, if he'd seen it coming?"

"We know a part of the ceiling fell on him. Maybe that happened before he could escape. Maybe he was drugged, or drunk. Who knows? You'll not get me speculating on this. I'm afraid you'll have to wait till the postmortem and toxicology screens for answers to your questions."

"Any signs of a container or igniter?"

"There are plenty of possible containers," said Hamilton, "but not one with ACCELERANT written in capital letters on it. They'll all have to be tested. Odds are he used a match as an igniter, and sadly there won't be anything left of that by now."

"Deliberate, then?"

"I'm not committing myself yet, but I don't like the looks of it. It's hard to predict what happens with fires. Maybe he was drunk and spilled some accelerant on his clothes and set fire to himself and panicked. People do, you know. I've seen it before. And smoke inhalation can cause disorientation and confusion. Sometimes it looks as if people have run into the flames rather than away from them. Let's just call it *doubtful* origin for now, okay?"

Banks looked at the blackened figure. "If the doctor can tell us anything from what's left of him."

"You'd be surprised," said Hamilton. "Rarely is a body so badly damaged by fire that a good pathologist can't get something out of it. You'll be having Dr. Glendenning, I imagine?"

Banks nodded.

"One of the best." Hamilton instructed Terry Bradford to take more samples, then they moved toward the bow of the barge, to the point where it almost touched its neighbor's stern. They waited while Peter Darby changed the film in his camera and the cassette in his camcorder.

"Look at this," Hamilton said, pointing to a clearly discernible strip of deeply charred wood that started in the living quarters, near the main seat, and continued to the bow, then over to the stern and living quarters of the other boat. "Another streamer," he said. "A line of accelerant to spread a fire from one place to another. In this case, from one *barge* to another."

"So whoever did this wanted to burn *both* barges?"

"It looks like it." Hamilton frowned. "But it's not very much. Just one narrow streamer. It's like . . . I don't know . . . a flick of the wrist. Not enough. An afterthought."

"What are you getting at?"

"I don't know. But if someone had *really* wanted to make sure of destroying the second boat and anyone on it—and I'm not saying that's what happened—then he could have done a more thorough job."

"Maybe he didn't have time?" said Banks.

"Possible."

"Or he ran out of accelerant."

"Again, it's a possible explanation," said Hamilton. "Or maybe he simply wanted to confuse the issue. Either way, it cost another life."

The body on the second barge lay wrapped in a charred sleeping bag. Despite some blistering on her face, Banks could see that it was the body of a young girl. Her expression was peaceful enough, and if she had died of smoke inhalation, she would never have felt the fire scorching her cheeks and burning her sleeping bag. She had a metal stud just below her lower lip, and Banks imagined that would have heated up in the fire too, explaining the more deeply burned skin radiating in a circle around it. He hoped she hadn't felt that, either. One charred arm lay outside the sleeping bag beside what looked like the remains of a portable CD player.

"The body should be fairly well preserved inside the sleeping bag," Hamilton said. "They're usually made of flame-resistant material. And look at those blisters on the face."

"What do they mean?" Banks asked.

"Blistering is usually a sign that the victim was alive when the fire started." Making sure that Peter Darby had already videotaped and photographed the entire scene, Hamilton bent and picked up two objects from the floor beside her.

"What are they?" Banks asked.

"Can't say for certain," he said, "but I think one's a syringe and the other's a spoon." He handed them to Terry Bradford, who put them into evidence bags, taking a cork from his accessory bag first, and sticking it over the needle's point. "The fire's sure to have sterilized it," he said, "but you can't be too careful handling needles."

Hamilton bent and scraped something from the floor beside the sleeping bag and Bradford put it in another bag. "Looks like she was using a candle," Hamilton said. "Probably to heat up whatever it was she injected. If I wasn't so certain the fire started on the other barge, I'd say that it could have been a possible cause. I've seen it more than once, a junkie nodding off and a candle starting a fire. Or it could even have been used as a crude timing device."

"But that's not what happened here?"

"No. The seats of the fire are definitely next door. It'd be just too much of a coincidence if the two fires started simultaneously from separate causes. And this one caused so much less damage."

Banks felt a headache coming on. He glanced at the young girl's body again, nipped the bridge of his nose above the mask between his thumb and index finger until his eyes prickled with tears, then he looked away, into the fog, just in time to see Dr. Burns, the police surgeon, walking toward the barges with his black bag.

Chapter 2

*A*ndrew Hurst lived in a small, nondescript lockkeeper's cottage beside the canal, about a mile east of the dead-end branch where the fire had occurred. The house was high and narrow, built of red brick with a slate roof, and a satellite dish was attached high up, where the walls met the roof. It was still early in the morning, but Hurst was already up and about. In his early forties, tall and skinny, with thinning, dry brown hair, he was wearing jeans and a red zippered sweatshirt.

"Ah, I've been expecting you," he said when Banks and Annie showed their warrant cards, his pale gray eyes lingering on Annie for just a beat too long. "It'll be about that fire."

"That's right," said Banks. "Mind if we come in?"

"No, not at all. Your timing is immaculate. I've just finished my breakfast." He stood aside and let Banks and Annie pass. "First on the left. Let me take your coats."

They gave him their overcoats and walked into a room lined with wooden shelves. On the shelves were hundreds, perhaps thousands, of long-playing records, 45-rpm singles and EPs, all in neat rows. Banks exchanged a glance with Annie before they sat in the armchairs to which Hurst gestured.

"Impressive, aren't they?" Hurst said, smiling. "I've been collecting sixties vinyl since I was twelve years old. It's my great passion. Along with canals and their history, of course."

"Of course," said Banks, still overwhelmed by the immense collection. On any other occasion he would have been down on his hands and knees scanning the titles.

"And I'll bet I can lay my hands on any one I want. I know where they all are. Kathy Kirby, Matt Monro, Vince Hill, Helen Shapiro, Joe Brown, Vicki Carr. Try me. Go on, try me."

Christ, thought Banks, an anorak. Just what they needed. "Mr. Hurst," he said, "I'd be more than happy to test your system, and to explore your record collection, but do you think we could talk about the fire first? Two people died on those barges."

Hurst looked disappointed, like a child denied a new toy, and went on tentatively, not sure if he still held his audience. "They're not filed alphabetically, but by date of release, you see. That's my secret."

"Mr. Hurst," Annie echoed Banks. "Please. Later. We've got some important questions for you."

He looked at her, hurt and sulky, but seemed at last to grasp the situation. He ran his hand over his head. "Yes, I know. Pardon me for jabbering on. Must be the shock. I always jabber when I'm nervous. I'm really sorry about what happened. How did . . . ?"

"We don't know the cause of the fire yet," said Banks, "but we're definitely treating it as suspicious." *Doubtful* was Geoff Hamilton's word. He knew as well as Banks that the fire hadn't started on its own. "Do you know the area well?" he asked.

Hurst nodded. "I think of this as *my* stretch of the canal, as my responsibility."

"Including the dead-end branch?"

"Yes."

"What can you tell me about the people who lived on the barges?"

Hurst lifted up his black-rimmed glasses and rubbed his right eye. "Strictly speaking, they're not barges, you know."

"Oh?"

"No, they're narrow boats. Barges are wider and can't cruise on this canal."

"I see," said Banks. "But I'd still like to know what you can tell me about the squatters."

"Not much, really. The girl was nice enough. Pale, thin young thing, didn't look well at all, but she had a sweet smile and she always said hello. Quite pretty, too. When I saw her, of course. Which wasn't often."

That would be Tina, Banks thought, remembering the blistered body in the charred sleeping bag, the blackened arm into which she had injected her last fix. "And her boyfriend, Mark?"

"Is that his name? Always seemed a bit furtive to me. As if he'd been up to something, or was about to get up to something."

In Banks's experience, a lot of kids Mark's age and younger had that look about them. "What about the fellow on the other boat?" he asked.

"Ah, the artist."

Banks glanced at Annie, who raised her eyebrows. "How do you know he was an artist?"

"Shortly after he moved there, he installed a skylight and gave the exterior of his boat a lick of paint, and I thought maybe he'd actually rented or bought the boat and was intending to fix it up, so I paid him a courtesy visit."

"What happened?"

"I didn't get beyond the door. He clearly didn't appreciate my coming to see him. Not very courteous at all."

"But he told you he was an artist?"

"No, of course not. I said I didn't get past the door, but I could *see* past it, couldn't I?"

"So what did you see?"

"Well, artist's equipment, of course. Easel, tubes of paint, palettes, pencils, charcoal sticks, old rags, stacks of canvas and paper, a lot of books. The place was a bloody mess, quite frankly, and it stank to high heaven."

"What of?"

"I don't know. Turpentine. Paint. Glue. Maybe he was a glue-sniffer? Have you thought of that?"

"I hadn't until now, but thank you very much for the idea. How long had he been living there?"

"About six months. Since summer."

"Ever see him before that?"

"Once or twice. He used to wander up and down the towpath with a sketchbook."

A local, perhaps, Banks thought, which might make it easier to find out something about him. Banks's ex-wife Sandra used to work at the Eastvale Community Centre art gallery, and he still had a contact there. The idea of meeting up with Maria Phillips again had about as much appeal as a dinner date with Cilla Black, but she would probably be able to help. There wasn't much Maria didn't know about the local art scene, including the gossip. There was also Leslie Whitaker, who owned Eastvale's only antiquarian bookshop, and who was a minor art dealer.

"What else can you tell us about him?" he asked Hurst.

"Nothing. Hardly ever saw him after that. Must have been in his cabin painting away. Lost in his own world, that one. Or on drugs. But you'd expect that from an artist, wouldn't you? I don't know what kind of rubbish he painted. In my opinion, just about all modern—"

Banks noticed Annie roll her eyes and sniffle before turning the page in her notebook. "We know his first name was Tom," Banks said, "but do you know his surname?"

Hurst was clearly not pleased at being interrupted in his critical assessment of modern art. "No," he said.

"Do you happen to know who owns the boats?"

"No idea," said Hurst. "But someone should have fixed them up. They weren't completely beyond repair, you know. It's a crying shame, leaving them like that."

"So why didn't the owner do something?"

"Short of money, I should imagine."

"Then he could have sold them," said Banks. "There must be money in canal boats these days. They're very popular with the holiday crowd."

"Even so," said Hurst, "whoever bought them would have had to go to a great deal of extra expense to make them appeal to tourists. They were horse-drawn boats, you see, and there's not much call for them these days. He'd have had to install engines, central heating, electricity, running water. Costly business. Tourists might enjoy boating along the canals, but they like to do it in comfort."

"Let's get back to Tom, the artist," said Banks. "Did you ever see any of his work?"

"Like I said, it's all rubbish, isn't it, this modern art? Damien Hirst and all that crap. I mean, take that Turner Prize—"

"Even so," Annie interjected, "some people are willing to pay a fortune for rubbish. Did you actually *see* any of his paintings? It might help us find out who he was, if we can get some sense of the sort of thing he produced."

"Well, there's no accounting for taste, is there? But no, I didn't actually see any of them. The easel was empty when I paid my visit. Maybe he was some sort of eccentric. The tortured genius. Maybe he kept a fortune under his mattress and someone killed him for it?"

"What makes you think he was killed?" Banks asked.

"I don't. I was just tossing out ideas, that's all."

"The area looks pretty inaccessible to me," Banks said. "What would be the best approach?"

"From the towpath," Hurst said. "But the nearest bridge is east of here, so anyone who came that way would have had to pass the cottage."

"Did you see anyone that night? Anyone on the towpath heading toward the branch?"

"No, but I was watching television. I could easily have missed it if someone walked by."

"What would be the next-best approach?"

Hurst frowned for a moment as he thought. "Well," he said finally, "short of swimming across the canal, which no one in his right mind would want to do, especially at this time of year, I'd say from the lane through the woods directly to the west. There's a lay-by, if my memory serves me well. And it's only about a hundred yards from there to the boats, whereas it's nearly half a mile up to where the lane meets the B-road at the top."

The fire engines had parked where the lane turned sharply right to follow the canal, Banks remembered, and he and Annie had parked behind them. He hoped they hadn't obliterated any evidence that might still be there. He would ask DS Stefan Nowak and the SOCOs to examine that particular area thoroughly. "Ever see any strangers hanging around?" he asked.

"In summer, plenty, but it's generally quiet this time of year."

"What about around the branch? Any strangers there?"

"I live a mile away. I don't spy on them. I sometimes saw them when I cycled by on the towpath, that's all."

"But you saw the fire?"

"Could hardly miss it, could I?"

"How not?"

Hurst stood up. "Follow me." He looked at Annie and smiled. "I apologize for the mess in advance. It's one of the advantages of the bachelor life, not having to keep everything neat and tidy."

Annie blew her nose. Banks was hardly surprised to hear that Hurst was a bachelor. "Except your record collection," he said.

Hurst turned and looked at Banks as if he were mad. "But that's *different,* isn't it?"

Banks and Annie exchanged glances and followed him up

the narrow creaky stairs into a room on the left. He was right about the mess. Piles of clothes waiting to be washed, a tottering stack of books by the side of the unmade bed, many of them about the history of canals, but with a few cheap paperback blockbusters mixed in, Banks noticed, Tom Clancy, Frederick Forsyth, Ken Follett. The smell of unwashed socks and stale sweat permeated the air. Annie was lucky she was stuffed up with a cold, Banks thought.

But Hurst was right. From his bedroom window, you could see clearly along the canal side, west, in the direction of the dead-end branch. It was impossible to see very far now, because of the fog, but last night had been clear until early morning. Hurst wouldn't have been able to see the branch itself because of the trees, but Banks had no doubt at all that it would have been impossible for him to miss the flames as he went to draw the curtains at bedtime.

"What were you wearing?" Banks asked.

"Wearing?"

"Yes. Your clothes. When you cycled out to the fire."

"Oh, I see. Jeans, shirt and a thick woolly jumper. And an anorak."

"Are those the jeans you're wearing now?"

"No. I changed."

"Where are they?"

"My clothes?"

"Yes, Mr. Hurst. We'll need them for testing."

"But surely you can't think . . . ?"

"The clothes?"

"I had to wash them," said Hurst. "They smelled so bad, with the smoke and all."

Banks looked again at the pile of laundry waiting to be washed, then he looked back at Hurst. "You're telling me you've already washed the clothes you were wearing last night?"

"Well, yes . . . When I got home. I know it might seem a bit strange, but how was I to know you'd want them for testing?"

"What about your anorak?"

"That, too."

"You *washed* your anorak?"

Hurst swallowed. "The label said it was machine washable."

Banks sighed. Traces of accelerant might well survive the firefighters' hoses, but they used only cold water. He doubted that anything would survive washing powder and hot water. "We'll take them anyway," he said. "What about your shoes? I suppose you put them in the washing machine as well?"

"Don't be absurd."

"Let's be thankful for small mercies, then," Banks said as they set off downstairs. "What time do you usually go to bed?"

"Whenever I want. Another advantage of the bachelor life. Last night, I happened to be watching a rather good film."

"What was it?"

"Ah, the old police trick to see if I'm lying, is it? Well, I don't have an alibi, it's true. I was by myself all evening. All day, in fact. But I did watch *A Bridge Too Far* on Sky Cinema. War films are another passion of mine."

Hurst led them into the tiny kitchen, which smelled vaguely of sour milk. The anorak lay over the back of a chair, still a little damp, and the rest of his clothes were in the dryer. Hurst dug out a carrier bag and Banks bundled the lot inside, along with the shoes from a mat in the hallway.

"What time did the film finish?" he asked, as they returned to the living room.

"One o'clock. Or five past one, or something. They never seem to end quite on the hour, do they?"

"So when you looked out of your bedroom window around one o'clock—"

"It would have been perhaps one-fifteen by the time I'd locked up and done my ablutions."

Ablutions. Banks hadn't heard that word in years. "Okay," he went on. "At one-fifteen, when you looked out of your bedroom window, what did you see?"

"Why, flames, of course."

"And you knew where they were coming from?"

"Immediately. Those wooden boats are death traps. The wood above the water line's as dry as tinder."

"So you knew exactly what was happening?"

"Yes, of course."

"What did you do?"

"I got on my bike and rode down the towpath."

"How long did it take?"

"I don't know. I wasn't timing myself."

"Roughly? Five minutes? Ten minutes?"

"Well, I'm not that fast a cyclist. It's not as if I was going in for the Tour de France or something."

"Say ten minutes, then?"

"If you like."

"What did you do next?"

"I rang the fire brigade, of course."

"From where?"

He tapped his pocket. "My mobile. I always carry it with me. Just in case . . . well, the Waterways people like to know what's going on."

"Do you work for British Waterways?"

"Not technically. I mean, I'm not officially employed by them. I just try to be of use. If those narrow boats hadn't been in such sorry shape, and if they hadn't been moored in such an out-of-the-way place, I'm sure BW would have done something about them by now."

"What time did you make the call?"

"I don't remember."

"Would it surprise you to know that your call was logged at one thirty-one A.M.?"

"If you say so."

"I do. That's fifteen minutes after you first saw the flames and cycled to the boats."

Hurst blinked. "Yes."

"And what did you do after you rang them?"

"I waited for them to come."

"You didn't try to do anything in the meantime?"

"Like what?"

"See if there was anyone still on the boats."

"Do you think I'm insane? Even the firefighters couldn't risk boarding either of the boats until they'd sprayed water on them, and they were wearing protective clothing."

"And it was too late by then."

"What do you mean?"

"Everybody was dead."

"Yes . . . well, I tried to tell them how dangerous it was, living there. I suspect one of them must have had a dodgy heater of some sort, too, as well as the turpentine. I know it's been a mild winter, but still . . . It *is* January."

"Mr. Hurst," Annie asked, "what were you thinking when you saw the fire's glow above the tree line and got on your bike?"

Hurst looked at her, a puzzled expression on his face. "That I had to find out what was happening, of course."

"But you said you already *knew* at once what was happening."

"I had to be certain, though, didn't I? I couldn't just go off half-cocked."

"What else did you think might have been causing the orange glow?"

"I don't know. I wasn't thinking logically. I just knew that I had to get down there."

"Yet you didn't *do* anything when you did get down there."

"It was too late already. I told you. There was nothing I could do." Hurst sat forward, chin jutting aggressively. He looked at Banks. "Look, I don't know what she's getting at here, but I—"

"It's simple, really," said Banks. "DI Cabbot is puzzled why you decided to cycle a mile—slowly—down to the canal branch, when you already knew the boats were on fire and that the wood they were made of was so dry they'd go up in no time. I'm puzzled, too. And I'm also wondering why you didn't just do what any normal person would have done and call the bloody fire brigade straight away. From here."

"Now there's no need to get stroppy. I wasn't thinking clearly. Like I said, you don't when . . . when something like that . . . The shock. Maybe you're right. Looking back, maybe I should have phoned first. But . . ." He shook his head slowly.

"I was waiting for you to say you hurried down there to see if there was anything you could do," Banks said. "To see if you could help in any way."

Hurst just stared at him, lower jaw hanging, and adjusted his glasses.

"But you didn't say that," Banks went on. "You didn't even lie."

"What does that mean?"

"I don't know, Andrew. You tell me. All I can think of is that you wanted those narrow boats and the people who lived on them gone, that you didn't call the fire brigade the minute you knew they were on fire, and that as soon as you got home you put your clothes in the washing machine. Perhaps nobody can fault you for not jumping on board a burning boat, but the fifteen minutes it took you to cycle down the towpath and make the call could have made all the difference in the world. And I'm wondering if you were aware of that at the time, too." Banks looked at Annie, and they stood up, Banks grabbing the bag of clothes. "Don't get up," he said to Hurst. "We'll see ourselves out. And don't wander too far from home. We'll be wanting to talk to you again soon."

* * *

Banks wasn't the only one who saw his weekend fast slipping away. As Annie pulled up outside the Victorian terraced house on Blackmore Street, in south Eastvale, blew her raw nose and squinted at the numbers, she realized that the fire on the barges, or narrow boats, as Andrew Hurst had insisted they were called, was probably going to keep her well occupied for the next few days. She had been hoping that Phil Keane, the man she had been seeing for the past few months—when work and business allowed, which wasn't all that often— would be coming up from London for the weekend. Phil had inherited a cottage in Fortford from his grandparents, though he had grown up down south, and he liked to spend time there no matter what the season. If Phil didn't make it, Annie had planned to spend her free time getting over her cold.

Annie got out of the car and looked around. Most of the houses in the area were occupied by students at the College of Further Education. The area had been tarted up a lot since Annie had started working in Eastvale. What had once been a stretch of marshy wasteground between the last straggling rows of houses and the squat college buildings was now a park named after an obscure African revolutionary, complete with flower beds that rivaled Harrogate's in spring. A number of cafés and a couple of fancy restaurants had sprung up there over the past few years, too. Students weren't as poor as they used to be, Annie guessed, especially the foreign students. Many of the old houses had been renovated, and the flats and bed-sits were quite comfortable. Like the rest of Eastvale, the college had grown, and its board knew they had to work to attract new students.

This morning, though, in the clinging January fog, the area took on a creepy, surreal air, the tall houses looking like a Gothic effect in a horror film, rising out of the mist with their steeply pointed slate roofs and elaborate gables. Through the bare trees across the park Annie could see the lonely illuminated red sign of the Blue Moon Café and Bakery offering cheap breakfasts. For a moment, she considered going in and ordering fried eggs, mushrooms and beans on toast—skipping the sausage and bacon because she was a vegetarian—but she decided against it. She'd grab something more healthy later, back in the town center. Besides, she thought, looking up at the looming house, she had an alibi to check.

She walked up the steps and peered at the names on the intercom box. Mandy Patterson. That was the person she wanted. She pressed the bell. It seemed to take forever, but eventually a sleepy voice answered. "Yes? Who is it?"

Annie introduced herself.

"Police?" Mandy sounded alarmed. "Why? What is it? What do you want?"

Annie was used to that reaction from members of the public who either felt guilty about some driving or parking offense or didn't want to get involved. "I just want to talk to you, that's all," she said in as convincing a friendly voice as she could manage. "It's about Mark."

"First landing, flat three, on your left."

Annie heard the door release click and pushed it open. Inside, the place was far less gloomy than out. The thick-piled stair carpets looked new, the hallway was clean and well kept, the interior well lit. Better than the student digs of her days, Annie thought, even though those days had been only about fifteen years ago.

Annie climbed the steep stairs and knocked on the door to flat three. Fit as she was, she was glad Mandy didn't live all the way at the top. The damn cold was sapping her energy, making her feel dizzy when she exerted herself. She couldn't meditate, either. All she experienced when she sat in the lotus position and tried to concentrate on the breath coming and going as it passed the point between her eyebrows was either a stuffed-up nose or a thick, phlegmy sniffle.

The girl who opened the door looked as if she had just been woken up, which was probably the case. She rubbed her eyes and squinted at Annie. "So you're the police?" she said, looking at Annie's army greatcoat, long scarf and high boots.

"Afraid so."

Annie followed her into the room. Perhaps because Mandy had heard over the intercom that Annie was female, or perhaps because seminudity didn't concern her, she hadn't bothered putting anything on other than a long white T-shirt with a George and Dragon logo on the front. Annie thought it was too cold for such scanty clothing, but she could soon feel that the bed-sit was centrally heated. Another change from her own student days, when she had braved a dash from the piled blankets to the gas fire and hoped to hell her five pee from last night hadn't run out. She took off her overcoat and found that she was warm enough without it.

"You woke me up, you know," Mandy said over her shoulder.

"Sorry about that," Annie said. "Part of the job." The messed-up sheets on the mattress under the window testified to what Mandy said.

"Cup of tea? I'm having one myself. Can't think in the morning without a cup of tea."

"Fine," said Annie. "If you're brewing up anyway." Mandy had a posh accent, she noticed. What had she been doing with Mark, then? Slumming it? A bit of rough?

The kitchenette was separated from the rest of the bed-sit by a thin green curtain, which Mandy left open as she filled the electric kettle. Annie sat in one of the two small armchairs, which were arranged around an old fireplace filled by a vase full of dried purple-and-yellow flowers and peacock feathers. There was a poster of Van Gogh's *Sunflowers* on the wall, and the radio was playing quietly in the background. Annie recognized an old Pet Shop Boys number, "Always on My Mind." That had been a hit back during her own student days in Exeter. She had liked the Pet Shop Boys.

A vivid memory of Rick Stenson, her boyfriend at the time, came to her as the music played. A handsome, fair-haired media studies student, he had always put her down for her musical tastes, being into Joy Division, Elvis Costello, Dire Straits and Tracy Chapman. He thought he was a cut above the Pet Shop Boys, Enya and Fleetwood Mac fans. He even used to go on about the original Fleetwood Mac, when Peter Green played with them. What had she seen in him? Annie wondered now. He'd been nothing but a bloody arrogant snob, and he hadn't been an awful lot of good in bed, either, showing some slight flair for the obvious and no imagination whatsoever beyond. Ah, the mistakes of one's youth.

Mandy came in with the tea and sat in the other armchair, legs curled up, the hem of her T-shirt barely covering the tops of her slim, smooth thighs. Curly brown hair, messy from sleep, framed a heart-shaped face with thin lips, a small nose and loam-brown eyes. She had beautiful Brooke Shields eyebrows, Annie thought with envy, her own being definitely on the thin and skimpy side.

"What did you do last night?" Annie asked.

"Do? What do you mean? Why do you want to know?"

"Would you just let me ask the questions?" Annie didn't know why she was becoming testy with Mandy, but she was; she could feel the irritation building at the girl's voice, the thighs, the eyebrows. She took out a paper handkerchief and blew her nose. The room felt hot now; she could feel the sweat prickling under her arms. Or maybe it was a fever that came with her cold.

Mandy sulked and sipped some tea, then she said, "Okay. Ask away."

"Was Mark here with you?"

"Mark? Of course not. That's ridiculous. What's he supposed to have done? If he said—"

"You do *know* him, don't you?"

Mandy toyed with a strand of hair, straightening and curling. "If you mean Mark Siddons, yes, of course I know him. He comes by the pub sometimes when he's working on the building site."

"Which building site?"

"Over the park. They're putting up a new sports center for the college."

"And are you friendly with Mark?"

"Sort of."

Annie leaned forward. "Mandy, this could be important. Was Mark here with you last night?"

"What kind of girl do you think I am?"

"Oh, for crying out loud," Annie said, feeling her head spin with the fever and the irritation. "This is supposed to be a simple job. I ask you the questions and you give me honest answers. I'm not here to judge you. I don't care what kind of girl you are. I don't care if you just fancied a bit of rough and Mark—"

Mandy reddened. "It wasn't like that!"

"Then tell me what it *was* like."

"What's this all about? What has Mark done?"

Annie didn't want to give Mandy any reason for prevarication, and she knew that every piece of information altered the equation. "You answer my questions first," she said, "then I'll tell you why I'm asking them."

"That's not fair."

"It's the only deal you'll get. Take it or leave it."

Mandy glared at her, then settled down to playing with her curls again. She let the silence stretch before answering. "Mark came to the pub a few times, at lunchtime, like I said. It was the holiday period, so I was working extra shifts. I liked him. He wasn't a bit of rough." She gave Annie a harsh glance. "Maybe he seemed like that on the surface, but underneath, he's . . . well, he's a nice bloke, and you don't get to meet many of those."

So cynical so young, Annie thought, but Mandy had a point. Annie thought of Banks. He was a nice bloke, but she had split up with him. Maybe she should have hung on to him instead. He had another girlfriend now, she knew, even though he didn't like to talk about her. Annie was surprised at the flash of jealousy she felt whenever she knew he was going away for the weekend. Was she younger than Annie? Prettier? Better in bed? Or just less difficult? Well, she had her reasons for doing what she did, she told herself, so let it be.

"He'd flirt a bit and we'd chat," Mandy went on. "You know what it's like."

"What about last night?"

"He came to the pub late. He seemed a bit upset."

"Why?"

"He didn't say. He just seemed depressed, like he had a lot on his mind."

"What time was this?"

"About a quarter to eleven. Nearly closing time. He only had the one pint."

"Then what?"

"I invited him back here for a coffee."

"So he *was* here?"

"Yes."

"Why did you lie to me?"

"Because I didn't want you to think I was a tramp or a slag or anything. It wasn't like that at all. I only asked him up for a coffee because I felt sorry for him."

"What happened?" Annie asked.

"We talked, mostly."

"Mostly?"

Mandy looked down, examining her thumbnail. "Well, you know . . . One thing led to another. Look, I don't have to spell it out, do I?"

"What did you talk about?"

"Life."

"That's a big subject. Can you narrow it down a bit for me?"

"You know, relationships, hopes for the future, that sort of thing. We'd never really talked like that before." She frowned. "Nothing's happened to him, has it? Please tell me he's all right."

"He's fine," said Annie. "Did he tell you about Tina?"

"Tina? Who's that?"

"Never mind," said Annie. "What did he talk about?"

"Does he have a girlfriend? He never told me. The two-timing bastard."

"Mandy, can you remember what he talked about?"

It took Mandy a few moments to control her anger and answer. "The boat. Living on the boat. How he was only working on a building site, but he wanted to get into masonry and church-restoration work. He told me he had a sister on drugs, and he wanted to help her. That sort of thing. Like I said, relationships, dreams. Wait a minute! Was that Tina? His sister?"

"I don't know," said Annie. "Did he say anything about someone called Tom?"

"Tom? No. Who's that?"

"A neighbor. An artist who lived on the boat next to Mark's."

Mandy shook her head. Her curls bounced. "No," she said. "He never mentioned any Tom. Apart from saying how he liked it there, and how peaceful it was, he just complained about some interfering old anorak who kept trying to get him to move."

That would be Andrew Hurst, Annie thought, smiling to herself at the description. "What time did he leave here?"

"I don't know. Late. I was half asleep. I hardly noticed him go."

"How late?" Annie persisted. "One o'clock? Two o'clock?"

"Oh, no. Later than that. I mean we really *did* talk for hours, until two at least. It was only *after* that . . ."

"What?"

"You know. Anyway, he seemed edgy later, said he couldn't sleep. I told him to go because I needed my sleep for work."

"So it was after two?"

"Yes. Maybe around three."

"Okay," said Annie, standing to leave.

"Your turn now," said Mandy, at the door.

"What?"

"You were going to tell me why you're asking these questions."

"Oh," said Annie. "That. You can read all about it in the papers," she said, and headed down the stairs. Then she added over her shoulder, "Or if you can't wait, just turn up your radio."

It was late morning by the time Banks had put in motion the complex machinery of a murder investigation. There was a team to set up, actions to be assigned, and they would need a mobile unit parked down by the canal. Banks had already arranged for a dozen constables to search the immediate area around the narrow boats, including the handiest point of access and the woods where Mark had been hiding. If they found anything, they would tape it off for the SOCOs. Unfortunately, the closest house to the boats was Andrew Hurst's, and the village of Molesby lay half a mile south of that, across the canal, in a hollow, so he didn't expect much from house-to-house inquiries in the village. They still had to be carried out, though. Someone might have seen or heard something.

Banks went to his office. His left cheek still stung from where the twigs had cut him as he'd chased Mark through the woods, and his clothes and hair all smelled of damp ash. His chest felt tight, as if he'd smoked a whole packet of cigarettes. There was nothing he wanted more than to go home, take a long shower and have a nap before getting back to work, but he couldn't. The pressure was on now.

Geoff Hamilton was still at the fire scene and had already put a rush on forensics to find out what accelerant had been used. The gas chromatograph ought to provide speedy results. Dr. Glendenning, the Home Office pathologist, would conduct the postmortems later that afternoon, starting with Tom, the artist, as it was his boat where the fire had started.

Banks knew he was being premature in treating the incident as a double murder before Geoff Hamilton or Dr. Glendenning gave him the supporting evidence necessary for such a decision, but he had seen enough on the boats. It was important to act quickly. The first twenty-four hours after a major crime are of vital significance, and trails quickly go cold after that. He would take the heat from Assistant Chief Constable McLaughlin later, if he turned out to be wrong and to have wasted valuable budget funds, but Area Commander Kathleen Finlay and Detective Superintendent Gristhorpe had agreed with him on the necessity of an early start, so things were in motion. Banks was senior investigating officer and Annie his deputy.

There was one more thing that Banks had to do before he could even think of lunch. He rang down to the custody officer and asked him to send up Mark—whose full name, it turned out, was Mark David Siddons—to his office, not to an interview room. Mark's hands had checked out negative for accelerants. His clothes were at the lab waiting in line for the gas chromatograph, and would take a bit longer. He wasn't out of the running yet, not by a long chalk.

While he waited, Banks found a chamber music concert on Radio 3. He didn't recognize the piece that was playing, but it sounded appropriately soothing in the background. He didn't imagine that Mark would be a fan of classical music, but that didn't matter. Mark wouldn't be listening to the music. Banks remembered an article he'd read recently about playing classical music in underground stations to discourage mobs of youths from gathering and attacking people. Apparently it drove the yobs away. Maybe they should blare Bach and Mozart out of city center loudspeakers, especially around closing time.

Banks glanced at his *Dalesman* calendar. January's picture was of a snow-covered hillside in Swaledale dotted with black-faced sheep.

Finally, a constable knocked on the door and Mark walked over the threshold.

"Sit down," Banks said.

Mark looked around the room apprehensively and perched at the edge of a chair. "What's going on?" he asked. "You know something, don't you? It's about Tina."

"I'm sorry, Mark," Banks said.

The loud wail that rang out of Mark's small body took Banks by surprise. As did the violence with which he picked up his chair and threw it at the door, then stood there, chest heaving, racked with sobs.

The door opened, and the constable poked his head around it. Banks gestured for him to leave. For a long time, Mark just stood there, his back to Banks, head down, fists clenched, body heaving. Banks let him be. The music played softly in the background, and now Banks thought he recognized the adagio of one of Beethoven's late string quartets. Finally, Mark wiped his arms across his face, picked up the chair and sat down again, staring at his knees. "I'm sorry," he mumbled.

"It's all right," said Banks.

"It's just . . . I suppose I knew. All along I knew, soon as I saw it, she couldn't have got away."

"It didn't look as if she suffered, if that's any help."

Mark ran the back of his hand under his running nose. Banks passed him the box of tissues that had been languishing on his desk since his December cold had cleared up.

"Well, at least she won't suffer anymore," Mark said, sniffling. He looked up at Banks. "Are you sure she didn't? I've heard terrible things about fires."

"The way it looked," said Banks, "is that she probably died in her sleep of smoke inhalation before she even knew there was a fire." He hoped he was right. "Look, Mark, we've still got a long way to go. If there's anything else you can tell me, do it now."

Mark shot him a glance. "There's nothing else," he said. "I was telling you the truth about where I was. I only wish to God I hadn't been."

"So you were gone from ten-thirty to four in the morning?"

"About that, yes. Look, surely the tests—"

"I need to hear it from you." Banks felt sorry for the kid, but procedures had to be followed. "We're looking at murder here," he said, "two murders, and I need a lot more information from you."

"Someone *murdered* Tina? Why would anyone want to do that?" Mark's eyes filled with tears again.

"She probably wasn't the intended victim, but it amounts to the same thing, yes."

"Tom?"

"It looks that way. But there's something else, another criminal matter."

Mark wiped his eyes. "What?"

"Are you a user, Mark?"

"What?"

"A drug addict, a junkie."

"I know what it means."

"Are you?"

"No."

"Was Tina?"

"Tina was . . ."

"What?"

"Nothing."

"Look, Mark, we found a syringe beside her, on the boat.

I'm not looking to bust you for anything, but you've got to tell me. It could be important."

Mark looked down at his shoes.

"Mark," Banks repeated.

Finally, Mark gave a long sigh and said, "She wasn't an addict. She could take it or leave it."

"But mostly she took it?"

"Yes."

"What?"

"Whatever. Heroin, if it was around. Morphine. Methadone. Demerol. Valium. Downers. Anything to make her oblivious. Not uppers. She said those only made her too alert, and alertness made her paranoid. And she stayed away from pot, acid and E. They made her see things she didn't want to see. You have to understand. She was just so helpless. She couldn't take care of herself. I should have stayed with her. She was so scared."

"What was she scared of?"

"Everything. Life. The dark. Men. She's had a hard life, has Tina. That's why she . . . it was her escape."

"Did Tina have any drugs when you left?"

"She had some heroin. She was just fixing up." Mark started to cry again. Banks noticed his hands had curled into tight fists as he talked. He had tattoos on his fingers. They didn't read LOVE and HATE like Robert Mitchum's in *The Night of the Hunter*, but TINA on the left and MARK on the right.

"Where did she get the heroin?"

"Dealer in Eastvale."

"His name, Mark?"

Mark hesitated. Banks could tell he was troubled by the idea of informing on someone, even a drug dealer, and the inner struggle was plain in his features. Finally, his feelings for Tina won out. "Danny," he said. "Danny Corcoran."

Banks knew of Danny "Boy" Corcoran. He was strictly a small-time street dealer, and the drugs squad had been watching him for weeks, hoping he might lead them to a large supplier. He hadn't done yet.

"How did you know about Danny Corcoran?"

"A contact in Leeds, someone from the squat where we used to live."

"How long had Tina been using?"

"Since before I met her."

"When was that?"

"About six months ago."

"How did you meet?"

"At the squat in Leeds."

"How did you end up on the boat?"

"We didn't like the squat. There were some really ugly characters living there, and one of the bastards kept putting his hands on her. We got into a fight. And the place was always dirty. Nobody bothered cleaning up after themselves. Think what you like of Tina and me, but we're decent people, and we don't like living in filth. Anyway, the boat needed a lot of work, but we made it nice."

"How did you find the boat?"

"I knew about it. I'd seen them before. I used to go for walks on the towpath and sometimes I'd stop and wonder what it would be like, living on the water like that."

"When was that?"

"A year or so back."

"So you're from around here? From Eastvale?"

Mark gave a quick shake of his head. Banks didn't pursue the matter. "Carry on," he said.

"We just wanted to be together, by ourselves, without anyone to rip us off or fuck up our lives. I was trying to get Tina off drugs. I loved her. I don't care if you believe me or not. I did. I looked out for her. She needed me, and I let her down."

"What about her parents? We'll need to contact them. Someone will have to identify the body."

Mark glanced sharply at Banks. "I'll do it," he said.

"It needs to be a relative. Next of kin."

"I said I'll do it." Mark folded his arms.

"Mark, we'll find out one way or another. You're not doing anybody any favors here."

"She wouldn't want those bastards anywhere near her," he said.

"Why not?"

"You know."

"Was she abused?"

He nodded. "Him. Her stepfather. He used to do it to her regularly, and her mother did nothing. Too frightened of losing the miserable bastard. I swear I'll kill him if I ever see him again. I mean it."

"You won't see him, Mark. And you don't want to go talking about killing anyone. Even in grief. Now, where do they live?"

"Adel."

"La-di-da," said Banks. Adel was a wealthy north Leeds suburb with a fine Norman church and a lot of green.

Mark noticed Banks's surprise. "He's a doctor," he said.

"Tina's stepfather?"

"Uh-huh. That's how she first got addicted. She used to nick morphine from his surgery when he'd . . . you know. It helped her get over the shame and the pain. He must have known about it, but he didn't say anything."

"Did he know where she lived, on the boat?"

"He knew."

"Did he ever visit you there?"

"Yes. To try to take Tina back. I wouldn't let him."

Mark probably weighed no more than eight or nine stone, but he looked wiry and strong. People like him often made deceptively tough scrappers, Banks knew, because he'd been like that himself at Mark's age. He was still on the wiry side, despite all the beer and junk food. A matter of metabolism, he supposed. Jim Hatchley, on the other hand, seemed to show every pint he supped right in his gut.

"So Tina's father knew about you?"

"Yes."

"When was the last time he paid you a visit?"

"About a week ago."

"You sure he didn't come yesterday?"

"I don't know. I was at work. On the building site. Tina didn't say anything."

"Would she have?"

"Maybe. But she was . . . you know . . . a bit out of it."

A little chat with Tina's stepfather was definitely on the cards. "What's his name?" Banks asked.

"Aspern," Mark spat out. "Patrick Aspern."

"You might as well give me his address."

Mark gave it to him.

"And stay away," Banks warned him.

Mark looked sullen, but he said nothing.

"Is there anything else you can tell me about Tom on the next boat? What did he look like?"

"Ordinary, really. Short bloke, barrel-chested. He had long fingers, though. You couldn't help but notice them. He didn't shave very often, but he didn't really have a beard. Didn't wash his hair much, either."

"What color was it?"

"Brown. Sort of long and greasy."

Maybe the victim wasn't Tom after all. Banks remembered the tufts of red hair that had somehow escaped the flames and made a note to talk to Geoff Hamilton about the discrepancy.

"Did he have any visitors?"

"Just a couple, as far as I know."

"At the same time?"

"No. Separate. I saw one of them two or three times, the other only once."

"What did he look like, the one you saw a few times?"

"Hard to say, really. It was always after dark."

"Try."

"Well, the only glimpse I got of him was when Tom opened his door and some light came out. He was thin, tall-ish, maybe six foot or more. A bit stooped."

"See his face?"

"Not really. I only saw him in the shadows."

"What about his hair?"

"Short. And dark, I think. Or that could have just been the light."

"Clothes?"

"Can't say, really. Maybe jeans and trainers."

"Would you recognize him if you saw him again?"

"Dunno. I don't think so. There was one thing, though."

"What's that?"

"He carried one of those big cases. You know, like art students have."

"An artist's briefcase?"

"I suppose that's what you'd call it."

So if Tom was an artist, Banks thought, then this was probably his dealer or agent. Worth looking into. "When did you last see him?" he asked.

"Yesterday."

"Yesterday when?"

"Just after dark. I hadn't been home from work long."

"How long did he stay?"

"I don't know. I went back inside before he left. I was having a smoke and Tina doesn't like me smoking indoors. It was cold."

"So he could have still been there after you left for the pub?"

"He could've been, I suppose. I didn't hear him leave. We did have the music on, though."

"What about the other visitor?"

"I can't really say. It was just the once, maybe two, three weeks ago. It was dark that time, too."

"Can you remember anything at all about him?"

"Only that he was shorter than the other bloke, and a bit fatter. I mean, not really fat, but not skinny, if you know what I mean."

"Did you see his face?"

"Only when Tom opened the door. I can tell you his nose was a bit big. And hooked, like an eagle. But I only saw it from the side."

"Did you ever see any cars parked in the lay-by through the woods?"

"Once or twice."

"What cars?"

"I remember seeing one of those jeep things. Dark blue."

"Jeep Cherokee? Range Rover?"

"I don't know. Just a dark blue jeep. Or black."

"Anything else?"

"No."

"But you never saw anyone getting in or out of it?"

"No."

"Was it there yesterday, when the man came?"

"I didn't see it, but I didn't look. I mean, it was dark, I'd have had to have been walking that way. I'd seen it there before when he visited, though. The tall bloke."

"Can you remember anything else that happened before you went out yesterday?" Banks asked.

"That sad bastard from the lockkeeper's cottage was round again on his bike."

"Andrew Hurst? What was he doing here?"

"Same as always. Spying. He thinks I can't see him in the woods, but I can see him all right."

Just like we saw you, Banks thought. "Who is he spying on?"

"Dunno. If you ask me, though, he's after seeing Tina without her clothes on."

"Why do you say that?"

"The way he ogles her whenever he's around. He just looks like a perv to me, that's all, and he's always lurking, spying. Why else would he do that?"

Good question, Banks thought. And it was interesting that Andrew Hurst had specifically mentioned that he *didn't* spy on the people on the boats. He also hadn't told Banks and Annie about his earlier visit during their conversation that morning. Banks would have to have another chat with the self-styled lockkeeper.

"What's going to happen to Tina now?" Mark asked.

Banks didn't want to go into the gory details of the postmortem, so he just said, "We'll be hanging on to her until we've got this sorted."

"And after? I mean, there'll be a funeral, won't there?"

"Of course," said Banks. "Don't worry. Nobody's going to abandon her."

"Only once we were talking, like you do, and she said when she died she wanted 'Stolen Car' played at her funeral. Beth Orton. It was her favorite. She wanted to be a singer."

"I'm sure that can be arranged. But that's a while off yet. What are you going to do in the meantime?"

"Find somewhere to live, I suppose."

"The social will help out. With your clothes and money and accommodation and all. Talking about that, have you got any money?"

"I've got about ten quid in my wallet. There was some money we'd saved on the boat, a couple of hundred. But that's gone now, along with everything else. I'm not a sponger. I've got a job. I'm not afraid of hard work."

Banks remembered what Annie had told him about her interview with Mandy Patterson, about Mark's dreams. "Someone said you wanted to be a stonemason, do church-restoration work. Is that right?"

Mark looked away, embarrassed. "Well, I don't have the qualifications, but I'd like to have a go. I just like old churches, that's all. I'm not religious or anything, so I don't know why. I just do. They're beautiful buildings."

"What about clothes?"

"The clothes you took are all I've got," he said. "Everything else went up with the boat."

"We're about the same size," said Banks. "I can let you have some old jeans and stuff till you get yourself sorted."

"Thanks," said Mark, looking down at the red low-cost suspect overalls he had been issued with. "Anything would be better than this."

"Can you go home for a while? To your parents?"

Mark gave a sharp shake of his head. Again, Banks knew better than to pursue the subject, no matter how curious he was to know what made Mark react in such a frightened manner at the mention of his parents. Same as Tina, most likely. There was too much of it about, and most of it still didn't get reported.

"What about mates? Someone from the building site, perhaps?"

"I suppose there's Lenny."

"Do you know his address?"

"No, but he's in the George most lunchtimes. Besides, the people at the site know him."

"Do you think he'd be willing to put you up for a couple of nights until you find a flat, get on your feet again?"

"Maybe. Look, don't worry about me," Mark said. "I'll be all right. I'm used to taking care of myself. Can I go back to my cell now? I didn't sleep, and I'm dog-tired."

Banks glanced at his watch. "It's lunchtime. I hear they do a decent burger and chips."

Mark stood up. The two of them walked downstairs, where Banks handed Mark over to one of the constables on duty, who would escort him down to the basement custody facilities. Then Banks walked out into the market square and headed for the Queen's Arms. He fancied a beef burger and chips, too, but he'd have to miss out on his usual lunchtime pint. He was going to Adel to talk to Tina's parents, and he didn't want the smell of beer on his breath when he spoke to Dr. Patrick Aspern.

Chapter 3

After stopping off at home for a quick shower and a change of clothes, Banks headed down to Adel early that afternoon, listening to the same Beethoven string quartet that had been playing on the radio during his talk with Mark: number 12 in E flat.

The fog had thinned to a mere gauze, except in patches, so it wasn't a difficult drive, and the temperature was heading toward double figures. One or two hardy souls were out playing on the golf course near Harrogate, dressed in sweaters and jeans.

Banks turned off the Leeds ring road onto Otley Road and stopped by the imposing gates of Lawnswood Crematorium to consult his map. A little farther along the main road, he turned right and drove into the affluent community of winding streets that was Adel.

He soon found the large detached corner house, which also doubled as the doctor's surgery. This wasn't going to be an easy job, Banks reflected as he got out of his car. Mark's allegations against Patrick Aspern might be groundless, and Banks was there to tell the parents that their daughter was dead and ask them to identify the body, not to interrogate the stepfather over sexual abuse. That might come later, though, Banks knew, so he would have to be alert for anything out of the ordinary in Aspern's reactions to his questions.

Banks took a deep breath and pushed the doorbell. The woman who answered looked younger than he expected. About Annie's age, early thirties, with short layered blond hair, pale, flawless skin and a nervous, elfin look about her. "Mrs. Aspern?" he asked.

The woman nodded, looking puzzled, and put her hand to her cheek.

"It's about your daughter, Tina. I'm a policeman. May I come in for a moment?"

"Christine?" Mrs. Aspern fingered the loose neck of her cable-knit sweater. "She doesn't live here anymore. What is it?"

"If I might come in, please?"

She stood aside and Banks stepped onto the highly polished hardwood floor. "First on the right," said Mrs. Aspern.

He followed her direction and found himself in a small sitting room with a dark blue three-piece suite and cream walls. A couple of framed paintings hung there, one over the decorative, but functional, stone fireplace, and the other on the opposite wall. Both were landscapes in simple black frames.

"Is your husband home?" Banks asked.

"Patrick? He's taking afternoon surgery."

"Can you fetch him for me, please?"

"Fetch him?" She looked alarmed. "But . . . the patients."

"I want to talk to you both together. It's important," Banks said.

Shaking her head, Mrs. Aspern left the room. Banks took the opportunity to stand up and examine the two paintings more closely. Both were watercolors painted in misty morning light, by the looks of them. One showed the church of St. John the Baptist, just down the street, which Banks happened to have visited once with his ex-wife Sandra during his early

days in Yorkshire. He knew it was the oldest Norman church
in Leeds, built around the middle of the twelfth century. Sandra had taken some striking photographs. A plain building, it
was most famous for the elaborate stone carvings on the
porch and chancel arch, at which the painting merely hinted.

The other painting was a woodland scene, which Banks assumed to be Adel Woods, again with that wispy, fey early-
morning light about it, making the glade look like the
magical forest of *A Midsummer Night's Dream*. The signature "Keith Peverell" was clear enough on both. No connection to "Tom" there, not that he had expected any.

Mrs. Aspern returned some minutes later, along with her
clearly perturbed husband. "Look," he said, before any intro-
ductions had been made. "I can't just leave my patients in the
lurch like this. Can't you come back at five o'clock?"

"I'm afraid not," said Banks, offering his warrant card.

Aspern scrutinized it, and a small, unpleasant smile
tugged at the corners of his lips. He glanced at his wife.
"Why didn't you say, darling? A detective chief inspector, no
less," he said. "Well, it must be important if they sent the organ grinder. Please, sit down."

Banks sat. Now that Aspern was pleased he'd been sent
someone he thought commensurate with his social standing,
though probably a chief constable would have been prefer-
able, the patients were quickly forgotten. Things were likely
to go a bit more easily. If Banks let them.

Aspern was a good fifteen years or so older than his wife,
Banks guessed. Around fifty, with thinning sandy hair, he
was handsome in a sharp-angled way, though Banks was put
off by the cynical look in his eyes and the lips perpetually on
the verge of that nasty little superior smile. He had the slim,
athletic figure of a man who plays tennis and golf and goes to
the gym regularly. Being a doctor, of course, he'd know all
about the benefits of exercise, though Banks knew more than

one or two doctors, the Home Office pathologist Dr. Glendenning among them, who smoked and drank and didn't give a damn about fitness.

"I'm afraid it's bad news," he said, as Dr. and Mrs. Aspern faced him from the sofa. Mrs. Aspern was chewing on a fingernail already, looking as if she was expecting the worst. "It's about your daughter, Tina."

"We always called her Christine. Please."

"Out with it, man," Aspern prodded. "Has there been an accident?"

"Not quite," Banks said. "Christine's dead. I'm sorry, there's no easier way to say it. And we'll need one or both of you to come and identify the body."

They sat in silence, not looking at each other, not even touching. Finally, Aspern found his voice. "Dead? How? What happened?"

"There was a fire. You knew she was living on a canal boat just outside Eastvale?"

"Yes. Another foolish idea of hers." At last, Aspern looked at his wife. Tears were running from her eyes as if she'd been peeling an onion, but she made no sound. Her husband got up and fetched her a box of tissues. "Here you are, dear," he said, putting them down on her knees. She didn't even look at them, just kept staring ahead into whatever abyss she was seeing, the tears dripping off the edges of her jaw onto her skirt, making little stains where they landed on the pale green material.

"I appreciate your coming yourself to tell us," said Aspern. "You can see my wife's upset. It's been quite a shock. Is that all?"

"I'm afraid not, sir," Banks said. "The fire was of doubtful origin. I have some questions I need to ask you as soon as possible. Now, in fact."

"It's all right, Patrick," Mrs. Aspern said, coming back from a great distance. "Let the man do his job."

A little flustered by her command of the situation, or so it seemed to Banks, Aspern settled back onto the sofa. "If you're sure . . ." he said.

"I'm sure." She looked at Banks. "Please tell us what happened."

"Christine was living with a boy, a young man, rather, called Mark Siddons, on an abandoned narrow boat."

"Siddons," said Aspern, lip twisting. "We know all about him. Did he do this? Was he responsible?"

"We have no evidence that Mark Siddons had anything to do with the fire," said Banks.

"Where was he? Did he survive?"

"He was out at the time of the fire," Banks said. "And he's unharmed. I gather there was no love lost between you?"

"He turned our daughter against us," said Aspern. "Took her away from home and stopped her from seeing us. It's as if he took control of her mind like one of those religious cults you read about."

"That's not what he told me," Banks said, careful now he knew he was walking on heavily mined land. "And it's not the impression I got of him."

"Well, you wouldn't expect him to admit it, would you? I can only imagine the lies he told you."

"What lies?"

"Never you mind. I'm just warning you, that's all. The boy's no good. Don't believe a word he says."

"I'll bear that in mind," said Banks. "How old was Christine?"

"Seventeen," said Aspern.

"And how old was she when she left home?"

"She was sixteen," Mrs. Aspern answered. "She went the day after her sixteenth birthday. As if she just couldn't wait to get away."

"Did either of you know that Christine was a drug user?"

"It doesn't surprise me," said Aspern. "The crowd she was hanging around with. What was it? Pot? Ecstasy?"

"Apparently she preferred drugs that brought her oblivion rather than awareness," Banks said softly, watching Patrick Aspern's face closely for any signs of a reaction. All it showed was puzzlement. "It was heroin," Banks continued. "Other narcotics, if she couldn't get that, but mostly heroin."

"Oh, dear God," said Mrs. Aspern. "What have we done?"

Banks turned to her. "What do you mean?"

"Fran," her husband said. "We can't blame ourselves for this. We gave her every opportunity. Every advantage."

Banks had heard this before on so many occasions that it slipped in one ear and out the other. Nobody had a clue what their kids really needed—and how could they, for teenagers are hardly the most communicative species on earth—but so many parents assumed that the advantages of wealth or status were enough in themselves. Even Banks's own parents, working-class as they were, thought he had let them down by joining the police force instead of pursuing a career in business. But wealth and status rarely were enough, in Banks's experience, though he knew that most kids from wealthy families went on to do quite well for themselves. Others, like Tina, and like Emily Riddle and Luke Armitage, cases he had dealt with in the recent past, fell by the wayside.

"Apparently," Banks went on, cutting through the husband-wife tension he was sensing, "Christine used to steal morphine from your surgery."

Aspern reddened. "That's a lie! Did Siddons tell you that? Any narcotics in my surgery are safely under lock and key, in absolute compliance with the law. If you don't believe it, come and have a look for yourself right now. I'll show you. Come on."

"That won't be necessary," said Banks. "This isn't about Christine's drug supplies. We know she got her last score from a dealer in Eastvale."

"It's just a damn shame you can't put these people away *before* they do the damage," said Aspern.

"That would assume we know who the criminals are going to be before they commit their crimes," said Banks, thinking of the film *Minority Report,* which he had seen with Michelle a few weeks ago.

"If you ask me, it's pretty bloody obvious in most cases," said Aspern. "Even if this Siddons didn't start the fire, you can be damn sure he did *something*. He's got criminal written all over him, that one."

More than once Banks, like his colleagues, had acted on the premise that if the person they had in custody hadn't committed the particular crime he was charged with, it didn't matter, because the police *knew* he had committed other crimes, and had no evidence to charge him with them. In police logic, the crime they were convicted for, the one they didn't commit, made up for all the crimes they had committed and got away with. It was easier in the old days, of course, before the Police and Criminal Evidence Act gave the criminals more rights than the police, and the Crown Prosecution Service wouldn't touch anything with less than a hundred-percent possibility of conviction, but it still happened, if you could get away with it. "We'd have to overhaul the legal system," he said, "if we wanted to put people who haven't done anything away without a trial. But let's get back to the matter in hand. Did you know of anyone who'd want to hurt Christine, Mrs. Aspern?"

"We didn't know her . . . the friends she made after she left," she answered. "But I can't imagine anyone would want to harm her, no."

"Dr. Aspern?"

"Me, neither."

"There was an artist on the adjacent boat. All we know is that his name was Tom. Do you know anything about him?"

"Never heard of him," said Patrick Aspern.

"What about Andrew Hurst? He lives nearby."

"I never saw anyone."

"When did you last visit the boat?" Banks asked him.

"Last week. Thursday, I believe."

"Why?"

"What do you mean, why?" Aspern said. "She's my step-daughter. I was concerned. I wanted to persuade her to come home."

"Did you ever see the neighbor on one of your visits?"

"Look, you're making it sound as if I was a regular visitor. I only went up there a couple of times to try to persuade Christine to come home, and that . . . thug she was with threatened me."

"With what?"

"Violence, of course. I mean, I'm not a coward or a weakling or anything, but I wouldn't put it past someone like him to have a knife, or even a gun."

"You didn't go there yesterday?"

"Of course not."

"What kind of car do you drive?"

"A Jaguar XJ8."

"Did you ever visit the boat, Mrs. Aspern?" Banks asked.

Before Frances Aspern could answer, her husband jumped in. "I went by myself," he said. "Frances has a nervous disposition. Confrontations upset her. Besides, she couldn't bear to see how Christine was living."

"Is this true, Mrs. Aspern?" Banks asked.

Frances Aspern nodded.

"Look," said Dr. Aspern, "you can see we're upset over the news. Can't you just go away and leave us in peace for a while, to grieve?"

"I'm afraid you'll have to save that for later," said Banks. "When I've finished here, I'd like one or both of you to follow me up to Eastvale and identify the body."

Mrs. Aspern touched her chalklike cheek. "You said it was a fire."

"Yes," said Banks. "I'm sorry. There is some disfiguration. Not much, but some."

"I'll go, darling," said Aspern, resting his hand on her knee. "I can cancel surgery. I'm sure everyone will understand."

She shook him off. "No. *I'll* go."

"But you're upset, dear. I'm a doctor. I can deal with these things. I've been trained."

She shot him a scornful glance. "*Deal with?* Is that all this means to you? I said I'll go, Mr. Banks. Can you take me and have someone bring me back? I'm afraid I'm far too upset to drive myself."

"At least let me drive you," her husband pleaded.

"I don't want you there," she said. "Christine was *my* daughter."

There. It was said. And it lay heavily between them like an undigested meal. "As you wish," said Patrick Aspern.

"Are you certain it couldn't have been an accident?" Mrs. Aspern asked, turning to Banks. "I still can't believe that anyone would want to harm Christine."

"Anything can happen when drugs enter the equation," said Banks. "And that's another angle we'll be looking at. There's also a strong possibility that Christine wasn't the intended victim."

"What do you mean?" asked Aspern.

"I can't say much more at this point," said Banks. "We still have a lot of forensic tests to do and a lot of questions to ask. At the moment, we're simply trying to get as much information as possible about the people who lived on the boats. When we know more, we'll know where to focus our investigation, which line of inquiry to follow."

"I can't believe this is happening," said Aspern.

His wife stood up. "I'm ready to go," she said to Banks,

then added, looking at her husband, "you can get back to your patients now, Patrick."

He started to say something, but she turned her back and walked out of the room.

Mark's cell was small and basic, but comfortable enough. It smelled a bit—a hint of urine, vomit and stale alcohol—but they were old smells. At least it was clean, and he wasn't shut in with a gang of sexually frustrated bikers with fourteen-inch penises. There were a couple of drunks down the corridor, even at that time in the afternoon. One of them kept singing "Your Cheatin' Heart" over and over again until one of the officers made him shut up. After that, Mark could hear them snore or call out in their sleep from time to time, but other than those few irritations, things remained fairly quiet. All in all, it wasn't so bad. The only thing was, he couldn't go out when he wanted. It was like home, until he plucked up the courage to take on his mother and Crazy Nick and made his final break.

Mark tried, but sleep just wouldn't come. Most of his thoughts centered on Tina and the news the policeman had given him of her death. Of course, he had known it, known as soon as he got to the woods and saw the firemen and the smoldering barges that she had to be dead. But he had tried to deny it to himself; now he had to face it and accept it: he would never see Tina again.

And it was *his* fault.

Tina. So gentle, so frail and so birdlike, it broke his heart that he had been unfaithful to her and hurt her and would never get the chance to put things right, to tell her he was sorry and that he loved her, only her, not Mandy or anyone else. Tina trusted him, needed him and depended on him. He got her through the bad times, and when there were good times—which there were—they laughed together, and sometimes went on walks in the country and drank screw-top wine and ate cheese-slice sandwiches beside a crystal stream.

Sometimes they seemed to live an almost normal life, the kind of life Mark wanted for them. In his dreams, he got a steady job in Eastvale, maybe working on church restoration, got Tina straight, then they rented a little flat. When the first baby came, they had saved enough for a small semi, maybe by the sea. At least that was how he saw their life developing. He knew he'd be taking care of Tina forever, because she would always need that, even if she got straight, she was so badly scarred inside; but he could do it, he wanted to do it, and once she kicked the habit she couldn't help but get stronger. She was intelligent, too, much brighter than he; maybe she could get into the college like Mandy and get a job as a secretary or something. He bet she could work with computers if she put her mind to it.

Sometimes they even made love, but that was hard for Tina; she was never far from the hunger and the darkness at the center of her being. The wrong word or gesture, and she was burrowing deep inside herself again, scrunching up in the fetal position with her thumb in her mouth, on the nod. And when she was like that, it didn't matter if he was there or not. Which was why he hadn't been there last night.

Tina wasn't much interested in sex, partly because drugs do weird things to your sex drive, but mostly because of her stepfather. When Mark thought of Patrick Aspern, his stomach knotted and rage surged through him. One day he'd . . .

Despite what the policeman had said, Mark wondered if Tina could have started the fire accidentally. She heated her spoon over a candle to prepare her fix, and she'd been careless once or twice in the past. But he'd been there then, not like this time.

But no, he realized; it couldn't have happened that way. He remembered that he had been careful to snuff out the candle himself before leaving her on the nod, in a sleeping bag, her eyes glazed, pupils dilated, to all intents and purposes lost to the world, wrapped in a warm cocoon of safety and oblivion, without a care, until it started to wear off and she started to itch and her stomach knotted up and her every pore oozed with craving for more. He'd been through it all with her so many times, and he knew he'd have gone through it again when he got home, if it hadn't been for the fire.

He'd told Tina he was sick of her and her junkie ways, and if she didn't get into some sort of rehabilitation center or methadone program he was leaving her. She didn't care when he said it because the heroin was kicking in and flooding her veins and that rush, that golden warmth, was the only thing she cared about in the whole world when it spread through her like an orgasm. So he stormed out. Out to Mandy and her tantalizing, lithe young body. Tina didn't know where he was going, of course, and she never would now. But *he* knew, and that was more than enough.

At least he knew the fire couldn't have started on their boat. Did she know it was happening, that the flames were creeping closer, the smoke enveloping her? Even if she had come round when she smelled the smoke or saw the flames, would she have had time to get her head together and jump for land? Or water? Perhaps then she would have drowned. Tina couldn't swim.

Mark curled up on the hard bunk, and the thoughts and fears tumbled around in his tired brain. When the drunk started up again with "Your Cheatin' Heart," he put his hands over his ears and cried.

"Is the music all right?" Banks asked Frances Aspern.

"Pardon?"

"The music. Is it okay?"

They were entering the Dales landscape beyond Ripon,

and the distant shapes of the hills rose out of the mist in shades of gray, like whales breaking the water's surface. Banks was playing Mariza's *Fado em Mim,* traditional Portuguese songs, accompanied by classical guitar and bass, and he realized they might not be to everyone's taste. Frances Aspern had been staring out of the window in silence the whole way so far, and he had almost given up trying to start a conversation. He couldn't help but be aware of the weight of her grief beside him. Grief or guilt; he wasn't certain which.

"Yes," said Mrs. Aspern. "It's fine. She sounds very sad."

Indeed she did. Banks didn't understand a word of the songs without the translations on the CD booklet, the print of which was daily getting too small for him to read without glasses, but there was no mistaking the sense of loss, sadness and the cruelty of fate in Mariza's voice. You didn't need to know what the words meant to feel that.

"I didn't want to ask you while your husband was present," Banks said, "but is Christine's birth father still around?"

She shook her head. "I was very young. We didn't marry. My parents . . . they were good to me. I lived with them in Roundhay until Patrick and I married."

"We'll still need to talk to him," said Banks.

"He's back home. In America. We met when he was traveling in Europe."

"Can you give me the details?"

She looked out of the window, away from Banks, as she spoke, so that he could barely hear her. "His name is Paul Ryder. He lives in Cincinnati, Ohio. I don't have his address or telephone number. We haven't been in contact since . . . well . . ."

Banks made a mental note of the name and city. It might be hard to track down this Paul Ryder after so long, but they'd have to try. "How did you and Dr. Aspern meet?" he asked.

"Patrick was a colleague of my father's, a frequent visitor to our house when I was at home, when Christine was only a baby. My father is also a doctor. I suppose, in a way, he was Patrick's mentor. He's retired now, of course."

Banks wondered how well that marriage had gone down with Mrs. Aspern's family. "Were you both at home last night?" he asked.

She turned to look at him. "What do you expect me to say to that?"

"I expect you to tell me the truth," Banks said.

"Ah, the truth. Yes, of course we were both at home." She turned to look out of the window again.

"Did your husband go out at all yesterday?"

Mrs. Aspern didn't reply.

"Is there anything else you want to say?" Banks asked. "Anything at all you want to tell me?"

Mrs. Aspern glanced at him again. He couldn't make out the expression on her face. Then she turned back to look out of the window. "No," she said, after a long pause. "No, I don't think so."

Banks gave up and drove on, Mariza singing against a backdrop of the misty Dales landscape, a song about sorrow, longing, pity, punishment and despair.

The scene looked different in the late afternoon, Annie thought as she walked through the woods to the canal branch. The area was still taped off, and she had to show her warrant card and sign in before entering, but the firefighters and their equipment were gone, and in their stead was an eerie silence shrouding the two burned-out narrow boats and the scattering of men in hooded white overalls patiently searching the banks. The smell of ashes still hung in the damp air.

She found Detective Sergeant Stefan Nowak poking through debris on the artist's boat. Stefan was their crime scene coordinator, and it was his job to supervise the collection of possible crime scene evidence by his highly trained team and to liaise between the special analysts in the lab and Banks's team.

Stefan looked up as Annie approached. He was a handsome, elegant man—no doubt a prince, Annie thought, as so many exiled Poles were—and he looked aristocratic, even in his protective clothing. There was a certain remoteness about him, which stopped on just the polite side of aloofness, and made him seem regal in some way. He had a faint Polish accent, too, which served to heighten the mysterious effect. He was friendly enough to be on a first-name basis with both Annie and Banks, but he didn't hang out in the Queen's Arms with the rest of the lads, and nobody knew much about his private life.

Annie sniffled. "Found anything?" she asked.

Stefan gestured toward the murky water. "One of the frogmen found an empty turps container in there," he said. "Probably the one used to start the fire. No prints or anything, though. Just your regular, commercial turps container. Anyway, I'm finished here," he said. "Come on, I'll show you what we've found so far."

Annie wrapped her scarf more tightly around her sore throat as they took the narrow path through the woods. Wraiths of fog still drifted between the trees like elaborate spiderwebs, and here and there they had to step around a patch of muddy ground or a shallow puddle.

About halfway to the lane, Annie saw the plastic retaining frames around faint imprints in the mud, each with a ruler lying next to it. "Luckily, the ground was just muddy enough in places," Stefan said. "Probably protected by the trees. Anyway, we got reasonably fresh shoe impressions, but they could be anybody's."

"How many?"

"Just the one person, by the looks of it."

"Did the firefighters use this path?"

Stefan pointed. "No, down there. This is the path you'd take from the lay-by. They parked farther down, closer to the canal. This part of the woods is riddled with paths. I gather it's a popular spot in summer."

Annie looked down at the markings. "So they could be our man's?"

"Yes, but don't get your hopes up. Anyway, they've all been carefully photographed, and casts have been made. They're drying out right now, but tomorrow we'll run them through SICAR."

SICAR was an acronym for Shoeprint Image Capture and Retrieval, which combines a number of scanned databases to match footwear files with specimens, primarily the "Solemate" database of over three hundred common brands of shoes and two thousand different sole patterns. Stefan's expert would have sprayed the muddy impression with shellac or acrylic lacquer, then he would have made a cast in dental stone. Back at headquarters, he would enter the details of the shoe impression on the computer, coding by common patterns such as bars, polygons and zigzags, and by manufacturers' logos, if any were present. From these reference databases, they could find out what type and brand of shoe caused the imprint, and they could also search the crime and suspect databases to see if it matched the shoe of a person taken into custody, or a footprint left at a previous crime scene.

Of course, what everyone really hoped for was something more than just class characteristics, some sort of unique markings, the kind that come from wear and tear, a nice drawing pin embedded in the sole, for example, something that could be matched with a specific shoe. Then, once you have your suspect and his shoe, you have solid evidence that links him to the scene.

They got to the lay-by, beside which the police mobile unit was parked, completely blocking the lane. It didn't matter much, though, as the track was hardly ever used and it led only toward a narrow bridge over the canal about two miles west. Anyone wanting to get there was advised to take the next turning by a diversion sign posted at the junction of the lane and the B-road half a mile north.

Annie noticed more retaining frames, measures and markers on the lay-by itself.

"Impressive," she said. "You have been busy."

"We'll see," said Stefan. "Trying to process a crime scene like this is like peeling the layers off the onion, and you don't know which layer is the important one." He pointed to one of the imprints. "Here we've got parallel tire tracks," he said. "And that should be enough to tell us who the manufacturer was. From these we can also get the track width and wheelbase measurements, which might even help us identify the make of the car. If there are a number of individual characteristics present in the tire impressions, which may be the case, then we should be able to match them to the specific tire, and vehicle, too."

"If and when we find it," said Annie.

"Naturally. We've also collected soil samples from the entire area. No rare wildflowers at this time of year, of course, but there are some unique mineral features, and they should also help us tie in the shoes and tire to the scene, should we find them."

"And should they still be dirty."

Stefan narrowed his eyes. "Trace evidence can be microscopic sometimes. You ought to know that. You'd be surprised how little we can work with."

"I'm sorry," said Annie. "I don't mean to be negative. It's just . . . I have a feeling we're not dealing with an amateur here."

"And we're not amateurs, either. Besides, we don't know *what* we're dealing with here yet."

"True enough," Annie agreed. "I'm just suggesting that

he'll have done his best to cover his tracks, and the longer it takes us to find him . . ."

"The more tracks he'll manage to cover. Okay, I'll grant you that. But it'll take more than a car wash and a good polishing to get rid of every atom of soil he might have picked up here. Besides, don't forget, we've got the tire impression to go on. There's an oil stain, too, by the looks of it." He pointed to another protected area on the lay-by. "We'll have that back for analysis by the end of the day. It's certainly beginning to look as if *someone* parked here recently, and if it wasn't you or the fire brigade . . ."

Annie knew that it was neither she nor Banks. They had been concerned to preserve as much of the scene as they could when they arrived, almost by instinct, so they had left their cars farther up the lane and made their way through the woods without benefit of using a marked path. All in all, then, things were looking promising. Even if the evidence that Stefan and his team painstakingly collected didn't lead them directly to the arsonist, it would come in useful in court when they did find him.

"Any chance it was a Jeep Cherokee?" Annie asked, remembering what Banks had told her Mark said he'd seen. "Or something similar?"

Stefan blinked. "Know something I don't?"

"Just that something resembling a Jeep Cherokee has been reported seen in the area. Not last night, but recently."

Stefan looked down at the tire tracks. "Well," he said, "it's something to go on. We can certainly compare wheelbase and track width. Anyway," Stefan said, opening the door of the mobile unit with a flourish, "it's not exactly the Ritz, but the heater works. How about coming in for a cuppa?"

Annie smiled, her body leaning toward the source of heat the way a sunflower leans toward the sun. "You must be a mind reader," she said, and followed him in.

* * *

By the time Banks and Frances Aspern got to Western Area Headquarters after Mrs. Aspern's positive identification of Christine at the mortuary of Eastvale General Infirmary, Annie had already left to talk to the SOCOs at the canal. Banks arranged for a uniformed constable to drive Mrs. Aspern back home, and he had just settled down to review the findings so far, with Gil Evans's Jimi Hendrix orchestrations playing quietly in the background, when Geoff Hamilton appeared at his office door. Banks invited him in and Hamilton sat down, glancing around.

"Cozy," he said.

"It'll do," said Banks. "Tea? Coffee?"

"Coffee, if you've got some. Black, plenty of sugar."

"I'll ring down." Banks ordered two black coffees. "Anything new?"

"I've just come from the lab," Hamilton said. "We carried out gas chromatograph tests this afternoon."

"And?"

Hamilton took two sheets of paper and a videotape from his briefcase and laid them out on Banks's desk. The sheets of paper looked like graphs, with peaks and valleys. "As you know," he said, looking at Banks, "I took debris samples from a number of places, especially on boat one, Tom's boat, the main seat of the fire. I don't know how much you know about it," he went on, "but gas chromatography is a relatively simple and quick process. In this case, we put the debris in large cans, heated them and used a syringe to draw off the headspace, the gases given off, and we then injected that into the chromatograph. This"—he pointed to the left graph—"is the chromatogram we got from the point of origin." He then pointed to the graph beside it, which, to Banks, looked almost identical. Both showed a series of low to medium peaks with one enormous spike in the middle. "And this is the chromatographic representation of turpentine."

"So we were right," Banks said, studying the chromatograms. "What about the other boat?"

"Apart from the streamers I noted on my initial examination," Hamilton said, "there are no other signs of accelerant. Anyway, that's the physical evidence so far. Turpentine is your primary accelerant. Its ignition temperature is 488 degrees Fahrenheit, which is quite low. As we found no evidence of timing or incendiary devices, I'd say someone used a match."

"Deliberate, then?"

Hamilton looked around, as if worried that the room was bugged, then he let slip a rare smile. "Just between you and me and these four walls," he said, "not a shred of doubt."

The coffee arrived and both remained silent until the PC who delivered it had left the office. Hamilton took a sip and lifted up the videotape. "Want to watch a movie?" he asked.

Videotaped evidence and interviews were so common these days that Banks had a small TV/Video combination in his office. Hamilton slipped the tape in and they both got a driver's-seat view as the fire engine raced to the scene.

Most engines, or "appliances," as the firefighters called them, were fitted with a "silent witness," a video recorder that taped the journey to the source of the call. It could come in useful if you happened to be really quick off the mark and spotted a getaway vehicle, or arrived at the scene and got a picture of the arsonist hanging about enjoying his handiwork. This time, there was nothing. The fire engine passed a couple of cars going the other way, and it would probably be possible to isolate the images and enhance the number plates. But Banks didn't hold out much hope they would lead anywhere. The fire was well under way by the time Hurst called it in, and the arsonist would be well away, too. It was an exhilarating journey, though, and Hamilton ejected the tape when the appliance came to a halt at the bend in the lane.

"There's one thing that bothers me," Banks said. "The boy, Mark, described the artist's hair as brown but what little of it we saw on the boat was more like red."

"Fire does that," said Hamilton.

"Changes hair color?"

"Yes. Sometimes. Gray turns blond, and brown turns red."

"Interesting," said Banks. "What about Tina? Could she have survived?"

"If she'd been awake and aware, yes, but the state she was in . . . not a chance."

"The way it looks, then," said Banks, "is that the artist on boat one was the primary victim, yet some small effort had been made to see that the fire spread to boat two, where Mark and Tina lived. But why Mark and Tina?"

"I'm afraid that's your job to find out, not mine."

"Just tossing ideas around. Elimination of a witness?"

"Witness to what?"

"If the arsonist was someone who'd visited the victim before, then he might have been seen, or worried he'd been seen."

"But the young man survived."

"Yes, and Mark *did* see two people visit Tom on different occasions. Maybe one of them was the killer, and he had no idea that Mark was out at the time. He probably thought he was getting them both, but he was in a hurry to get away. Which means . . ."

"What?"

"Never mind," said Banks. "As you said, it's my job to find that out. At the moment I feel as if we've got nothing but assumptions."

Hamilton tapped the graphs and stood up. "Not true," he said. "You've got confirmation of accelerant usage in a multi-seated fire."

Hamilton was right, Banks realized. Until a few minutes

ago, all he'd had to go on were appearances and gut instincts, but now he had solid scientific evidence that the fire had been deliberately set.

He looked at his watch and sighed. "Dr. Glendenning's conducting the postmortem on the male victim soon," he said. "Want to come?"

"What the hell," said Hamilton. "It's Friday evening. The weekend starts here."

Chapter 4

"*D*o you know that it takes about an hour or an hour and a half at between sixteen and eighteen hundred degrees Fahrenheit to cremate a human body?" Dr. Glendenning asked, apropos of nothing in particular. "And that the ordinary house—or, in this case, boat—fire rarely exceeds twelve hundred? That, ladies and gentlemen, is why we have so much material left to work with."

The postmortem lab in the basement of Eastvale General Infirmary was hardly hi-tech, but Dr. Glendenning's experience more than made up for that. To Banks, the blackened shape laid out on the stainless-steel table looked more like one of those Iron Age bodies preserved in peat bogs than someone who had been a living, breathing human being less than twenty-four hours ago. Already, the remnants of clothing had been removed to be tested for traces of accelerant, blood samples had been sent for analysis, and the body had been X-rayed for any signs of gunshot wounds and internal injuries. None had been found, only a belt buckle, three pounds sixty-five in loose change, and a signet ring without initials engraved on it.

"Thought you wouldn't know that," Glendenning went on, casting an eye over his audience: Banks, Geoff Hamilton and Annie Cabbot, fresh from the scene. "And I hope you appreciate my working on a Friday evening," he went on as he examined the body's exterior with the help of his new assistant, Wendy Gauge, all kitted out in blue scrubs and a hairnet. Glendenning looked at his watch. "This could take a long time, and you also probably don't know that I have an important dinner engagement."

"We realize you're a very important man," said Banks, "and we're eternally grateful to you, aren't we, Annie?" He nudged Annie gently.

"We are, indeed," said Annie.

Glendenning scowled. "Enough of your lip, laddie. Do we know who he is?"

Banks shook his head. "All we know was in the report I sent you. His name's probably Tom, and he was an artist."

"It would help if I knew something about his medical history," Dr. Glendenning complained.

"Afraid we can't help you," said Banks.

"I mean, if he was a drug addict or a drunk or on some sort of dodgy medication . . . Why do you always make my job so much more bloody difficult than it needs to be, Banks? Can you tell me that?"

"Search me."

"One day I probably will," Glendenning said. "Inside and out." He scowled, lit a cigarette, though it was strictly forbidden, and went back to work. Banks envied him the cigarette. He had always smoked at postmortems. It helped to mask the smell of the bodies. And they always smelled. Even this one would smell when Dr. Glendenning opened him up. He'd be like one of those fancy, expensive steaks: charred on the outside and pink in the middle, and if he'd got enough carbon monoxide in his system, his blood would look like cherryade.

"Anyway," Glendenning went on, "if he was an artist, he was probably a boozer. Usually are in my experience."

Annie said nothing, though her father, Ray, was an artist, and a boozer. She stood beside Banks, eyes fixed on the doctor, already looking a little pale. Banks knew she didn't like postmortems—nobody really did except, arguably, the pathologist—but the more she attended, the sooner she'd get used to them.

"He's got burns over about seventy-five percent of the body's surface area. The most severe burning, the greatest combination of third- and fourth-degree burning, occurs in the upper body area."

"That would be the area closest to the point of origin," said Geoff Hamilton, cool and glum-looking as ever.

Dr. Glendenning nodded. "Makes sense. Mostly what we've got is full-thickness burning on the front upper body. You can see where the surface looks black and charred. That's caused by boiling subcutaneous fat. The human body keeps on burning long after the fire's been put out. Sort of like a candle, burning in its own fat."

Banks noticed Annie make an expression of distaste.

"Farther down," Glendenning continued, "on the legs and feet, for example, you can see the skin is pink and mottled in places, covered with blisters. That indicates brief exposure and lower temperature."

When Dr. Glendenning got to the external examination of the victim's head, Banks noticed what looked like skull fractures. "Found something, Doc?" he asked.

"Look, I've told you before not to call me Doc. It's lacking in respect."

"But have you found evidence of blows to the head?"

Glendenning bent over and probed the wounds, examining them carefully. "I don't think so," he said.

"But that's what they look like to me," Annie said.

"To you, lassie, maybe. But to *me,* they look like fractures caused by the heat."

"The heat causes fractures?" Annie said.

Dr. Glendenning sighed. Banks could imagine the sort of teacher he'd be and how he'd terrify the poor medical students.

"Of course it does," he said. "Heat contracts the skin and causes splits that may easily be interpreted as cuts inflicted during life. It can also cause fractures in the long bones of the arms and legs, or make them so bloody brittle that they're fractured while the body is being moved. Remember, we're sixty-six percent water, and fire is a great dehydrator."

"But what about the skull?" Annie asked.

Glendenning looked at her, a glint in his eye. "The fractures are caused by pressure. The brain and the blood start to boil, and the steam needs an outlet, so it blows a hole in the skull. Pop. Just like a bottle of champagne."

Annie shuddered. Even Banks felt a little queasy. Dr. Glendenning went back to work, a mischievous grin on his face.

"Anyway," he went on, "skull fractures caused by fire often radiate along suture lines, the weakest point in the skull's surface, and that's the case here. Also, the skull splinters haven't been driven *into* the brain matter, which would most likely be the case if blunt-instrument trauma were present. They've been forced outward."

"So you're saying he *wasn't* hit over the head?"

"I'm saying nothing of the kind," Glendenning said. "I'm only saying it seems unlikely. That's typical of you, Banks, jumping to conclusions when you've got only part of the evidence, going off half-cocked. What about a bit of scientific method, laddie? Haven't you been reading your Sherlock Holmes lately?"

"I know that when you have eliminated the impossible, whatever remains, however improbable, must be the truth. Or something like that."

"Well, in this case," said Glendenning, "almost anything's still possible. Your report mentioned that the body was covered by debris, and I've seen the crime scene photos and sketches. The damage might have been caused by a section of the ceiling falling on the deceased after his death."

"I suppose it could have happened that way," said Banks.

"Definitely possible," said Geoff Hamilton.

"I'm glad you both agree," Glendenning said.

"On the other hand, though," Banks argued, "wouldn't you expect to find skull splinters in the brain if that were the case?"

Glendenning graced him with a rare smile. "You're learning, laddie. Anyway, we don't even know whether the injury was post- or antemortem yet. That's my point."

"Do you think you could find out?"

Glendenning rolled his eyes. "Do I think I could find out?" he mimicked, then went back to the body. "Well, why don't we start by looking for signs of smoke inhalation?" He held out his hand theatrically. "Scalpel."

Wendy Gauge suppressed a smile as she handed him the required instrument, and the pathologist bent over the corpse. The nose had burned away, along with enough skin and flesh to allow the chin and jawbone to show through in places. Glendenning worked away at exposing the tracheal area and bronchial passage, parts of which Banks could see were black with soot or charring, then he bent over the body again. "There's definitely some thermal injury to the mouth, nose and upper airways," he said, "but that's not unusual, and it doesn't tell us much." He poked around some more. "There's soot present, but not a great deal. In fact, in this case, there's little enough to conclude that he was still breathing, but shallowly."

"Was he unconscious?" Banks asked.

"Very likely."

"So that blow to the head might have been administered prior to the starting of the fire? It might have *caused* the unconsciousness?"

"Hold your horses." Dr. Glendenning bent over the body again. "I've already told you; that blow was more likely caused by the fire or falling debris than by human force. Deposition of soot on the tongue, in the nares, the oropharynx and the nasopharynx, all of which we have here, cannot be held to imply life during the fire."

"So he could have been already dead?"

Glendenning gave Banks a nasty look and went on. "Traces of soot below the larynx would indicate that the victim was alive at the start of the fire."

"And is there any?" Banks asked.

"A little. Right now, we need to dig deeper." Glendenning gave the go-ahead and Wendy Gauge wielded her own scalpel and made the customary Y-shaped incision. The blackened skin, which had been dried by the fire and then wetted by the firefighters' hoses, peeled back like burned paper. And there it was, the sickly smell of death. Cooked or raw, it amounted to the same thing. "Hmm," said Glendenning. "You can see how deep the burning goes in some places. It's never uniform, for a number of reasons, including the fact that your skin's thicker in some places than in others."

"Needs to be around you," said Banks.

Glendenning pointedly ignored him. "There's some exaggerated redness of the blood," he said, "which indicates the presence of carbon monoxide. We'll know the exact amounts when that incompetent pillock Billings brings the results back from the lab."

Banks remembered the day he found his old chief constable, Jimmy Riddle, dead in his garage from carbon monoxide poisoning. Suicide. His face had been cherry-red. "How much carbon monoxide does it take to cause death?" he asked.

"Anything over forty percent is likely to cause impaired judgment, unconsciousness and death, but it depends on the person's state of health. The generally accepted fatal level is fifty percent. All right, Wendy, you can go on now."

"Yes, Doctor." Wendy Gauge pulled up the chest flap and took a bone cutter to the rib cage, which she cracked open to expose the inner organs.

At that moment, the door opened and Billings appeared from the lab. The scene of carnage being played out on the stainless-steel postmortem table didn't faze him, but he was clearly terrified of Dr. Glendenning and developed a stutter whenever he had to deal with him. "H-here it is, Doctor," he said. "The c-carbon monoxide results."

Glendenning glared at him and studied the report. "Do you want the short answer or the long one?" he said to Banks, after dismissing Billings with an abrupt jerk of his head.

"The short one will do for now."

"He has a CO level of twenty-eight percent," Glendenning said. "That's enough to cause dizziness, a nasty headache, nausea and fatigue."

"But not death?"

"Not unless he had some serious respiratory or heart disease. Which we'd know about if we had his medical history. In general terms, though, no, it's not enough to cause death. And given the levels of soot and particulate matter in the airways, I'd say he was alive, but most likely unconscious, when the fire started, in which case the cause is probably asphyxia caused by smoke inhalation. And don't forget, there are plenty of other nasty gases released during fires, including ammonia and cyanide. A full analysis will take more time."

"What about tox screening?"

"Don't try to tell me my job, laddie," Dr. Glendenning growled. "It's being done."

"And dental records?"

"We can certainly get impressions," said Glendenning, "but you can hardly check his chart against every bloody dentist in the country."

"There's a chance he may have been local," said Banks, "so we'll start with the Eastvale area."

"Aye, well, that's *your* job." Glendenning glanced at the clock and turned back to the body. "There's still a lot to be done here," he said, "and I'm afraid I can't promise you I'll get to the second victim tonight. I might even miss my dinner engagement as it is."

Wendy Gauge removed the inner organs en bloc and placed them on the dissecting table.

"Well," said Banks, looking at Hamilton and Annie, "whether our victim was hit on the head, whether his brains blew out through his skull, or whether he had a bad heart and died of low-level carbon monoxide inhalation, we know from the evidence so far that *someone* set the fire, so we're looking at murder. The best thing we can do now is try to find out just who the hell he was." Banks glanced again at the loathsome hulk on the table, the charred and leathery skin, the exposed intestines and dribbles of reddish-pink blood. "And," he added, "let's hope we're not dealing with a serial arsonist. I wouldn't want to be attending any more of these post-mortems if I could help it."

"Isn't this intimate?" said Maria Phillips, settling into her chair at a dimpled copper-topped table in a quiet corner of the Queen's Arms. "Go on, then, I'll be a devil and have a Campari and soda, please."

Banks hadn't asked her if she wanted a drink yet, but that didn't seem to bother Maria as she set her faux fur coat on the chair next to her, patted her bottle-blond curls, then reached into her handbag for her compact and lipstick, with which she busied herself while Banks went to the bar. He had given her a ring at the community center that afternoon and discovered she was working late, which suited him fine. He was glad to be in a friendly pub after the ordeal of the post-mortem and wanted nothing more than to be surrounded by ordinary, living people and to flush the taste of death by fire out of his system with a stiff drink or two.

"Evening, Cyril," he said to the landlord. "Pint of bitter

and a large Laphroaig for me and a Campari and soda for the lady, please."

Cyril raised his eyebrows.

"Don't ask," Banks said.

"You know me. The soul of discretion." Cyril started pulling the beer. "Wouldn't have said she was your type, though."

Banks gave him a look.

"Nasty fire down Molesby way."

"Tell me about it," said Banks.

"You involved already?"

"From the start. It's been a long day."

Cyril looked at the scratch on Banks's cheek. "You look as if you've been in the wars, too," he said.

Banks put his hand up and touched the scratch. "It's nothing. Just a disagreement with a sharp twig."

"Pull the other one," said Cyril.

"It's true," said Banks.

"But you can't talk about the case, I know."

"Nothing much to say, even if I could. We don't know anything yet except two people died. Cheers." Banks paid and carried the drinks back to the table, where Maria sat expectantly, perfectly manicured hands resting on the table in front of her, scarlet nails as long as a cat's claws. She was an unfashionably buxom and curvaceous woman in her early thirties, and she would look far more attractive, Banks had always thought, if she got rid of all the war paint and dressed for comfort rather than effect. And the perfume. Especially the perfume. It rolled over him in heavy, acrid waves and soured his beer. He took a sip of Laphroaig and felt it burn pleasantly all the way down. He didn't usually drink shorts in the Queen's Arms, but this evening was an exception justified by a particularly nasty postmortem and Maria Phillips both within the space of a couple of hours.

Maria made it clear that she noticed the scratch on Banks's cheek, but that she wasn't going to ask about it, not yet. "How's Sandra doing?" she asked instead. "We do so miss her at the center. Such energy and devotion."

Banks shrugged. "She's fine, far as I know."

"And the baby? It must be very strange for her, becoming a mother all over again. And at her age."

"We don't talk much these days," said Banks. He did know, though, through his daughter Tracy, that Sandra had given birth to a healthy seven-pound girl on the third of December, not much more than a month ago, and that she had named her Sinéad, not after the bald pop singer, but after Sean's mother. Well, good luck to her. With a name like that, she'd need it. As far as he knew, via Tracy, both mother and daughter were doing fine. The whole business churned his guts and changed everything, especially the way he related to his past, their shared life together. In a strange way, it was almost as if none of their twenty-plus years together had happened, that it had all been a dream or some sort of previous existence. He didn't know this woman, this child. It even made him feel different about Tracy and his son, Brian. He didn't know exactly why, how, or in what way, but it did. And how did they feel about their new half sister?

"Of course not," Maria said. "How insensitive of me. It must be very painful for you. Someone you spent so many years with, the mother of your children, and now she's had a baby with another man."

"About this artist, Tom?" Banks said.

Maria waved a finger at him. "Clever, clever. Trying to change the subject. Well, I can't say I blame you."

"This *is* the subject. At least it's the one I intended to talk about when I asked you for a drink."

"And here's silly old me thinking you just wanted to talk."

"I do. About Tom."

"You know what I mean."

"Have you ever encountered or heard of a local artist whose first name is Tom?"

Maria put her hand to the gold necklace around her throat. "Is this what you're like when you interrogate suspects?" she said. "You must terrify them."

Banks managed a weak smile. He hadn't been lying when he told Cyril it had been a long day, and it was getting longer. Every minute spent with Maria felt like an hour. "It's not an interrogation, Maria," he said, "but I *am* tired, I don't want to play games, and I really do need any information you might have." He felt like adding that he had just seen the charred remains of a corpse, watched Dr. Glendenning peel away the blackened flesh and pull out the shiny organs, but that would only make things worse. Patience. That was what he needed. And plenty of it. Problem was, where could he get it?

Maria pouted, or pretended to pout, for a moment, then said, "Is that all you know about him? That his name was Tom?"

"So far, yes."

"What did he look like?"

Banks paused, again recalling the ruined face, melted eyes, exposed jawbone and neck cartilage. "We only have a vague description," he said, "but he was fairly short, thick-set, with long greasy brown hair. And he didn't shave very often."

Maria laughed. "Sounds like every artist I've ever met. You'd think someone capable of creating a thing of beauty might take a little more pride in his appearance, wouldn't you?"

"Oh, I don't know," said Banks. "It must be nice to be able to wear what you want, not to have to put a suit on and worry about shaving every morning when you go to work."

Maria looked at him, her blue eyes twinkling. "I don't suppose you'd have to wear anything at all, would you, if it was really warm?"

"I suppose not," said Banks, gulping more Laphroaig, followed by a deep draft of beer. "But does that description ring any bells?"

She gazed at him indulgently, as if he were a wayward schoolboy, then frowned. "That *could* be Thomas McMahon," she said. "He's certainly the shortest artist I've ever met. I suppose Toulouse-Lautrec was shorter, but he was before my time." She smiled.

Banks's ears pricked up. "But he fits the description, this Thomas McMahon?"

"Sort of. I mean, he was short and squat, a bit toadish, really. He had a beard back then, but his hair wasn't really long. One thing I do remember, though . . ."

"What?"

"He had beautiful fingers." She held out her own hand, as if to demonstrate. "Long, tapered fingers. Very delicate. Not what you'd expect for such a small man."

Wasn't that what Mark had said about Tom? That he had long fingers? It wasn't a lot to base an identification on, but it was the best they had so far. "Tell me more," Banks said.

Maria waved her empty glass. "Well, I could be bribed," she said.

Banks had finished his Laphroaig and he still had half a pint left, but he wasn't having any more, as he had to drive home. He went to the bar and bought Maria another Campari and soda. The pub was filling up now, and he had to wait a couple of minutes to get served. Someone put an old Oasis song on the jukebox. The Queen's Arms was certainly a lot different from the previous summer, Banks thought, when foot-and-mouth had emptied the Dales, keeping even the locals away, and Cyril hardly had a customer from one day to the next. And this was only January, most of the people here local. Maybe the coming summer would be a boom time for the Dales businesses. They certainly needed it. Back at the table he handed Maria her drink and said, "Well?"

He was surprised when she opened her handbag and

brought out a packet of Silk Cut and a slim gold lighter. He didn't remember her as a smoker. "Do you mind?" she asked, lighting up.

It wouldn't have mattered if he did mind; the smoke was already drifting his way, along with the perfume. "No," he said, surprised to find that instead of a craving, for the first time he felt revulsion. Was he going to turn into one of those obnoxious, rabid antismokers? He hoped to hell not. He sipped some beer. It helped a little.

"I can't tell you much about him," Maria said. "If indeed he is the one you think he is."

"Let's assume that he is, for the sake of argument," said Banks.

"I mean, I wouldn't want to be responsible for sending you off in the wrong direction, wasting police time."

Banks smiled again. "Don't worry about that. I won't arrest you for it. Just tell me what you know and leave the rest to us."

"It must have been about five years ago," Maria said. "Sandra was still with us at the time. She used to talk to him quite a bit, you know. I'm sure she'd remember even better than me."

Wonderful! Banks thought. Was he going to have to go and talk to his ex-wife to get information about a case? Maybe he'd send Annie. No, that would be cruel. Jim Hatchley, then? Or Winsome? But he knew, if it came to it, that he'd have to go himself. It would be rude and cowardly not to. No doubt he'd get to see the new baby, bounce little Sinéad on his knee. Maybe Sean would be there, too, and they'd ask him to stay for dinner. Happy families. Or he might end up baby-sitting while they went out to the cinema or the theater for the evening. On the other hand, maybe it could be avoided altogether if he pressed Maria just a little harder. "Let's start with what you remember," he said.

"Well, as I said, it was a long time ago. McMahon was a

local artist, lived on the eastern edge of town, as I recall. It was part of our job to encourage local artists—not financially, you understand, but by giving them a venue to exhibit their work."

"So Thomas McMahon had an exhibition of his work at the community gallery?"

"Yes."

"And there'd be records of this? A catalog, perhaps? A photograph of him?"

"I suppose so. Down in the archives."

"Was he any good?"

Maria wrinkled her nose. "I won't pretend to be an expert on these matters, but I'd say not. There was nothing distinguished about his work, as far as I could see. It was mostly derivative."

"So he'd have a hard time making a career of it?"

"I imagine he would. He sneaked a couple of ghastly abstracts in, too, at the last moment. I have a feeling they were what he really wanted to paint, but you can't make a living from that sort of thing unless you have real talent. On the other hand, you can make a fair bit from selling local landscapes to tourists, which he did."

"Any chance that his death might affect the value of his work?"

Maria's eyes widened. "My, my, you do have a devious mind, don't you? What a delicious motive. Kill the artist to increase the value of his paintings."

"Well?"

"Not in his case, I shouldn't think. A bad watercolor of Eastvale Castle is a bad watercolor of Eastvale Castle, whether the painter is alive or dead. Perhaps a dealer might know more than I do, but I think you'll have to look elsewhere for your motive."

"Was he a drinker?"

"He liked his drink, but I wouldn't say he was a drunk."

"Drugs?"

"I wouldn't know. I saw no signs, heard no rumors."

"And you've neither seen nor heard anything of him since?"

"Oh, yes. He's dropped by a couple of times, for other artists' openings, that sort of thing. And he was at the Turner reception, of course."

"I see," Banks said. The Turner. By far the most valuable and famous painting ever to be housed in the modest community center gallery, a Turner watercolor of Richmond Castle, Yorkshire, believed lost for many years, had spent two days there after being discovered under some old insulation during a cottage renovation. Nobody knew how it had got there, but the speculation was that the original owner died and whoever had the insulation put in didn't know the value of the small painting. There had been a private reception for local bigwigs and artsy types. Annie had been involved in the security, Banks remembered. It had happened last summer, while Banks had been in Greece, and he had missed all the excitement.

"Other than that?"

"No. He dropped out of the local scene shortly after the exhibition, five years ago. I understand that his dealer had trouble selling his work, and that McMahon went through some sort of personal crisis. I don't know the details. Leslie Whitaker might be able to help. I know they were friends, and he tried to sell some of McMahon's serious paintings as well as the junk he painted for the tourist trade."

"So Whitaker was McMahon's agent?"

"Sort of, I suppose."

"Recently, too?"

"Yes. I've seen Thomas McMahon coming out of Leslie Whitaker's shop once or twice this month. He looked as if he'd been buying some books. He was carrying a package, at any rate."

"Did you talk to him?"

"Only to say hello."

"How did he seem?"

"Remarkably fit, actually. Though, as you mentioned earlier, his hair was a bit long, and it could have done with a wash. He also hadn't shaved for a few days, by the look of him."

"Do you think you could dig out a catalog and give me the names of the artists whose openings he attended?"

"Why?"

"The catalog might help identify any of his works that show up, and we'd like to talk to anyone who might have known him. A photograph would help, too."

"I can try. I'd have to look at the center's records, though."

"Could you do it first thing?"

Maria eyed him for a moment and sipped some Campari and soda. Her glass was almost empty again. "I suppose I could. You do realize it's Saturday tomorrow, though, don't you?"

"The center's open."

"Yes, but it's my day off."

"I'll send one of my DCs along then," said Banks. "It might take him a bit longer, but . . ."

"I didn't say I *wouldn't* do it."

"Then you will?"

"All right, yes. If you want."

"And you'll ring me at the station, send anything you find down there?"

"Yes." She held out her glass. "You never know; I might even deliver it myself."

"You want another drink?" Banks asked.

"Please."

"All right. But I'm afraid you'll have to drink this one by yourself. I've got a long drive home."

Maria looked disappointed. "Oh, well, in that case I won't bother . . . But I thought . . ."

"What?"

"Well, I don't live that far away. Maybe you'd like to come for a nightcap, or just a coffee or something?" She wrinkled her nose. "It might perk you up a bit."

"Thanks for asking," Banks said, hurriedly finishing his beer. "But perking up's the last thing I need right now. I really do have to get some sleep."

"Never mind, then. Some other time." Maria gathered her things together and stood up to put on her coat. "I'll ring you in the morning," she said, and made a hasty exit.

Oh, shit, thought Banks, embarrassed by the looks he was getting from others in the pub. Surely he had never given Maria Phillips any reason to think he wanted more from her than information about the artist? He had only seen her two or three times since Sandra had left, and on those occasions they had simply bumped into each other on the street, or he had visited the community center for one reason or another and had seen her there. They had done nothing but exchange small talk. Still, she had always been a strange one, he remembered, always superficially flirtatious, even when he was married to Sandra. He had thought it was just her way of relating and had never taken her seriously. And maybe that's all it was, even now. He picked up his overcoat and briefcase. At least she was going to ring him with the information he wanted in the morning, information that might take him a bit closer to the mystery that was Tom.

Annie drove her aching bones home after the postmortem, on Banks's advice. There was nothing more to be done tonight, he had told her, so best get some rest. That was exactly what she intended to do, she thought, as she locked the door of her small Harkside cottage behind her, the cottage that seemed to be at the center of a labyrinth of narrow winding streets, as Banks had once pointed out. She would have a glass of Chilean cabernet and a long hot bath, then take a couple of nighttime cold-relief capsules and hope for a peaceful night's sleep. Maybe she'd feel better in the morning.

There was one message waiting for her on her answering machine, and she was absurdly pleased to hear that it was from Phil. He would definitely be coming up to Swainsdale tomorrow and would be staying a few days at his cottage in Fortford. Would Annie care to have dinner with him one evening over the weekend, perhaps, or even early next week, if she wasn't too busy?

Well, she would, but she didn't know if she could commit herself right now, what with a big new case on the go and this damn cold dragging on. Still, being a DI gave her some perks, even if it did mean no overtime, and her evenings should be free, barring the necessity to head out somewhere overnight. If she felt well enough, there was no reason why she shouldn't tentatively agree to dinner tomorrow.

Annie dropped her keys on the table, poured herself a glass of wine and picked up the telephone.

When Banks arrived home after his drink with Maria Phillips, he also found one message waiting for him. It was from Michelle Hart, whom he realized he had forgotten to call. She just wanted to tell him that she wouldn't be able to see him this weekend as they were all working overtime on a missing-child case. Banks could well understand that. Missing children were the worst, every policeman's nightmare. It was while Michelle was looking into the disappearance of Banks's childhood friend, Graham Marshall, whose bones had been discovered the previous summer, over thirty-five years since he had disappeared, that they had met.

Even though he couldn't get away either, he still felt disappointed. This sort of thing was happening more and more often lately, so much so that they felt and acted like strangers for the first few hours every time they did meet. It was no way to sustain a relationship. First the distance, the long winter drives in fog, driving rain or hail; then the Job, the unpredictable hours. Sometimes he wondered if it was possible for a copper to have anything but the most superficial and undemanding of relationships.

He had also wondered more than once over the past few months where things were going with Michelle. They met up when they could, usually managed to have a good time, and the sex was great. But she always seemed to hold a part of herself back. Most people did, Banks realized, including himself, but with Michelle it was different, as if she were carrying around some great weight she couldn't, or wouldn't, share, and in a way it made their relationship feel superficial.

With Annie, Banks had developed a deeper relationship. That was the problem, what had made Annie run: the intimacy, and Banks's residual feelings for Sandra. And the kids, of course. The idea of Banks's two children seemed to scare Annie to death. Michelle never talked about children. Banks wondered if she had been deeply wounded by her past in some way. Annie had been raped, and they had talked about that, got it out in the open, but with Michelle . . . she just wouldn't open up.

Banks sorted through his post, pleased to see that his copies of *Gramophone* and *Mojo* had both arrived, and poured a wee dram of ten-year-old cask-strength Laphroaig, which DS Hatchley had bought him at a duty-free shop. Talk about a drink with teeth; it bit deep into your tongue, throat and gut and didn't let go. The aroma alone was enough to make you feel pissed.

Banks thought about Michelle again. Was he attracted only to wounded women? he wondered. Did he see himself as some sort of healer, a Travis McGee figure, remembering the books he'd read with prurient interest as an adolescent, along with James Bond, the Saint, Sexton Blake and Modesty Blaise. Just a few days on the *Busted Flush* with old Travis and you'll be right as rain. Well, if he did see himself that way, he wasn't making a very good job of it, was he? And you didn't get to his age, or Michelle's, without taking a hefty emotional, even physical, knock or two along the way. Especially if you happened to be a copper. Banks laughed at himself, tilted his head back and tipped his glass.

He phoned back, but Michelle was out, so he left a message of regret on her answering machine. Maybe next weekend, he said, though he doubted either of their cases would have wound down by then.

At least he had had one bit of good news when he called back at the station after his little chat with Maria Phillips: their body was *definitely* Thomas McMahon. There was only one dentist in the village of Molesby, the nearest settlement to the narrow boats, and DC Templeton had had the good sense to check there first with the dental impression. Thomas McMahon had been there for a filling less than a week before.

Sometimes it was that easy.

It was cold in the cottage, and Banks considered lighting a peat fire. Then he decided it wasn't worth it; he was sure he wouldn't be able to stay awake long enough to enjoy it. Besides, after today, there was something about the idea of even the most innocent domestic fire that frightened him. He checked the smoke detectors to see if they were both still working. They were. Then he turned on two bars of the electric fire and poured himself another drink.

He thought of watching a movie on DVD. He had recently bought a player and it had revitalized his interest in movies. He was starting to collect them the way he did CDs. In the end he decided that it was too late; he knew he would fall asleep on the sofa halfway through. Instead he put on Cassandra Wilson's *Belly of the Sun* CD and browsed through the *Gramophone* reviews. God, what a deep, rich sensuous voice Cassandra had, he thought, like melting chocolate as she worked each syllable for all she could get, stretched them out until you thought they'd break, dropped on them from high or crept up underneath them and licked and chewed them out of shape.

The whiskey tasted good, sharp, peaty and a little bit medicinal, and he wished he could go outside and stand by Gratly Falls and look down the daleside to the lights of Helmthorpe the way he did when the weather was good, but it was too cold. Oh, certainly it was mild enough for January, but after dark a chill came to the air that defied even the properties of a fine single malt whiskey to warm the cockles of one's heart. A wind had sprung up, too, and he felt as if he were marooned in his little cottage, straining against its ropes to stay on the ground.

As he put the magazine aside and settled back with his feet up, only a dim table light on, Cassandra singing Dylan's "Shelter from the Storm," his mind drifted over the day's events, as it often did at times like this. He wasn't so much thinking as just riffing, improvising on a theme, the way a jazz player did, or the way Elgar had written his *Enigma* variations.

Enigma was a good place to start. Everything about today's events seemed infused by that very quality. Elusive, inchoate, equivocal. On the one hand, it appeared as if Thomas McMahon had been the intended victim, but there were no signs of external injury other than the fire damage, and they knew nothing about any possible motive. On the other hand, Mark Siddons had had a row with his drug-addict girlfriend Tina and stormed off, but his alibi held tight, and the physical evidence exonerated him.

Tina, or Mark, had also bought drugs from Danny Boy Corcoran, and wherever drugs are concerned you have to look closely at everyone involved. Then there was Tina's stepfather, Dr. Patrick Aspern. Banks hadn't particularly liked him, but that didn't mean much in itself. He had disliked innocent people before. But if what Mark said about

Aspern and his stepdaughter was true, that was enough to give the doctor a strong motive. And both Aspern and his wife had been evasive, to say the least, when it came to alibis. On the other hand, perhaps something in Mark's own background had made him only too eager to believe Tina's story without question. That background might well be worth looking into, Banks thought, making a mental note to put DS Hatchley on it in the morning.

Andrew Hurst was another problem. Hurst haunted the canal side, he had lied about his activities, he had washed his clothes, and he had no alibi. But what motive did he have? Perhaps he didn't need one. He had first approached the scene, then he had rung the fire brigade. Maybe he was an arsonist who just liked to start fires, a pyromaniac. From what Banks knew of the basic psychology of pyromaniacs, many of them liked not only to report, hang around and watch their own handiwork, but they liked to take part in the firefighting operation, too, and help the police. Banks would see just how helpful Andrew Hurst wanted to be.

Banks thought about another Laphroaig as the CD came to an end, but decided against it. Instead, he took himself off to bed.

Chapter 5

*D*anny Boy Corcoran lived in a small flat off South Market Street, on the fringes of the student area. He had once been a business student at Eastvale College, but he had discovered a more lucrative career in selling drugs and dropped out before finishing his diploma. His flat had been under surveillance all night, and Danny and his girlfriend hadn't arrived home until eight in the morning, so Banks and Annie had the advantage. Banks felt surprisingly well rested after his early night, and even Annie looked and sounded more cheerful than she had in days. The cold still lingered, Banks could tell, by her red nose and the occasional sneeze, but it was on the wane.

Danny Boy, on the other hand, looked like crap. He had clearly just gone to bed and was wearing only a red sweatshirt with a Montego Bay logo and Y-fronts, his scrawny hairy legs sticking out below. Danny was a wannabe bad-boy Jamaican drug dealer, but unfortunately for him, in reality he had been born to white middle-class parents in Blandford Forum. His dreadlocked hair stuck out in all directions, and his bloodless face seemed paler than a vampire's in a time of famine. "Can we come in, Danny?" Banks asked, as they showed their warrant cards.

"Why? Whaddya want?"

"I'll tell you if you let us come in."

Danny's lanky frame still blocked the doorway. "Gor-rawarrant?"

"We don't need one. We just want to talk."

A figure appeared behind Danny, framed by his out-stretched arm and the doorpost, similarly thin, and pale enough to make her flesh-toned bra and panties look like a suntan. Banks could see she had goose bumps on her arms. And needle marks. "Danny, who is it? Tell them to go away and come back to bed."

"Fuck off, Nadia," Danny said without turning around. "It's business."

Nadia made a face at his back, turned and shambled away.

"Look, I don't know what you've come here disturbing my rest for," he said. "I've not done anything wrong."

"Spare us the poor, wronged-youth act, Danny. You spent last night peddling your wares in the pubs on York Road and South Market Street, then you ended up at a party on the East Side Estate."

Danny first looked puzzled, then affronted. "You've been *watching* me?"

"Someone else has. I wouldn't waste my time. Listen, Danny, how about if I tell you we're not drugs squad and this isn't about drugs? Not really. We don't *have* to search the flat, but we can if you like."

"Look, you told me . . ."

"I told you what, Danny?"

"Never mind."

"I've never spoken to you before in my life," Banks said, gently easing Danny's arm out of the way and walking into the flat. The living room was a mess, with clothes and CD cases strewn around the place, but at least it was clean and didn't smell of smoke, or worse. There was a big poster of Bob Marley smoking a spliff on one wall, probably the clos-est Danny Boy had ever got to Jamaica, and a few sad-looking potted plants on the windowsill, none of them marijuana.

"Just a few questions, Danny, that's all."

"I've always cooperated with you in the past, haven't I?"

"Like I said, I've never clapped eyes on you before in my life, but I'm sure your conduct has been exemplary," Banks said. "Let's keep it that way. Perhaps you might answer one or two little questions? Mind if we sit down?"

Danny looked suspicious, as well he might, and nodded toward two winged armchairs. He scratched his head. "You're not going to trick me, you know," he said. "I wasn't born yesterday."

"No," said Annie, making herself comfortable. "You were born on the ninth of August, 1982. We know that. We know plenty about you, Danny."

Danny was still standing, hopping from foot to foot. "Look," he said, "it's cold. Can I put the fire on and get dressed?"

"Course you can," said Banks. "It *is* a bit nippy in here."

Danny turned on the gas fire and headed to the bedroom to get dressed. Banks followed him. "What you doing?" Danny asked.

"Just routine," said Banks. "We've sort of developed a habit of not letting suspects out of our sight."

"*Suspect?* You said this wasn't about drugs."

"Get dressed, Danny."

Nadia lay in bed in the half-dark with the sheets and blanket pulled right up to her chin. "What's going on, Danny?" she asked in a whiny voice. "Come back to bed. Please."

"Go to sleep, Nadia. This won't take long." Danny pulled on a pair of jeans.

"What were you wearing on Thursday night?" Banks asked.

"Thursday? Dunno. Why?"

"I'd like to see."

"Whatever it was, it'll likely still be in the laundry basket over there. Nadia takes care of all that shit." He glared over at Nadia. "When she can be bothered."

"Oh, Danny . . ."

The laundry basket was only half full. "Got a plastic bag, Danny?" Banks asked. "A bit bigger than the ones you use for the stuff you sell."

"Very funny." Danny reached into the wardrobe and found a bin liner. "This do?"

"Nicely." Banks filled it with the clothes from the laundry basket, then followed Danny back into the living room, which was warming up a treat now.

When they had all sat down, Banks asked, "Did you hear about the boat fire just south of town?"

"I might have heard something in the pub last night. Why?"

"Two people died in that fire," said Annie.

"That's a tragedy, but it's nothing to do with me."

"You think not?" Annie took a folder from her briefcase and opened it on her knees. "We have a statement here from a young lad called Mark Siddons to the effect that you supplied him with heroin for his girlfriend, Tina Aspern. What do you have to say about that, Danny?"

Danny looked mystified. "Look, you *know* I do people little favors like that once in a while. Like I do for you. You know I'm not some big-time drug dealer. I don't understand this. What's going on? You say you're not drugs squad. You said this wasn't about drugs."

"It isn't, Danny," Banks explained. "Not exactly. I think I know what you've been trying to say. You're not sure about us, about DI Cabbot and me, so you're being very shy about it, but you've got a nice little deal going with the drugs squad, haven't you? In exchange for information about the big guys from time to time, they leave you alone. You've got protection. You're immune. It's a dangerous game, Danny. Those big guys always seem to find out where the leak is in the end, and they're not forgiving types. But that's your business. I'm sure you know the risks already. Thing is, you're not immune from me and DI Cabbot here. We've got nothing to do with the drugs squad. We're Major Crimes. What we're concerned about is the fire. It's murder we're investigating, Danny. That's why we want your clothes. Arson, not drugs. Unless there's a connection?"

"That fire was nothing to do with me. I wasn't even near the place. Nadia and me was down in Leeds till yesterday evening."

"Picking up more smack to sell this weekend?"

Danny scratched one of his underarms. "Seeing some friends."

"Getting the itch, are you?" Banks asked.

"You don't think I use that shit myself, do you?"

"Look," Annie said, "did you supply Mark Siddons with heroin for his girlfriend Tina Aspern?"

"I don't know who it was, do I? Wait a minute." He looked from one to the other. "There was nothing wrong with that shit. Nobody overdosed on that stuff. It was well cut."

"So you did?"

"Where's this going?"

Annie looked at Banks and raised her eyebrows. Banks took over. "It's serious, Danny," he said. "You see, Tina Aspern was one of the people who died in that boat fire."

"I didn't know that. I mean, I hardly even knew her. Poor kid."

"But if you supplied the heroin, Danny . . . You see, if she hadn't been under the influence, she might have survived."

"You're not sticking me with that. No way." He folded his arms.

"It's a matter of culpability, Danny," said Banks, stretching the truth and the law quite a bit. "See, if you sold her that stuff and it resulted in her death, even indirectly, then you're responsible. You don't think we'd bring you in just for selling a bag here and there, do you? This is serious business, Danny. Serious jail time."

"That's a load of bollocks and you know it," said Danny. "You must think I'm stupid, or something. I didn't make her shoot the stuff. I didn't even sell it to her. It was him who bought it from me, the boyfriend. He probably stuck the needle in her, too. How does that make me guilty of anything?"

"It's the law."

"Yeah, well, we'll wait to hear what my brief has to say about that, won't we?" He picked up a mobile phone from the coffee table. Before he could dial a number, Banks slapped it out of his hand and it bounced on the hardwood floor into the corner by the stereo.

"Hey, if you've broken that . . ." Danny started to rise from his chair but Banks leaned forward, put his hand on the boy's chest and pushed him back. "I haven't finished yet."

"Now, you wait—"

"No. *You* wait a minute, Danny. Hear me out. What happened? Did Mark and Tina rip you off, or did you figure they had more money stashed away on the boat and you'd go over there and help yourself while they were on the nod? You weren't to know Mark wasn't a user."

"I never—"

"Did you go down there last night while Tina was stoned and steal the money? Did the man from the next boat see you? Did you get into a scuffle and knock him out? What made you think of the fire, Danny? Was it the bottle of turpentine just sitting there, so inviting? It was very clever of you, by the way, leading us to think the other bloke was the victim. Very clever."

Danny just sat there shaking his head, jaw open.

"Or maybe it was one of the big guys who found out about your deal with the drugs squad? Was that it? A warning to you, Danny? 'You'll be next'?"

Banks knew he was winging it, just throwing out the line

and hoping for a bite, and the farther he went, the more he could see that he wasn't going to get one. Danny Boy Corcoran hadn't been near the boats; he hadn't killed Tina Aspern or Thomas McMahon. All he'd done was what he usually did, sell a few quids' worth of low-grade smack to weekend thrill-seekers and, in this case, the boyfriend of a more serious addict. But there was still a chance that he might know *something*.

"What kind of car do you drive?" Banks asked.

"Red Mondeo. Why?"

"Ever heard of an artist called Thomas McMahon? He lived on the next boat."

"I've never been down there. I don't like water."

"You didn't sell McMahon heroin, too?"

"No way."

"How did Mark and Tina find you in the first place?"

"It's not difficult, if you want what they wanted. Word of mouth usually works just fine. Anyway, as it happens, there's this mate in Leeds, said they're all right."

That was what Mark had told him, Banks remembered. "What's his name?"

"Come off it!"

"His name," Annie said. "If you don't tell us, Mark Siddons will. His girlfriend's been killed, remember?"

Danny looked from Annie to Banks, then down at the floor. "Benjamin Scott," he whispered. "And don't tell him I told you. He can be a nasty piece of work, can Benjy." Danny clutched his stomach. "My guts hurt. Are you nearly finished?"

"Address?" Annie asked.

Danny gave her an address in Gipton. Banks would phone DI Ken Blackstone at Millgarth in Leeds and ask him to check out Mr. Benjamin Scott.

"One more thing, Danny," Banks said as they stood up to leave.

"What?"

"As of now, you're out of business."

"What do you mean?"

"You heard."

"You can't—"

"I can do what I want, Danny. And I will. Let me put it simply: I don't like drug dealers. You'll be watched. Not by me, and not by the drugs squad, but by people I trust. And if anyone sees you dealing smack again you'll be pulled in before your feet can touch the ground. Got it?"

"I don't—"

"And if that doesn't work, pretty soon Benjy and his friends will find out you've been two-timing them with the drugs squad. Is *that* clear enough?"

Danny paled.

"Is it?" Banks pressed.

Danny swallowed and nodded.

At that moment, Nadia walked in again and stood over Danny, rubbing her pale thin arms. "Danny," she said, "please hurry up. I need something. I need it bad."

Danny rolled his eyes. "Oh, for fuck's sake."

Banks and Annie left with their bag of laundry.

Mark signed for his belongings: money, penknife, keys and the portable CD player he'd stuck in his pocket with an old David Bowie CD in it, the only CD he had left now. He liked Bowie; the man never stood still long enough for anyone to pigeonhole him; he was always changing, moving on. *Ziggy Stardust. The Thin White Duke.* Maybe Mark would be like that now. When Tina was around, there had been someone worth working for, worth settling down with. But now . . . what was the point in going on without her?

"What about my clothes?" he asked.

"Not back from the lab yet," said the custody officer.

"But they've done the tests. They've proved I didn't set the fire. It's cold out there. I'll need my jacket."

"It's the weekend. These things take time. Try coming back next week. In the meantime . . ." With obvious disapproval, the officer brought out a carrier bag from under the desk and handed it over to Mark. "DCI Banks said to give you this." He gestured with his thumb. "You can change in there."

Mark went into the room they used for fingerprinting and photographing suspects and took off his red overalls. Banks's jeans fitted him okay around the waist, but they were a bit long, so he rolled up the bottoms. The sleeves of the old three-quarter-length suede overcoat with the worn fleece lining were also too long, and it was hardly top of the line as far as youth fashion was concerned. Still, it looked warm enough, and it was decent of the copper to remember his promise, Mark thought.

This was all he had now, what he was wearing, borrowed as it was, and what had been in his pockets. He didn't even have any cigarettes left, and given how expensive they were, he probably shouldn't go spending what little money he had left on them. So this was it, then. Oh, there was stuff back at home, of course, if Crazy Nick hadn't destroyed it all. Old clothes, toys, some CDs. But he'd never be going back there. Certainly not now his mum had died of lung cancer, as his Auntie Grace had told him, and there was only Crazy Nick left.

At last he walked through the front doors of the police station to freedom, though it was a freedom blighted by loss and uncertainty. To be honest, Mark wouldn't have complained if they'd locked him up for a bit longer. He'd been warm and well-fed in the nick, and no one had mistreated him. Outside, in the gray Tina-less world, who knew what lay ahead?

A couple of passersby edged around him and looked down their noses, as if they knew exactly where he'd just come from. Well, sod them, he thought, taking a deep breath of cool air. Sod them all.

The copper, Banks, had just come out of the Golden Griddle and was walking across Market Street toward him. "Mark," he said. "How do they fit?"

"All right," said Mark. "They'll do for now. I mean, thanks."

"You're welcome. Just a quick word."

"What?"

"It might be nothing," Banks said, "but I've been thinking about the fire, the way it was spread to your boat."

"And?"

"Well, I don't want to alarm you, but it might have been a sort of shot across the bows, so to speak, a warning shot."

"What do you mean?"

"Maybe whoever did it didn't know whether you could identify him or not. Maybe he didn't even know Tina was there, but he was just sending you a message."

"What message?"

"Not to say anything, or else."

"But I don't know anything."

"Are you sure, Mark? Are you certain you didn't get a better look at Tom's visitors?"

"No. I told you the truth."

"All right," said Banks. "I believe you. Like I said, I don't want to alarm you, but if he thinks you know who he is, you could be in danger. Go carefully. Keep your eyes open."

"I can take care of myself," said Mark.

"Good," said Banks. "I'm glad to hear it. Just watch your back, that's all." He gave Mark a card. "And here's my number if you think of anything. Mobile, too."

Mark took the card and Banks disappeared inside the police station.

It was market day and the canvas-covered stalls were all set up in the cobbled square, chock-a-block with cheap clothes, car accessories, washing-up liquid, batteries, the cheese van, the butcher, the greengrocer, crockery, cutlery, toys, used books and videos. The older cloth-capped, waxed-jacketed punters milled around with the younger leather-and-denim crowd, fingering the goods while barkers shouted out the virtues of their unbreakable tableware or infallible electric bottle openers.

There was nothing Mark wanted at the market, so he set off down the street, hands thrust deep in his pockets, head down, thinking about what Banks had just told him. He'd never realized that *he* might be in danger. Now, though, he looked at everyone with a keener eye, though he didn't really know whom he was looking for. Still, if what Banks had said was right, and if the killer did believe that Mark might have seen him, then he'd better watch himself.

Mark felt something in one of the pockets of Banks's suede overcoat. He pulled it out. A packet of Silk Cut, with two left, and a disposable lighter. What a piece of luck. Mark lit up. At least he had a fag, old and dry as it tasted.

He went through the other pockets to see if Banks had left any money, but all he found was a couple of old parking stubs and a note with "Schoenberg—Gurrelieder—del Mar/Sinopoli" written on it, which meant bugger all to him. Mark had always admitted he wasn't much when it came to the brains department. He was a hard worker, good with his hands, and he'd tackle anything within reason, but when it came to brains and spelling, leave him out of it. The copper must be a brainy fellow if he'd written that, Mark thought. It didn't even look like English. Maybe it was somewhere he went on his holidays. Mark had never been abroad, but he'd probably do that one day, too, he thought. Somewhere really weird like Mongolia. Ulan Bator. He'd seen it on a map in the squat and liked the sound of it. *Ulan Bator*. See, he wasn't so stupid after all.

He put the headphones over his ears and turned on the CD player as he made his way among the Saturday-morning shoppers on South Market Street. Bowie came on singing

"Five Years," one of Mark's favorites. It was nice to have real music again, better than that fucking drunk singing "Your Cheatin' Heart." Even so, he felt numb and aimless, as if the music were coming down a long tube from far away. Everything had seemed like that since he knew Tina was dead. He was going through the motions, but really he wasn't going anywhere.

After walking for about half an hour, Mark arrived at the construction site. The outside of the new gym complex was mostly completed, but there was a lot to be done inside—laying the floors, drywalling, fixtures and fittings, plumbing, electrics, painting—and it could all be done in winter, even if the weather was bad. The door was open and Mark went in. Things weren't going full-tilt because it was a Saturday, but a lot of blokes worked weekends—Saturdays, at any rate, to get their jobs done by the deadline.

Inside, the place had the smell of newness about it. Not paint, because that hadn't been applied yet, but just a melange of various things, from new-cut wood to the slightly damp cardboard boxes that things came in, to the sawdust that scattered the floors. Mark used to like the smell, the way he liked the smell of cut stone, but he couldn't say why, only that it sparked something instinctive in him, something beyond words, beyond brains. There was a music to all the activity, too, a unity. Not David Bowie's music, but hammers, drills and electric saws. To some it was noise, but to Mark it used to have pattern and meaning, the pattern and meaning of something being made. A symphony. It made him feel the same way as the music of the sea, which formed the background of some of his only happy childhood memories. He thought he must have been there when he was very young with his mother, before the drinking, before Crazy Nick. He thought it was Scarborough, had a vague memory of the castle on the hill, the waves crashing over the promenade. But he couldn't remember for certain. None of it mattered now, anyway.

Lenny Knox was a subcontractor, a big, burly Liverpudlian with a face like red sandpaper, who usually worked every day God sent until the job was done. Sure enough, he was having a smoke by what were to be the showers and locker rooms when Mark came over. Vinnie Daly, one of his other workmates, put down his spanner when he saw Mark.

"Where you been, mate?" Lenny asked. "We was worried sick when we heard about the fire, weren't we, Vinnie? They wouldn't say on the news who got hurt, like. You all right?"

"I'm all right," said Mark. "Police took me in, didn't they? Kept me overnight."

"The bastards."

"It wasn't so bad."

"What about your young lass?"

Mark looked down at the unfinished floor. "She's dead, Lenny."

"Oh, no," said Lenny, touching Mark on the shoulder. "Poor wee devil. I'm sorry, son, really I am. She were a nice lass."

Mark looked at him, holding back the tears. "I wasn't there, Lenny. I wasn't there for her."

"It's not your fault, what happened. Look, if you need somewhere to kip, you know, for a couple of days, like, I'm sure my Sal won't mind."

"You sure, Lenny? 'Cos I've got nowhere else to go right now."

"Yeah, it's okay. Look, you don't want to be here today. Take yourself off, if you like, and come round to ours later."

"No. I want to work. What else would I do? Where would I go? Besides, it'll take my mind off things for a while at least. And I need the money." The last was certainly true, but whether work would take his mind off his problems, Mark didn't know. How could anything stop him from thinking about Tina?

Lenny looked down at him. "Of course," he said. "Of course. Right. Look, why don't you pick up those shower-heads over there and come with me."

Late Saturday morning, after warning Mark Siddons and setting a slowly recovering DS Hatchley the task of digging into the boy's background, Banks headed for Adel again. Maria Phillips, true to her word, had left him the catalog and the names of three local artists whose openings Thomas McMahon had attended in Eastvale over the past five years. Unfortunately, there was no photograph of McMahon in the catalog. Apparently, people were not particularly interested in what artists looked like unless they painted self-portraits.

Banks wanted another crack at Dr. Patrick Aspern, without his wife present this time, if possible, and with the gloves off. Aspern wasn't off his suspect list yet, not by a long chalk.

As Banks drove, he listened to Bob Dylan singing about being in Mississippi for a day too long and thought he knew the feeling. Not so much being in Yorkshire too long—he was still happy there—but staying with something or someone until long after you should have left, let go, when it all falls to pieces and the real damage gets done.

He pulled up outside the Tudor-style house, and this time Patrick Aspern himself answered the door, casually dressed in gray trousers, white shirt and a mauve V-neck sweater. He looked as if he was dressed for a round of golf, and he probably was. Banks suspected there would be no surgery on weekends.

"My wife's lying down," said Dr. Aspern, clearly surprised to see Banks back so soon. "This has all been a great shock to her, you know, especially seeing Christine, the state the body was in. If only she'd listened to me, at least she might have been spared that."

"A shock to you, too, I should imagine?" said Banks. "I mean, Christine's death."

"Yes, of course. But we men realize we have to get on with our jobs, don't we? Can't afford to dwell on our emotions the way women do. Anyway, I can't imagine how I can help you, but do come in."

Banks followed him into the same room he had been in the previous day. The clock ticking on the mantelpiece was the only sound.

"Have you found anything out yet?" Aspern asked.

"Not much, I'm afraid," said Banks. "We do know that the man on the other boat was an artist called Thomas McMahon, and that he was most likely the intended victim. Have you ever met him or heard of him?"

"McMahon? Can't say as I have."

"I'd like to talk to you about Mark Siddons a bit more," Banks said.

Aspern's expression darkened. "If anyone's responsible for what happened to Christine, it's him," he said. "I've been thinking about it. If he'd been with her, as he should have been, she'd be alive today. He knew she was ill, for crying out loud, knew she needed taking care of."

"I thought you didn't like the idea of their being together?"

"That's not the point. If he was supposed to be with her, he should have been there. He knew she wasn't capable of looking after herself properly. Where was he, anyway?"

Banks was damned if he was going to tell Patrick Aspern that Mark had been in bed with Mandy Patterson at the time of the fire. "His alibi's been checked," was all he said. "I take it your surgery is attached to the house?"

Aspern looked surprised by the abrupt change of subject. "Yes. Actually, it was two houses knocked into one. I know it's rather old-fashioned, but people around here like it. It's so much more civilized than some anonymous clinic. That's one of the reasons we bought the houses in the first place."

"Pretty expensive proposition."

"Not that it's any of your business, but Fran's father helped us out."

"I see. Very nice of him. Anyway, what I'm getting at is that Christine *could* have had access to drugs here, couldn't she? They were in the house, after all."

Aspern crossed his legs and tugged at the crease of his trousers. "As I told you last time, I keep everything in my surgery under lock and key. The surgery itself is also securely locked when I'm not there."

"Yes, but presumably the keys are somewhere around?"

"On my key chain. In my pocket."

"So they're always with you?"

"Well, almost always. I mean . . . not when I'm asleep or in the bath . . ."

"So Christine could have got access, for example, while you were asleep, or out somewhere?"

"I'd have my keys with me if I was out."

"But there is a possibility, isn't there? She could even have had copies made."

"I suppose there's the possibility. But it didn't happen."

"Did you ever notice any drugs missing from your surgery? Specifically morphine?"

"No. And, believe me, I would have noticed."

"Didn't you ever notice anything unusual about Christine's behavior while she was living at home?"

"No, not particularly. She seemed tired, listless, spent a lot of time alone, in bed. You know teenagers. They seem to need sixteen hours' sleep a day. To be honest, I didn't even see that much of her."

"But you're a *doctor*. You're trained to spot signs other people might miss."

Aspern gave a grim smile. "We're not infallible, you know, despite what some people think."

"So you had no idea that Christine was taking drugs?"

"None at all. Like I said, she was a teenager. Teenagers are surly and uncommunicative, whether they're on drugs or not."

"What about her eyes? Didn't you notice dilated pupils?"

"I might have done, but I wouldn't necessarily jump to the conclusion that my stepdaughter is a drug addict. Would you?"

Banks wondered. What would he think if he noticed those signs in Tracy or Brian? As a policeman, he had certainly been trained to look for them. But if he challenged either of his children and the explanation was innocent, such a challenge could cause irreparable damage to their relationship. They'd never trust him again. On the other hand, if he were right . . . Fortunately, he had never been put to the test. Brian played in a rock band, so he was probably the one with the best access to drugs. Banks didn't doubt that his son had tried marijuana, perhaps even Ecstasy. Banks could live with that. Maybe Brian had also taken the odd upper on the road to stay awake. But nothing stronger, surely? Not heroin. And Tracy? No, she was far too sensible and conventional, wasn't she?

"Didn't you ever notice needle marks on her arms?" Banks paused. "Or in other places, perhaps?"

Aspern stared at him. His expression was hard to read: cold but quizzical. "That's a strange question," he said finally. "If I had, then I would have known what was going on. I said I didn't know, ergo I can't have noticed anything."

"I suppose she must have worn long-sleeved tops," Banks said.

Aspern got up, walked over and leaned on the mantelpiece by the watercolor of Adel Woods. He looked as if he were posing for a photograph. "Indeed she must have," he said. "Look, I understand you have your job to do and all that, and I think I've been more than patient with you. But I've just lost my stepdaughter, and I'm beginning to get a very suspicious feeling about this conversation. If this artist on the other boat was the intended victim, why are you asking so many questions about Christine? She was merely an innocent bystander."

"Oh, nothing's obvious yet," Banks said. "It's still early days. Believe me, we're gathering as much information as we can about Thomas McMahon, but we have to follow every lead we have and avoid jumping to conclusions. I said it *looked* as if Christine wasn't the intended victim, but criminals can be very clever at misdirecting investigations, especially if they've had a chance to think out and plan their crimes ahead of time."

"You think that's how this happened? It was planned?"

"It's beginning to look that way to me."

"I still don't understand why you're questioning *me* this way. You can't think I had anything to do with it, surely?"

"Where were you on Thursday night?"

Aspern laughed. "I don't believe this."

"Humor me."

"I was here, of course. With my wife. Just like I told you the last time you asked."

"Nobody else? No dinner guests?"

"No. We ate by ourselves, then we watched television. It was a quiet evening at home."

"What time did you go to bed?"

"Eleven o'clock, as usual."

"You always go to bed at eleven o'clock?"

"Weeknights, yes. We sometimes stay up a bit later at weekends, or we may go to the opera, dine with friends. Believe it or not, my job can be rather tiring, and I do need my wits about me."

"Of course. Wouldn't want the hand that holds the needle to be shaking, would we?" Banks was wondering how he could get around to Mark's accusation that Aspern had sexually abused Christine. If there was an easy way, he couldn't think of it. He decided to jump right in. "Mark Siddons had something else to say about Christine," he said.

"Oh?"

"He said that one of the reasons she left home was that you were sexually abusing her."

At least Aspern didn't act outraged, Banks noticed. He seemed to take the accusation calmly and consider it. "And you believe him?"

"I didn't say that."

"Then why mention it, especially at a time like this? Can't you see how upsetting an accusation like that can be to a grieving relative, however groundless?"

Banks stood up and looked Aspern in the eye. "Dr. Aspern, this is a murder investigation. We might not know exactly who the intended victim was, or victims were, but we do know that two people died. One of them was your stepdaughter. Now, I'm very sorry for your loss, but as you said earlier, we men have to get on with our jobs, don't we? That's what I'm doing. And anything that I think might be relevant to the investigation, I ask questions about. That's not unreasonable, is it?"

"Put that way," Aspern said, "I suppose not."

"So will you answer my question?"

"It's hardly worth dignifying with a denial."

Banks looked into his eyes. "Try anyway."

"Very well. The accusation is absurd. I never touched my stepdaughter. Will that do?"

He was lying, Banks knew it. In that instant, he knew that Tina and Mark Siddons had been telling the truth. But who would believe him? And how could it be proved? What could he do about it?

So intent was he on registering his awareness of Patrick Aspern's body language and facial signals that he didn't notice the figure in the doorway until she spoke.

"What is it?" Frances Aspern asked, her face still soft and puffy from sleep. "What's going on?"

They both turned to face her. Patrick Aspern looked at his wife and said, "It's nothing, darling. Just a few more questions, that's all."

The look that passed between them said more than enough.

Chapter 6

*B*anks had loved the smell of old bookshops ever since he was a child, and Leslie Whitaker's Antiquarian Books and Prints, in the maze of cobbled alleys at the back of the police station, was no exception. It stood in a row of particularly ancient shops with low, crooked beams and mullioned bay windows thick as magnifying glass. On one side was a tobacconist's, with its wooden bowls of exotic pipe tobaccos, and on the other, J. W. Allen, apothecary, with the antique blue, green and red bottles in the window. Purely for the tourists, of course.

The bell jangled over the door as Banks entered. It was hard to define the smell, a mix of dust, leather and paper, even a spot of mildew, perhaps, but its effect was as comforting to Banks as that of freshly mown hay, or bread straight from the baker's oven. Something to do with a childhood spent in the children's library and many days as a teenager spent browsing in secondhand bookshops. He paused on the threshold to inhale and savor the sensation, then presented his warrant card to the man shelving books across the room.

"A chief inspector, indeed," Whitaker said. "And on a Saturday afternoon, too. I am honored."

"We're short-staffed," Banks said. While this was partly true, it was not the real reason he often made such routine calls himself. Most chief inspectors spent their careers behind desks piled high with paper, or in meetings thrashing out details of budget and manpower, paper clips and databases, cost-effective policing, flow charts and value assessments. While Banks had plenty of that to do, he also liked to keep his hand in, liked to stay close to the street policing he had grown up with. It was partly a matter of solidarity with the troops, who appreciated that their boss would often carry out the same tedious, dead-end tasks as they did, even get his hands dirty; and partly selfishness, because Banks hated paperwork and loved getting out there and sniffing out the lie or the possible lead. Some of the young turks who had come up through accelerated promotion schemes didn't understand why he just wouldn't settle down to "administrative" duties, which was what many of them aspired to in the long run.

Banks's instincts as a working detective had developed enough over the years, and his success rate was high enough, that neither Detective Superintendent Gristhorpe nor Assistant Chief Constable Ron McLaughlin stood in his way. And if Banks also chose to interview a suspect— a task usually carried out by a lowly DC, or DS at the highest, and one which most people above the rank of inspector had forgotten how to do—then that was fine with his bosses, too, as he had a knack for the thrust and parry, or the subtle persuasiveness of a good interrogation.

All Banks knew so far was that Leslie Whitaker had taken over the business from his father, Ernest, who had died two years ago. There was a framed photograph of what Banks took to be the two of them on Whitaker's desk. He didn't correspond with Banks's mental image of an antiquarian book dealer, though the picture of the wispy-haired man in the ill-fitting sweater was a bit of a stereotype. Whitaker was in his early forties, dressed in a light-gray suit, white shirt and maroon tie. His short dark hair was thinning a bit at the temples, but the look suited him. He looked fit and well muscled. Banks supposed that, with his strong chin and clear blue eyes, women, and perhaps even men, found him handsome. He had no criminal record, and DS Hatchley, who knew everything about these matters, hadn't been able to unearth any gossip about him.

"What can I do for you?" Whitaker asked. "Do please sit down."

He sat behind his ancient polished desk at the rear of the shop and gestured Banks to a hard-backed chair. Banks sat. "It's information I'm after, really," he said.

"Some crime in the book world?"

"Art world, actually. Or so it appears."

"Well, that would certainly make more sense. The art world's rife with crime."

"I suppose you've heard about the fire on the canal boats?"

"Yes. Tragic. Terrible business."

"We have reason to believe that one of the victims was an artist called Thomas McMahon. I believe you knew him?"

"Tom McMahon? Good Lord. I had no idea."

"So you did know him?"

"Tom? Well, yes, vaguely. I mean, I'd no idea where he was living or what he was up to, but I know him—knew him—yes."

"From what context?"

"I sell his work. Or rather, I liaise between Tom and the various craft markets, shops and boutiques throughout the dale that sell the landscapes he paints. And a few years ago, when he was regarded as an up-and-coming artist, I collected a couple of his paintings and even managed to sell a few."

"What happened?"

"He just never took off. It happens more often than you'd think. The art world's brutal, and it's very difficult to break into. He had a big exhibition at the community center, and I thought maybe he had a chance, but . . . in the end he just didn't make the grade."

"Was he talented?"

"Talented?" Whitaker frowned. "Yes, of course. But what does that have to do with anything?"

Banks laughed. "Well, I've seen enough squiggles on blank canvases selling for thousands to know what you mean, but it was a genuine question."

Whitaker pursed his lips. "Tom's technique was excellent," he said, "but derivative. When it came right down to it, he just wasn't very original."

That was exactly what Maria Phillips had said. "Derivative of whom?"

"He was all over the map, really. Romantic landscapes. Pre-Raphaelites. Impressionism. Surrealism. Cubism. That was the problem with Tom; he didn't have any particular distinctive style, nothing you could point to with any amount of certainty and say *that's* a Thomas McMahon."

"So the paintings you bought . . . ?"

"Worthless."

"Doesn't his death change that?"

Whitaker laughed. "I see what you're getting at. Many artists didn't get famous until after they were dead. Van Gogh, for one. But he *was* an original. I don't think death is going to make Thomas McMahon's works immortal, or valuable. No, Mr. Banks, I'm afraid I have no motive for getting rid of Tom McMahon, and I didn't exactly pay a fortune for the paintings in the first place."

Again, it was much the same as Maria had told him. "I wasn't implying that you had a motive," said Banks. "I'm simply trying to get at who might benefit from his death."

"Nobody I can think of. It can't have been easy for him, though," mused Whitaker.

"Why not?"

"Failure's never easy to handle, is it?"

Banks, who had missed nabbing more than one obvious villain in his career, knew how true that was. He remembered the failures more than the successes, and every one of them galled him. "I suppose not," he said.

"I mean you head out of a successful exhibition thinking you're Pablo Picasso, and the next day people don't even bother reading your name in the bottom right-hand corner of the canvas. Then all you've got left to give them is nothing more than a sort of glorified photograph to remind them of their holiday in the Dales. So much for artistic vision and truth."

"Is that how McMahon felt?"

"I can't say for certain. He never talked about it. But I know it's how I'd feel. Forgive me, I'm just extrapolating."

"But you sell these 'glorified photographs'—or at least you help to."

"For a commission, yes. It's a business."

"I understand McMahon was also a customer of yours?"

Whitaker shifted in his chair and glanced at the top shelf of books. "He dropped by the shop from time to time."

"What did he buy?" Banks looked around at the leather-bound books and the bins of unframed prints and drawings. "I'd have thought your fare was a bit pricey for the likes of Thomas McMahon," he said.

"They're not all expensive. Many books and prints, even old ones, are hardly worth more than the paper they were printed on. It's actually quite rare to come across the sort of find that makes your pulse race."

"So McMahon bought cheap old books and prints?"

"Inexpensive ones."

"Why?"

"I've no idea. I suppose he must have liked them."

"What did he buy the last time you saw him?"

"An early-nineteenth-century volume of natural history. Nothing special. And the binding was in very poor shape."

"How much did it cost?"

"Forty pounds. A steal, really."

Yes, Banks thought, but what was a man squatting on a narrow boat doing spending forty pounds on an old book? He remembered the wet, charred pages he'd seen on the boat with Geoff Hamilton. Well, McMahon *was* an artist, and perhaps he just loved old books and prints. "Can you tell me anything about his state of mind?"

"He seemed fine whenever I saw him. In very good spirits, really. He even so much as hinted that things might be on the up for him."

"Was he specific?"

"No. It was just when I asked him how he was, you know, as you do. Well, you don't really expect much more than 'fine, thanks' as a reply, do you? But he said he was thriving and that they might think they could grind old Tom down but he'd still got a trick or two up his sleeve. He often referred to himself in the third person."

"Who are 'they'?"

Whitaker shrugged. "Didn't say. The world in general, I assumed. The ones who refused to recognize his talent and buy his masterpieces."

"And what trick did he have to show them?"

"No idea. I'm merely reporting what he said. Tom always tended to talk a good game, as they say."

"You think there was any truth to it, that his fortunes were improving?"

"Who can say? Not from sales to the tourists, they weren't."

"So you hadn't noticed any decline in him? In his appearance or mental state?"

"Quite the opposite, really. I mean, Tom was never the

model of sartorial elegance—he was always a bit paint-stained and disheveled—but his clothes sense seemed to have improved. He'd also lost a bit of weight. And mentally, I'd say he was in good spirits."

"Was he ever married?"

"I think he might have been, once upon a time, but if he was, it was long before he fetched up here in Eastvale."

"Womanizer?"

"No, not really."

"Men? Little boys?"

"No, don't get me wrong. Tom wasn't that way inclined. He liked women, even had the occasional girlfriend, but nothing lasted. There was only one love for him, and that was art. It was always his art that came first—came even before such mundane matters as punctuality and thoughtfulness, if you see what I mean. And it was such a damn shame that his art wasn't really worth much to anyone else."

Banks nodded. Whitaker might as well have been describing a policeman's lot. He'd forgotten his share of dates and anniversaries because he'd been too involved in a case. That was partly why his marriage had ended. The miracle was, he realized only later, that it had lasted so long in the first place. He had assumed everything was fine because Sandra was an independent spirit and got on with her own life. And so she did—ultimately to the extent of taking up with Sean, dumping Banks and getting pregnant in her mid-forties. And now she was a mother again. "Any particular girlfriends you remember?" he asked.

"Well, he was rather taken by young Heather. Can't remember her second name. Worked in the artists' supplies shop down York Road. I can't say I blame him. She was quite a stunner. Real page-three material. I don't think she's there anymore, though the owner might know where she is. Much too young for Tom, of course. He was asking for grief, there."

"How old was he?"

"It was about five years back, so he'd have been in his late thirties."

"And Heather?"

"Early twenties."

"Serious?"

"On his part. He was quite broken up when she traded him in for a more successful artist. That was one of the few times I saw him pissed. I think it really depressed him, you know, feeling all washed-up as an artist, and then his girl chucks him for someone more successful. That was about as low as I ever saw him."

Well, that would do it, thought Banks. "Who did she leave him for?"

"Jake Harley. Glib bastard, I must say. Up-and-comer at the time, but I'm happy to report that he went nowhere, too. He didn't have the guts to live with his failure, though. He committed suicide about eighteen months ago down in London. Of course, he'd split with Heather ages before then."

"And you don't know where she is now?"

"Sorry. Haven't clapped eyes on her in about three years. Sam Prescott might know, though. He still runs the shop."

"You don't know of any more recent girlfriends?"

Whitaker shook his head.

"Was he ever with anyone when he came in here, male or female?"

"No. He was always alone."

"Did he ever mention anyone, any names at all?"

"No, not that I can recall. But he was always a bit of a loner, especially after Heather."

Banks stood up and stretched out his hand. "Well, thanks very much, Mr. Whitaker. You've been a great help."

"I can't see how, but you're welcome, I'm sure."

"Can you think of anyone else we might talk to about McMahon?"

Whitaker thought for a moment. "Not really." He mentioned a couple of artists whose names Banks had already heard from Maria Phillips. It sounded to Banks as if McMahon had shed his earlier life and friends and cut off all contact with the old world, the world that had burned him, had refused to recognize his talent. Whether he had found new friends or adopted the life of a recluse, the way it seemed, remained to be seen. And why had he been buying worthless old books and prints from Leslie Whitaker?

Annie had been around enough artists in her time to recognize the type. Baz Hayward had adopted the persona of the suffering, world-weary, misunderstood, dissolute genius, justifying all his excesses and his total lack of talent and social graces by his devotion to art—right down to the beard, the ragged clothes and the body odor. Whether he really did have any talent or not, she didn't know. Some of the most obnoxious people she had ever known possessed immense talent, though many of them squandered it.

Hayward bade her wait for a moment while he finished off some essential brushstrokes to a painting he was working on. Smiling to herself over the pathetic arrogance of his need to seem important, Annie wandered over and looked out of the window. She knew she could play the heavy if she wanted, but luckily she was in a good mood because she was going to dinner with Phil tonight, all being well.

Hayward lived in a converted barn on the high road between Lyndgarth and Helmthorpe. It was an isolated spot with a spectacular view down the slope past the stubby ruins of Devraulx Abbey to the drizzle-darkened flagstone roofs of Fortford, where Phil's cottage was. Smoke from chimneys drifted slowly eastward on the faint breeze, bringing a hint of peat to the air. On the steeply rising slopes of the south daleside, beyond the clustered cottages of Mortsett and Relton, Annie could see the imposing symmetry of Swainsdale Hall.

It was odd to see the hall from this perspective, she realized. Only last summer, she had spent some time there, heading the search for a missing boy. Today, no smoke came from the high chimneys. Annie guessed that ex-footballer Martin Armitage was in Florida or the West Indies with his wife, ex-model Robin Fetherling. Well, good for them. There wasn't much left for them at Swainsdale Hall now.

Hayward's loft was chilly and Annie kept her greatcoat on. The cold didn't seem to bother Hayward himself, though, who was prancing around waving his paintbrush, wearing torn jeans and a dirty white T-shirt. If he'd been at the Turner reception, Annie didn't remember him.

She had been surprised to hear from Banks that Thomas McMahon had also been there, and when she cast her mind back, she thought she remembered a short, burly fellow with a glass of wine in his hand chatting to some of the center's committee members. It had been a crowded room, though, and she had been there partly to keep an eye on the painting in the adjoining room, so she could easily have missed both McMahon and Hayward.

Annie had met Phil Keane at the reception. He was there in his professional capacity as an art researcher to help authenticate the find. They hadn't talked much that evening, but Phil had phoned her a few weeks later and asked her out to dinner. She'd been busy—it wasn't an excuse—but he had phoned again a week later, as she suggested. That time, she accepted. They had seen each other only four or five times since then, because of the pressures of their work, but each time Annie found herself becoming more and more attracted to his charm, his consideration and his intellect—not to mention his graceful and finely honed body. She was also inordinately pleased to find that Phil had heard of her father's work.

Finally, she heard Hayward throw down the brush and play himself a brief fanfare. "Finished."

"It's a wonderful view," Annie said, gesturing toward the window.

"What?" Hayward looked confused. "Oh, yes," he said, catching on, "I suppose it is, if you like that sort of thing. Personally I think landscapes are vastly overrated, and landscape painting died with the invention of the camera. It just hasn't had the decency to roll over and accept the fact. A good digital camera can do anything the Impressionists ever did."

"That's an interesting way of looking at it," said Annie, perching on the edge of the only uncluttered chair. Discarded clothes littered the floor and mold grew in a half-empty coffee cup on the low table. She was glad he didn't offer her tea or coffee. But it was the walls that disturbed Annie most of all. They were covered with what she could only assume to be Hayward's own sketches and paintings, all looking like Rorschach tests painted by Francis Bacon on drugs. The whole effect was dizzying and disturbing, and it made her vaguely queasy, though she wasn't at first sure why. Still, they must sell, she thought, or he wouldn't be able to afford this place.

"It is, isn't it?" said Hayward, waving his hand dismissively. "I try to break free from conventional ways of thinking and living. Anyway, it's the isolation I like. I keep the curtains closed most of the time."

"Good idea," said Annie. "Thomas McMahon. You were friends once. What happened?"

"Tom? Friends?" He ran his hand through his lank, greasy hair. "Yes, I suppose we were, in a way."

"Did you have a falling-out?"

"I disagreed with his artistic direction, or lack of one—the kind of abstract effects he was working on went out with the Cubists, and then there were those dreadful landscapes he churned out for the tourist trade."

"To pay the rent?"

"I suppose so. But rent's not that important in the grand scheme of things, is it?"

Annie felt glad she wasn't Hayward's landlord. "When did you last see him?"

"Must have been four, five years ago."

"Not since?"

"No. He just sort of dropped out of the scene. What scene there is." Hayward scratched his crotch. "I saw less of him. He became more distant and moody. In the end, I didn't even know where he was living. I thought he'd left town."

"You didn't bump into him at the Turner reception last summer, then?"

Hayward pulled a face. "Do me a favor. *Turner?* You think I'd waste my time with that sort of tripe?"

"Of course," Annie said. "Forgive me. I should have known. Despite the fact that you didn't approve of McMahon's art, did you have any sort of personal falling-out?"

"No. We were always on good terms. Polite terms, at any rate. And whatever it was he did, it wasn't art."

"But you've no idea what he was up to more recently?"

"None at all."

"His work hasn't appeared anywhere?"

"Thank God, no."

"Would it surprise you to hear that we think he was squatting on a boat on the canal, a boat that was set on fire on Thursday night, killing him and the girl on the neighboring boat?"

If Annie had any hopes of shocking Hayward into some sort of decent human reaction, they were soon dashed. "No," he said. "Nothing really surprises me anymore. Except art. And even that doesn't surprise me as often as it used to. As Diaghilev said to Jean Cocteau, *'Étonne moi.'* Ha! If only."

"Do you have any idea why anyone would want to kill Tom McMahon?"

"For painting bad pictures?"

"Mr. Hayward."

Hayward grinned. "A bit too brutal for you, that, was it? Too close to the bone?"

"You seem to be very aware of the effects you're striving for," Annie said. "I'd be careful that it doesn't give a sort of stiff, wooden aspect to your art. That kind of arrogant, straining self-consciousness can be quite counterproductive, you know."

"What would you know about it?"

"Nothing. Just an opinion."

"Uninformed opinion is about as interesting as a Constable landscape."

"Ah," said Annie, who thought Constable landscapes quite interesting. More interesting than what was on Hayward's walls, anyway. She was getting nowhere here, and Hayward was clearly far too wrapped up in himself to be capable of noticing anyone else's existence, let alone killing anyone. It was time to go.

"Look," said Hayward, when Annie got up to walk to the door, "I'm sorry I can't be of more help to you, but I really haven't seen Tom in years, and I've no idea what he did with his life. He just wasn't a very original painter, that's all."

"That's okay," said Annie. "Thanks for your time."

Hayward stood in the doorway, leaning on the jamb and blocking the exit. "Maybe your visit wasn't entirely wasted, though," he said.

Annie felt her breath tighten in her throat. "Oh?" she said.

"No. I mean, there are often other purposes, aren't there? Hidden purposes. You do something for one reason, at least on the surface, but it turns out there's an underlying, deeper reason you just weren't conscious of. A more important reason. Fate, perhaps."

"Speak English, Baz. And get out of my way."

Hayward stood his ground. "I'd like to paint you," he announced, beaming, as if offering her a place on the Queen's honors list.

"Paint me?"

"Yes. We could start now, if you like. Perhaps some preliminary sketches?"

Annie looked around at the walls. She knew now what it was that disturbed her about the artwork hanging there. Every piece, either charcoal sketch or color painting, was of a gaping vagina. It was hardly an original idea—the flowerlike symmetry and individuality of female genitals had excited artists for years—and Annie was open-minded as far as most things were concerned. But being in this room, surrounded by garish paintings of them, and knowing that the odious Baz Hayward was now quite openly staring at the inverted V of her jeans between her legs, where her greatcoat gaped open, gave her the creeps.

She grabbed his wrist so quickly he had no time to stop her, twisted his arm behind his back and pushed him into the room. He stumbled into the easel, knocking the painting he had been working on to the floor. Then Annie pulled her coat tight around her waist, fastened the belt, said, "Fuck off, Baz," and left.

When Banks walked down the front steps of Eastvale General Infirmary, it was already dark, and the drizzle had turned into a late-afternoon mist that blurred the shop lights on King Street. For some reason, he was overcome with a vivid memory of a similar afternoon when he was fifteen or sixteen, when he'd been upstairs on a bus coming home from town, a copy of the *Fresh Cream* album and the latest *Melody Maker* tucked under his arm. Looking out at the yellow halos of the streetlights and the hazy neon signs, he had lit a cigarette and it had tasted magnificent, by far the best cigarette he had ever smoked. He could taste it now, and he automatically reached in his pocket. Of course, there were no cigarettes in his pocket. He looked across King Street at the light in the newsagent's window, bleary in the late-afternoon mist, strongly tempted to dash over and buy a packet. Just ten. He'd smoke only the ten and then no more. But he got a grip on himself, turned his collar up and trudged up the hill to the station.

Christine Aspern's body had been in far better shape than Tom McMahon's. In fact, the skin that had been covered by the sleeping bag was not charred, but pale and waxy, like that of most corpses. It was only her face and hands, where she had suffered second-degree burns, that had been at all blackened or blistered by the fire. The blisters were also a sign, Dr. Glendenning said, that the victim was probably alive when the fire began, though a small amount of blistering can occur after death. Given the other evidence, though, he would surmise that the blistering in Tina's case was postmortem.

Dr. Glendenning had approached the autopsy with his usual concern for detail and confirmed that, pending toxicology results that probably wouldn't be in until Monday afternoon at the earliest, this being the weekend, she had died, like Thomas McMahon, of asphyxiation due to smoke inhalation, and most likely not from a heroin overdose.

As in the case of McMahon, Glendenning had also found thermal injury to the mouth and nose but not lower down, in the tracheal area. He had found only trace amounts of soot below the larynx, indicating that Christine was most likely unconscious when the fire started.

There was always the chance that Danny Boy's heroin had been unusually pure and that she had died of an overdose before or during the fire, but Banks was willing to bet she was probably just on the nod. Mark had already told him that she had injected herself that evening. She wouldn't have been the first junkie to lie there in the cocoon of safety and emptiness she had created for herself while the flames consumed her flesh. Either way, there was no evidence of foul play other than the starting of the fire itself, and going by the splash patterns and accelerant tests Geoff Hamilton had carried out, the arsonist had probably not even set foot on Mark and Christine's boat.

It was late Saturday afternoon and the duty constables were bringing in a couple of drunken Eastvale United supporters when Banks got to the station. Eastvale was hardly a premier-division team, but that didn't stop some fans from acting as if they were at a Leeds versus Manchester United match. Banks edged around the wobbly group and headed upstairs to the relative peace of his office, grabbing the handful of completed actions from his pigeonhole on the way. He slipped off his raincoat, kicked the heater to get it started and turned on his radio to a Radio 3 special about Bud Powell on *Jazz Line Up*.

As he listened to "A Night in Tunisia," he flipped through the actions and found only one of immediate interest.

According to her ex-employer Sam Prescott, Heather Burnett, the girl from the art supplies shop who had left Thomas McMahon for Jake Harley, had later left Harley himself for an American installation specialist called Nate Ulrich, and they now lived in Palo Alto, California. Well, it had been a long shot in the first place, Banks thought.

Because it was the weekend, things were slow. Banks didn't expect any preliminary forensic results, including analysis of clothing samples and toxicology, until early Tuesday. He still needed to know who had owned the boats, but as yet DC Templeton hadn't got very far with his inquiries. There was a good chance he might have to wait until Monday or later to find someone who knew, maybe someone from British Waterways.

Then there was the car to consider, the dark blue Jeep Cherokee, or Range Rover, whatever it was, that had been seen parked in the lay-by nearest the boats. It was probably a waste of time, as there would be so many of them to check out, but Banks issued the actions anyway. He also ordered a survey of all the car-rental agencies in the area. There was a good chance that if someone was out to break the law, he might not want to use his own car when visiting McMahon in case he was spotted. Also, if he knew the roads in the immediate area of the boats, he would know that a Jeep was a much better option than an ordinary car, especially in winter.

Banks had no sooner issued the action than his phone rang.

"Alan, it's Ken." DI Ken Blackstone, phoning from Leeds. "We sent a couple of lads over to interview that dealer you mentioned, Benjamin Scott."

"That was quick. Must be a slow day down there."

"United's away this week. Anyway, we leaned on him a bit—seems there were small amounts of suspicious substances in his flat—and he's got a watertight alibi. He was in Paris with his girlfriend when the fire started."

"How the other half lives. You're sure?"

"She verified it, and they showed us used tickets, credit card receipts, gave us the number of the hotel. Want me to phone?"

"No, it's all right, Ken. It was only a vague possibility. Look, do you happen to know anything about a bloke called Aspern, a Dr. Patrick Aspern?"

"I can't say I do, not off the top of my head. Why?"

"He's the dead girl's stepfather, and her boyfriend's made a rather serious accusation. There might be something in it. Think you could check around, see if there's anything on him?"

"Can do."

"And there's no need to be *too* discreet about your inquiries."

"Understood. Where's he live?"

"Adel."

"That'll be Weetwood station. I know a DI there. I'll get

back to you after the weekend. It's been a while. How's things?"

"Not bad," said Banks.

"Sandra?"

"A distant memory."

"She's had the baby?"

"She's had the baby. Sinéad. Nice of you to ask, Ken. Mother and child are doing fine."

"Sorry, I didn't know it was still such a touchy point. Any chance you'll be down in my neck of the woods again soon?"

"Depends on how the case goes. And what you dig up on Aspern, of course."

"Well, if you've got time, give me a bell. We can go out for a curry and a piss-up. My sofa's yours anytime. You know that."

"Thanks, Ken. I'll likely take you up on that soon. Talk to you later."

"Bye."

Banks tapped his ballpoint on the desk. He didn't really expect anything to come of inquiries into Patrick Aspern. If Mark's accusation was to be believed, whatever went on was a family matter, in more ways than one, and they might never be able to find any evidence. Frances Aspern knew something, Banks was certain, but she didn't seem very likely to talk. Whatever the reason, her relationship with Aspern was important to her; she needed him enough to sacrifice her daughter to him, if, indeed, that was what had happened.

Banks did, however, want Aspern to know that the local police were on his case, which was why he had told Ken Blackstone not to worry about discretion. It would be interesting to see how the good doctor reacted to that. He glanced at his watch. Time to get a few more actions issued, have a chat with Annie about progress so far, then go home. And what would he do there? Well, it wasn't always Laphroaig and *La Cenerentola* for Banks. He did, at times, give in to his baser instincts, and tonight he felt like an evening alone with a Chinese take-away, a James Bond DVD—Sean Connery, of course—and a few cans of lager. Ah, the lush life.

Lenny Knox and his wife, Sally, lived on Eastvale's notorious East Side Estate, a living testament to the fact that it wasn't only big cities that had problem areas. But like all the big city estates, the East Side Estate also had its share of decent people just trying to make the best of a bad situation, and Lenny was one of them. He was a founding member of the local neighborhood watch, keeping an eye out for drug deals and vandalism. He'd had his own problems when he was a teenager, Mark knew from their conversations, but a short prison sentence in his early twenties had turned him around.

They'd done a fair day's work when Lenny pulled his rusty old Nissan up outside the terraced house on the estate's central artery. Street parking wasn't especially safe in the area, but everyone knew Lenny's car, and no one dared touch it. Lenny probably thought that was because everyone was scared of him, but Mark thought it more likely because the car was a piece of crap no respectable thief would waste a second glance on. Mark looked around warily as he got out of the car, and it wasn't because of what Banks had warned him about. He had bad memories of the East Side Estate, and even though he didn't think Crazy Nick was around anymore, it still paid to be careful. He knew that Nick would kill him if he found him. That was why the boat had been safe. Nick would never think to look anywhere rural like that; if anything, he had even less upstairs than Mark himself.

Mark followed Lenny inside and saw Sal's look of surprise when he entered. She welcomed her husband with a perfunctory kiss on the cheek and disappeared into the kitchen to make tea. A black cat with half its left ear missing rubbed up against Mark's leg, then slunk off upstairs.

"Make yourself at home," Lenny said, pointing to a threadbare armchair.

"Are you sure it's all right?" Mark asked. "I don't want to be a bother."

"Oh, don't worry about Sal," he said. "She'll come around. She always does."

Mark had seen the expression on Sal's face, and he wasn't too certain about that.

Lenny offered Mark a cigarette. "We'll have a cuppa first," he said, "just to wash the dust out, then I'll go get us all some fish and chips and a few cans of lager. Okay?"

Mark reached in his pocket. "I've got some money . . ."

Lenny waved it away. "Don't be daft. My treat."

"But—"

"No arguments. You can buy us pizza on payday, all right?"

"Okay."

Lenny tuned the television set to a snooker game and settled back in his chair. The house smelled faintly of burned bacon and cat's piss. Mark couldn't concentrate on the game; he'd never been a big snooker fan, anyway. He couldn't stop thinking of Tina, couldn't quite get his head around the fact that she was dead, gone, kaput, and that they'd never again be able to snuggle up to each other against the winter chill in their sleeping bag. His home was gone, too. It might not have been much, but it had meant a lot to them. It was their very own place, an escape from the miserable squat in Leeds, and they'd added a little personal touch here and there—a nice candlestick, a Primus stove to boil water and cook tinned foods on, a framed photo of the two of them on the wall, a mini CD player and a few of their favorite CDs: Beth Orton, David Bowie, Coldplay, System of a Down, Radiohead, Ben Harper.

Tears pricked Mark's eyes. He couldn't cry, not in front of Lenny, but he felt like it. What would he do now, without Tina to look after? What was the point of it all? Until he'd met her, his life had been nothing but an aimless mess, and that's what it would turn into again. He knew people had looked at the way they lived and judged them, but he didn't care what people thought. One day he and Tina were going to get it all together: home, kids, the lot. Let them laugh. But now . . . And it was all his fault.

The snooker game droned on. Sal poked her head around the door and said, "Tea's ready. Can I talk to you a minute, Len?"

Len pulled a long-suffering face for Mark's benefit, as if to say, *Women!* Then he dragged himself away from the TV set and went into the kitchen.

When Mark thought of Tina's stepdad, he felt the voiceless anger boil in him until his hands shook. He had no doubt that Aspern was responsible for Tina's drug addiction. She had told him that she started doing morphine to dull the pain and humiliation of his sexual advances, and when Aspern caught her at it one day, he started using the drugs as a reward for sexual favors. He'd already given her sedatives before, to make her easier to handle. And he was supposed to be a doctor. The mother knew more than she let on, but she was scared shitless of Aspern, Tina had told him. A mouse. If he so much as raised his voice at her, her lower lip would start to tremble and she'd run away in tears. Tina had nobody to stand up for her. Nobody but Mark. But now it didn't matter anyway.

"What the hell do you think you're doing?" he heard Sal saying in the kitchen. "Bringing him here. The kid's just come out of jail, for Christ's sake. It's been all over the news. I knew it was him when I first heard about that fire."

"I've been in jail myself, love," Lenny said, "but it doesn't make me a criminal."

"That's different. That was years ago. *We* can't be responsible for him."

"Have a heart. The poor kid's just lost his girlfriend and his home."

"Home! A clapped-out boat. Lenny, what's got into you? You're not usually such a soft touch."

"What do you mean?"

"Oh, no doubt he's spun you a sob story of some sort. Got you thinking he's the son you never had—"

"Now, wait a minute!"

"No! *You* wait a minute. You bring him here without asking, without even ringing first to let me know, and you expect me to cook for him, clean up after him? What do you think I am, Lenny, a skivvy? Is that all I am to you? A bloody skivvy?"

"Come on, love."

"Don't you 'love' me."

"Sal . . ."

"Have you thought for just one moment, has it even crossed that tiny little brain of yours, that *he* might have been the one who set the fire? Have you thought of that?"

"For crying out loud, Sal, Mark wouldn't do anything like that. Besides, the police let him go."

"The police are always letting murderers go. Just because they don't have enough evidence. But it doesn't mean they don't know *someone* did it."

"Oh, come on. He's a good kid."

"Good kid! You won't be saying that when the bloody house is burning down around you, will you!"

"Sal, I'm not—"

But Mark didn't hear any more. Tears finally blurring his vision and anger seething inside him, he snatched up his overcoat and dashed out of the door. He was halfway down the street before he heard Lenny shouting after him, but he ignored the calls and ran on, under the railway bridge, away from the town.

* * *

The Angel was reputed to have the finest chef east of the Pennines, and he was even rumored to have something of a flair for vegetarian dishes. Thoughtful of Phil to take that into account. Annie had dressed accordingly, toning down her sartorial flamboyance a bit with her little black number in deference to Phil's decidedly more conservative-but-casual look. She hadn't worn the frock in ages and felt a bit self-conscious in it. She was pleased to find that it still fitted. The last time she wore it, she remembered, was on one of her dinner dates with Banks. And that reminded her: something he'd said in their brief meeting a short while earlier had rung a bell somewhere, and she wanted to ask Phil about it.

She had also done the best she could to hide her red nose with cunningly applied makeup and had taken Nurofen so she didn't have to reach for her hankie all evening, although she could still feel that irritating tickle at the back of her throat. From experience, she knew that it responded best to red wine, but they were driving to the restaurant separately and she would have to take it easy on the alcohol. Before she left, she made sure she had her beeper and mobile, though she hoped to hell she wouldn't have to use either.

Phil was already waiting at the bar, a half pint in front of him, and he waved her over. "They're just preparing the table," he said. "Won't be a minute. Drink?"

"Mmm, I think I'll just have a grapefruit juice for now, thanks." That way, Annie thought, she'd be able to have a couple of glasses of wine with dinner.

Phil ordered the drinks without comment. That was one of the things she liked about him. He never questioned you or made a snarky comment the way some people did when you didn't order real booze, or if you happened to be a vegetarian. All he'd asked her the first time they went out to dinner was whether her reasons for not eating meat were humanitarian or health. A bit of both, she had replied.

"Busy day?" he said.

Annie nodded. "The boat fire. You must have heard about it by now."

"Yes, of course. Any leads yet, or shouldn't I ask?"

"Probably best not to," Annie said, with a smile, "but no, nothing really."

The maître d' came over and led them to their table. It was in a quiet corner of the restaurant, a table with a scarlet cloth, lit by a shaded lamp, polished silverware gleaming. Wallpaper music piped softly in the background, Beatles via Mantovani, not loud enough to interfere with conversation, but audible enough to create an atmosphere of soporific calm. Cozy and intimate.

Annie watched Phil as he studied the menu: the small, boyish mouth, slightly receding dark hair, just showing a tinge of gray here and there, the watchful and intelligent gray eyes. He must be seven or eight years older than her, she thought, probably in his early forties. Banks was older than her, too. Why was it she went for older men? Did she feel safer with them? Was she looking for a father figure? She almost laughed out loud thinking what Ray, her dad, would have to say about that.

In some ways, Annie thought, Phil was actually quite similar to Banks: a little traditional, conservative, even, on the surface, but broad-minded and free-spirited underneath it all. Besides, it wasn't so much age that mattered to her, but intelligence, maturity and a sense of culture. Not that career and money didn't matter, but most of the mobile-flaunting men she had dated of her own age had been interested in them to the exclusion of other things, and it was the other things that interested Annie most.

She decided on a salad with pears, walnuts and crumbled

blue cheese to start, and a wild mushroom risotto as her main course, then put the menu aside. Phil was still studying his.

"Problem?" Annie asked.

"Just can't decide between the venison and the guinea fowl."

"Sorry, can't help you there."

Phil laughed and put his menu down. "I don't suppose you can." He took out a coin from his pocket, spun it in the air and caught it. "Heads," he said, looking at the way it had landed. "Venison."

"How do I know you didn't cheat?"

"Actually, I did," he confessed. "It was supposed to be heads for the guinea fowl but I realized at the last moment I really wanted venison. Wine?"

"Please."

Phil chose a bottle of 1998 Chianti Classico. Not too ostentatious, Annie thought, but not cheap, either.

"How's the Turner?" she asked when they had given their orders.

"Still resting comfortably. It should be up for auction soon. The Tate's interested, naturally, but so are the V and A and several private collectors."

"It's definitely genuine, then?"

"Oh, yes. So the team of experts attests."

"It wasn't just your opinion?"

"You must be kidding. Not a chance. It would be immodest of me to say my voice doesn't carry some weight, but a discovery like that comes under incredible scrutiny. Any art forger worth his salt wouldn't pick a big-name artist like Turner or Constable to copy. Forgers with any sense stick to less famous artists. Turner's a national treasure. You might as well try and pass off a Da Vinci or a Van Gogh."

"It has been done, though, hasn't it?"

"Oh, yes. It has been done. Tom Keating, for one, comes to mind. He did Rembrandt, among others. And Eric Hebborn did all right with Corot and Augustus John. But that was in the fifties and sixties. These days, there are far more forensic tests and, as I said, a battery of experts to get past. This one's been verified through fingerprints, among other things."

"Fingerprints?"

"I thought that might interest you. They can last a very long time, you know. Prints have even been found on prehistoric cave paintings and pottery unearthed at archaeological digs."

"But how can you verify them? Turner's been dead for more than a hundred and fifty years."

"Painting can be a messy business. You get your hands dirty, and as often as not an artist applies his fingers to the paint and the paper or canvas during the process of painting. Especially oils, but even with watercolors like this one. If you examine the surface carefully with a magnifying glass— a bit like Sherlock Holmes, I suppose —you can often find very good fingerprints."

"But how do you check against the artist's original?"

"That's the problem. It's not always possible, and the results are sometimes dubious, but in the case of Turner, it actually works very well."

"Why?"

"His prints are on file in the Tate archives."

"Of course," said Annie.

"Naturally, you need an impeccable source. A painting with credible provenance leading right back to the artist. But not many other people would have been in a position to get their fingerprints in the paint on a Turner canvas. He was known to work alone, without assistants."

Annie nodded.

"And it's been done before," Phil went on. "A Canadian called Peter Paul Biro pioneered the whole technique some years ago. He worked with the West Yorkshire Police to identify a Turner called *Landscape with Rainbow* in 1995. I'm surprised you didn't hear about it."

"In 1995 I was a mere DC in Somerset and Avon."

"Well, that explains it."

"We tend not to notice that much outside our immediate areas," Annie explained. "You get focused on the job in hand and—"

"I understand," said Phil.

"How much do you reckon it will go for?"

Phil pursed his lips and thought for a moment, then said, "About three hundred thousand. Maybe a bit more, seeing as it's part of a set."

The wine came and the waiter first showed off the bottle, then presented the cork and a tiny splash in Phil's glass. "Just pour it," said Phil. "I'm sure if it's corked you'll bring us another bottle."

"Of course, sir," said the waiter. Annie wasn't used to such deference in Yorkshire restaurants, or restaurants anywhere, for that matter. But there was something about Phil that seemed to bring it out in people. Maybe he looked like someone famous, though Annie couldn't think who. Stefan Nowak was the only other person she could think of who had the same sort of aura. She could imagine waiters being deferential around Stefan, too.

Phil sipped some wine and looked around. "Turner actually dined here once," he said, "on the same tour he did the sketches for that watercolor."

"Really? I knew the place was old but . . ."

"Well, I don't think it was the same chef. Mostly he complained about the weather. Bit of a miserable bugger, was J.M.W. Bit of a miser, too."

"He'd fit in well up here, then."

"I've never found Yorkshire folk to be anything less than generous."

"I agree, actually. It's just one of the myths around these parts, and people sometimes seem quite proud of it, the parsimony."

"They're canny with their money, I'll give them that. But there's no harm in not being a wastrel, as my grandfather always used to say."

Annie almost asked him about his Yorkshire grandparents, but she held herself back. She didn't feel like getting into family histories and reminiscences tonight. There was something about other people's families that always disturbed her a bit.

The starters arrived and both ate in silence for a while. "One thing I never got around to asking you is why this painting went missing for so long," Annie said, when she had finished the last walnut. "I mean, seeing as it was a Turner, and part of a set."

"There are plenty of Turners unaccounted for," said Phil. "As you know, this one was part of a series of twenty watercolors Turner painted for the *History of Richmondshire*. He delivered the first twelve to the publisher for engraving in spring 1817, and the other eight in December of the same year. After that, the originals were sold to various buyers. The one we saw, *Richmond Castle and Town,* was one of six that the publishers of the history were selling off at cost. Twenty-five guineas. Can you believe it? Previously the only record of it seems to have been at an exhibition of the Northern Society in Leeds in 1822. After that, nothing. Anyway, three of the twenty went missing, two untraced—until last summer—and one destroyed in a fire."

Annie's ears pricked up. "A fire?"

"Ah, I see. You're thinking about the boat fire you're investigating, aren't you? Well, I hate to disappoint you, but this was decades ago. There's no connection."

"But there's still one more missing from the set?"

"Yes. *Ingleborough from Hornby Castle Terrace.* Hasn't been seen since the turn of the last century. It fetched a record price when it was sold at Christie's in 1881 to a certain W. Law, Esquire. Two thousand guineas, in fact. It would be nice to find it and complete the set, of course, but it's not as if they're all collected in one place."

"Real *Antiques Roadshow*."

"You may well laugh, but it happens more often than you think. That dusty old frame in the attic. The ugly landscape old Aunt Eunice's grandad hid away in the cellar."

Annie laughed. "You could hardly call the Turner ugly."

"Of course not. But somebody thought little enough of it to bury it under a couple of layers of insulation."

As they ate their meals, they talked about paintings and films they liked, and Annie discovered that they were both fans of Alec Guinness in the old Ealing comedies, though Phil preferred *The Captain's Paradise* to Annie's favorite, *The Lavender Hill Mob*. They both loved *The Horse's Mouth*, though.

When it was time for dessert, Annie decided to hell with her diet—not that she was really on one, but she was always full of good intentions—and went for the crème brûlée. She resisted the cognac, though, and chose café au lait. She was pleased that she had managed to restrict herself to only one glass of wine.

"Have you ever heard of a local artist called Thomas McMahon?" she asked Phil after her first mouth-watering spoonful.

Phil frowned. "McMahon? Can't say I have, no. Why? He any good?"

"I probably shouldn't be telling you," she said, "but it'll be in the papers tomorrow, and probably on the radio and TV tonight. He's most likely the victim in the boat fires. One of the victims. I just wondered if you'd heard of him at all, come across him in your line of business?"

"I don't come across many living artists, I'm afraid," said Phil.

"From all accounts, after a promising start he dropped out

of the scene some years ago, made a living painting land-scapes for tourists."

"Then I'd have even less reason to have heard of him. Always the detective, eh, Annie?"

Annie blushed. There was some truth in that. She was slowly and indirectly getting around to what she had wanted to sound him out on. "One thing we found out—my boss discovered it, actually—was that he frequented an antiquarian bookshop on Market Street and that he bought a number of old books and prints."

"Nothing unusual in that, surely?"

"We don't think he was very well off, and besides, most of the stuff he bought was worthless. Worthless but old."

Phil looked at her, and she saw the beginnings of understanding in his eyes. "I was just thinking," she went on, "that " Right then, her beeper went off. The station. One or two of the other diners gave her dirty looks. "Oh, shit," she said. "Sorry. I mean, I'd better . . . I won't be long."

"Okay. Don't worry. I'll be waiting."

Annie hustled outside and fumbled with her mobile. "Yes?"

"DI Cabbot?"

"Yes."

"DCI Banks said to tell you there's been another one—another fire, that is—and he wants you to get out to Jennings Field ASAP. You know where it is?"

"I know it," said Annie. "Thanks. I'm on my way."

Bollocks, she thought, putting her phone away and reentering the restaurant. Inconsiderate arsonist, spoiling her evening. She just had time to make a quick apology to Phil before heading out.

"Can I give you a lift?" he asked.

"No, thanks," said Annie. "I'll go in my own car." She could just imagine the expression on Banks's face if she turned up at a crime scene in Phil's BMW. She wasn't even dressed for standing around in an open field on a cold night, she realized, as she threw on her elegant but lightweight black overcoat.

Just to end their evening together on a perfect note, Annie found herself unable to get her handkerchief to her mouth fast enough to stop a sneeze and ended up spraying the entire table with germs. Phil just smiled and gestured for her to go. Red-faced now, as well as red-nosed, Annie went.

Chapter 7

*J*ennings Field lay on the eastern outskirts of Eastvale, beyond the East Side Estate and the railway lines, where the landscape flattened out toward the fertile vale that lay between the Yorkshire Dales and the North York Moors. It was a clear, cold night; the day's light mist had completely dissipated. The stars shone icily bright, and lights twinkled from distant villages, where the good citizens would all be sitting nice and warm in front of their tellies watching Des Lynam. A half-moon dripped its milky light on the far woods, silvering the bare lattices of the treetops.

The call had disturbed Banks partway through *Goldfinger*—the bit where the laser is slowly creeping up toward Bond's privates—takeout chicken fried rice and his second can of lager. He stood with his hands in his pockets breathing out plumes of air and watched Annie get out of her car and sign in with the uniformed officer at the perimeter. A couple of reporters shouted questions at her, but she ignored them. One of them whistled as she ducked under the police tape, and Annie froze for just a moment, then carried on walking. She was nicely dressed, Banks noticed when she got in range of the lights the fire department had erected, and was she wearing a bit more makeup than usual? Out with her new boyfriend, then? Well, it *was* Saturday night, after all.

She caught him looking and blushed. "What?"

"Nothing," Banks said. "You look nice."

Annie rolled her eyes. "So what have we got?"

The remains of a caravan, the sole dwelling in the field, parked at the far end, just under the shelter of a couple of beech trees, still smoldered, and an acrid stink of burned rubber and plastic wafted their way. There was nothing left of the roof and sides; only a skeleton of soot-blackened metal struts remained, and the innards lay open to the elements. Water from the fire hoses dripped to the ground and puddled.

"Anyone inside?" Annie asked.

"We've got one body," Banks told her. "And luckily this time we think we know who it is."

Annie blew on her bare hands. She was wearing simple black court shoes, tan tights and a long black coat, elegant rather than practical, Banks noticed. Going-out-for-a-meal clothes. Her feet must be cold.

Banks pointed to a man talking to DC Winsome Jackman over by the group of parked cars and two gleaming red fire appliances. "That's Jack Mellor. He's a regular at the Fox and Hounds, about half a mile down the road, in the nearest village, and he reported the fire. He's still pretty shaken. He says he saw the flames as he was walking his dog down the road at about nine o'clock for a couple of pints and a chat with his mates as usual." Banks pointed away from the village lights. "He lives in Ash Cottage, about two hundred yards in that direction. Says the chap who lived in the caravan was another Fox and Hounds regular. Quiet bloke, by all accounts. Harmless. Name of Roland Gardiner."

"He lived alone in the caravan?"

"Yes. Been there at least a couple of years now, according to our Mr. Mellor. There's no car in evidence. Not even any wheels on the caravan. See the way it's propped up on blocks? Anyway, this field's common land, despite its name. Nobody knows who the hell Jennings was. I'm sure the local council's been trying to squeeze Gardiner out, just like British Waterways was trying to get rid of the barge squatters, but for better or for worse . . . this was Gardiner's home."

"What the hell's going on?" Annie said. "Is someone trying to set fire to all the eyesores and down-and-outs in the area?"

"It certainly looks that way, doesn't it?" said Banks. "But let's not jump to conclusions. We've no evidence yet that there's any connection between the fires. And they weren't down-and-outs, despite their living conditions. Don't forget that Thomas McMahon was an artist who managed to make a living painting local landscapes for the tourist trade. I think he *chose* to live the way he did. Even Mark Siddons works at the Eastvale College building site. None of the victims were really spongers or bums."

"The girl was a junkie, though."

"Well," said Banks, watching Geoff Hamilton guide the SOCO in packaging debris from the caravan, "there might be any number of reasons for that." He was thinking, as Mark had been thinking earlier that evening, about Dr. Patrick Aspern, with whom he was far from finished. "Besides, in my book, that makes her ill, not criminal."

"You know what I mean," Annie said. "And you also know that I agree with you. All I'm suggesting is that a junkie loses a certain . . . strength of will, that someone who needs something so much will do whatever it takes to get it, sponging being the least of it."

"Point taken," said Banks.

The local constable, PC Locke, came over to them. "Mr. Mellor wants to know if he can go to the Fox and Hounds," he said. "Says the dog's freezing its balls off—if you'll pardon my language, ma'am—and he needs a pick-me-up."

"I can understand that," said Banks. "Look, this isn't exactly kosher," he went on, taking Locke aside and lowering his voice. "Strictly speaking, we have to consider Mellor a suspect, but why don't you accompany him to the Fox and Hounds and wait for us? We've got to talk to him somewhere, and it might as well be there. At least I suppose it'll be warm."

"Yes, sir."

"And keep a sharp eye on his alcohol intake. He's allowed one, a small one, for the shock, but no more. I don't want him pissed when we get there to question him, okay?"

"Understood, sir."

"And one more thing."

"Sir?"

Banks gestured over to the road, where the phalanx of media people jostled for space and pointed cameras. "Avoid them. Mum's the word."

"I think I can manage that, sir. We'll go the back way."

PC Locke walked over to Mellor and they headed toward the back lane, the dog on its leash trotting along beside them, and before they had got very far, they vanished over a stile into the darkness. Banks hoped that no bright spark of a reporter decided to go and check out the local pub. They'd get there eventually, he knew, but they wouldn't leave the scene yet, not while there was still some action.

"Are you sure that was wise?" Annie asked.

"Probably not, but I don't think Mellor started the fire. Let's have a look at the damage."

They walked closer to the burned-out caravan. In the bright artificial light, it was easy to spot the pooling at the center of the floor, one sign of accelerant use, and Banks fancied he could even smell a whiff of petrol on the air. Geoff Hamilton's electronic "sniffer" had already detected something and confirmed that some sort of accelerant had been used. The damage to the caravan was far worse than that to the boats. It was also such a small scene, and the remains of the floor were so unstable, that Hamilton and DS Stefan

Nowak were trying to do the best they could by working their ways in from the outside edges, not trampling on the flimsy caravan floor at all. Peter Darby was videotaping their progress, occasionally swapping his camcorder for his trusty Pentax and taking a flurry of stills.

At the center of it all, by the pooling that marked the seat of the blaze, lay a blackened body, this one on its side, curled in the familiar pugilistic pose. It had been hard to spot at first among the charred furniture and fixtures, but once you managed to separate it from its context, you couldn't miss it. Hamilton said that the warped and cracked object beside the body was a glass. There had been a glass lying beside Tom McMahon's body too, Banks remembered, wondering if it was relevant. He noticed Annie give a little shiver, and he didn't think it was caused by the cold.

Hamilton and Stefan Nowak came walking toward them.

"Anything?" Banks asked.

"Pooling, traces of accelerant," said Hamilton.

"Same as before?"

"Looks like it."

"Anything to connect the two?"

Hamilton shifted from foot to foot. "Well," he said, "apart from the fact that we've had two suspicious fires in out-of-the-way places in two days, when we're usually only unlucky enough to get two a year, I'd say no."

It was an important point. Banks needed to know whether they were now running two separate arson investigations or just one. "How long would it take for a caravan that size to be reduced to that state?" he asked.

"Half an hour or so. Whatever caused it, it was hot and fast."

"What about the accelerant used?"

"This one smells like petrol to me—you can smell it yourself—though I'd rather wait for the chromatograph results and the spectral analysis, just to be certain."

"The previous victim, or one of them, was an artist," Banks mused aloud. "So it was reasonable to assume that he'd have turpentine somewhere around. We don't know what Mr. Gardiner was yet, but the killer clearly brought his own accelerant this time. Maybe he *knew* both victims, knew that McMahon would have turpentine handy to start the fire, but also knew that he had to bring his own to Gardiner's caravan. But why bring petrol instead of turps?"

"Probably had some on hand," said Hamilton. "Most people do, if they've got a car. It'd be easy enough to siphon a little off. And safer than going to a shop to buy turpentine. Someone might have remembered him."

"Good point," said Banks. "What about the victim?"

"What about him?"

"Well, he didn't just lie there and let himself burn to death, did he?"

"How the hell would I know what he did?"

"Speculate. Use your imagination."

Hamilton snorted. "That's not my job. I'll wait for the test results and the postmortem, thank you very much."

Banks sighed. "Okay," he said. "If the victim had been conscious, and capable, might he have been able to escape this fire?"

"He might have been," Hamilton conceded. "Unless he was overcome by smoke or fumes. They can disorient a person very quickly."

"Whoever set the fire had to have been inside the caravan at the time, hadn't he?"

"It looks that way from the pattern of pooling. If he'd poured it through the window or tossed it through the door, for example, you'd see evidence of that in the trail, and in the charring."

"And there isn't any?"

"Not that I can see."

"And whoever set the fire got out?"

"Well, there's only one body."

"What about access, escape route?"

"There's a lane runs by the back, behind the trees and the wall."

"Okay," said Banks. He turned from Hamilton and looked at the charred, smoking caravan again. There wasn't much more they could do at the scene. Best leave it to Stefan and his team, see what they could turn up, if anything.

Banks turned to Annie. "Let's go and talk to Mr. Mellor," he said. "I could do with a bloody stiff drink."

Annie looked at her watch. "It's after closing time," she said.

Banks smiled. "Well, I think being a copper ought to have *some* advantages, don't you?"

Mark ran fast, away from the fire, until he was exhausted, and then slowed to walking speed. All the time his mind was filled with echoes and rage. The voices of Lenny and Sal became those of his mother and Crazy Nick as they argued about him drunkenly downstairs, getting louder and louder until they ended in blows and screams. *Get rid of him! Get rid of him! Get rid of him! He should have been drowned at birth!*

Mark put his hands over his ears as he ran, but it didn't do any good. The voices went on, from inside. *Always in the bloody way. Can't you do something about him?* He remembered the nights spent locked in the dank, spidery cellar alone, with no light, no warmth, no human company. And he remembered the time when he was sixteen and got brave enough to fight back, how he had smacked Crazy Nick right in the mouth and how both of them were too stunned to do anything when they saw the blood start to flow.

You little fucker! Look what you did.

Mark knew right there and then that he was fighting for his

life, so he laid into Crazy Nick with all he'd got, punching and kicking until Nick was on the floor gargling blood, and Mark's mother was beating on his back with her hard little fists. He smashed a chair over Crazy Nick's head and that was it, the last night he spent at home, the night he ran, with his mother's screams of revenge and hatred burning in his ears. Just as he was running now.

He stopped for breath and looked around, realized he didn't have a clue where he was. He had headed east from Lenny's, he knew that much, beyond the town limits, so he was out in the country now. If he looked behind him, he could see the lights of Eastvale, even hear a distant train going by. He wished he had enough money to take a train somewhere. Or a plane. That would be even better. *Ulan Bator*. But then he realized he didn't even have a passport, so he was stuck here. Stuck here forever. But not in Eastvale. He was never going back there. Not if he could help it.

He was on a dark country road with trees and drystone walls on either side. The flames were well behind him now, and he thought he could hear the sirens of fire engines. Good luck to them. They didn't do Tina much good. He thought of her fragile, pretty face, her slight form. Tina hadn't had a chance. Tears stained Mark's face as he felt the waves of guilt tearing him apart for the hundredth time. If only he hadn't gone chasing after Mandy; if only, if only, if only . . .

Dark winter fields stretched away from him on both sides of the road, bare branches clawing like talons at the starlit sky, and now and then he could make out the lonely glow of a distant farmhouse or the clustered lights of a small village. For a moment, Banks's words of warning came back to him, that he might be in danger, that he might be the next victim, and he felt a tremor of fear. Shadows moved and rustling sounds came from behind him. But it was only the wind in the trees. Why would anybody want to kill him? He didn't know anything. But Tina hadn't known anything, either.

Mark didn't know where he was going; all he could do was keep walking. If he kept going on, eventually he'd end up at the seaside. Maybe he'd live there. It was easy enough to get a job at the seaside, no questions asked, with all those tourists to take care of. Drake from the squat had told him that. Drake had lived in Blackpool and worked at the Pleasure Beach on one of the rides. Made a fucking pile, he said, and pulled plenty of talent, too. But not in January. Blackpool was a cold and lonely place in January. Still, maybe there'd be some building work. There was always building. And there was the sea. Mark loved the sea.

Running had warmed him up, but now, as he slowed his pace, he realized he was cold, cold as the night he'd watched the fire on the boats. Was it only the other day? It seemed like years ago. Tina had only been dead for two days. And was the rest of his lifetime without her going to be as miserable as it was now? Maybe he should just do away with himself. That would serve them all right, wouldn't it? His mother—bless her miserable little soul and may she rot in hell—Crazy Nick, Lenny, Sal, the police, the lot of them. That's what he'd do; he'd top himself. Join Tina. Even save the bloke who'd killed her from having to kill him, too. But he knew he didn't really have the guts to do it. Besides, no matter what the religious people said, Mark didn't believe in reunions beyond the grave.

He pulled the fleece-lined coat tight around him, tightened up the collar around his neck. Wearing a copper's clothes. That was one for the books. It would serve them all right if he did die, though, wouldn't it? He wasn't even sure anymore whether he cared or not, whether it wasn't such a good idea after all. Everything inside was going numb, like his feet, and he realized he didn't even need to do anything painful to die. It would be easy. All he had to do was find an out-of-the-way spot—plenty of them around here—and lie down in the cold. They said it was just like falling asleep. You got cold, then numb, so you couldn't feel it, then you went into a coma and died. Especially as he was halfway there already. He saw a stile and the silhouette of a ruined barn in the next field, a little moonlight shining through the empty windows. That would do, he thought, at least for the night. That would do just fine. And if he died there . . . well, that would serve the bastards right, wouldn't it?

It was well after official closing time when Banks and Annie joined Jack Mellor at the table nearest the fireplace in the Fox and Hounds, but the landlord was not in any hurry to lock up as long as the police were drinking there.

Banks dismissed PC Locke, who had been baby-sitting Mellor since his initial questioning at the scene, and ordered three double brandies, breaking any number of laws and police rules in doing so. He didn't give a damn. It was bloody freezing out there and he needed something to warm him up. Annie seemed glad of the fire, too, and sat as close as she could. She didn't seem to mind the brandy, either, judging by the way she knocked back her first sip. Only Mellor, the dog sleeping curled on the floor by his side, let his glass sit without touching it, but he'd had one already, and his moon-shaped face was looking a little less pale than it had at the scene. The landlord tossed a couple more logs on the fire. They crackled and spat, throwing out enough heat for Banks to take off his overcoat. Annie crossed her legs and took her notebook out, giving Banks a look when she caught him glancing at the gold chain on her ankle.

"Can you start by telling us exactly what happened tonight?" Banks asked.

Mellor stared into the flames. "It's still quite a shock," he said. "Seeing something like that . . . even from a distance . . . someone you know."

Thank God he hadn't seen the body close up, Banks thought. "I'm sure it is," he said. "Take your time."

Mellor nodded. His cheeks wobbled. "I was walking Sandy here as usual. We always drop by the Fox for a couple of jars of an evening, ever since my wife died."

"I'm sorry to hear it," said Banks.

"Well, these things happen." Mellor reached forward and took a sip of brandy. "Anyway, as I said, it was habit. Creatures of routine. Boring sort of life, I suppose."

"And tonight?"

"I saw the fire through the trees. I think Sandy must have smelled it first because he was acting strange." He leaned over and stroked the dog's glossy ruff. Banks could see from the light ginger fur how he had got his name. Sandy stirred, opening one brown eye and cocking an ear, then drifted off again. "Anyway, we hurried over there, but . . . I could see immediately there was nothing I could do."

"What time was this?"

"I usually set off at nine, pretty much on the dot, and it's about ten minutes from home, so . . ."

"Ten past nine, then?"

"About that, yes."

Banks knew that the emergency call had been logged in at 9:13 P.M. "Where did you call from?"

"Phone box down the road. It's only a short distance. I hurried as best I could, but . . ." He patted his stomach. "I'm afraid I'm not built for speed."

Banks had seen the phone box and estimated that Mellor's timing was pretty much accurate.

"I don't have a mobile phone," he explained. "No need for one, really. No one to call and no one who'd want to ring me."

That didn't stop most people owning a mobile, Banks thought, remembering the sad, pointless conversations he'd overheard during the last few years: "It's me. I'm on the

train. We're just leaving the station now. It's raining up here."
And so on, and so on.

"I take it you were by yourself at home?"

"Yes. I live alone now, apart from Sandy, of course."

"What did you do after you'd rung the fire brigade?"

"I just waited."

"Where?"

"By the gate."

"You didn't approach the caravan?"

Mellor sniffed and wiped his eyes with the back of his hand. "I knew there was nothing I could do by then," he said. "Just watch it burn. I felt so useless. The firemen were very fast getting here."

"It's all right, Mr. Mellor," Banks assured him. "Nobody could have done anything by then." Geoff Hamilton had said the fire would have taken less than half an hour to do the damage it did, and it was well under way by the time Mellor saw it. That would mean that it had probably been set between about eight forty-five and nine o'clock. "Did you see anyone in the area?" he asked.

"Nobody."

"Nobody passed you on the road?"

"No. I didn't see a soul. Never do at that time of night."

"Any cars?"

"One or two. We get a fair bit of traffic, especially on a Saturday night. It's the main road between Eastvale and Thirsk."

"Remember anything about them?"

"I'm afraid not."

"Anything suspicious or unusual happen?"

"No."

Banks took a sip of fiery brandy. His knees were getting hot from the fire, and he noticed Annie's shins turning red under her tights. "All right, Mr. Mellor," he went on. "What can you tell us about the victim?"

"Roland? Not much. He was rather a reserved sort of man."

"But you drank with him regularly?"

"Well, neither of us is a big drinker. We'd pass the time of evening over a couple of halves, maybe."

"How often?"

"Two or three times a week. Though sometimes I didn't see him for days."

"Did he ever say where he was on those occasions?"

"No."

"But the two of you must have talked quite a bit?"

"Oh, yes. Current events. Politics. Sports. That sort of thing. Roland was very well informed."

"Did he ever tell you anything about himself?"

"A little, I suppose. It's . . ."

"Mr. Mellor," Banks said, sensing some sort of generic regard for the confidences of a dead friend, "it looks very much as if Mr. Gardiner is dead. And anything you tell us would be in the strictest confidence, of course."

"What do you mean, it looks as if Roland is dead? Is he or isn't he?"

"There was a body found inside the caravan," Banks said carefully. "It's dead. Unfortunately, we haven't been able to identify it yet, so we're being cautious. Can you think of anyone else who might have been in the caravan?"

Mellor shook his head. "No. Roland valued his privacy, and he lived alone, like me."

"Then we're assuming it's him, just between you and me, but we can't make any official statement until there's been a positive identification. Right now, anything you can tell us will be a great help. What did he look like?"

"Nothing to write home about, really. I suppose he was about five foot seven or eight, a little overweight." He patted his belly. "Not quite as much as me, though. Receding hair, a touch of gray here and there. Hooked nose. Not really big, but hooked. Pale blue eyes."

Mark Siddons had seen a man with a hooked nose visiting Tom McMahon's boat on one occasion, Banks remembered. "How old was he?"

"Early-to-mid-forties, I'd say."

"Go on."

"That's about it, really. Dressed casually most of the time. At least, I never saw him in a suit. Just jeans and a cotton shirt. Soft spoken. Polite. Didn't laugh much."

"Did he have any living relatives?"

"Not that I know of. He never talked about his family. I think his parents are dead, and he never mentioned any brothers or sisters."

"Was he married?"

"Well, you see, that's just it, that's the problem," said Mellor. "Roland was divorced. About two years ago, just around the time he came to Jennings Field."

"What happened?"

"He lost his job, and his wife walked out on him. Another man. All he had left were the caravan and the car, the way he told me, and he drove around until he found somewhere he could stay, and he's been there ever since."

"How did he survive?"

"He was on the social."

"Was he from around these parts?"

"Yes. Not broad-spoken, though, but as if he'd traveled a bit. You know, spent time down south or abroad."

"What happened to the car?"

"Roland just left it there, where he'd parked his caravan. He said he'd no use for it. He'd given up on life. He didn't want to go anywhere. In the end it just fell apart."

"How long ago?"

"Maybe a year or so."

"Where is it now?"

"Hauled away for scrap metal and spare parts."

"Do you know what Mr. Gardiner did for a living?"

"Yes. He worked for a small office supplies company."

"What happened?"

"Competition got too big and too fierce. They couldn't afford the kind of discounts and delivery the big boys were offering, so they started cutting costs. Roland was quite bitter about it."

"Do you know where he lived when he was with his wife?"

"They lived in Eastvale, down on that new Daleside Estate. I'm sorry, but he never told me the actual address."

"I know it," said Banks. The Daleside Estate was a mix of council and private housing built on the site of the old Gallows View Fields on the western edge of town. There had been a short debate in council over the name of the place, some suggesting they stick with Gallows View for historical purposes, others arguing that it would put off potential buyers. In the end, progress won out, and it became officially "Daleside," but most Eastvalers still called it the Gallows View Estate. It was the area where Banks had worked on his first case in Eastvale, although he felt no sentimental attachment. The old row of cottages and the corner shop had all been demolished now to make way for the newer houses.

"Is she still there?"

"He never said otherwise. I assume she stayed on in the house."

Annie made a note. The ex-wife wouldn't be hard to find, Banks thought.

"How did he feel about his wife?" Banks asked.

"I got the impression that he'd had a hard time supporting her taste for exotic holidays abroad and creature comforts as much as anything else. Then, when he loses his job, she chucks him and walks out. Talk about kicking a bloke while he's down."

"Yes, I suppose I'd feel pretty bitter about that myself," said Banks. It certainly gave Gardiner a good motive for killing his wife, but that was not what had happened.

Annie looked at Banks. His situation wasn't quite the same, but he knew—and he knew that Annie knew—that it was close enough to all intents and purposes. Maybe the only real difference was that Banks hadn't pushed so hard at his career only for Sandra's sake—Lord knows her tastes were pretty modest—but more for his own needs. Still, she had left him—out of the blue, it had seemed at the time—and he had almost lost his job and his sanity, and now she was living with Sean and Sinéad in London. Banks certainly understood bitterness and betrayal.

"Did she ever visit him at the caravan?" Banks asked.

"Not that I know of. He never said."

"Were they actually divorced, or just separated?" Banks was wondering whether the ex–Mrs. Gardiner needed her husband permanently out of the way for some reason.

"He said divorced. In fact, I saw him the day he told me the decree came through and he got quite maudlin at first, then angry. He had a bit too much to drink that night, I remember."

There went one theory. "Did he ever have any visitors at all?"

"He never spoke of any, and I can't see the caravan from my cottage. I do remember seeing someone leaving the place once while I was walking down the lane, but that's all."

"When was this?"

"Few months ago. Summer."

"A man or a woman?"

"A man."

"What did he look like?"

"Too far away to see, and he was walking away from me."

"Tall or short, black or white?"

Mellor raised his eyebrows. "White. And maybe a bit taller than you. Not a big man, though. Carried himself well."

"But you didn't see what he looked like."

"No, I'm only going on the way he walked. It can tell you more than you think, you know, sometimes, the way a man walks. They do say when you're in the cities to walk as if you know where you're going, no-nonsense and all, and you're less likely to get mugged. That sort of walk."

"Which direction did he take?"

"Toward the car park off the lane, behind the caravan. It's quite handy, really. There's some waterfalls across Jennings Field. Not more than a trickle, really, but you know what tourists are like. So the council cleared a small car park. Pay and display."

It was the area of easiest access to the caravan. The SO-COs had taped it off and would be searching come daylight. "Did you see him drive away?"

"I'm afraid not. The exit's on the lane behind the field, behind Roland's caravan. It's hidden by the trees and a wall. I must admit, though, I was a little curious, as I hadn't seen or heard of a visitor to Roland's place before."

"Did you ever see a dark-colored Jeep in the area?"

"No. Sorry."

"Thanks anyway," Banks said. "Did you ask Mr. Gardiner about his visitor?"

"Yes, but he just tapped the side of his nose. Said it was an old friend. You know," Mellor said, swirling the remains of the brandy in his glass, "when I first got to know Roland, I worried about him a lot."

"Why is that?"

"He seemed prey to fits of depression. Sometimes he wouldn't leave the caravan for days, not even to come here. When he did come and you asked him if he was all right, he'd shrug it off and say something about taking the 'black dog' for a walk."

Black dog. Winston Churchill's term for the depression that hounded him all his life. "Do you think he might have been suicidal?"

Mellor thought for a moment. "There were times," he said. "Yes. I worried he might do himself harm."

Fire wasn't a common method of suicide, Banks knew. The last case he'd come across was of a man chaining himself to the steering wheel of his car, pouring petrol all around and setting it alight. He'd left the windows closed, though, and there wasn't enough oxygen in the interior of the car for a fire to take hold, so when the brief flames had consumed it all, the man died of asphyxiation, with hardly a mark on him. Still, Banks had to consider every possibility. "Do you think he might have done this himself?" he asked Mellor.

"Start the fire? Good Lord, no. Roland wouldn't do anything irresponsible like that. Someone else might have got hurt. One of the firemen, for example. And it would certainly be a painful way to go. No. He had some strong pills from the doctor, he told me once. Sleeping pills. I don't know what they were called. Apparently he had terrible trouble sleeping. Nightmares and so on. If he was going to go, that was the way he would have done it."

Black dog. Nightmares. Roland Gardiner certainly sounded like a troubled man. Was it all down to him losing his job and his wife leaving him, or were there other reasons?

"Besides," Mellor went on, "things had been looking up for him recently."

Banks glanced at Annie. "Oh?"

"Yes. He seemed a lot more cheerful, a lot more optimistic."

"Did he say why?"

"Just that he'd met an old friend."

"What old friend?"

"He didn't elaborate on it. Like I said, Roland was a secretive sort of chap."

"The same old friend who visited him at the caravan?"

"Might have been. It was about the same time."

"Last summer?"

"Yes."

"When was the last time you saw Roland?"

Mellor thought for a moment. "Last Wednesday, I think it was. He lent me a book."

"What book was that?"

"Just a history book. We were both interested in Victorian England."

Banks stood up. "Thanks very much, Mr. Mellor. You've been a great help. Need a ride home?"

"Thank you. Normally I'd walk, but it's late, cold, and I've had a bit of a shock. You've got room for Sandy, too?"

"Of course. No trouble."

Annie's car was still back at Jennings Field, so they all crammed into Banks's Renault, Sandy curling up beside Mellor on the backseat, and headed toward Ash Cottage, the heater on full. In a few minutes the interior of the car was warm and Banks found himself feeling sleepy from the brandy. He knew he wasn't over the limit, just tired. They dropped off Mellor and Sandy, and Banks handed over his card. "In case you remember anything else." Then Banks drove Annie back to the field. They sat a moment in his car, the engine running and heater still on, watching the activity around the burned-out caravan. Things were definitely on the wane, but Stefan was still there, as were Geoff Hamilton and a group of firefighters. Both appliances had gone.

"Christ, I *hate* fires," said Banks.

"Why? Have you ever been in one?"

"No, but I have nightmares about it." He massaged his temples. "Once, way back when I was on the Met, I got called to an arson scene. Terraced house in Hammersmith. Some sort of arranged marriage gone wrong and the offended family pours petrol through the letter box of the other lot." He paused. "Nine people died in that fire. Nine people. Most of the time you couldn't tell the bodies from the debris, except for one bloke who still had a boiling red blister on his skull. And the smell . . . Jesus. But you know what stuck in my mind most?"

"Tell me," said Annie.

"It was this little girl. She looked as if she was kneeling by her bed with her hands clasped, saying her prayers. Burned to a crisp, but still there, stuck forever in that same position. Praying." Banks shook his head.

Annie touched his arm gently.

"Anyway," Banks went on, shaking off the memory. "What do you think?"

"I don't know what to think, really. I've got to admit it seems to be stretching coincidence to have two similar fires so close together. But where's the link?"

"That's what we have to find out," said Banks. "Unless we're dealing with a pyromaniac, a serial arsonist who likes starting fires in out-of-the-way places, then there *is* a connection between the victims, and the sooner we find it, the better. We'll get Kevin Templeton on it. He's good at ferreting out background. I'm going back to the station."

"I'll follow you."

"Okay. It's late, but I want to set a few things in motion while they're fresh in mind. For a start, I want to know about Mark Siddons's and Andrew Hurst's alibis for tonight. And Leslie Whitaker's. I'm not at all certain about him yet. Then we'll have to track down Gardiner's ex-wife. And let's not forget Dr. Patrick Aspern, Tina's stepfather."

"Surely you can't think he had anything to do with all this?"

"I don't know, Annie. Serious allegations were made, at least as far as his conduct toward his stepdaughter is concerned. And neither he nor his wife have solid alibis for the boat fires. He's not off my list yet. I think I'll send Winsome down to talk to him in the morning, ask him for an alibi. That should be interesting."

Annie sighed. "If you think it's necessary. It's your neck."

"And I want to put a rush on toxicology, too. These people didn't just lie down and let themselves be burned."

"Alan?"

"Yes?"

"I was talking to a friend of mine earlier, a chap called Philip Keane. He operates a private art authentication company, the one that was involved in the Turner find up here last July. I think he might be able to help, at least as far as the art angle is concerned. I'm sure he'd be happy to have a chat with you."

Banks looked at her. He knew she was seeing someone, but not his name. Was he the one? Was this why she had dressed up specially tonight and put a little extra makeup on? The timing was right, and he knew she'd helped the local gallery out with security for the brief period the Turner was housed there. "Did he know McMahon?"

"No, nothing like that. It's just something that crossed my mind earlier, and Phil might have some ideas, that's all."

"All right," said Banks. "Tell him to come to the station tomorrow."

"Oh, come on, Alan. He's a friend, not a suspect. How about the Queen's Arms? Lunch?"

"If we've got time. Tomorrow might be a busy day."

"If we've got time."

"Okay," said Banks.

Annie opened the door, and when she moved, Banks caught a whiff of her Body Shop grapefruit scent, even over the fire smells and the smoke from the pub that lingered in her hair and on her clothes. Annie stepped over to her own car. Banks slipped Tom Waits's *Alice* in the CD player and headed back through the dark lanes to the station listening to the croaking voice sing about shipwrecks, ice and dead flowers.

Chapter 8

*D*C Winsome Jackman hated Yorkshire winters. She didn't think much of the summers, either, but she really hated the winters. As she got out of her nice warm car in front of Patrick Aspern's house on Sunday morning, she felt a pang of longing for home, the way she often did when the cold and damp got to her even through her thick sweater and lined raincoat. She remembered the humid heat back home, way up in Jamaica's Cockpit Country, the lush green foliage, the insects chirping, the bright flame trees, banana leaves click-clacking overhead in the gentle breeze from the ocean, remembered how she used to walk up the steep hill home from the one-room schoolhouse in her neat uniform, laughing and joking with her friends. She missed her mother and father so much she ached for them sometimes. And her friends. Where were they all now? What were they doing?

Then she remembered the shanties, the crippling poverty and hopelessness, the way so many men treated their women as mere possessions, chattels of no real value. Winsome knew she had been lucky to get out. Her father was a police corporal at the Spring Mount station, and her mother worked at the banana-chip factory in Maroon Town, sitting out back in the shade with the other women, gossiping and slicing bananas all day. Winsome had worked for two summers at the

Holiday Inn just outside Montego Bay, and she had often talked to the tourists there. Their stories of their homelands, of America, Canada and England, had excited her imagination and sharpened her will. She had envied them the money that allowed them to have luxurious holidays in the sun, and the opportunities they must have at home. These countries, she had thought, must indeed be lands of plenty.

And it wasn't only the white folk. There were handsome black men from New York, London and Toronto, with thick gold chains hanging around their wrists and necks, their wives all dressed up in the latest fashions. What a world theirs was, with all the movies, fashions, cars and jewelry they wanted. Of course, the reality fell a long way short of her imagination, but on the whole she was happy in England; she thought she had made the right move. Apart from the winters.

She sensed, rather than saw, a number of curtains twitch as she walked up the path to ring Aspern's doorbell. A six-foot-one black woman ringing your doorbell was probably a rare event in this neighborhood, she thought. Anyway, winter or not, it was nice to get away from the computer for a while, and out of the office. And she was on overtime.

A man answered her ring, and she was immediately put off by the arrogant expression on his face. She had seen looks like that before. Other than that, she thought he was probably handsome in a middle-aged English sort of way. Soft strands of sandy hair combed back, unusually good white teeth, a slim, athletic figure, loose-fitting, expensive casual clothes. But the expression ruined everything.

He arched his eyebrows. "Can I help you?" he asked, looking her up and down, the condescension dripping like treacle from his tongue. "I'm afraid there's no surgery on Sundays."

"That's all right, Dr. Aspern," Winsome said, producing her warrant card. "I'm fit as a fiddle, thank you very much. And I probably couldn't afford you, anyway."

He looked surprised by her accent, no doubt expecting some sort of incomprehensible patois. The Jamaican lilt was still there, of course, but more as an undertone. Winsome had been in Yorkshire for seven years, though she had only been in Eastvale for two since her transfer from Bradford, and she had unconsciously picked up much of the local idiom and accent.

Aspern examined her warrant card and handed it back to her. "So first they sent the organ-grinder, and now they send the monkey."

"Excuse me, sir?"

"Never mind," said Aspern. "Just a figure of speech. You'd better come in."

Winsome got the impression that Aspern scanned the street for spies before he shut the door behind them. Was he worried what the neighbors might think? That he was having an affair with a young black woman? Drugs, more likely, Winsome guessed. He was concerned that they would think he was supplying her with drugs.

He showed her into a sitting room with cream wallpaper, a large blazing fireplace and a couple of nice landscape paintings on the wall. A recent medical journal lay open on the glass-topped coffee table beside a half-empty cup of milky tea.

"What is it this time?" he asked.

Winsome sat in one of the armchairs without being asked and crossed her long legs. Aspern perched on the sofa and finished off the tea.

"Where were you last night, sir?" Winsome asked.

"What?" Aspern's superior expression was replaced by one of puzzlement and anger.

"I think you heard me."

"Let's say I just didn't believe what I'm hearing."

"Okay," said Winsome, "I'll repeat the question. Where were you last night?"

"Has *he* put you up to this?"

"Who?"

"You know damn well who I'm talking about. Banks. Your boss."

"DCI Banks issues the actions, sir, and I just carry them out. I'm merely a humble DC. I'm not privy to his inner thoughts. As you so accurately put it yourself, the monkey, not the organ-grinder." She smiled. "But I *do* need to know where you were last night."

"Here, of course," Aspern answered after a short pause. "Where the hell else do you think I'd be, with my daughter so recently deceased? Out for a night on the town?"

"I understand she was your stepdaughter?" Winsome said.

"I always thought of her as my own."

"I'm sure you did. No blood relation, though. Probably a good thing."

Aspern's face darkened. "Now, look here, if Banks has been putting ideas in your head . . ."

"Sir?"

Aspern took a few calming breaths. "Right," he said. "I see. I understand what you're up to. Well, it won't work. Last night Fran and I both stayed in and watched television, hoping for something to take our minds off what's happened."

"Did you succeed?"

"What do you think?"

"What did you watch?"

"A film on Channel Four. I'm sorry, but I can't remember the title. I wasn't really paying attention. It was set in Croatia, if that helps."

"Is your wife here at the moment?"

"She's resting. As you can imagine, this has been very hard on her. Anyway, she'd only corroborate my statement."

"I'm sure she would," said Winsome. "We'll let her rest for now."

"Very good of you, I'm sure."

"But you must admit it's not a very strong alibi, is it? It's been my experience that wives will often stand by their husbands, no matter what horrors or atrocities they might be guilty of."

"Well, I'm not guilty of anything," said Aspern, getting to his feet. "So if that's all, I'll bid you good-bye. I don't have to sit around and listen to your filthy insinuations."

Winsome held her ground. "What insinuations would those be, sir?"

"You know what I'm talking about. Banks obviously briefed you on his groundless suspicions, and you're here to do his dirty work for him. It won't wash. I'll be complaining to my MP about the both of you."

"That's your prerogative," said Winsome. "But you have to understand that our job can be difficult at times, insensitive, even. I really *am* sorry for your loss, Dr. Aspern, but I still have questions to ask."

"Look, I've told you what I was doing. What more do you want?"

"What clothes were you wearing?"

"Come again?"

"You seem a bit hard of hearing this morning, sir. I asked what clothes you were wearing last night."

"I don't see how that's relevant to anything."

"If you'd just tell me. Or, better still, fetch them for me."

Aspern narrowed his eyes, then stomped out of the room. A few moments later he returned and flung a dark-blue cotton shirt and a pair of black casual trousers over the arm of the chair beside her. "Unless you want my underwear, too?" he said.

"That won't be necessary," said Winsome. She knew it was a farce, that he could have given her any old clothes and said he'd worn them last night, or that he could have washed and dried them in the meantime, but that wasn't the point of the exercise. The point was to shake him up, and in that she thought she was succeeding remarkably well. "What about your jacket and overcoat?" she asked.

"What jacket and overcoat? I told you we stopped at home last night. Why would I need a jacket and overcoat?"

"Of course, sir. My mistake." Winsome stood. "Mind if I take these?"

"Take them where? What for?"

"For forensic testing."

"And what do you hope to find?"

"I don't *hope* to find anything, sir. It'll just help us eliminate you from our inquiries."

"I love the language you people use. 'Eliminate you from our inquiries.' Talk about bureaucratese."

"That's a very good word for it, sir. Sometimes it does sound a bit overly formal, doesn't it? Anyway, if you could lay your hands on some sort of a bag . . Plastic would be best. Bin liner, or something like that."

Aspern went into the kitchen and found her a white plastic kitchen bag.

"Thanks. That'll do just fine," Winsome said.

"Eliminate me from *what* inquiries?" Aspern asked.

"What do you mean, sir?"

Aspern sighed. "You said earlier that this would help eliminate me from your inquiries. I'm asking exactly *what* inquiries you're talking about."

"I'm surprised you haven't heard," she said. "It's been all over the news. There was another fire last night, remarkably similar to the one in which your stepdaughter died, and not too far away."

"And I'm a suspect?"

"I didn't say that, sir, but we'd look pretty unprofessional if we didn't cover every possibility, wouldn't we?"

"I don't care what you'd look like; this is discrimination, pure and simple."

"Against what group? Doctors, for a change?"

"Now, look here, you fucking—"

Winsome raised a finger to her lips. "Don't say it, Doc," she said. "You know it'll only get you into trouble in these politically correct times."

Aspern ran his hand over his hair and regained his composure, and his arrogant air. "Right," he said, nodding. "Right. Of course. I apologize." He spread his hands. "Take whatever you like."

"That's all right, sir," she said, lifting the bag of clothes. "This is all I need. I'll be on my way now."

"I'm sorry you've had such a wasted journey. It's a long way to come for so little."

"Oh, I wouldn't call it wasted," said Winsome. "Not at all."

She felt absurdly pleased with herself as she walked down the path to her car. Curtains twitched again and Winsome smiled to herself as she hefted the bag onto the seat beside her and drove off.

Annie tracked down the ex–Mrs. Gardiner easily enough— she was now Mrs. Alice Mowbray, wife of Eric—and by mid-morning she was knocking on the door of their semi on Arboretum Crescent. The woman who answered the door looked about forty, and she had a hard-done-by air about her. The red cashmere jumper and black skirt she was wearing looked a bit Harvey Nicks, the gold necklace wasn't cheap, either, and her blond hair definitely came from a bottle.

"Who is it, Alice?" a voice from inside the house called. "If it's those bloody Jehovah's Witnesses again, tell them to bugger off!"

Annie showed her warrant card and Alice stood back to let her in. "It's the police," she called out.

A man came out of the room on the left of the hall, a curious expression on his face. Annie put him at about the woman's age, or maybe five years younger. It was hard to tell. He didn't have a gray hair on his head and was, she supposed, handsome in a way, the sort of bloke who's full of confidence and tries to pick up women in the better class of pub. Well, some women fall for the brash, sleazy charm, Annie realized.

"What do you want?" he asked. "If it's about that speeding ticket, then—"

"It's your wife I want to see, sir," said Annie.

"I can't imagine why," said Alice, "but let's talk in the conservatory. I know the weather's not very good, but it's a nice view, and we've got an electric heater."

"That'll be fine," said Annie, aware of Eric Mowbray breathing down her neck as she followed Alice to the conservatory. Well, it wouldn't do any harm to talk to him, too, she thought. He looked the type who would get nervous easily and blab, if there was anything to blab.

They settled in the conservatory, which was warm enough and did indeed have a magnificent view looking west into Swainsdale, the distant hills shrouded in light mist. Alice Mowbray sat down on a wicker chair and tugged her skirt over her plump knees. The skirt was at least two inches too short for someone with her thighs, Annie thought, and in conjunction with the peroxide-blond hair it gave her a definite look of mutton dressed as lamb. Her husband, black hair slicked back with a little gel, jeans too tight over the slight paunch he was already beginning to show, looked as if he didn't mind. Unbidden, an image of the two of them disco-dancing under a whirling glittering globe, Eric waving his hands in the air and doing his best John Travolta imitation, came into her mind, and she had to hold back the laughter.

"What is it, then?" Alice Mowbray asked.

"I'm afraid I've got some rather bad news for you," she said. Alice put her hand to her necklace. "Oh?"

"It's about your ex-husband. I don't know if you've seen or heard any news this morning . . . ?"

"Only the Sunday papers," Alice said.

Annie knew the Jennings Field blaze had been too late to make the national Sunday papers. "Well, I'm afraid there's been a fire at the caravan where your ex-husband was living."

"Oh, no," said Alice. "Is Roland hurt?"

"There was one person in the caravan at the time. As yet, we can't be certain if he was Mr. Gardiner, but I'm afraid that person is dead, whoever he is."

"I don't believe it. Not Roland."

"I'm sorry, Mrs. Mowbray, but it's true. If it is him. Are you all right?"

Alice had turned pale, but she nodded. "Yes, I'll be fine." She looked at her husband. "Darling, can you fetch me a glass of water, please?"

Eric didn't look too happy at being asked to fetch and carry in front of another woman, but there wasn't much he could do about it without looking a complete arsehole, except his wife's bidding.

"I'm sorry to spring such a shock on you like this," Annie said, "but there are some questions I need to ask."

"Of course. I understand. We've been apart for over two years now, but it's not as if I don't . . . well, still have some feelings for Roland. Was he . . . you know . . . ?"

Annie knew all about divorced men's feelings for their ex-wives at first hand, through Banks, and they could be complicated. She felt lucky that Phil had never been married. "I'm afraid the body was badly burned," she said, "but if it's any consolation we think he was unconscious before the fire started."

Alice frowned. "Unconscious? But how . . . ?"

"Sleeping pills, perhaps. But we don't know anything for certain yet. That's why I need to talk to you."

Eric came back with a glass of water and a pill and handed them to Alice. "What's this?" she asked, looking at the pill.

"Your Valium," he said. "I just thought you might need it."

Alice set the pill aside. "I'm fine," she said, and sipped some water.

"He was a useless pillock," Eric said.

"Pardon?" Annie said.

"Her ex. Roly-poly. He was a prize pillock."

"Eric, don't be so disrespectful."

"Well, he was. I'm only telling the truth, Allie, and you know it. Why else are you here with me while he was off living in a poky caravan in a godforsaken field somewhere? He was a loser."

"Mr. Mowbray," Annie said, "I don't think you've quite grasped the situation here. A man, possibly Roland Gardiner, is dead."

"I heard you the first time round, love. And I say it doesn't make a scrap of difference. He was a useless pillock while he was alive, and he's a useless pillock dead."

Annie sighed and turned back to Alice, who was glaring at her husband. "I don't know what's wrong with him," she said. "He's not usually rude like this."

"Never mind," said Annie, giving Eric Mowbray a dirty look. "Maybe he's just trying to hide his grief." *Or something else,* she thought. She turned back to Alice. "One problem we do have is with identification. Dental records are often useful in such cases. Could you tell me who your family dentist is? Doctor, too."

"I don't know if Roland ever went after he left," said Alice, "but we went to Grunwell's, on Market Street. Our family doctor's Dr. Robertson, at the clinic on the Leaside Estate."

Annie knew the place.

"We don't know much about your ex-husband," Annie went on. "Is there anything you can tell us that might be of any use?"

"He was just ordinary, really," said Alice.

"You can say that again," said Eric Mowbray.

"Shut up, Eric," said Alice.

Annie was fast starting to think that Eric Mowbray had outstayed any usefulness she might have erroneously attributed to him in the first place. "Mr. Mowbray," she said, "perhaps you could leave us for a while? I have some questions to ask your wife."   •

Mowbray got up. "Fine with me. I've got work to do, anyway."

After he'd left the conservatory, the two women let the silence stretch a few moments, then Alice said, "He's a good sort, really, Eric. Just got a bit of a sore spot where Roland's concerned."

"Oh? Why's that?"

"Because he's my ex. Eric's the jealous type."

"I see," said Annie. "Does he have any reason to be?"

"Not of Roland."

"What does Mr. Mowbray do for a living?"

"He's in computers. He makes very good money. Look at this conservatory. It certainly wasn't here when me and Roland were together. Nor the Volvo. And we're having our holidays in Florida in February. We're going to Disney World."

"Very nice. Do you own any other vehicles?"

"Eric used to have a Citroën, but he sold it."

"No Jeep or Range Rover?"

"No. Why?"

"Was Roland a successful businessman?"

"I often thought he was in the wrong business," Alice said. "He just wasn't that much of a salesman. Didn't have the oomph. Didn't have an ounce of ambition in his entire being. No get-up-and-go at all. Sometimes I thought he'd have been far better off as a schoolteacher, maybe. And happier. Still, he wouldn't have earned much money at that, either, would he?"

Money seemed to figure large in Alice Mowbray's view of the universe, Annie gathered, and perhaps in her second husband's, too. Jack Mellor had already hinted as much the previous night. "Did he not try to get another job?" she asked.

"It would have been a bit difficult for him, wouldn't it?"

"Why? Lots of people get made redundant and find new jobs."

"Redundant? That's a good one. Where on earth did you get that idea?"

"Your husband *didn't* lose his job?"

"Oh, Roland lost his job, all right, but it wasn't through redundancy. No. He was fired. You could have knocked me over with a feather. I never thought he had it in him."

"Had what in him?"

"He'd been on the fiddle, hadn't he?"

"Had he?"

"Yes. Something to do with forging orders and cooking the books. Stealing from the company. I must say he didn't have a lot to show for it, but that's typical Roland, that is. Small-time, even as a crook. No ambition."

"Can you tell me the name of the company he worked for?"

Alice told her. Annie wrote it down.

"Did Roland have any enemies?"

"Enemies? Roland? He was too much of a mouse to make enemies. Never offended a soul. He'd never stand in anyone's way enough to make an enemy. No, Roland was likable enough, I'll give him that. He had a natural charm. People liked him. Perhaps because he was so passive, so easygoing. He'd do anything for anyone."

"This forgery business, did he have a partner?"

"Did it all by himself. As I said, you could have knocked me over with a feather."

"How long were you married?"

"Ten years."

"Quite late in life, then?"

Alice narrowed her eyes. "For Roland, yes. He was thirty-two when we married."

Annie didn't dare ask Alice how old *she* was. "Had he been married before?"

"Neither of us had. I must admit, he turned my head. He could be a real charmer, could Roland. Until you got to know him, of course, then you saw how empty it all was."

"Was the divorce amicable?"

"As amicable as these things go. He didn't have anything I wanted, despite his little business on the side, and he seemed quite willing to let me keep the house."

"You didn't want the caravan?"

"The caravan? I hated the bloody thing! That was typical Roland, though. Soon as we did have a bit of extra cash, off he goes and buys a bloody caravan. That was his idea of a good time: two weeks in a caravan at Primrose Valley or Flamborough Head. I ask you."

"So there was no unsettled business between you?"

"I got on with my life, and he got on with his."

"Mr. Mowbray, your present husband, when did he come on the scene?"

"What do you mean?"

"Did you meet him before or after you split up with Roland?"

Alice paused a few moments before answering. "Before," she said. "But things were already over for Roland and me."

Annie supposed that Alice needed someone to go off with, an excuse to end her marriage, and somewhere to go. Many people did. They didn't want to stay in a relationship, but they didn't want to go it alone, either.

"What did you do last night?"

If Alice found the question offensive, she didn't let on. "We were out to dinner at a friend's house."

"Can you give me the address? Just routine, for the paperwork."

Alice gave it to her.

"Do you think Roland might have committed suicide?"

"I don't think he had the guts. It might have been something he'd think of, but when it came to it, he'd bottle out. And certainly not in a fire. He wasn't exactly the most physically brave man I've ever met. He used to make enough fuss about going to the dentist's, for crying out loud."

"Can you give me a list of his friends?"

"Friends? Roland? There was no one close. I can probably come up with a few names of people who knew him, mostly from work, but I don't think they'll be able to tell you any more than I can."

"Was he secretive, then?"

"I suppose so. Just quiet, though, mostly. I don't think he really had much to talk about."

"Do you happen to have a photograph of him? As recent as possible?"

"I might have one or two," Alice said. "Would you excuse me for a moment?"

Annie heard her go upstairs. She also heard her husband question her as she went. Annie sat and admired the view as two sparrows fluttered in the birdbath out in the garden. She thought she could see a hawk circling over distant Tetchley Fell. A couple of minutes later, Alice came back with a handful of photographs.

"These were taken at the last office Christmas party we went to," she said. "Three years ago."

Annie flipped through them and picked one of the few that was actually in focus: Gardiner sitting at a table, a little flushed from the wine, raising his glass to the photographer and smiling. It was good enough for identification purposes.

"Has anyone been around asking for him since he left?" she asked.

"No. But there was a phone call."

Annie's ears pricked up. "When?"

"In July, I think."

"Did the caller identify himself?"

"No. That was the funny thing. When I told him Roland no longer lived here, he just asked me if I knew where he did live."

"What did you say?"

"I told him. I mean, I knew where Roland was. I had to, with the divorce, the solicitors and everything."

"Did he ever call back?"

"No. That was all."

Interesting, Annie thought. July. Around the time Roland Gardiner started being a bit more optimistic, according to Jack Mellor, and the same time Thomas McMahon got a spring in his step. What happened last summer? Annie wondered. She asked Mrs. Mowbray a few more questions about Roland's past: where he went to school, where his parents lived, and so on; then she left. She didn't see Eric Mowbray on her way out, and she couldn't say it bothered her.

"One of the main problems an art forger faces," Phil Keane explained to Banks and Annie that Sunday lunchtime at the Queen's Arms, "is getting hold of the right period paper or canvas."

Banks looked at him as he talked. So this was the mysterious man Annie was now seeing? She had referred to Phil merely as a friend, but Banks sensed a bit more chemistry than Platonic friendship between them. Not that they were fawning over each other, playing kissy-face or holding hands, but there was just something in the air—pheromones, most likely, and something in the way she listened as he spoke. Not so much hanging on his every word, but respectful, *involved*.

Banks had noticed that one or two of the women in the place had cast appraising glances when Phil walked in ten minutes late and insisted on going to the bar to buy a round of drinks. He was handsome, Banks thought, but not outrageously so, well dressed but not showy, and he talked with the easy charm and knowledge of a habitual lecturer. He did, in fact, give occasional lectures, Annie said, so it was hardly surprising that he seemed so confident, even a bit pedantic, in his delivery. What was there not to like about this man? Banks wondered. This man who was probably shagging Annie. Let it go, Banks told himself; they'd moved on ages ago, hadn't they? And he had Michelle.

The trouble was that Michelle was far away right now, and here was Banks sitting in the Queen's Arms with Annie and her new fancy man, desperately looking for things to dislike. In his experience, anything or anyone who seemed too good to be true *was* too good to be true. Well, the man was too old for her, for a start, but then so had *he* been too old for her, and Phil Keane was a few years younger than he.

"Anyway," Phil went on, "not everyone can do a John Myatt and forge modern masters with emulsion paint on any old scrap of paper he finds lying around, so the typical forger tends to be careful, especially in these days of scientific testing. He has to make sure his materials, and not just his techniques, pass all the requisite requirements. Not always an easy task."

"You were saying about the paper . . . ?"

"Was I? Oh, yes." Phil scratched the crease between the side of his nose and his cheek. It was a gesture Banks immediately disliked. It said, *Until I was so rudely interrupted.* The pontificator's irritation at being interrupted in his digressions. He was damned glad he'd found *something* to dislike about the man at last, even though it wasn't much.

"Well, until the end of the eighteenth century, all paper was made by hand, usually from rags, and after that it was slowly replaced by machine-made paper, some of it made from wood pulp."

"What's the difference?" Banks asked.

"Wood pulp makes far inferior paper," Phil replied. "It's weaker and discolors more easily." He leaned forward and tapped the table. "But the point I'm trying to make is that if you want to forge an artist's work, you'd damn well better make sure you use the same materials he did."

Banks took a sip of his Theakston's bitter. Phil was working on a half of XP, slowly, and Annie stuck with fruit juice. "Makes sense," Banks said. "Go on. Where do you find that sort of thing?"

"Exactly the problem. There are several places he might look for the paper," Phil went on, "and one of the best sources is an antiquarian book and print dealer. Not everything they sell is expensive, but a lot of it is old. The endpapers of old books are especially useful, for example, and books usually have a publication date to guide you as to the age of the paper you're using."

"What about prints?" Banks asked. "I mean, wouldn't some old drawings be dated, too?"

"Yes, but that's not always reliable. They could easily be copies of etchings, made posthumously, in another country, even, and until you've developed a very good nose for the genuine article, you wouldn't want to slip up by believing what you read on an old print."

"What about canvas?" Banks asked. "Aren't most paintings done on canvas?"

Here Phil allowed himself a slight smile, which Banks pounced on as not being entirely devoid of condescension. He was starting to like the man less and less moment by moment, and he was enjoying the feeling very much.

"Quite a lot are," said Phil, "but the same applies as to paper, except you don't find canvas in books. You try to seek out old worthless canvases. Quite often what you find determines which artist you forge."

"I see," said Banks. "And you think Thomas McMahon was a forger?"

Phil glanced at Annie, a concerned expression flitting across his face.

"Phil only said that could be one possible explanation of McMahon's odd purchases from Whitaker's," Annie said.

"Yes," Phil added. "I'm not making any accusations or anything. I didn't even know the man."

"Wouldn't matter if you did make accusations," said Banks. "McMahon's dead. He can't sue you."

"Even so . . ."

"The problem is," Banks went on, "does any of this have anything to do with his murder, and if so, how? Shall we order lunch?"

Phil looked around. "Look, I know a cozy little place out Richmond way that serves the most tender roast lamb you've ever tasted in your life." He looked at Annie. "And I hear they do a delicious vegetable curry, too. What say we head out there?"

Mark awoke the next day still very much alive, and he realized that he probably had the fleece-lined overcoat to thank for that. Even in his favorite leather jacket, he would have been too cold in the barn. He didn't know what time it was because he didn't have a watch, but it was daylight, and a hell of a lot warmer than it had been during the night.

He had slept surprisingly well, he thought, but exhaustion will do that for you. He must have run and walked well into the night. And it was the first real sleep he'd had since the fire. Rubbing his bleary eyes, he cast a look around at his surroundings, a half-demolished barn littered with rubble and sheep droppings. It stank of piss, too. Time to move on. He wished he could have a hot cup of tea and something to eat, some bacon and eggs, perhaps. He wouldn't get far on the ten quid in his pocket and a bit of loose change, but at least he could buy himself a couple of small meals. It would be nice to find a proper toilet, too, somewhere he could wash his hands and face. If only he could find a café. Hardly likely in the sort of classy villages you got around this part of the world. No greasy spoons or lorry drivers' cafés.

It was nearly one o'clock, he saw by the church clock in the first village he came to. Christ, he hadn't realized he'd slept in *that* long. You could hardly call the place picturesque. This was one the tourists would drive straight through without even slowing down. There was one Tarmac main street of squat red brick houses with the red pantile roofs so common in East Yorkshire, a post office, general store and newsagent's.

The village was dead quiet, apart from some faint pop music coming from the shabby-looking local pub, the Farmer's Inn. There was a blackboard outside advertising bar food, and Mark noticed that he could get a ham-and-cheese sandwich for £2.99, or a roast beef lunch with Yorkshire pudding, vegetables and roast potatoes for £5.99. What should he do? Go carefully and save enough for another sandwich later, or blow nearly everything on a hearty lunch? Finally, he decided on the latter course, mostly because he was starving. He hadn't eaten since they kicked him out of jail.

Cautiously, he walked inside. It wasn't one of those places where all conversation stops and everyone looks at you when you walk in, as in that werewolf film he'd seen on the telly in the squat, but he still felt exposed in his ill-fitting clothes, no doubt with a twig or two stuck on the hem of his overcoat and a smear of sheep shit on his jeans. He just hoped he didn't smell too bad.

The pub was exactly the slightly down-at-heels local you'd expect in such a village, which was probably why the food was so cheap. It smelled of last night's beer and cigarette smoke and was mostly full of hard-looking unemployed farmhands, who wouldn't be squeamish about a bit of sheep shit here and there. The landlord was a surly bugger, but he copied down Mark's order and gave him a number, only turning his nose up when Mark ordered a small lemonade to drink. He didn't want to waste his money on beer. With the change in his pocket, he now had a little over four pounds left, and that might buy him a roll and a cup of tea for dinner, if he could find anywhere serving such fare. He'd worry about tomorrow when it came.

He realized he'd have to do something about the money situation soon, and it might mean a bit of burglary. He didn't like it, but he'd done it before, and he'd do it again if he had to. It was the one thing Crazy Nick had taught him, when he had forced Mark to come out on jobs with him. There was hardly a house he couldn't get into. Mark would never beg, but he would thieve if necessary. At least thieving took guts, and you didn't look like you'd just given up and sat down with your hand sticking out permanently.

Mark had one cigarette left, he realized, courtesy of the copper who had given him the clothes. He decided to smoke it *after* his lunch. He sat in a deserted corner by the window and looked out through the greasy glass on the empty high street. People would be eating their roasts behind their dusty net curtains, perhaps watching football or racing, as Crazy Nick did when he came back from the pub. If his team lost he used to smack Mark around. Mark's mother, too, sometimes, though she was a tough old bird, and you could tell Crazy Nick had to be really pissed to have a go at her. As often as not, he came out the worse for wear.

The telly was on behind the bar in the pub, sound off, and Mark was just in time to catch the local news. A tart with a microphone was standing by a burned-out caravan dripping with water the fire hoses had sprayed on it. Was that what he had seen last night, when he was running from Lenny's place? Then the screen displayed a still photograph of a man Mark had never seen before. The tart talked on for a while as the cameras lovingly panned over the scene of desolation, then the film cut to footage of the two boats. Mark felt his breath catch in his throat as he looked on his former home again, now in daylight, with men in protective clothing going over the scene.

There was another reporter by the canal side, a man, this time. His name was captioned at the bottom of the screen, but it was too small for Mark to read. He was wearing a heavy overcoat and a scarf wrapped around his neck. He talked and gestured as the others, police officers, Mark supposed, went about their work.

Next came an old picture of Tom in the next boat, the man they said was an artist. He was barely recognizable from the photograph, but it was definitely Tom.

And then came the picture that grabbed ahold of Mark's heart and squeezed. He'd never seen it before, but it was Tina, maybe taken two or three years ago, before they met. Her blond hair was long, over her shoulders, and it seemed to glow with health. She was smiling at the camera, but Mark could tell it was a bit forced. If you didn't know her well, though, didn't know that telltale clenching of the jaw and shadows behind her eyes, then you'd never know. Time hung suspended. He almost felt as if she could see him, was looking right at him, and he wanted to call out to her, tell her he was sorry he had failed her, sorry he hadn't been there for her.

When the picture vanished as quickly as it had appeared, and the program cut back to the reporter by the canal, Mark stood up so quickly he knocked his drink over and ran out into the street.

Banks bowed out of the excursion to the pub out Richmond way, allowing Annie to go with Phil, which was probably what she wanted anyway, ate a hurried roast pork lunch at the Queen's Arms alone and returned to the station. Because it was a Sunday, things were slow, especially as far as forensics went, but a major investigation was under way, and Banks's Major Crimes core team was hard at work.

At this point, while each fire was being investigated separately for cause and motive, every possible effort was being made to find the link between them that everyone suspected was there. When Banks dropped by the incident room, Winsome was back entering the green sheets into the HOLMES computer system; DC Gavin Rickerd was making sure everything was in its place, neatly logged and filed; DC Kevin Templeton was chewing the end of a pencil as he tried to gather information on any similar fires; and DS Hatchley was pondering over the bits and pieces he had dug up on Mark David Siddons. The phones rang from time to time, computer keyboards clacked and fax machines hummed. Everything was ticking over nicely, but just ticking over. Of course, everyone was on overtime except Banks. A DCI didn't get paid overtime.

Banks hadn't been back in his own office more than a couple of minutes when Stefan Nowak tapped at the door. "A moment?"

Banks looked up. "Good news, I hope?"

"I don't know," said Stefan, standing at the open door. "But there's something you might like to see, if you've got a minute or two to spare."

Curious, Banks followed Stefan down the corridor into the "new" part of the building, which they called the annex. It was just as old, in fact, but it used to be a hotel before Eastvale expanded from divisional HQ into Western Area Headquarters and knocked through the walls. Now it housed fingerprints, photography, scenes-of-crime and computers, among other departments.

Stefan stopped at a lab bench. "I thought you might be interested in this," he said, pointing to a blackened cube about the size of a computer monitor. "We retrieved it from the caravan. Looks as if it was hidden in one of the cupboards."

"What is it?" Banks asked.

"Well, it looks to me like a fire-resistant safe," said Stefan.

"A fire-resistant safe? What on earth is a bloke living on his wits in a dilapidated caravan doing with a fire-resistant safe?"

"You tell me," said Stefan. "I only found it and identified it."

"Can you open it?"

"It might take a bit of brute force."

"Any reason to treat it gently?"

"No. We've already checked for prints. Nothing."

"So let's do it."

Stefan had already got his hands on a small crowbar—from the police garage, he told Banks—and he proceeded to wedge it in the lock area and exert pressure. Nothing happened. He looked up at Banks. "Any safecrackers down in the cells?"

"I wish," said Banks. "Keep at it. Fire-resistant or not, the fire must have weakened the lock a bit, at least."

Stefan kept at it. Still nothing happened. "I think we might have to dynamite it," he said.

Banks laughed. "Let me have a go."

Stefan handed him the crowbar and Banks shifted it to the side opposite the lock, where the deep-seated hinges were. It was hard to see exactly what he was doing because of the fire damage, but he thought he had succeeded in inserting the sharp flat end of the crowbar between the body of the safe and the hinged door. Gently at first, he worked the crowbar up and down and managed to get it in another few millimeters. Finally, the first hinge cracked and it was only a matter of time before he broke the second one, too.

"Fireproof, but not Banks-proof," he said, pulling open the door. He reached into the dark interior. "Looks like something's there."

"What is it?" Stefan asked.

Banks pulled out the safe's contents, wrapped in black plastic bin liner, and placed them on the lab bench. Both men looked down in astonishment. On the table in front of them lay some rolled-up tubes of paper and three bundles of twenty-pound notes, fastened with rubber bands, probably five hundred quid or more in each of them. Banks unfolded the tubes and saw a number of sketches of a castle, and a finished watercolor painting, about eleven by sixteen, of a view along a valley from the castle terrace.

"That's Hornby Castle," said Stefan.

"How do you know?"

He glanced sideways at Banks. "I've been there. I do a lot of walking. It's near Kirkby Lonsdale. And this"—he pointed to the watercolor—"is the view from the castle. That's Ingleborough, one of the Three Peaks. I've walked them."

The Three Peaks walk was a popular one, but it had always seemed just that little bit too eccentric for Banks. Not to mention exhausting. You had to walk more than twenty miles in twelve hours, climbing three bloody great hills—Pen-y-Ghent, Whernside and Ingleborough—as often as not in the pouring rain.

Banks looked at the sketches and the watercolor again. They looked old. There was no signature, but it was obvious enough, even to Banks's untrained eye, that he was looking at the work of J.M.W. Turner, or a close facsimile.

"Bloody hell," he said, "I'd better ring Annie."

"I don't think your boss likes me very much," Phil Keane said to Annie that evening. They were at her place and were just finishing a light evening meal of pasta primavera, neither being terribly hungry after their big lunch.

Annie poured them each another glass of Sainsbury's Montepulciano D'Abruzzo. "What makes you say that?" she asked.

"Oh, I don't know. Just a feeling. Do you think he might be jealous?"

Annie felt herself blush. She hadn't told Phil about her and Banks. "Why would he be?"

"Maybe he's got designs on you himself?"

"Don't be silly." Annie drank some wine rather too quickly and it went down the wrong way. Along with her cold, that set her coughing. Phil brought her a glass of water and watched her concernedly as she took a few seconds to get it under control.

"Okay?" he said.

"Fine. Look, Alan and I, we . . . well . . ."

Phil looked at her, interested.

"Do I have to spell it out?"

"Of course not," Phil said. "And I'm sorry for bringing it up. You could have told me sooner, though. It's not as if I expected you to have lived the life of a nun, you know."

"You didn't?"

"Well, *I* certainly haven't. The life of a monk, I mean."

"You haven't?"

"No."

"Anyway, it was a while ago."

"It just surprises me, that's all."

"Why?"

"I don't know," Phil said. "I suppose because he doesn't seem your type."

"What *is* my type?"

"I don't know. He just . . . what's he like?"

"What do you mean?"

"What did you like about him?"

"Alan? Well, he's fun to be with. Most of the time, at any rate. He loves music, likes single malt whiskey, has tolerable taste in films, apart from an unfortunate fondness for action adventure stuff—you know, James Bond, Arnold Schwarzenegger and dreadful macho stuff like that. Which is odd because he's not really a macho kind of bloke. I mean he's sensitive, kind, compassionate, and he's got a good sense of humor."

"Did you live together?"

Annie laughed. "No. I stayed in my little hovel at the center of the Harkside labyrinth, as he used to put it, and he's got a lovely little cottage near Gratly. He's a bit of a loner, actually, so it suits him quite well."

"What went wrong?"

"I don't know. It just didn't work out. Too much baggage. Alan's recently divorced, and his family's still on his mind a lot. It just didn't work out. Oh, we work well together. That's not a problem. Except . . ."

"What?"

"Well, you know. Sometimes you can't help but be aware of your history. It can make things difficult. But it's manageable. And he's a good boss. Gives me a lot of freedom. Respects my opinions."

"About those fires?"

"About anything."

"And what are your opinions?"

"I don't have any yet. Early days."

"You're not comfortable talking about your work with me, I can see. I'm sorry."

Annie reached out and squeezed his arm. "Oh, it's all right," she said. "To tell the truth, I was just getting used to having no one to talk to outside the station. I do have to exercise some discretion, but it's not as if I've signed the Official Secrets Act or anything. Anyway, as I said, I don't have any theories yet. Not enough evidence. All we know is that they seem to be the work of an arsonist. Which is hardly a bloody secret." She wasn't going to tell Phil about the Turner and the money that Banks had phoned her about just yet, not until she had talked to Banks about possibly getting Phil involved as a consultant.

"Not even the tiniest suspicion?"

"I could hardly tell you if I suspected someone, could I?"

"Then you *have* signed the Official Secrets Act?"

Annie laughed and topped up her glass. She felt a little tipsy, but it had been a long weekend, and she was still fighting off the remnants of her cold. "It's like doctors and patients," she said.

"Until your suspect is arrested?"

"Ah, then the rules change, yes. Look, you haven't told me how long you're staying up north this time."

"I don't know," said Phil. "It's fairly quiet at the office, but something could come up and I might get called back."

"A suspicious Sickert, perhaps? Or a dodgy Degas?"

Phil laughed. "Something like that. Look, do you fancy a weekend in New York?"

"New York!" Annie had never been to America. She and Phil had been to Paris in September, and she'd had a hard time getting him to let her pay her own way. She didn't think she could afford New York, and she didn't want him to pay.

"Yes. Next weekend. Business, mostly, I'm afraid. I've a few gallery owners and dealers to meet with. But we could take in a Broadway show, dinner later."

"I'm not sure I'd be able to get away next weekend."

"The case?"

"Yes. And there's the money . . ."

"Oh, don't worry about that. It's a business trip. On the company."

"Both of us?"

"Of course. You'd be my security adviser."

Annie laughed and carried their empty dishes over to the kitchen sink. "It sounds wonderful, but . . ."

"Tell me you'll at least think about it."

"I'll think about it." Annie sensed Phil behind her before she felt his hands on her hips and his lips nuzzle the hollow between her neck and shoulder. She wriggled and he circled his arms around, holding her to him tightly enough so she could feel his erection pressing at the base of her spine. She couldn't help but experience a moment of fear and panic as she felt his hardness against her. Images of the rape of three years ago flashed through her mind and set her nerves on edge. But she had learned to control the emotions and, if not to enjoy sex as fully as she might, at least not to run away from it.

"Leave those dishes for now," Phil said, loosening his grip.

Annie turned to face him, surprised to feel the panic dissipating so quickly, the warmth spreading like wetness between her legs, her knees weak. It hadn't been like this with Alan, she thought, then felt ashamed for making the comparison. Phil put his arms around her and she smiled up at him. "Okay," she said. "Stay the night?"

"I don't have my toothbrush."

Annie laughed and buried her face in the soft cotton of his shirt. "Oh, I think I've got an unused one in the bathroom," she said.

"In that case . . ." Phil said. He let his arms fall by his side, then Annie took him by the hand and led him toward the stairs.

Chapter 9

*A*nnie looked pleased with herself on Monday morning, and Banks guessed it wasn't entirely to do with her job. She sat down opposite him in his office and crossed her legs. She was wearing tight black jeans and a red shirt made of some silky sort of material, which seemed to whisper when she moved. Her hair looked tousled, and her cold seemed to be on the wane. There was a glow about her that Banks wasn't sure he liked.

"Anyway," she said, "I talked to Roland Gardiner's ex-employer and it seems as if Roland was playing a minor variation on the long firm fraud."

"Was he, indeed?" A long firm fraud involves setting up a fraudulent company—easy enough to do these days with computer software—and acquiring goods or services without paying. A true long firm fraud takes a long time to get going—hence its name—and requires a bit of capital. You first have to pay your bills promptly to gain the trust of the companies you purchase from. "How did he manage that?" Banks asked. "I thought you told me his ex-wife said he never had a penny to spare."

"He didn't. That was the beauty of it. He bought from himself."

"What do you mean?"

"From the company he worked for. Office products. Good market. Easy to get rid of. Gave himself a nice line of credit and took it from there. He didn't need to establish trust over a long period."

"He can't have made much," Banks said.

"He didn't. I think that's what bothered his ex-wife, too. I get the impression that if he'd made a bit more money she wouldn't have minded too much where he got it from."

"What happened when his boss found out?"

"Offered the honorable way out. Pay back and resign. No police. Seems he was well liked enough around the office."

"So where does this get us?" Banks asked, talking to himself as much as to Annie.

"Well," Annie answered. "We've got a dead art forger, and now it seems as if the second victim was a different kind of fraudster. And he had a Turner watercolor and about fifteen hundred quid in a fire-resistant safe. It seems like too much of a coincidence to me. Whatever it was, they must have been in it together."

"Sounds logical," said Banks. "But what? And what's the link between them? How did they know one another?"

"I can't answer those questions yet," said Annie. "Not enough information. But if there's a link, we'll find it. What interests me right now is who else was involved."

"The third man?"

"Yes. Someone killed them."

"Unless they fell out and Gardiner killed McMahon."

"Still doesn't explain who killed Gardiner."

"His ex? Her new husband?"

"Possible," said Annie.

"But unlikely?"

"In my opinion. What about Leslie Whitaker?"

"He's another possibility," said Banks. "I'm not entirely

convinced that he didn't know exactly what McMahon was up to. I think we should have another crack at him, anyway. Let's have him in, this time."

"Good idea." Annie paused. "Alan, about this Turner . . . ?"

"Yes?"

"I was just wondering, before we do anything else, you know, if we should perhaps bring Phil in, let him have a look at it? After all, it is his line of expertise."

"I think we'd be better going through correct channels," said Banks, feeling about as stiff and formal as he sounded.

"That's not like you," Annie said. "Besides, it could take ages. Phil might be able to tell us something useful right away."

"Don't forget there's Ken Blackstone," said Banks. "He's got a strong background in art forgery."

"But he's West Yorkshire," Annie argued. "And that was ages ago. Phil knows the business, and he's here right now."

"I gathered that," said Banks.

Annie's mouth tightened. "What's that supposed to mean?"

"Nothing. Only that I think we should go through official channels."

"Oh, for crying out loud, we use consultants all the bloody time. What about that psychologist? The redhead who fancies you?"

Banks felt himself flush, partly with anger and partly with embarrassment. "You mean Dr. Fuller? She's a professional psychologist, a trained criminal profiler."

"Whatever. Phil's a trained art authenticator."

"We don't know *what* Phil is. You've hardly known him five minutes."

"You know what your problem is?" Annie said, running her hand through her hair. "You're bloody jealous, that's what it is. You're playing dog in the manger. What you can't have, nobody else should get either, right?"

"He can have you as much and as often as he wants, for all I care," said Banks, "but I won't compromise this investigation because of your private life."

"Oh, pull the carrot out of your arse, Alan. Can you hear yourself? Do you have any idea what you sound like?"

Banks felt as if he'd taken a wrong turn and the brick wall was looming dead ahead. "Look . . ." he began, but Annie cut in, after a deep breath.

"All I'm saying is let him have a look at the Turners, that's all," she said, softening her tone. "If you're worried he's going to run off with them, you can chain them to your wrist."

"Don't be absurd. I'm not worried about anything of the kind."

"Then what is your objection? What can it possibly be?"

"He's an unknown quantity." Banks felt that his objections were inadequate, and he knew he was well on the defensive, partly because he also knew he was acting irrationally, out of jealousy, and he didn't know how to get out of the situation without admitting it.

"I know him," Annie said. "And I can vouch for him. He knows his business, Alan. He's no dilettante."

Banks thought for a moment. He knew he had to give in gracefully, knew that he'd brushed against dangerous ground indeed during their little exchange. Much as he didn't like the idea of bringing Annie's boyfriend into the investigation, it was certainly true that Phil Keane might be able to help them with the art forgery angle, had in fact helped them already in elaborating on the possible reasons why McMahon had bought useless old books and prints from Whitaker. Besides, he *was* objecting because he was jealous, and that was unprofessional.

"All right," he said. "I'll put it to Detective Superintendent Gristhorpe. I can't be fairer than that."

"*You'll* put it to him? Are you sure you won't put it to him the way you've just put it to me?"

"Annie, this stops now. Okay? I said I'll put it to him. Take it or leave it."

Annie glared at Banks, then she snatched up her files. "Fine," she said. "I'll take it. You put it to him."

"Look, what's all this about?" said Leslie Whitaker, clearly uncomfortable to find himself on the receiving end of a police interrogation. "You've kept me waiting over an hour. I've got a business to run."

"Sorry about that, Mr. Whitaker," said Banks, arranging his folders neatly on the desk in front of him. They were in interview room two, which was hardly any different from interview rooms one and three, except that it let in even less light from the high, grille-covered window. Banks had brought DS Hatchley in to assist. Annie was digging up more background on Roland Gardiner, then she would be going to see Phil Keane with the Turners. Besides, she and Banks were barely speaking, and that was not conducive to the teamwork required for a successful interview.

"Can you get on with it, then?" said Whitaker, tapping his left hand against the desk. His foot was jumping, too, Banks noticed. Nervous, then. Something to hide? Or just angry?

Banks glanced at Hatchley, who raised his eyebrows. *"Get on with it?"* Hatchley repeated. "It's not often we get someone telling us to get on with it, is it, sir?"

"That's true," said Banks. "Still, we'll do as you say, Mr. Whitaker, and get on with it. If you've nothing to hide, and if you're truthful with us, you'll be opening up that shop again in no time."

Whitaker leaned back in the chair. He was wearing a beige jacket over a dark blue polo-neck sweater. Banks tried to match him with the description he had of McMahon's visitor from Mark Siddons, but all he could conclude was that the description was vague enough to fit Whitaker and a hundred or more others.

"When we talked to you the other day," Banks said, "you told us that you sold books and prints on occasion to Thomas McMahon."

"Yes. I did. So what?"

"Do you know why he wanted them?"

"I already told you, I had no idea."

"I think you do, Mr. Whitaker."

Whitaker's eyes narrowed. "Oh?"

"Yes," said Banks. "Want to know what I think? I think you deliberately sought out certain books and prints for Thomas McMahon, at his request."

Whitaker folded his arms. "Why would I do that?"

"You're an art dealer, aren't you?"

"In a small way, yes, I suppose so. More of a local agent, really."

"And you probably know a bit about forgery."

"Now, hang on a minute. What are you suggesting?"

Banks repeated the lecture he'd first heard from Phil Keane about the re-use of old endpapers and prints. Whitaker listened, making a very bad job of pretending he hadn't a clue what Banks was talking about.

"I still don't see what any of this has to do with me," he said, when Banks had finished.

"Oh, come off it," said Hatchley. "You were in it together. You and McMahon. You supplied him with the right sort of materials, he turned out the forgeries, you sold them, and then you split the profits. Only he got greedy, threatened to expose you."

"That's ridiculous. I did no such thing."

"Well, you must admit," said Banks, "that it all looks a bit dodgy from where I'm sitting."

"I can't help it if you have a suspicious nature. It must be your job."

Banks smiled. "The job. Yes, it does tend to make one a little less ready to accept the sort of bollocks you've been dishing out so far. Why don't you just admit it, Leslie? You had something going with McMahon."

Whitaker faltered a moment, but kept quiet.

"Maybe you didn't kill him," Banks went on. "But you know something. You knew why he wanted those books and prints, and I'll bet he paid *above* the odds for them. Your cut, nicely bypassing the taxman. What was Roland Gardiner's role?"

"I don't know who you're talking about."

"Come off it, Leslie. Roland Gardiner. He died in a caravan fire in Jennings Field on Saturday night."

"And you think I . . . ?"

"That's what I'm asking. Because if you didn't kill him, and if you didn't kill McMahon, then maybe you're next."

Whitaker turned pale. "You can't mean that. Why would you say that?"

"Stands to reason," said Hatchley. "These things happen when thieves fall out."

"I am *not* a thief."

"Just a figure of speech," Hatchley went on. "See, if you weren't the ringleader, as you swear you weren't, then you were just one of the underlings, and two of them are dead. See what I mean? Stands to reason."

"No," said Whitaker, regaining his composure. "It doesn't stand to reason at all. Your whole premise is rubbish, absolute rubbish. I've done nothing."

"Except supply Thomas McMahon with the paper necessary for his forgeries," said Banks.

"I didn't know what he was doing with the damn stuff."

"We think you did."

Whitaker folded his arms again. "Well, that's your problem."

"No. It's yours. What kind of car do you drive?"

"A Jeep. Why?"

"What kind of Jeep?"

"A Cherokee. Four-wheel drive. I live out Lyndgarth way. The roads can be bad."

A Jeep Cherokee was close enough to a Range Rover or any other kind of four-wheel drive station wagon for Banks, especially when the cars had only been spotted through the woods by people who had little knowledge of the various shapes and forms the vehicles took. "Color?"

"Black."

Again, close enough to dark blue. "Where were you last Thursday evening?"

"At home."

"Where's that?"

"Lyndgarth, as I said."

"Alone?"

"Yes. I'm recently divorced, if you must know."

"Not much of an alibi, is it?" Hatchley cut in.

Whitaker looked at him. "I wasn't aware I'd be needing one."

"That's what they all say."

"Now, look—"

"All right, Mr. Whitaker," said Banks, "you can argue with my sergeant later. We've got more important matters to cover right now. Where were you on Saturday evening?"

"Saturday? I . . ."

"Yes?"

Whitaker thought for a moment, then he looked at Banks, triumphant. "I was at a dinner in Harrogate. Yorkshire booksellers. We get together every month, about ten of us. They'll all vouch for me."

"What time did you arrive?"

"Eight o'clock."

Banks felt his hopes wane. If Whitaker really was with nine other people at eight o'clock Saturday, and the fire started around eight forty-five, it seemed to let him off. Especially as it took at least an hour to drive from Lyndgarth to Harrogate. But watertight alibis, in Banks's experience, were made to be broken.

"We will check, you know."

"Go ahead," said Whitaker. "Do you want their names? The others?"

"You can give them to Detective Sergeant Hatchley later."

"I don't see that we have anything more to talk about, do you?"

"Plenty," said Banks. "I still want to know what role Gardiner played in all this, and why he had to die, too."

"I've told you I never heard of any Gardiner. I'm an antiquarian bookseller. I occasionally deal in works of art. That's my only connection with Thomas McMahon. But I have no knowledge whatsoever of anyone called Gardiner."

Banks paused for a moment, whispered something in Hatchley's ear, mostly for effect, then turned back to Whitaker. "The way things look right now, Leslie," he said, "I think it's time to move on to the next stage."

"Next stage? What do you mean?"

"Well, this is just a preliminary interview, you understand. Just to get the lie of the land, so to speak. I'm not satisfied with what I've heard. Not satisfied at all. So now we take it a step further. We go over your finances, your car, your clothes, your business dealings, your life, with a fine-tooth comb, and if we find any of the evidence we're looking for, we haul you back in."

Whitaker swallowed. "You can't do that," he said, without much conviction.

Banks stood up. "Yes, we can," he said. "And we will. Detective Sergeant Hatchley will take down those names now."

On Monday afternoon, results started trickling in from the lab. First of all, Andrew Hurst's clothes were clean, as expected, and so were Danny Boy Corcoran's and Patrick Aspern's. None of this surprised Banks; apart from Hurst, who had washed his clothes, they had all been outsiders in the first place.

Banks would like to think that Aspern was involved somehow, but he very much doubted the good doctor had set the fires. Even so, he reminded himself that Patrick Aspern didn't have a decent alibi for either fire, and that he could have gone to see Tina on the day of the boat fires, then returned later. Perhaps she had threatened to tell the world what he'd done to her. He could have started the fire on McMahon's boat to draw the inquiry away from Tina. As yet, nobody had had any luck trying to locate Paul Ryder, Christine Aspern's birth father. Banks didn't imagine he was important to the case, as he had never even known his daughter, but at least he ought to know what had happened to her.

But there were other matters to consider. Banks would have liked to know why Andrew Hurst had washed his clothes in the middle of the night, for a start. As things stood, it just didn't make sense. DC Kevin Templeton was checking into Hurst's background, along with everyone else's, so maybe he would turn up something.

Then there were the Turner, the money, and the possible criminal activities of McMahon and Gardiner. Well, perhaps a closer look at Leslie Whitaker's business dealings would help turn up something there.

Banks sat in his office and browsed through reports and actions, a CD of Soile Isokoski singing Richard Strauss's orchestral songs playing in the background. Just when he was about to wander out for a coffee break, his phone rang. It was the front desk. Someone to see the man in charge of the fires on the boats. Someone called Lenny Knox.

Puzzled, Banks asked the duty officer to have him escorted upstairs, and he appeared at Banks's door, a burly, pock-marked, red-faced fellow, a couple of minutes later.

"Sit down," Banks said.

Knox sat. The chair creaked under his weight.

"What can I do for you, Mr. Knox?" Banks asked, leaning back and linking his hands behind his head.

"I'm worried about Mark, Mark Siddons," said Knox, traces of a Liverpool accent in his voice.

"Maybe you'd better start at the beginning."

Knox sighed. "Mark's a good kid. A pal of mine. He's a good grafter, too. Doesn't mind getting his hands dirty. We were doing a job together at the college—you know about that?"

Banks nodded. He knew about Mark's job.

"Anyway," Knox went on, "when you let him out of jail, the poor kid had nowhere to go, and he'd just lost his girlfriend, so I invited him home with me."

"That was a kind gesture," Banks said.

Knox looked at him and sighed. "It was meant to be. Backfired, though, didn't it?"

"How?"

"You've got to understand, Sal's a good girl, really, but she's . . . well, she doesn't like to feel put-upon. Likes to think she's part of things, decisions and suchlike. And she likes things planned out, doesn't like surprises."

"Sounds reasonable."

"Anyway, it was my fault. I brought Mark home with me, told him he could stay without even consulting her. She hit the roof. Mark must have heard us arguing in the kitchen, and the next thing I knew he'd legged it. I yelled after him but he didn't pay it any mind."

Banks reached for his notepad. "When did this happen?" he asked.

"Saturday evening."

"What time?"

"About half past seven."

"Which direction did he go?"

"Toward the railway tracks."

Banks tapped his pencil on his pad. Jennings Field lay a short distance east of town, beyond the tracks. For a number of reasons, Banks hadn't considered Mark to be a strong candidate for the boat fires, but this put a different complexion on things. Mark could easily have made it to the field by the time the fire started. But why? Was he a pyromaniac? Was there something that triggered him? Anger? Rejection? He had been angry at Tina, too, before he left for Mandy's flat on Thursday night. But the alibi . . . the timing . . . the clothes . . . it just didn't make sense. Still, the important thing now was to find him and bring him in.

"Did Mark say anything to you about the fires?"

"Like what?"

"Anything at all."

"No. Only that he was cut up about Tina."

"He didn't voice any suspicions, any ideas about what happened?"

"Not to me, no. Look," said Knox, going on to echo Banks's own fears, "I'm not the sort to go blabbing to the police, which is why I didn't come straight here, but I'm worried about Mark, I thought he might have got in touch, but he hasn't, and there's no one else to report him missing. Like I said, at bottom of it all he's a good kid. Not like some you see around these days. And he's had it tough. He doesn't have any money, and he's got nowhere to go. You can bet he'll be sleeping rough. I know it's not exactly brass-monkey weather right now, but it's still bloody cold to be sleeping out in the open. And things can change pretty quickly up here."

"Too true," said Banks. And if Mark himself wasn't responsible for the boat fires, there was a good chance that whoever was wanted him out of the way. So he was out in the cold, possibly being hunted. Definitely not an ideal state of affairs. "Is there anything else?"

"No," said Lenny. "But perhaps you can find him, tell him

I'm sorry. Poor Sal was beside herself when she knew he'd heard her. Tell him he can come back to ours anytime he likes, she says now. I told you she was a good lass. It was just the shock, that's all, and her not being asked."

"What was Mark wearing?"

"A ratty old suede coat, fleece-lined, and jeans rolled up at the bottoms. Looked like hand-me-downs."

Banks smiled at the description of the clothes he'd given Mark: his own cast-offs. "We'll put out a bulletin for him."

"Don't frighten him, will you?" said Lenny. "I don't know what he'd do if he felt cornered. He's in a right state."

"We'll do our best, Mr. Knox," said Banks. "The important thing is to find him. I don't suppose you have a photograph?"

"Me? No. Didn't you take one when you had him in?"

"We don't do that as a matter of routine, Mr. Knox. We need a reason, and permission. In Mark's case, it simply wasn't necessary."

Knox stood up. "Right, then," he said. "You'll let me know?"

"Give me your telephone number. I'll see to it personally."

Knox gave him the number. "Thanks," he said.

When Knox had left, Banks walked over to his window. The CD had come to the *Four Last Songs* now, Banks's favorites. He remembered an occasion some years ago, before everything went wrong, when he had arrived home very late after attending the scene of a teenage girl's murder in an Eastvale cemetery. He had sat up smoking, drinking Laphroaig and listening to the *Four Last Songs,* Gundula Janowitz's version that time, and his daughter, Tracy, had woken up and come down to see what was wrong. They had talked briefly—Banks deliberately not telling her about the murder—then they had shared mugs of cocoa as they cuddled up on the sofa and listened to the Strauss songs. It was a moment forever etched in his memory, all the more so because it could never be repeated. Tracy was gone now, grown up, living her own life. Sandra was gone, too. And Brian.

The day was still gray but fairly warm outside. Lucky for Mark. There were plenty of people crossing the market square, shopping along Market Street and York Road. The church facade was covered in scaffolding, like an exoskeleton, and the weather was good enough for the restorers to get up there and work away at the ancient stonework and lead roofing. He thought of Mark, who had said he wanted to do church restoration work. Banks knew Neville Lauder, the stonemason in charge of the project, from the Queen's Arms. Maybe he could put in a word. He had to maintain his objectivity, though. Much as he thought Lenny was right in his assessment of Mark, and much as Banks liked the kid, felt sorry for him, there was still a chance that Mark Siddons was a killer.

"Got a minute, sir?"

Banks looked up. DS Hatchley. "Come in, Jim," he said. "How you doing?"

"Not too badly, thanks." Jim Hatchley sat down and ran his hand over his untidy straw-colored hair. He still looked tired, Banks thought, with bags under his eyes and puffy, blotchy skin. Still, not only was he just recovering from a nasty bout of flu, but his youngest was teething. Having babies would do that to you. Would Sandra lose sleep? he wondered. She had looked good when he last saw her, but that could change when little Sinéad started teething.

"What is it?" Banks asked. "Anything on Whitaker's alibi?"

"Checks out so far," Hatchley said. "But it's early days yet. Anyway, that other job you asked me to do. Mark David Siddons."

"Yes?"

Hatchley shook his head. "Poor bastard," he said.

"What can you tell me?"

"His mother's Sharon Siddons, a right slag if ever there was one. I thought the name rang a bell. They lived on the East Side Estate, where else? She died a year ago. Lung cancer."

"Father?"

"Dunno," said Hatchley. "Sharon was an alcoholic as well as a slag. Started young. She worked as a prossie for a while, till she got pregnant at seventeen. After that there was a long line of men in her life. Most of them losers, and none of them lasting very long. Last one was a charmer by the name of Nicholas Papadopoulos. Perhaps you've heard of him?"

"Crazy Nick?"

"One and the same."

Banks had indeed heard of Crazy Nick. You couldn't be a copper in Eastvale for five minutes without hearing of him. Disturbing the peace, breaking and entering, assault, GBH, drunk and disorderly. You name it, and if it took no brains, Crazy Nick had done it. Stopping just short of murder. The last time he'd been arrested it had taken four strapping PCs to hold him down and bring him in. He never stopped swearing and struggling the whole time, and once he was in the cell he drove the custody section insane with his nonstop stream of curses and banging.

"Isn't he a guest of Her Majesty at the moment?"

"Indeed he is," said Hatchley. "Strangeways. And he won't be out for quite a while. Whacked a night watchman with a hammer during a warehouse break-in and fractured his skull."

"How long was he with the Siddons woman?"

"Until she started to show the cancer symptoms," said Hatchley. "Then he was off like a shot. Died alone, and in agony, poor cow."

"Was he around when Mark ran off?"

"Yes. Probably the reason. Believe it or not, Mark gave him a bloody good hiding. Enough to put him in hospital for a couple of days, at any rate. Broken nose. Couple of ribs.

Twenty stitches in his scalp. Concussion. Took him by surprise. Went crazy on him, according to the neighbors. Even his mother couldn't drag him off."

"Good for him," Banks said. "And Nick didn't take his revenge? That's not like him."

"Couldn't find the kid, then he got caught for that warehouse job."

"But Mark's got no form, himself?"

"No. We've had him in on sus for a couple of housebreakings, and he once got caught shoplifting in HMV. Charges dropped. That's all."

"Anything important we *haven't* got him for?"

"No. At least I can't find any rumors."

And if anyone could, Banks knew, it was probably Hatchley, with his long list of snitches and a pair of eyes in practically every pub in Eastvale. "So he's basically a clean kid?" he said.

"Looks that way," Hatchley agreed. "He attended Eastvale Comprehensive, but was truant as often as not. Didn't get into much trouble there, apart from a bit of a shoving match with one teacher, but he didn't exactly shine academically, either. Good at games, though. Want me to keep on digging?"

"Anything to do with fires come up in connection with him?"

"Not that I can find."

"He didn't try to set fire to the school, or to the house after he beat up Crazy Nick?"

"Just ran off. Never went back."

"Sensible," said Banks. Given the sort of background Mark had endured, both with his mother and her earlier men friends, and with Crazy Nick Papadopoulos, it was no surprise that he was willing to believe Tina's tale of woe without question. It didn't mean she wasn't telling the truth, however, and Banks had certainly sensed *something* wrong in the Aspern household. There was another thing, too; from what

Hatchley had told Banks, Mark certainly had a violent temper, no matter how justifiable his uprising against Crazy Nick had been. The lad needed watching.

"Okay, Jim," Banks said. "Thanks very much."

"Cheers," said Hatchley. "My pleasure."

By Monday afternoon, Mark was close to Sutton Bank, and starving. He was glad he had gone back into the pub for his lunch the previous day after the shock of seeing Tina's image on the TV screen. The landlord had given him a dirty look, but other than that, his abrupt departure and return hardly raised an eyebrow. That evening he had eaten fish and chips and kipped down in another old barn. He had got up earlier on Monday morning, with only enough money for a chocolate bar left in his pocket. After walking a few miles, he realized he wasn't trying to do the coast-to-coast walk, that was for anoraks, so he might as well at least try to get a lift.

Just outside Northallerton, a man towing a horse box gave him a lift to Thirsk. All the way he had been aware of the horse shifting nervously behind him, and he thought he could smell manure. The driver hadn't said much, just dropped him off in the High Street, and now he was on the Scarborough Road hoping for another kind soul to stop for him.

It was a gray afternoon, the clouds so low and the air so moist it was almost, but not quite, raining. "Mizzling," they called it in Yorkshire, describing that bone-chilling combination of mist and drizzle. There wasn't much traffic, and most of the cars and vans that passed just whizzed by without even slowing down. If he got to Scarborough, Mark knew, there was a good chance he'd be able to pick up some casual laboring work. It didn't matter what—ditch-digging, demolition, construction—he could turn his hand to almost anything as long as it didn't involve being educated. School had hardly been more than a mild distraction throughout his childhood and adolescence.

A police patrol car cruised by and seemed to slow down a bit just ahead of him. Mark tensed. He knew the coppers weren't going to give him a lift. Most likely beat the shit out of him and leave him lying bleeding in a field. He must have been imagining things, though, because the car carried on and disappeared into the distance.

Mark trudged on, hardly bothering to stick out his thumb. He must have walked a couple of miles, the steep edge of Sutton Bank looming before him, when he heard a car coming and remembered to stick out his thumb. The car slowed to a halt about ten yards in front of him. It was quite a posh one, he noticed, an Audi, and shiny, as if it had just been cleaned. It would make a nice change from the horse box. For a moment, Mark worried that it might be the killer, but how could anyone know where he was?

The driver leaned over and opened the passenger window. He was a middle-aged bloke, Mark saw, wearing a camel overcoat and leather driving gloves. Mark didn't recognize him.

"Where you going?" he asked.

"Scarborough," said Mark.

"Hop in."

He seemed a pleasant enough bloke. Mark hopped in.

Chapter 10

*B*anks grabbed his leather jacket, left by the back door and slipped behind the wheel of his 1997 Renault, thinking it was about time he had a new car, maybe something a bit sportier, if he could afford it. Nothing too flashy, and definitely not red. Racing green, perhaps. A convertible wasn't much use in Yorkshire, but maybe a sports car would do. His midlife crisis car, though he didn't particularly feel as if he were going through a crisis. Sometimes he felt as if his life was on hold indefinitely, but that was hardly a crisis. The only thing he knew for certain was that he was getting older; there was no doubt about that.

A snippet of interesting information about Andrew Hurst had just come to his attention. Annie was showing Roland Gardiner's Turners to Phil Keane, Detective Superintendent Gristhorpe having easily agreed to the consultation, so Banks decided to head out to the canal by himself.

He slipped in an old Van Morrison CD to dispel the January blues—not entirely convinced that they were caused by the weather—and drove off listening to "Jackie Wilson Said." It was just over a mile to the edge of town, past the new-look college, and another couple of miles of mostly open countryside to the canal. The road wound by fields of cows and sheep, drystone walls on either side, an occasional wooded area and stiles with signposts pointing the direction for ramblers. Not that it was rambling weather. You'd soon catch a chill and probably get bogged down in the mud before you got too far in open country. To his right, he could see the far-off bulk of the hills, like the swell before the wave frozen in a gray ocean.

The landscape flattened out toward the canal, which was why the channel had been dug there, of course, and Banks soon found the lane that ran down to the side of the lock-keeper's cottage. He parked by the towpath and turned off Van just as he was getting going on "Listen to the Lion."

It seemed an age before Hurst answered the doorbell, and when he did he looked surprised to find Banks standing there.

"You again," he said.

"Afraid so," said Banks. "You weren't expecting me?"

Hurst avoided his eyes. "I told you everything I know."

"You must think we're stupid. Can I come in?"

"You will anyway." Hurst opened the door and moved aside. The hallway was quite low, and he had to stoop a little as he stood there. Banks walked into the same room they had been in before, the one with Hurst's extensive record collection. Helen Shapiro was singing "Lipstick on Your Collar." Hurst turned off the record as soon as he followed Banks into the room, as if it were some sort of private experience or ritual he didn't want to share.

He was fastidious in his movements. He lifted the needle off gently, then stopped the turntable, removed the disc and slipped it lovingly inside its inner sleeve. It was an LP called *Tops With Me,* Banks noticed, and on the cover of the outer sleeve was a picture of the smiling singer herself. Banks had forgotten all about Helen Shapiro. Not that he had been much of a fan to start with, not enough to know about her LPs, at any rate, but he did remember buying an ex-jukebox copy of "Walkin' Back to Happiness" at a market stall in Cathedral

Square, Peterborough, when he was about ten, before the covered market opened. It was one of those 45s with the middle missing, so you had to buy a plastic thingamajig and fix it in before you could play it.

Banks perched on the edge of an armchair. He didn't take his leather jacket off because the house was cold, the elements of the electric fire dark. Hurst was wearing a thick gray, woolly polo-neck sweater. Banks wondered if he was too poor to pay the electricity bills.

"You should have told us you had a criminal record," Banks said. "You could have saved us a lot of trouble. We find out things like that pretty quickly, and it looks a lot worse for you."

"I didn't go to jail. Besides, it wasn't—"

"I don't want to hear your excuses," Banks said. "And I know you didn't go to jail. You got a suspended sentence and probation. You were lucky. The judge took pity on you."

"I can't see what it has to do with present events."

"Can't you? I think you can," said Banks. "You were charged with conspiracy to torch a warehouse. The only reason you got such a soft sentence was because the person who co-opted you was your boss, and he was the one who actually lit the match. But you helped him, you gave him a false alibi, and you lied for him throughout the subsequent investigation."

"It was my job! He was my boss. What else was I supposed to do?"

"Don't ask me to solve your moral dilemmas for you. In any situation, there are a number of possible choices. You made the wrong one. You lost your job, anyway, and all you gained was a criminal record. When the insurance company got suspicious and called the police in, the company went bankrupt. Since then you've had a couple of short-term jobs, but mostly you've been on the dole." Banks looked around.

"Lucky you'd paid off most of your mortgage. Was that with the cash your boss gave you for helping with the arson?"

Hurst said nothing. Banks assumed he was right.

"Was that where you got your taste for fire?"

"I don't have any taste for fire. I don't know what you're talking about."

"The narrow boats, Andrew. The narrow boats."

Hurst shot to his feet. "You can't blame that on me." He stabbed his chest with his thumb. "I was the one who called the fire brigade, remember?"

"When it was way too late. You've been seen skulking around in the woods, probably spying on Tina Aspern. You have no alibi. You washed your clothes before we could get a chance to test them. Come on, Andrew, how would it look to you? Why did you do it? Was it for the thrill?"

Hurst sat down again, deflated. "I didn't do it," he said "Honest, I didn't. Look, I know it *looks* bad, but I'm telling you the truth. I was here by myself all evening watching videos. It's what I do most evenings. Or sit and read a book. I hardly have an active social life, and I don't have a job. What else am I supposed to do?"

"Do you feel inadequate, Andrew? Is that what it's all about? Do the anger and rage just build up in you until they get so strong that you just have to go out and burn something?"

"That's ridiculous. You're making out that I'm some sort of pyromaniac or something."

"Aren't you?"

"No. Of course I'm not. That other fire, which I *didn't* start, by the way, was purely a business thing. Nobody got hurt. Nobody got any weird gratification in setting it. It was just a way of dealing with a financial problem."

"Maybe this one was, too."

"Oh? Now you're changing your approach, are you? Now I'm not a drooling pyromaniac but a cold, practical businessman dealing with a problem." He folded his arms. "And what problem might that have been?"

"Maybe Tina Aspern was your problem."

"I don't know what you mean."

"Perhaps she was going to tell on you. You used to spy on her, didn't you?"

"No."

"Where were you on Saturday evening?"

"Saturday? Same place as usual. Here."

"Watching another war video?"

"*Force Ten from Navarone,* as a matter of fact. Very underrated film."

"Andrew, get this clear: I don't care about your fucking film reviews. All I care about is that three people are dead and that you might be responsible. Ever heard of a man called Gardiner? Roland Gardiner?"

"No."

"Leslie Whitaker?"

"No."

"What kind of car do you drive?"

"I don't. I can't afford to run a car, and I don't need one."

That would have made it very difficult for Hurst to have got to Jennings Field and back on Saturday night, Banks realized, but there were buses. "In all your nosing about the area," he asked, "have you ever seen a car of any kind parked in the lay-by closest to the boats?"

"A few times. Yes."

"What kind of car?"

"Different ones. Picnickers in summer, mostly."

"And more recently?"

"Only once or twice."

"What make, do you remember?"

"A van of some kind. You know, a Jeep Cherokee, Land Cruiser, or a Range Rover, that sort of thing. I'm not very well up on the latest models."

"But it was definitely that kind of vehicle?"

"Yes."

"Color?"

"Dark. Blue or black."

"Ever see the driver?"

"No."

"Okay. Let's get back to the fires. Why did you hang around the boats so much? Was it the girl?"

Hurst looked away, scanning the rows of his LP collection, lips moving as if he were silently reading the names off the covers to himself. Banks's mobile rang. He excused himself and walked outside to answer. It was DC Templeton calling from headquarters. "Sir, we've identified the owner of the boats."

"Good work," said Banks.

"It's some bigwig in the City. Name's Sir Laurence West. Merchant banker."

"Can't say I've heard of him," said Banks, "but then I don't exactly move in those kinds of circles."

"Anyway," Templeton went on, "I've already been on the phone to him, and he's agreed to grant an audience at his office tomorrow, but you'll need to make an appointment."

"Good of him."

"Yes," said Templeton. "I think he also believed he was being magnanimous about it."

"I see. Okay then, Kev, thanks. I'll go down there myself tomorrow morning, seeing as he's so important." Besides, thought Banks, it would be nice to get away, if just for a day. He'd take the train, if the trains happened to be running. It was actually faster and far less hassle than driving to London, and train journeys could be relaxing if you had a good book to read and some CDs to listen to. "Make an appointment for one o'clock, would you?"

"Yes, sir."

"Any first impressions?"

"Only that this is all a terrible intrusion into his valuable time, and he needed reminding he even owned the boats."

"Okay," said Banks. "I don't suppose we can expect much from him, then, but it's got to be done."

"And, sir?"

"Yes."

"A woman called."

"Which woman?"

"Maria Phillips, from the art gallery. Wants to talk to you again. Says she'll be in the Queen's Arms at half six. I think maybe she fancies you, sir."

"I'll deal with her. Anything else?"

"DS Nowak wants to see you as soon as you can make it."

"Where is he?"

"Here, in his office."

"Right. Tell him to hang on. I'll be back in half an hour."

"Will do, sir."

Banks hung up and went back to Andrew Hurst, who was in the same chair, chewing on a fingernail. There was no point pursuing the peeping angle. If Hurst had been trying to get a peek at Tina naked, then he wasn't going to admit it. And even if he did, what could Banks do about it? It wasn't as if Tina were still around to press charges. But if she'd noticed and had threatened to tell on him . . . ? No, there was scant enough evidence to link Hurst with the first fire, and none at all with the second. Besides, the fire had definitely been set on McMahon's boat. Why risk tackling a grown, fit man when you could set fire to a junkie on the nod?

Banks thought Hurst was weird, and probably a peeper, but he was quickly coming to the realization that there was nothing he could do about it. The only obvious motive he might have had was revenge at McMahon's treating him so badly when he paid his neighborly visit, but that didn't seem a strong enough motive for murder unless Hurst had more than just one screw loose. Still, there were enough questions about him that needed answers to keep him on the list.

"Why did you wash your clothes, Andrew?" Banks asked. "Including the anorak. You must admit that looks suspicious."

Hurst looked at him. "I know it does. It's just . . ." He shook his head. "I don't know. Maybe I wasn't thinking straight. I mean, yes, of course I knew you'd find out I'd been arrested in connection with a fire. I don't think you're stupid. I just thought maybe that by the time you did find out about me you'd have caught whoever did it, so you wouldn't need to look at me as a suspect. I'd been close enough to the fire for my clothes to pick up traces. They stank of smoke and turpentine. I've heard how good your forensic tests are these days. I didn't want to spend a night at the police station."

"You smelled turpentine?"

"Yes. It was in the air."

"You didn't tell us at the time."

"I didn't want to get involved."

If Banks had a penny for every time he'd heard that from a member of the public, he would be a rich man. He stood up. "You're bloody lucky you don't get to spend a night in the nick," he said, "for wasting police time." He tossed Hurst a card. "Don't go on any holidays just yet, and if you think of anything else that might help us, give me a ring."

Hurst nodded gloomily and put the card on the table.

"You can get back to your Helen Shapiro now," Banks said, and left.

Annie was always amazed when she stepped inside Phil's cottage at how spick-and-span everything was. It wasn't as if all the men she had ever known were slobs—Banks's place was generally quite neat except for the CD cases strewn around the coffee table, usually next to an empty whiskey tumbler and an overflowing ashtray, when he used to smoke—but Phil's cottage had an almost military sparkle to it, along with the scent of pine air freshener. Still, it wasn't his main home and he didn't spend all that much time there. She wondered what his London flat looked like. Chelsea, he'd said. Maybe soon they'd have a weekend in London. Expensive as it was, it would be a hell of a lot more affordable than New York, especially if she didn't have to stop in a hotel.

"What a pleasure to see you," said Phil, closing the door behind her.

"It's not exactly a social call," said Annie, smiling to soften the words. "I need your help." She was still angry at Banks, but Phil didn't need to know about their exchange.

Phil raised his eyebrows. "Me? A consultation? Official?"

"Approved by the superintendent, no less," said Annie.

"But what can I possibly do to help you?"

Annie got him to fill out the necessary paperwork, then she unzipped her briefcase and laid out the Turner sketches and the watercolor, now safe inside their labeled and numbered plastic evidence covers.

"Well, well," said Phil. "These are a surprise. Where did you find them?"

"In a fire-resistant safe in that caravan that burned down over the weekend. It belonged to a man by the name of Roland Gardiner."

"The fire you had to leave dinner for?"

"That's right."

Phil leaned over and studied the drawings closely. Annie could see the concentration furrow his brow. When he had finished, he turned back to Annie. "Anything else found with them?"

"Only some money. No more drawings, if that's what you mean."

"No documents, letters, auction catalogs, nothing like that?"

"No."

"Pity." Phil took a large magnifying glass from a box on the bookshelf and went back to the sketches, studying them more closely. "It certainly *looks* like authentic period paper," he said. "I might get a better sense if I could touch it, too, though."

"Sorry," Annie said. "It's still to be tested for fingerprints."

"Whose fingerprints would you expect to find?"

"You never know. We might find the victim's. And Thomas McMahon's, if there's a link between them."

"You think McMahon forged these?"

"I don't know. That's partly why I came to you."

"But how would you know it was this McMahon's fingerprints? I mean, I assume if he'd been badly burned—both of them, in fact—then their hands . . ."

"Well, that's true," said Annie. "Unless either of them has a criminal record for some reason . . ." Then she remembered the book Jack Mellor said Gardiner had lent him. There was a good chance his fingerprints would be on that. Or perhaps even on some object from where he used to live with his wife, on the Daleside Estate. Thomas McMahon might be more difficult, but she was sure that if they looked they'd find his fingerprints somewhere. Whitaker's shop, for example. "We have to try," she said.

"How do you get fingerprints from paper? I mean, if they're not immediately visible through a magnifying glass."

"I leave it to the boffins," said Annie. "I think they usually use a chemical called ninhydrin, or something similar, but it's not my area of expertise."

"Isn't that a destructive process? Couldn't it damage the works? If these are genuine Turners . . ."

"I'm sure that's something they'll take into consideration.

They can probably use some sort of light source—laser or ultraviolet. I really don't know, Phil. The technology keeps changing. It's hard to keep up with. But don't worry, our fingerprint expert knows what he's doing. The last thing he'd want to do is to damage a work of art, especially if it's a genuine one."

"That's good," said Phil. "Then I assume you brought these to me because you want me to tell you if they're fake or real?"

"That would be a great help," said Annie. "In fact, *anything* at all you can tell us about them would be a help."

"It's not as easy as all that, you know, especially when they're covered in plastic. I mean, I can give an opinion off-the-cuff, mostly based on the style, but there are tests, other experts to be consulted, that sort of thing. And the provenance, of course. That would go a long way toward establishing whether it's genuine or not."

"I understand," said Annie. "Off-the-cuff will do fine for now."

"Well, they're similar to other Turner sketches in the large sketchbook and pocketbook he used on his 1816 Yorkshire tour, so it might also be possible to do a bit of comparison work with some bona fide originals. Later, of course, when you've finished with them."

"Was it unusual to do more than one sketch of the same sort of thing?"

"Not at all. Turner did dozens of sketches like this for the Richmondshire series. Three sketchbooks full. But that's the interesting thing: He usually worked in the books, not on loose sheets."

"So that's one mark against authenticity?"

Phil smiled at her. "It signals caution, that's all," he said. "But genuine or not," he went on, "this is certainly a beautiful watercolor. Look at that mist swirling around Ingleborough summit. You can almost see it moving. And there's not a soul around, see? It's very early in the morning, just after dawn. You can tell by the quality of the light. Turner was always very keen on reproducing time-of-day and weather conditions. And do you see that peacock in the right foreground? Marvelous detail."

Annie had looked at plenty of paintings in her time, many with her father's guidance, and was even a passable landscape artist herself, in what little spare time she had, but she lacked the training both in technique and in history and found she always learned something from Phil's point of view. It was one of the things she liked about him, his knowledge of and passion for art.

"May I ask exactly what makes you think it's a forgery?" he asked.

"Well, I'm certainly no expert," Annie said. "It's just the circumstances of its discovery. In the first place, it seems a bit of a coincidence that this should turn up so soon after the other Turner, don't you think? And what would Roland Gardiner—the victim in the caravan—be doing owning a Turner watercolor, several sketches and about fifteen hundred pounds in cash? When you consider what we talked about yesterday, about McMahon's buying up old eighteenth- and nineteenth-century books for the endpapers from Leslie Whitaker, then . . . I don't know. Perhaps we're trying to make a connection where none exists, but you have to admit, it's a bit of a strong coincidence when you put it all together. Two murders in two days—three, if you count the girl—an artist buying old paper, these Turners, the money."

"You think this Whitaker character might have something to do with it?"

"It's possible," said Annie.

"Did they know one another, Roland Gardiner and the artist?"

"We don't know. Not yet. But we're trying to link them. I

just wanted to get your take on whether we were dealing with the real thing here, the watercolor in particular."

"Well, it looks genuine enough to me on first examination. If not, then it's a damn good forgery. To be absolutely certain, though, I'd have to hang on to it for a while, perhaps show it to some colleagues, conduct a few tests. Fingerprints examination, as we did with the other one. Radiography, ultraviolet. Infrared photography. Computer image processing. Pigment analysis, that sort of thing. I'd also try to track down its provenance, if any exists. And I can't do that, can I?"

"I'm afraid not," said Annie. "Not yet, at any rate. As I said, there are fingerprints to be considered. And it may be evidence."

"Evidence of what?"

"I don't know." She grinned at him. "That's just the way the job is sometimes."

Phil smiled back. "Mine, too. I suppose you could say we're both detectives, in a way."

"That's one way of looking at it. Anyway, as soon as we're done with it, I'll ask you to look into its authenticity a bit further, if you'd still be willing to help."

"Of course. I've signed the Official Secrets Act, haven't I? Look, how rude of me. I never offered you any refreshments. It must have been the excitement of seeing the Turners. Tea, coffee, something stronger?"

"I can't," said Annie, carefully putting the papers back in her briefcase. "Too much on right now."

"Not even a tea break?"

Annie laughed. "Sometimes I don't even get dinner, as you know quite well." She leaned forward and kissed him quickly on the lips. He tried to make it into more, but she slipped free. "No. Really. I have to go."

He spread his hands. "Okay. I know when I'm beaten. See you tonight?"

"I'll give you a ring," Annie said, and hurried out to her car before she changed her mind about the tea, and whatever else was on offer.

"And be careful with your briefcase," he called after her.

It was DS Stefan Nowak's job to coordinate between the crime scene, the lab and the SIO, making sure that nothing was missed and priorities were dealt with as quickly as possible. He wasn't a forensic scientist by training, though he did have a degree in chemistry and had completed the requisite courses. As a result, he'd picked up a fair bit of scientific knowledge over his three years on the job, along with the ability to present it in layman's terms. Which was just as well. The best Banks had ever done at chemistry and physics was a grade-five pass in each at O-Level.

Though Stefan himself was elegant and always well-groomed, his office was a mess, with papers, plastic bags of exhibits and half-full mugs of coffee all over the place. Banks hardly dared move once he had sat down for fear the resulting vibration or disturbance of the air would bring a stack of reports, or beakers full of God knew what, toppling down.

"I trust you've got some positive results?" Banks said as he eased himself onto the chair. Nothing fell.

"Depends on how you look at them," Stefan said, the Polish accent barely audible in his cultured voice. "I've been over at the lab most of the afternoon, and we've finally got something on toxicology. I think you'll find it interesting."

"Do tell," said Banks.

"Luckily, in all three cases there was still enough fluid present in the bodies for tox analysis. McMahon, the artist, was the worst, but even there Dr. Glendenning found blood in the organs and traces of urine in the bladder. Unfortunately, the vitreous fluid in the eyes had evaporated in all victims."

"Go on," Banks urged him, not wishing to dwell on the evaporation of vitreous fluid.

"Let's take the girl first," Stefan said. "Christine Aspern. Because she was a known heroin addict we could be more specific in our search. As you probably know, heroin metabolizes into morphine once injected into the bloodstream, and it bonds to the body's carbohydrates. Only a small amount of morphine is secreted unchanged into the urine. Sometimes none at all."

"So you can't tell whether she injected heroin or morphine?"

"I didn't say that. Only that heroin becomes morphine once it's in the blood. Besides, heroin's a morphine derivative, made through a reaction with acetyl chloride or acetic anhydride. Anyway, spectral analysis indicated traces of heroin. The presence of other substances, such as quinine, bears out the result."

Banks knew that quinine was often used to pad heroin for sale on the streets. "It's what we expected," he said. "How much?"

"The stuff was around thirty percent pure, which is pretty much the norm these days. And there wasn't enough to cause death. At least, the lab results make that seem unlikely."

"So the fire killed her one way or another?"

"Asphyxia did. Yes."

"What about the other two?"

"Ah, there it gets a little more interesting," Stefan said. He leaned forward and a pile of books teetered dangerously. "Alcohol was present in the urine in both cases, though none was present in the girl's system."

"How much?"

"Not a lot in McMahon's case, maybe between one and two drinks."

"Not enough to make him pass out, then?"

"Unlikely."

"And Gardiner?"

"About twice as much. But there's more."

"I hoped there would be. Go on."

"During general screening, spectral analysis also discovered the presence of flunitrazepam in the systems of Thomas McMahon and Roland Gardiner. Comparisons indicate it's the same drug in both cases."

"Flunitrazepam?" said Banks, remembering one of the drugs circulars he'd read in the past few months. "Isn't that Rohypnol?"

"Rohypnol is one form of it, yes. The 'date rape' drug. Recently upgraded from Class C to Class A. It's a form of benzodiazepine, a tranquilizer about ten times stronger than Valium. It causes muscle relaxation, drowsiness, unconsciousness and amnesia, among other things. It also impairs basic motor skills and lowers the blood pressure. It's often used to spike drinks because it's colorless, odorless and tasteless and it dissolves in alcohol. At least it used to. The problem is that since 1998, La Roche, the chief manufacturer, has added a component that makes any drink you add it to turn bright blue. The drug itself also dissolves more slowly and forms small chunks."

"Which makes it a lot harder to sneak into people's drinks."

"Yes. Even dark drinks will turn cloudy. Anyway, if that were the case, one or both victims might have noticed."

"Which means?"

"Which means it's either counterfeit, bootleg Rohypnol, or another member of the benzodiazepine family. Remember, this test took a bit more time because they had to do a general tox screen. They're still working on it to pin down specifics, but I thought you'd like some sort of advance notice of what you're dealing with."

"Thanks, Stefan," said Banks. "Much appreciated. How long does it take to act?"

"Twenty minutes to half an hour."

"Any idea what quantities they were given?"

"Certainly enough to be effective. One odd thing."

"Yes?"

"Gardiner, the caravan victim, also had a significant amount of Tuinal in his system. Tuinal's—"

"I know what Tuinal is, Stefan. It's a form of barbiturate."

"Yes. It's not prescribed very often these days."

"We know who Gardiner's doctor is. We can make inquiries. He's the one who had more to drink, too?"

"Yes. Just thought you'd like to know."

"Interesting," said Banks. "I wonder why?"

"Search me. One more thing," said Stefan as Banks walked toward the door.

Banks paused and turned. "Yes?"

"The tire tracks are consistent in all their dimensions with those of a Jeep Cherokee, and if you ever find a suspect, he was wearing Nike trainers with a very distinctive pattern of crisscross abrasions on the right heel."

As Banks left the office, he had a mental image of McMahon in his cabin and Gardiner in his caravan, each welcoming an old friend, chatting, making plans for whatever it was that was going to make their fortunes, drinking to it, then after a while starting to feel drowsy, finding it hard to move. At which point their faceless killer splashes turpentine or petrol about the place, drops a match and leaves. Couldn't be easier.

Or crueler.

Chapter 11

"*I*'m Clive," said the driver.

"Mark."

"Pleased to meet you, Mark."

"Likewise. And thanks for the lift."

"My pleasure." Clive turned and flashed Mark a quick smile. "I'd stop awhile so we could admire the view when we get to the top, but I'm afraid we wouldn't see much today."

They were climbing the winding road up Sutton Bank now, the Audi moving easily despite the one on five and one on four gradients. The higher they got, the mistier it became, as if they were ascending into the very clouds themselves. Mark's ears started to feel funny. He was enjoying the warm, plush interior of the car.

Sutton Bank forms the western edge of the North York Moors, and when you get high up, you can look back over your shoulder and see all the way from the Vale of York to the Dales. Only on a clear day, of course.

When they finally crested the top after about a mile or so, Mark managed a quick look behind and saw nothing but vague shapes through a gray veil. Ahead was mostly rough moorland, similarly mist-shrouded. It was an eerie landscape, and the occasional sheep that materialized out of thin air only made it seem eerier. Sheep gave Mark the creeps. He didn't know why, but they did.

"What do you do, Mark?" Clive asked.

"I'm looking for work."

"What sort of work?"

"Restoration. Old buildings. Churches and stuff."

"That's interesting. Where do you live?"

"Eastvale," Mark said. It was the first thing that came to his mind.

"Lovely town," said Clive. "Have you got a girlfriend?"

Mark said nothing, thought of Tina, the way she had looked at him from the TV screen. He felt his heart shrivel in his chest.

Clive turned and flashed him another quick smile. Mark didn't like the way he did that. He didn't know why, just a feeling.

"A handsome, strong lad like you surely must have a pretty girlfriend?" Clive went on. He patted Mark's knee, and Mark stiffened instinctively.

"It's all right, you know," Clive said. "You can be frank with me. I'm a doctor. Look, I know you young people today. You're always at it, aren't you? I do hope you practice safe sex, Mark."

Mark said nothing. He was thinking of another doctor, Patrick Aspern, and how he'd like to smash the bastard's face in. He was aware of Clive chuntering on beside him, but he wasn't really paying much attention. He just hoped they'd get to Scarborough soon. The sea.

". . . very important to be circumcised, you know," Clive went on. "I know it's not always fashionable, but it's much more hygienic. There are plenty of germs around that part of your body, you know, Mark. Your penis. And smegma. It's nasty stuff. Circumcision is much better all around."

"What?"

"Weren't you listening?" Clive glanced over at Mark. "I'm

talking about circumcision. It doesn't have to be painful, you know. Look, I've got some cream in the boot that will numb all feeling, like the dentist gives you, only it's not an injection. If you like, we could pull over into a lay-by and I can do it for you right now."

His hand slid over into Mark's lap, groping for his penis. Mark lashed out with his left fist and caught Clive a hard blow on the side of his head. Clive gasped and the car started to snake along the road. Mark hit him again, this time connecting with soft tissue near his nose and drawing blood. Then he did it again and thought he felt a tooth crack.

Clive barely had control of the wheel now. He was trying to talk, pleading, calling Mark a maniac, blood dribbling with the saliva from his mouth. But Mark couldn't stop. He wasn't even looking to see if there were any cars coming the other way; he just kept on pummeling at Clive, seeing Crazy Nick and Patrick Aspern and everyone who had ever hurt him.

Finally, they came to a sharp bend, and Clive had to slow down. He barely managed to change down in time, and as he gave all his attention to keeping control of the wheel, Mark slipped his hand into Clive's inside pocket, grabbed his wallet, then opened the passenger door and leaped out, rolling on the wet grass by the side of the road. A little dazed, he sat up ready to run, but he was just in time to watch Clive reach over and pull the door shut, then speed off into the mist. When the sound of the car's engine had faded, Mark was left with nothing but the occasional baaing of a distant sheep to break the silence in the gathering dark.

Banks was pleased to find the mercury pushing nine or ten as he walked down Market Street toward the main Eastvale Fire Station, where Geoff Hamilton had his office. January had been quite a month for ups and downs in temperature. He unbuttoned his overcoat, but he still felt a little too warm. The whiskey-soaked strains of Cesaria Evora came from the headphones of his portable CD player.

As he walked past the end of the street where he used to live with Sandra, Tracy and Brian, Banks couldn't resist the temptation to walk up to the old house and see how much it had changed. He stood by the low garden wall and looked at the front window. It hadn't changed. Not much. The curtains were closed, but he could see the flickering light of a television set in the living room. The most surprising thing was the "For Sale" sign on the lawn. So the new owners were selling already. Maybe it wasn't a happy home. But how many innocuous-looking houses on innocent streets ever were? Inner-city slums and tower blocks hadn't cornered the market in human misery yet.

Banks arrived at the fire station, put away his CD player and went inside. Two of the firefighters on shift were working on equipment maintenance, another was doing paperwork, and two were playing table tennis.

Banks tapped on Geoff Hamilton's office door and entered. Hamilton ran his hand across his hair and bade Banks sit down. Certificates hung on the wall, and an old-fashioned fireman's helmet rested on top of the filing cabinet. Hamilton's desk was tidy except for the papers he was working on.

"Report to the coroner," he said, noticing Banks looking at the papers. "What can I do for you?"

"Anything new?"

"Nothing yet."

"Look, Geoff," said Banks, "I know you don't like to commit yourself, but off-the-record, I'd just like to get some sense of motive, whether you think we're dealing with a serial arsonist here, if we can expect more of this sort of thing. Or might there be some other reason for what's happening around here?"

Banks noticed a hint of a smile pass over Hamilton's taciturn features. "And what would your guess be? Off-the-record."

"I don't know. That's why I'm here."

"You've uncovered no links between the victims yet?"

"We're working on it."

Hamilton rubbed his eyes. They had dark bags under them, Banks noticed. "What if you don't find any?"

"Then perhaps we're dealing with someone who just likes to start fires, and he's choosing relatively easy targets. Someone with a grudge against down-and-outs." Andrew Hurst came to Banks's mind, partly because of the way he seemed to disapprove of the narrow-boat squatters. "But I'm not sure if that's the case."

"Why not?" asked Hamilton.

"According to the toxicology results, both Roland Gardiner and Thomas McMahon were dosed with Rohypnol before the fires started."

"The glasses we found at the scene?"

"Most likely they contained alcohol, into which the drug had been introduced."

"And the girl?"

"We're pretty sure that Christine Aspern was high on heroin. Anyway, leaving Tina out of it for the moment, it looks as if both male victims admitted the killer to their homes and probably accepted a drink from him. If he didn't want to get rid of them for a reason, then he was doing it just for fun. What can you tell me about motivation in cases like this?"

"Fancy a coffee?"

"Wouldn't mind," said Banks. He followed Hamilton into the large, well-appointed kitchen, a white-tiled room complete with oven, fridge, microwave and automatic coffeemaker. A cook came in on weekdays and made the firefighters a meal, and the rest of the time they brought their own food or took it in turns to cook.

Hamilton poured the coffees into two large white mugs, adding a heap of sugar to his own, then they went back to his office and sat down. The coffee tasted good to Banks, dark and strong.

"As you know," Hamilton began, "there are plenty of motives for arson. Probably the most common is sheer spite, or revenge."

Banks knew this. About ninety percent of the arson cases he had been involved in during his career—including the very worst, the one that haunted him whenever the thought of fire raised its ugly head—arose out of one human being's disproportionate malice and rage directed toward another.

"These can vary between simple domestic disputes, such as a lover's quarrel, and problems in the workplace, or racial or religious confrontations."

"Is there any kind of profile involved in these sort of fires that compares to ours?"

"Well," said Hamilton, "they can be set by any age group, they're usually set at night, and they generally involve available combustibles or flammable liquids. Three out of three isn't bad."

"Aren't most fires set at night?"

"Not necessarily, but more often than not, yes."

"So what other possibilities do we have?"

"There's always the simple profit motive. You know, insurance frauds, eliminating the competition, that sort of thing. That's probably the next most common motive. But these weren't commercial fires."

"Not the caravan, certainly. It belonged to Gardiner. But I suppose the boats were commercial properties, to some extent," Banks said. "We've traced the owner and I'll be talking to him tomorrow. Even so, I can see someone burning empty boats for the insurance, but not deliberately drugging Thomas McMahon and setting fire to him in order to do so."

"Lives are often lost in commercial fires," Hamilton argued. "Often by accident—the arsonist didn't know there was anyone in the building—but sometimes deliberately. A nosy night watchman, say."

"Point taken," said Banks. "And we'll try to keep an open mind. What about pyromania as a motive?"

"Well, first of all you should bear in mind that pyromaniacs are extremely rare, and they're usually between fifteen and twenty."

"Mark Siddons is twenty-one," Banks said.

"I wouldn't rule him out, then. Anyway, they generally use whatever combustible comes to hand. I mean, they don't plan their fires. And there's no particular pattern in the kind of places they burn, or even where they strike. They're impulsive and often act for some sort of sexual gratification. The main problem here is that I can't see a pyromaniac doping or knocking someone out *before* starting a fire. They're usually loners and shun social company. Contrary to rumor, they don't usually stay at the scene, either. They'll be long gone by the time the fire brigade arrives. It's starting the fire gives them their thrill, not watching firefighters put it out."

"Any chance it was a woman?"

"There *are* female pyromaniacs," Hamilton said. "But they're even rarer. Oddly enough, they usually set their fires in daylight. They also set them fairly close to their own homes, often don't use accelerant, and they generally start small fires."

"I suppose we men like to start bigger ones?" said Banks.

"It would seem so." Hamilton sipped some coffee. "You know, I don't like to say it, but all these profiles are pretty much . . . well, I won't say a load of bollocks, they have been of some use to us on occasion, but they're pretty vague when you get right down to it."

"Under twenty-five, loner, bed wetter, harsh family background, absent father, domineering mother, not too bright, problems at school, problems at work, can't handle relationships."

"Exactly what I mean. Fits any sociopath you'd care to point out. From all that, you'd think we'd be able to spot them *before* they strike."

"Oh, we can," said Banks. "We just can't do anything about it until they commit a crime. Anyway, I'm inclined to dismiss the pyromaniac in this case. I mean, from what you've seen, would you call these fires impulsive?"

"No. But there are also vanity fires, you know," Hamilton went on. "Someone wants to draw attention to himself through an act of heroism. Those are the sort of blokes who stick around and watch, or even help out."

"There weren't any heroes here, except the firefighters. Andrew Hurst hung around for a while, but he didn't get close enough to be a hero."

"What about the boy you found at the scene of the first fire?"

"Mark Siddons?"

"Yes."

"He hung around because his girlfriend was on one of the boats. His alibi held and his clothing and hands checked out clean. He also didn't have anywhere nearby he could have gone and cleaned up or changed. All his belongings, including his clothes, perished in the fire. I don't know, Geoff. I'm inclined to believe his story. Even so, he could have acted out of anger, I suppose, and covered his traces somehow. I just can't see the girl, Mandy, giving him an alibi if he wasn't, in fact, there. Annie said she had a tough enough time getting her to admit to having Mark in her bed in the first place. Didn't want to be known as 'that kind of a girl.' We could talk to her again. I don't suppose you found any trace of a timing device?"

"Not yet. But we're still sifting through the debris. Is it possible that the boy drugged McMahon, if that is indeed what happened, but someone else set the fire?"

"Possible," said Banks, "but highly unlikely, wouldn't you say? Don't forget, someone drugged Gardiner, too."

"Could that also have been the boy?"

"He was in the vicinity of Jennings Field at the right time," Banks admitted, "but there's no trace of a motive. Don't worry, though, we'll keep him on our list of suspects. I'm hoping to have another chat with him soon, when we find him."

"You let him go missing?"

"We had no reason to keep him locked up. He had an altercation with a friend and hoofed it. We'll find him. Okay?"

Hamilton put up his hands in mock surrender. "All right. All right."

Banks smiled. "So what's left as far as motive is concerned?"

"Well, there are fires started to conceal a crime."

"Which is also a distinct possibility here," Banks said. "Fire destroys evidence. Maybe not as much as the criminal thinks, but often it's enough."

"Evidence of what, though?" Hamilton asked.

"That's what we don't know yet. It looks as if Thomas McMahon might have been involved in art forgery, and Gardiner was fired for fiddling the company he worked for, but that's all we've got so far. We're still digging. First we need to know if there was any connection between the victims. If there was, and if we find it, that might lead us to some enemy they had in common."

"Sounds fair enough. I'm just hoping to hell there aren't any more fires."

"Me, too," said Banks.

"There is one ray of hope," said Hamilton.

"What's that?"

"The use of petrol as an accelerant might be a godsend."

"How come?"

"Well, you know that different brands of petrol contain

different additives, so you can tell, say, Esso from Texaco from Shell through spectral analysis?"

"I've heard about that," said Banks. "But it won't do us a lot of good in this case. Millions of people use Esso, Shell or Texaco."

"Yes, but it doesn't stop there," Hamilton went on. "When the petrol is pumped into a station's underground tank, then more contaminants are added unique to that tank."

"Are you telling me we can discover what *garage* the petrol came from through spectral analysis of the debris at the scene?"

"Not only that," said Hamilton, "but when you put the petrol in your fuel tank, another unique blend is created. By checking all local petrol stations and sampling each tank, we can actually determine which station the petrol came from and link it to the scene, or to a specific car's fuel tank."

"You're not serious?"

"I always take my work seriously, double-oh-seven."

Hamilton didn't crack a smile, so it took Banks a moment to catch on. A Bond reference. Geoff Hamilton clearly had hidden depths.

"But in order to find a possible match," Banks said, "we'd have to sample every underground tank in every petrol station in the area?"

"That's right. It helps if you have other information that helps you narrow down the search field."

"Not yet, we don't, but it's something to think about," Banks said. "Thanks."

"My pleasure," said Hamilton. He glanced at his watch. "And believe it or not, I'm going home now. My wife's beginning to wonder whether we're still married."

"I remember the feeling," said Banks, who planned on spending the evening at home catching up with the Sunday papers, maybe with a dram or two of Laphroaig. After meeting Maria Phillips in the Queen's Arms at half six, of course.

Later, just after nine, there was a modern version of *Great Expectations* on BBC, starring Gwyneth Paltrow. Banks liked the original Dickens novel, and he liked Gwyneth Paltrow, the way she sort of lit up the screen when she walked on.

Besides, he found watching television—*anything* on television—a great way of sorting out his thoughts and coming up with new hypotheses. The TV seemed to numb a part of his mind and leave the rest free to wander and make wild connections without too many inhibitions. At least that was the way it felt to him, and it had worked before.

Mark waited by the roadside for five minutes until he was certain Clive was gone, then he opened the wallet. It contained two hundred and fifty pounds in cash, all in nice crisp twenties and tens, fresh from the Cashpoint, along with credit cards, photos of a smiling woman and three blond children—Clive's family, no doubt—and a number of receipts for petrol and meals. Nowhere did it say that Clive was a doctor, and Mark guessed he was probably just a traveling salesman. And a pervert. Worried that the police would be after him after the incident, though, he thought of striking out across open country and avoiding the roads. But there was no way, he realized, that Clive was going to report what had happened. Even if he said Mark just attacked him in order to rob him, Mark could make enough noise to cause problems. And maybe others would come forward. Clive must know this; Mark doubted he was the first victim. And there was that smiling woman with the three blond children to consider. No, he thought, he was safe for the moment.

It was getting dark and he still had a long way to go. The moors became even eerier as the light faded and mist settled in patches. He knew he'd get lost if he headed for open country, probably die of exposure. Mark thought he could hear a dreadful howling in the distance. Weren't there ghostly hounds on the moors? Or werewolves? He thought about that film again, the one where the American tourist got bitten by a wolf on the moors and turned into a werewolf, and realized he had seen it when he was back with his mum and Crazy Nick, not at the squat. Or seen some of it. When Crazy Nick saw Mark was enjoying the film, he declared it was rubbish and switched to boxing. After that, Mark pretty much lost interest in television. There was no point, as he never got to watch anything he wanted anyway. He shivered and started to walk toward the nearest village, Helmsley, which he didn't think was very far.

When he got to the village, the lights in the houses and pubs were all on. It looked like a twee, tourist sort of place from what Mark could make out as he walked down the main street. He checked for Clive's car in the main car park and by the roadside, but thankfully couldn't see it. He laughed at himself, not sure why he was so paranoid. Clive had taken off like a bat out of hell and he wouldn't stop until he got to Scarborough. Mark had scared the shit out of him. Mark looked around to see that no one was watching, then he stopped and dropped Clive's wallet, minus the cash, down a grate.

There was a newsagent's shop still open at the corner, and Mark went in and bought a packet of cigarettes, twenty Benson & Hedges, seeing he was so flush, and a copy of the evening paper, just to see if there was any news about the fires. He was hungry and the cafés were all closed, the way they always seemed to be at teatime, so he ducked into a friendly-looking pub. He went first to the toilet, where he was able at least to clean up his hands and face and brush some of the muck off the suede overcoat. It was badly stained from his fall on the wet grass, though, and there was nothing he could do about that. Other than the overcoat, which he took off and carried over his arm so no one could see the stains, he reckoned he didn't look so bad.

Nobody paid him much attention as he sipped his pint of Guinness and ate the ham-and-cheese sandwich, which was all he was able to get there in the evening. The newspaper didn't tell him anything he didn't already know. The second fire was a caravan, and another man had been killed. Nobody would come right out and say it, but Mark could tell they thought it was deliberate, and that it had something to do with the fire on the boats.

It was half past six. The pub was warm and the log fire crackling in the hearth made him feel drowsy. He didn't want to move, didn't want to go anywhere. He lit his first cigarette in ages and inhaled the acrid smoke deep into his lungs. Heaven.

But what to do next? He knew he was about fourteen miles from the nearest railway station, back in Thirsk, but thought maybe he could get a bus from Helmsley to Scarborough. He'd have to find somewhere to stay when he got there, though, and that could be a problem if it was late and dark, especially as he was alone and without luggage or transport. He didn't want to draw attention to himself, even though he was almost a hundred percent certain Clive wouldn't report him to the police. He also had the killer to worry about, he realized. Somehow or other, he might have found out where Mark was, where he was going. He would have to be careful.

Then he saw the notice behind the bar: "B and B." The landlord had been friendly enough when he served Mark, even apologizing for the lack of hot meals, so Mark walked over to the bar and asked if there were any rooms vacant.

The landlord smiled. "It's not often we're full up at this time of year," he said. "I suppose it'll be a single you're wanting?"

"Yes," said Mark.

"I think we might be able to accommodate you. Rachel."

The woman helping behind the bar came over.

"Show this young lad the single, would you? Number six."

Rachel, a pretty young woman with fair hair and a peaches-and-cream complexion, blushed and said, "Of course, Mr. Ridley." She turned to Mark. "Come on."

Mark followed her up the narrow creaking staircase. At the top she opened a heavy door. The room looked magnificent to Mark, and he realized he must have been standing on the threshold with his mouth open. Rachel was expecting him to look around and say something.

"How much is it?" he managed to ask.

"Twenty-eight pounds, bed and breakfast," she said. "Breakfast's downstairs, between eight and nine o'clock. Well, do you want it?"

"Yes," said Mark, reaching in his pocket for the money.

"Tomorrow, silly," Rachel said. "You pay when you leave."

"Oh. Right," Mark said, amazed that someone would trust him not to run off without paying.

Rachel handed him the key and explained about the various locks and how he had to make sure he was in before they closed up the pub. He didn't even think he was going out, so that was no problem.

"Where's your rucksack?" she asked.

"Don't have one," he said.

She looked at him as if she thought he was daft, then shrugged and left, shutting the door behind her.

It was the nicest room Mark had ever been in in his entire life. It wasn't very big, but that was all right; he didn't need much space. The wallpaper was a cheerful flower pattern and the air smelled of lemons and herbs. It had a solid bed and a dresser and drawers for clothes and stuff. There were also a television and facilities for making tea and coffee. But best of all, there was a bathroom/toilet.

It had been difficult managing without running water on

the boat. Once a week they went to the public baths in East-vale, next to the swimming pool, but most days they did the best they could. Mark had found a bucket and a nice big enamel bowl in a junk shop, and usually he would walk half a mile west along the canal bank to the taps installed by the tourist board for the boaters, campers and walkers and get fresh water there, which he would carry back and heat on the stove. It was a hassle, but it was better than being dirty.

But now he had a bath to himself, and soap and shampoo and towels, too. First he turned on the television. It didn't matter what was on; he just wanted the sound for company. Then he started running a hot bath and made himself a cup of tea. When everything was ready he took his tea into the bathroom, climbed in the tub and lit a cigarette. It was wonderful. He could hear *Emmerdale* on the television through the half-open door as he lay back and luxuriated in the steamy warmth. This must be what it was like to be normal, he thought. He only wished Tina could be here with him. He knew it wouldn't all seem so special to her because she'd grown up with all these luxuries, but she would have loved it nonetheless.

He wished he could stay there forever, with the hot water enveloping him, the steam rising and the comforting voices on the television, but he knew he couldn't. Tomorrow he would have to find a way to get to Scarborough and get a job. Clive's money wouldn't last forever, especially if he had to pay so much for a room every night. But maybe he'd find somewhere cheaper in Scarborough. A little flat, even. And then he'd start putting his life back together.

Banks certainly felt as if he needed a drink when half past six came around, but left to his own devices he would have chosen other company than Maria Phillips. Still, he thought, pushing open the pub's door, duty calls, and she was harmless enough if you kept your distance.

The Queen's Arms was busy with the after-work crowd, most of whom seemed to prefer standing elbow to elbow at the bar. Banks was the first to arrive, so he managed to get Cyril's attention, bought himself a pint of bitter and settled by the window to read the paper.

Maria came dashing in ten minutes late, breathless and full of apologies. Someone hadn't turned up for an evening shift and she'd had to deal with it. Banks offered to get her a drink.

"You dear man," she said, unbuttoning her coat and unwinding her scarf. "I'll have the usual."

When he came back with her Campari and soda, she was composed, smoking a Silk Cut. A momentary pang of desire—for a cigarette, not for Maria—leaped through Banks's veins like an electric current, then passed as quickly as it came, leaving him feeling vaguely uneasy and fidgety.

"Cheers," Maria said, clinking glasses.

"*Slainte,*" said Banks. "So what is it you want to see me about?"

Her eyes sparkled with mischievous humor. "It's all business with you, isn't it?"

"It's been a long day."

"And I don't suppose there's a dear devoted woman waiting for you at home, ready to massage your neck and shoulders and run a nice warm bath for you, is there?"

"Afraid not," Banks said, thinking there was only Gwyneth Paltrow in *Great Expectations* and a tumbler of Laphroaig. But Gwyneth wouldn't be massaging him or running him a hot bath. "There's not even a faithful dog to fetch my slippers. Policing doesn't lend itself to pet-owning, especially when you live alone."

"Wives, either," Maria said.

"Well, I'd never claim to have *owned* a woman."

She slapped him playfully on the forearm. "Silly. You know what I mean. Your job. It must make relationships difficult."

Damn near impossible, thought Banks, realizing he hadn't even talked to Michelle in a day or two. He wondered how her missing child case was going. Better than his triple murder, he hoped. His train would pass through Peterborough on his way to London. Maybe she could come to the station and he could lean out of the window and kiss her like a scene in an old black-and-white film. All that would be missing would be the atmospheric steam from the engine. "Well," he said, "you should probably talk to Sandra about that."

"I would, except she seems to have deserted all her old friends."

"She's burned a few bridges, all right," said Banks. "So, Maria, what is it?"

"Nothing, really. It's just that after our little tête-à-tête the other day, well, you know how you start thinking back, trying to remember things?"

"Yes," said Banks. "That's why I usually give anyone I question my phone number. They often remember something later."

"You didn't give *me* your phone number."

"Maria! Stop doing your Miss Moneypenny imitation. You're just down the street."

"Just down the street. Story of my life. Ah, well." Maria laughed. "Oh, don't look so exasperated. I'm only teasing."

"You were talking about remembering something."

"So stern. Yes, like I said, I got to thinking, trying to play the scene in my mind's eye, so to speak."

"Which scene would this be?"

"The Turner reception, of course. There were quite a lot of people there, including that pretty young policewoman I've seen you with on occasion."

"Annie was involved in the security. As you well know."

"I'm surprised you two haven't . . ." Then she looked at Banks and opened her eyes wider. "Well, maybe you have. None of my business, anyway."

"That's right," said Banks. "The reception."

"I'm getting to that. I was trying to picture Thomas McMahon, what he was doing, who he was talking to. That sort of thing."

"And?"

"Well, he wasn't talking to anyone most of the time, but I did see him chat with Mr. Whitaker from the bookshop."

That made sense. Whitaker had told Banks that McMahon bought old books from him. For the endpapers, Phil Keane had suggested, perhaps to make forgeries of period sketches. And Banks was still keeping an open mind as to whether Whitaker was involved in some sort of forgery scam with McMahon and Gardiner, especially after Stefan Nowak had confirmed that the car parked in the lay-by on the night of McMahon's murder had been a Jeep Cherokee, the same model Whitaker owned. Thanks to Geoff Hamilton's expert knowledge, they could now check Whitaker's fuel tank against the accelerant used in the Gardiner blaze.

"What was Thomas McMahon doing?"

"Well, his wineglass was rarely empty, I can say that."

"But he wasn't drunk?"

"No. Maybe a little bit tipsy. But not so's you'd notice that much. I seem to remember he was the kind of chap who could hold his liquor, as they say in the movies. But that's not what I wanted to tell you."

"What is it, then?"

"Just that at one point he *was* talking to someone who might be able to tell you more about him than I can."

"Who?"

"That art researcher from London. Well-heeled, yummy-looking fellow. Do you know who I mean?"

Banks felt the hackles rise on the back of his neck. Annie's "friend" Phil. Philip Keane. "Yes," he said. "I know him. Why do you say well-heeled?"

Maria rolled her eyes. "Honestly, you *men*. His suit,

dearie. You can't get a suit like that off the peg in Marks and Sparks. That was a made-for-measure job, *bespoke*, tailor. Beautifully made, too. Best-quality material. Nice bit of schmatter. At a guess I'd say Savile Row."

"How do you know?"

She winked. "I've got hidden depths."

Banks imagined an art researcher probably made a fair income, and if Phil Keane wanted to spend it on Savile Row suits, good for him. "Go on," Banks said. "What were they talking about?"

"I don't know that, do I? I was some distance away doing my hostess routine, seeing that everyone's glass was full. It was just something I noticed, that's all, perhaps because most of the time McMahon *wasn't* talking to anyone."

"How long were they talking?"

"I don't know that, either. My attention was diverted. Next thing I knew, McMahon was studying one of the paintings on the wall and Mr. Art Researcher was chatting up Shirley Cameron."

"Which painting?"

"I can't remember. Just one of the ones we had on display in the reception room. Nothing fancy. Local, most likely."

"Did you get any sense of what their conversation was about?"

"Not really."

"I mean, were they arguing?"

"No."

"Exchanging pleasantries?"

"No."

"Intimate?"

"Not in that *sort* of way."

"An animated, passionate discussion?"

"No. More casual than that."

"Just passing the time of day, then?"

"Well, yes, except . . ."

"Except what?"

"When I was playing it back in my mind last night . . . I don't know if I'm imagining things, you know, embroidering on what I actually saw, but I could swear they were talking as if they *knew* one another."

"Not as if they'd just met?"

"No, that's it. You can tell, can't you, when there's a history? Even if you don't hear a word?"

"Sometimes," Banks said. "Body language can actually tell you quite a lot."

"Body language," Maria repeated. "Yes . . . Anyway . . ." She reached into her handbag. "He gave me his business card and I dug it out of the files, if that's any use."

Banks looked at the card. Some ornate sort of typeface, black and red. It gave Phil Keane's company name as Art-Search Ltd., along with an address in Belgravia. "Can I keep this?" Banks asked.

"Of course. It's no use to me, is it?"

Banks thanked her.

"Well, that's it, then." Maria spread her hands. "I've told you all I know. I have nothing left up my sleeve to keep you here with."

"Oh, I don't know," said Banks, suddenly feeling magnanimous toward Maria, and not in any great hurry to go home. After all, it was not yet seven o'clock and the film didn't start till nine. "What about the pleasure of your company?"

Maria looked puzzled. "You don't have to dash off somewhere?"

"No. Not yet, at any rate. As you pointed out, there's no wife waiting to massage my shoulders and neck and run a hot bath. How about another drink?"

Maria narrowed her eyes and looked at him suspiciously. "Are you sure?"

"Of course."

Maria blushed, then slid her empty glass toward him. "I'll have another Campari and soda then, please."

She actually seemed quite shy when *he* took the lead, Banks thought, as he made his way to the bar. As he stood there waiting for Cyril to pull his pint, he wondered about what he'd just heard. It didn't mean anything, necessarily, even if Maria's intuition was right, but why hadn't Phil told him? Why had he lied about knowing McMahon? And how could Banks go about checking into it without damaging his already fragile relationship with Annie?

Chapter 12

*O*n the train to London, Banks fretted about what Maria Phillips had told him the previous evening, and what to do about it. He couldn't even relax and enjoy his John Mayall CD for worrying, and he certainly couldn't concentrate on the Eric Ambler thriller he'd brought along.

There was no denying that Maria had told him Phil Keane was deep in conversation with Thomas McMahon, as if they already knew each other, and Keane had said he didn't know the artist. It could be a simple, honest mistake in identity—after all, it was a few months ago—but Banks didn't think so.

Maybe Keane, like anybody else, wanted to avoid any connection with a police investigation. It was a natural response, after all. Don't get involved. Leave me out of it. Leslie Whitaker had done the same thing, and Banks was convinced that he was in a lot deeper than he admitted.

But Phil Keane *was* involved. As a consultant, and as Annie's lover. Which meant he was supposed to be on *their* side, didn't it? The last thing Banks could do was talk to Annie about it. She would immediately turn on him for trying to come between her and Phil out of personal jealousy, making their last little set-to seem like a preliminary round.

Shortly after Grantham, Banks had an idea. He made a call

on his mobile to an old colleague on the Met, someone who might be able to help. After that, he had a bit more success putting the matter out of his mind and listening to *Blues from Laurel Canyon*.

King's Cross was the usual melee. Banks headed straight for the taxi rank and joined the queue. Within a few minutes he was on his way to Sir Laurence West's office in the City. The journey was slow, like most road journeys in London, and the mild weather seemed to have brought more people out onto the streets. Couriers on bicycles weaved in and out of the traffic with total disregard for safety—theirs or anybody else's—and pedestrians wandered across the streets no matter where, or what color, the traffic lights were. Many were wearing only their suits or Windcheaters and jeans.

There aren't many skyscrapers in the City, but Sir Laurence's offices were on the twelfth floor of one of them and offered a splendid view south over the river to Southwark, or would have done had the day not been so overcast.

When Banks finally made it past the security, receptionists, secretaries, office managers and personal assistants, he was beginning to wish he'd sent someone else instead. He didn't cope well with bureaucracy and soon found himself losing patience. When he was finally ushered into the inner sanctum he was ready to give Sir Laurence a hard time.

The office was about as big as the entire upper floor of Western Area Headquarters, and most of it was uncluttered open space. Thick carpets with intricate eastern designs covered most of the floor area, the rest being shiny hardwood, and a big teak desk sat at the center, a sleek laptop computer the only object on its surface. In one corner a black leather-upholstered three-piece suite was arranged around a low, glass-topped table, a cocktail cabinet nearby. There was a faint whiff of old cigar smoke in the air.

The man himself was tall and portly, bald-headed and bushy-eyebrowed, with more than a passing resemblance to

Robert Morley, probably in his early seventies, but well preserved. He was wearing a slate gray suit, white shirt and striped tie, no doubt representing some old school, exclusive club or regiment. He came forward with a genial smile on his face and shook hands, gesturing for Banks to sit in one of the armchairs.

"Drink?" he offered.

"No, thank you," said Banks.

"Hope you don't mind if I do."

"Not at all."

West poured himself some amber fluid from a cut-glass decanter and added a splash of soda. Banks got a whiff of brandy.

"I know it's a bit early," said West, "but I always make it a point to have a drink before lunch. Just the one, you understand. It helps sharpen the appetite."

Banks, who might have time to grab a burger at the nearest McDonald's, if he was lucky, nodded. "I'll have a Coke, if you've got any," he said.

"Of course." West opened what looked like a filing cabinet. It was a small fridge. He took out a can of Coke, poured it into a crystal tumbler and handed it to Banks, who thanked him and took a sip.

"Now, what can I do for you?" said West, sitting opposite Banks. He didn't have to explain that he was a busy man; it was evident from his body language. "The young man on the telephone didn't tell me very much. I do hope those wretched British Waterways people haven't been bothering you. They've been on at me for years, but I'm afraid I've rather ignored them."

Anyone else's boats would probably have been towed away long ago, Banks reflected. Wealth and power do have their privileges. Slowly, he explained about the fires and the deaths.

"Oh, dear," said West. "I hope you won't be holding me legally responsible for their condition?"

"That's not my department," said Banks. "All I'm interested in is who set the fire, and why."

"Then I'm afraid I can't help. You say there were squatters living on the boats? Perhaps they started the fire?"

"That's highly unlikely, given that two of them died."

"I wish I could help."

"How did you come to be the owner of the boats?"

West swirled his drink in his glass. "They were my father's," he said. "I suppose I inherited them."

"But you had no interest in his business?"

"No. He lived to be ninety-six years old, Mr. Banks. He died just two years ago, though he had been uncommunicative for some time. I know he was in the haulage business, but believe it or not, I didn't even know about those two boats until the Waterways people got in touch with me, after his death. I know I should have delegated, put someone on it, had something done, but I had more important things on my mind at the time. I didn't imagine they'd be doing any harm just sitting there."

"There was no reason you wanted to keep them?"

"Good Lord, no."

"Or sell them?"

"I suppose I might have got around to that eventually."

"Were they insured?"

"I imagine so. My father was a thorough man before his illness."

"But you don't know for how much?"

"I have no idea. I suppose the executor of his estate would know."

"Do you know of anybody who might have had a reason to set fire to them?"

"No. Surely you're not suggesting some sort of insurance fraud?"

"I'm not suggesting anything," said Banks. It was a patently absurd idea, anyway. West probably made a few billion a year, and the insurance on the boats wasn't likely to amount to more than twenty or thirty thousand. Still, stranger things had happened. The rich don't get richer by missing opportunities to make even more money. Or West might simply have got someone to torch them to get them off his hands.

"It's funny," said West, "but now you bring it up, I actually did receive an offer to buy one of the boats a few months ago. My secretary brought it to my attention, but I'm afraid I didn't take the offer very seriously."

"I thought you didn't need the money."

West laughed. "My dear man, that's no reason to let oneself be taken for a fool."

"How long ago was it?" Banks asked.

"Oh, not long. October, perhaps."

"Do you think you could find the letter?"

West called in his secretary, a buxom woman in a no-nonsense pinstriped skirt and matching jacket, who disappeared for a few moments and returned with a buff folder.

"How did the letter come to you?" Banks asked the secretary before she scurried off.

"It was forwarded through British Waterways," she said. She looked at Sir Laurence for guidance. He nodded, and she passed the folder to Banks. It contained just one sheet of paper, a letter dated the sixth of October. It was brief and to the point.

Someone wanted to buy the southernmost narrow boat—Tom's boat—moored on the dead-end branch off the Eastvale Canal, near Molesby. He was willing to pay ten thousand pounds—such a low sum, he explained, because the boat needed a lot of work—and that someone was Thomas McMahon himself.

* * *

Mark could smell and hear the sea as he made his way down the hill to the sands from Scarborough bus station just after eleven o'clock on Tuesday morning. After a breakfast of fried eggs, bacon, sausage, mushrooms and grilled tomatoes, he had paid his bill in Helmsley and wandered toward the bus stops in the square. There he had caught the half-past-nine bus and stared out of the window at the bleak, misty moorland landscape to the north, until the bus headed down from the moors near Pickering.

His plan, inasmuch as he had one, was to find a job as soon as possible. The money he had stolen from Clive would enable him to get a roof over his head and food in his belly for a while, at least. But he would need something more dependable in the long term. If there was going to be a long term.

Mark didn't know why, but he felt both apprehension and numbness at the same time. A part of him was numb because he had lost Tina, yet another part of him was afraid of what lay around the next corner, who might be lying in wait for him. There was still the guilt, too. If only he'd been on the boat with Tina instead of with that slut Mandy. Anger raged inside him somewhere, unfocused yet growing stronger. He might have killed Clive, he realized, if they hadn't slowed at the bend and he'd been sharp enough to seize his opportunity to grab the money and get away. He remembered what the policeman had said, about the fire not being an accident. That meant someone had killed Tina, whether she was the intended victim or not. The only person he could think of who had a reason to kill Tina was Patrick Aspern, and when Mark thought of Aspern, he felt his rage surge up again.

A cold wind blew off the North Sea, pushing inland a mass of cloud the color of dirty dishwater. There was no blue to be seen anywhere on the horizon, no rays of sunshine lancing through to make diamonds dance on the water; the whole world was wrapped in a gray shroud.

Down on the prom, all the amusements were closed for the

winter, the cafés and fish and chip shops shut up, Jimmy Corrigan's, the Parade Snack Bar, the sands deserted except for a man in a hooded overcoat walking his dog, hunched forward against the wind. The tide was high and waves like molten metal crashed on the beach, churning the brown sand. One or two other people were walking along the prom, old couples, a young family. Probably people who lived in town, Mark thought. After all, Scarborough was a big place, and the people who lived there had to go on even when the tourist season was over.

A solitary gray Vectra was parked across the street, outside the Ghost Train, with two men in it drinking tea and eating Kit Kats. They both glanced toward Mark, and he kept his face averted. He couldn't tell whether he recognized them or not, but there was no sense in falling right into their hands. Maybe two people had set fire to the boats, not just one, and these could be the ones. Hands in his pockets, he strolled on beside the harbor, where the nets were stacked and the fishing boats were all moored for the winter.

He tried to light a cigarette, but the wind was too strong, and after three matches he gave up. He'd have one later in a warm pub. It felt good to be near the sea. He didn't know why, but the sight of the water stretching out as far as the eye could see, until it met the sky way in the distance, evoked a feeling of awe in him: the way it was always changing, the surface swelling and dipping, the scudding whitecaps and huge breakers. It put you in your place, put things in perspective. He could watch it forever.

He imagined sailors years ago, in wooden ships with canvas sails bellied out, tossing on seas like this, no land in sight, and thought that was what he would have liked to have been if he'd lived then. A sailor on a whaling ship. Not throwing the harpoons, because he didn't particularly like the idea of killing whales, but maybe at the wheel, steering the rudder, discovering new worlds. Maybe even now he could join the

Merchant Navy, if they'd have him, and spend the rest of his days at sea. The ships were more modern, he knew, but they'd still be at the mercy of the waves.

Out of his peripheral vision, he noticed the Vectra start moving just behind him, to his left. He walked past the empty funfair and onto Marine Drive. The car didn't overtake him, but kept up a slow, steady pace, about twenty yards behind him. Were they following him? Mark risked a glance back and thought he saw one of them talking into a mobile phone.

Mark felt exposed, out in the open. Marine Drive curved around the base of Castle Hill, with nothing but the steep rocky slope on one side and the cold North Sea on the other. Nowhere to run. The wind howled in his ears and the waves crashed high over the seawall and the metal railings, and Mark was soaked in no time.

The Vectra remained twenty yards behind him, crawling along, no matter how much he altered his pace. A few other souls were braving the weather, all dressed in waterproof gear. Out in the distance, the dark shape of a ship bobbed on the water. Mark wondered what it was doing there, what it felt like, who was on it. Were they in danger? He couldn't see any danger signals flashing, any flares, or SOS lights. Weathering the storm. Just like him.

The car was still following him, no doubt about it. Mark picked up his pace, nearly running now, and it surged forward, pulling over onto his side of the road just a few feet in front of him, blocking the pavement.

Mark turned and ran the other way, back toward town, ignoring the doors slamming and the shouts behind him. He couldn't hear what they were saying anyway because of the wind and the crashing waves. He ran back toward the prom. If he could get into the maze of narrow streets behind the amusements, he might have a chance of losing them, whoever they were.

He hadn't got very far when he felt a hand on his shoulder.

He shook it off and kept going, but it was no use. Within seconds, his legs went from under him and he fell onto the hard surface, smashing his cheek against the stone. He felt a knee between his shoulders and his arm twisted up his back. The pain was excruciating, and he thought he screamed out, then he lay still. He could hear them talking but still couldn't grasp what they were saying, what they wanted. Mark could taste blood and salt on his lips and his tongue as they hauled him to his feet and back to the car. He cried out, but nobody came to help. One final, magnificent wave smashed against the seawall and drenched them all from head to toe before they got him inside the Vectra.

The garage was a mere stone's throw from the Askham Bar Park and Ride, off the outer ring road just west of York city center. Owner's name, Charlie Kirk. Handy place for a car rental agency, Annie thought. You could arrive at the train station and take the bus out, then you never had to worry about the murderous city center traffic, or the parking.

As it had done so many times before, legwork had paid off once again, and it looked as if this was the place where the killer might have rented his Jeep Cherokee. At least, the same person had rented the same vehicle on several occasions since the previous summer, including the past weekend. They had got lucky because not many local outfits had Cherokees for hire, but Charlie Kirk did. Now Annie was about to question the owner, with Stefan and his impressions expert in tow. They went off to the car park around the back with the mechanic while Annie went to talk to the clerical staff.

The small office was overheated and stuffy. Three people worked there, one up front, to deal with customers, and the other two, a young girl and an older man, farther back. The office was full of the usual stuff—computers, filing cabinets, phones and fax machines—and the walls were covered with posters of cars.

Annie slipped her overcoat off, laying it on a chair, and offered her warrant card to the woman at the front desk.

"I've been expecting you," the woman said, standing up to shake hands. "I'm Karen Talbot, office manager."

Annie put Karen Talbot at about thirty. She had blond highlights, glossy red lipstick and eyes so blue they had to be contact lenses, and she was wearing a black silk blouse, showing plenty of cleavage, and a short, tight red skirt. The effect was lost on Annie, but she imagined it wasn't on most of the male customers.

Karen sat down again, pulling her skirt as far over her thighs as it would go, which wasn't far.

"Is the owner around?" Annie asked.

"The captain isn't in today. This isn't his only outpost, you know. Quite the empire builder, our captain is."

"Captain?"

"Kirk. Captain Kirk. Our little joke. Only when he's not here, of course."

"I see," said Annie. "We'll talk to him later, then. Maybe you can help me for now?" She sat down opposite Karen.

Karen patted her hair. "I'll do my best. As a matter of fact, the captain wouldn't be able to tell you much, anyway. It's not as if he actually *works* here, if you know what I mean."

"So it's you who deals with the public?"

"Mostly, yes." Karen glanced behind at the other two. "But we take it in turns. That's Nick and Sylvia."

Annie said hello. Nick returned her greeting with a broad salesman's smile and Sylvia smiled shyly at her. Annie wondered how Nick, who must be well the wrong side of forty, felt working for a young upstart like Karen. She also found herself rather uncharitably wondering how Karen had got the job and what her relationship with the owner was. But such thoughts had little to do with the business on hand, so she pushed them aside and got down to business.

"We've been told that you've rented out a dark blue Jeep Cherokee, or a similar vehicle, to the same person on five different occasions since last summer. Is that correct?"

"Yes," said Karen. "Three times it was the Jeep, and twice we had to substitute a Ford Explorer."

"Did that cause a problem with the customer?"

"Not that I remember. He just wanted the same type of vehicle."

"Did you deal with this customer yourself?"

"Not every time."

"I did, twice," said Nick. "And Sylvia did once."

"First off," said Annie, "what were the dates?"

Karen went to the filing cabinet by her desk, flipped through the folders for a few seconds and pulled one out. Then she reeled off a string of dates in September, October, November and December, ending with the previous weekend.

"When did he take it out?" Annie asked.

"Thursday morning."

"And when did he return it?"

"Saturday morning."

So he had the Cherokee before the narrow-boats fire, but he took it back before the Roland Gardiner fire. Annie wondered why he would do that.

"Ever any problems when he brought it back?"

"No. It was always in excellent condition."

"Did he return it full or empty?"

"Empty. It costs a bit more, but it saves the customer having to search for a garage himself."

"You fill the cars here?"

"Yes. Of course."

That was a piece of luck, Annie thought. They could take samples from the garage's tank and from the Cherokee's. Banks had told her that forensics could identify the tank from which the petrol used in the Gardiner fire came. Whoever had rented the Cherokee would most likely not have needed to refill the tank anywhere else. If they came up with a match, that was solid evidence to use in court.

"What's the customer's name?"

"Masefield. William Masefield."

"What did he look like?"

"Ordinary, really."

"Let's see if we can improve on that, shall we?" said Annie with a sigh. She hated trying to get descriptions out of people. Most witnesses, in her experience, were neither observant nor good at expressing themselves in words. This time proved no exception. After about ten minutes, the best the three of them could come up with was that he was a little above medium height, generally in good shape though perhaps just a tad overweight, a little stooped, gold-rimmed glasses, graying hair and casual clothes—jeans, blue Windcheater. Nick thought he'd been wearing white trainers on at least one occasion, but didn't know if they were Nike or not. At least Annie ought to be grateful there were no glaring contradictions about height or hair color. It could have been the person Mark Siddons had described visiting Thomas McMahon, but it could have been a thousand other people, too.

"Any closed-circuit TV here?" Annie asked.

"Only out back, where the cars are," said Karen. "And it's only turned on at night, when no one's here. Otherwise we'd be changing the tapes every five minutes."

Too bad, Annie thought. But it was worth a try. "Was there anything else you remember about him?" Annie asked.

"No," said Karen.

"How did he pay?"

"Credit card."

"Can you give me the details?"

Karen quickly made a photocopy of William Masefield's file and passed it to Annie. The address, she noticed, was

Studley, a Midlands village in Warwickshire, not far from Redditch.

"Did he have any sort of accent at all?" she asked.

"Just ordinary," said Karen.

"What do you mean? What's ordinary? Yorkshire? Birmingham?"

"Sort of no accent, really. But nice. Educated."

Annie understood what she meant. They used to call it "Received Pronunciation," and it was what all the radio and television presenters spoke before regional and ethnic accents came into fashion. RP was generally regarded as posh and related to public schools, Oxford and Cambridge, and southeastern England, the Home Counties. Most accents tell you where a person comes from; RP only told you social status.

Stefan poked his head around the door and Annie noticed Karen immediately start to preen.

"Any luck?" she asked.

"It looks like the same vehicle," he said. "The measurements are the same, as are the tires, and there's some distinctive cross-hatching on the casts we took from the lay-by that appear to match this specific Jeep Cherokee. Mike's still working on it, and we'll be taking soil and gravel samples, but I thought I'd give you the breaking news."

"That's great," Annie said, tapping the sheet of paper in front of her. "William Masefield. We've got his details here. We've got him." In her mind, she could see them swooping in and making an arrest even before Banks got back from London, unrealistic as that was. Still, she *felt* jubilant. She could even see a possibility of that weekend in New York with Phil. *If* she could afford it, because she would insist on paying her own way.

"There's only one problem," Stefan said.

"Oh?"

"It's been thoroughly cleaned, inside and out."

Annie looked at Karen, who shrugged. "We always get the returns cleaned up as promptly as we can," she said.

"Shit," said Annie. "No forensics."

"Most likely not," Stefan agreed. "Though we can certainly take it in and try. We might pick up a print or a hair the cleaners missed."

"Wait a minute," said Karen. "What do you mean, 'take it in'? Take it where?"

"To the police garage," Annie said.

"But you can't take the Jeep. It's booked."

"Mr. Masefield again?"

"No. But they're good customers. Regular."

"It's evidence," said Annie. She turned to Stefan. "Tell Mike to take it to the police garage, but to make sure he gets that petrol sample first, along with a sample from the underground tank here."

"But the captain will—"

"Don't worry, Karen," said Annie, picking up a pad from the desk. "We'll give you a receipt. And you can always rent them the Explorer instead. I'm sure they'll understand."

"*Commander* Burgess? Well, bugger me!"

"Watch it with the vile language, Banks. And why such surprise?"

"The last time I saw you, you were a detective superintendent in National Criminal Intelligence. I thought they'd put you out to pasture for good."

"Things change. I'm resilient, me."

Not only that, Banks remembered, but "Dirty Dick" Burgess had been sent somewhere he could do little harm because he was accused of dragging his feet over a sensitive race-related investigation. The two had known each other for many years, and their relationship had changed significantly over the course of time. At first they had been like chalk and cheese: Burgess brash, right-wing, racist, sexist, cutting corners to get results; Banks trying his damnedest to remain a liberal humanist in a heartbreaking job, in demoralizing times. Now Banks cut more corners and Burgess toed the line more closely. They both came from a working-class background, and both had worked their way up the hard way, through the streets. Burgess was the son of an East End barrow boy. He had thrived in the Thatcher years, lain low during John Major's reign, and now he was thriving again in the Blair era. It just went to show what Banks had always believed; there wasn't much difference between Thatcher and Blair except for gender, and sometimes he wasn't too sure about that.

They were about the same age, too, and had managed to find a certain amount of common ground over the years. It was fragile ground, though, thin ice over a quagmire. Banks had phoned Burgess from the train, with an idea in mind, and Burgess had suggested that Banks buy him lunch. Thus they stood at the bar of a crowded pub near the Old Bailey, washing down the curry of the day with flat lager and rubbing elbows with barristers, clients and clerks. At least Burgess hadn't changed in one respect; he still drank like a fish and smoked Tom Thumb cigars.

What had changed most, though, was his appearance. Gone were the silver pony tail and the scuffed leather jacket; in their place a shaved head and a dark blue suit, white shirt and paisley tie. Shiny shoes. Burgess had also put on a few pounds, and his complexion was pink, the nose a little redder and more bulbous. The world-weary, seen-it-all look in his eyes had been replaced by one of mild surprise and curiosity.

"I can see you're doing all right for yourself," Banks said, pushing his plate away. He'd only eaten half of the curry, which wasn't very good. The sign read lamb, but he suspected it was mutton. And the spicing was so bland as to be immaterial.

"Can't complain. Can't complain. My old oppos at Special Branch didn't forget me, after all. I managed to pull off one or two coups that pleased a number of people in high places. I tell you, Banksy, this post-nine-eleven world is full of opportunities for a man of my talents."

"On whose side?"

"Ha, ha. Very funny."

"So where are you now? Back in Special Branch?"

Burgess put his finger to his lips. "Can't say. If I did, I'd have to kill you. Top secret. Hush hush. Actually, we're so new we haven't even got our acronym sorted yet. Anyway, what brings you down here? You were all mysterious on the phone." He offered Banks a Tom Thumb. Banks refused. Burgess's eyes narrowed. "What is it, Banksy? Have you stopped smoking? I haven't seen you light one up yet. That's not like you. You've quit, haven't you?"

"Six months now."

"Feel any better?"

"No."

Burgess laughed. "How's that lovely wife of yours? Ex, I should say."

"She's fine," said Banks. "Remarried now."

"And you?"

"Enjoying the bachelor life. Look, there was something I wanted to ask you. In complete confidence, of course."

"Of course. Why come to me otherwise?"

One thing Banks did know about Burgess was that he could be trusted to keep quiet and be as discreet as necessary. He had a network of informers and information-gatherers second to none, no matter who, or what, it was you wanted to know about. That was why Banks had rung him.

"It's rather delicate," said Banks.

"What's happened? Your girlfriend's chucked you and you want me to look into her new boyfriend's background, find some dirt on him?"

It was astonishingly close to home, but Banks knew Burgess was only casting stones in the dark to see if he could hit anything. His scattershot approach often worked wonders, but Banks was a little wiser to it than he used to be, and less inclined to react. He was still in awe of Burgess's uncanny ability to hit the right nerve, though.

"It's probably nothing," he said, "but I'd like a background check on a bloke called Philip Keane."

"Can you be a bit more specific?" Burgess said, thumbing through a soft black leather-covered notebook for a clean page. It wasn't standard issue, Banks noticed. Must be his private notebook. "I mean, unless he's related to that hothead who plays for Man U."

"Not as far as I know. Pretty cultured bloke. Oxford or Cambridge. One of the two. Works as an art researcher, checking pedigrees and provenance, mostly for private collectors, but does some work for the Tate and the National. As far as I know, it's his own business. I don't know if he has any employees or partners."

"Where's the office?"

"Belgravia." Banks gave him the address he'd got from the business card Maria Phillips gave him.

"Company name?"

"ArtSearch Limited."

"Anything else that might help?"

"Not really. He's in his early forties. Also owns a cottage in Fortford, North Yorkshire. Well-dressed, good-looking sort of bloke—"

"He *has* stolen your girlfriend, hasn't he, Banksy?"

"It's nothing like that."

"That pretty young DS you were bonking. What's her name?"

"If you mean Annie Cabbot, she's a DI now and—"

"Annie Cabbot, that's the one." Burgess grinned, not a pleasant sight, least of all for the glimpse it gave of his smoke-stained, crooked teeth. He shook his head. "Tut tut tut, Banksy. Will you never learn?"

"Look," said Banks, trying hard not to let Burgess's prodding and teasing exasperate him. "The bloke lied to me about something that might be important in a murder investigation. I want to know why."

"Why don't you ask him?"

"I'll do that. In the meantime, I want to find out as much about him as I can."

"You mean you want *me* to find out as much about him as *I* can."

"Okay. Will you do it?"

"You want me to find some dirt on him?"

"If there is any, I'm sure you'll find it. If not . . . I just want the truth."

"Don't we all? And you don't want Annie Cabbot to know about these discreet inquiries, I take it?"

"I don't want anybody to know. Look, maybe the lie's important and maybe it's not. What you find out, or don't, might help me to decide. It's a serious case."

"The Eastvale Canal fires?"

"You know about them?"

"Like to keep my finger on the pulse. And another thing: you paid a visit to Sir Laurence West this morning."

Banks smiled. "I don't suppose I should be surprised you know that already."

Burgess winked. "The walls have ears," he said. "Go carefully, Banksy. Sir Laurence has some very powerful connections."

"He told me what I wanted to know. I don't think I have a problem with him."

"Make sure you don't. These are difficult times. The

world's going to hell in a handbasket. You don't know who you can trust."

"You always seem to land on your feet."

"I'm a Weeble, me. Remember those when you were a kid? You could knock them down as many times as you wanted but they always rolled back to their feet."

"I remember," said Banks.

"Anyway, how's about another couple of pints? Unless you have to run."

Banks glanced at his watch. There was somewhere he wanted to go, but he didn't have to run. "Fine with me," he said.

"My shout this time."

Winsome was driving the unmarked police car down the M42, weaving in and out of the lanes of lorries with natural ease, windscreen wipers flapping like crazy to get rid of all the filthy spray. Annie, no mean driver herself, was surprised she didn't feel in the least bit nervous, considering the speed they were going and the narrow spaces Winsome seemed able to maneuver them in and out of.

"Where the hell did you learn to drive like this?" Annie asked.

Winsome flashed her a grin. "Dunno, ma'am," she said. "Back home, I suppose. I mean, I started when I was twelve, and I guess I just took to it. Some of those mountain roads . . ."

"But there aren't any motorways in Jamaica, are there?"

"You never been there, ma'am?"

"No."

"Well, there aren't. Not really. Not what you'd call motorways. But you can go pretty fast sometimes, and you get a lot of traffic in Montego Bay."

"What about Kingston?"

"Dunno," said Winsome. "Never been there. Mostly I learned driving here, though, on the job. I took a course."

"I'm glad to hear it. Look, Winsome . . ."

"What, ma'am?"

"About this 'ma'am' business. It makes me feel like an old woman. Do you think you could call me something else?"

Winsome laughed. "What do you recommend?"

"Up to you, really."

"Boss?"

"No. Don't like that."

"Chief."

"No."

"How about Guv?"

Annie thought for a moment. Banks didn't like "Guv," she knew. He said it sounded too much like television. But Annie didn't mind that. And she liked the sound of it. "Okay," she said. " 'Guv' will do fine."

"Right you are, Guv. What do you think?"

"About William Masefield?"

"Yes."

"I'm not sure," said Annie. "It can't be as easy as this, surely?"

"Sometimes it is. Easy, I mean."

"Not in my experience. If he's got any brains at all, he must have known we'd track him through the rental and the credit card eventually."

"Maybe he's not so bright as you think." Winsome dodged in and out of a convoy of about six articulated juggernauts with Spanish number plates, and Annie looked at the map. "We're nearly there. Get over in the left lane."

Winsome flashed her signal and edged over.

"You want Junction three. The A-435. Here it is."

Winsome took the exit and slowed down quickly. Annie turned to a more detailed map of the area she had bought before the journey and found the street in Studley. Winsome drove more sedately now, and there was little traffic on the road. They turned down a hill, then right into a network of streets, Annie looking for the address they had got from the garage.

Finally, Winsome pulled up in front of where the house should have been. The ones around were all detached. Not large, but comfortable enough, with bay windows and garages. The only problem was that where number eleven was supposed to be there was nothing but an empty lot.

They got out of the car, puzzled, and looked at the empty space.

"Help you, love?" said a voice behind them in a slightly nasal Midlands accent.

Annie turned and saw the woman had come out of the house across the street, a gray cardigan wrapped around her shoulders. "Maybe you can," she said, flashing her warrant card and introducing Winsome. "We're looking for a Mr. William Masefield."

"Ah, Mr. Masefield," the woman said. "I'm afraid you're a bit late, love. And so's he. He's dead."

"When?"

"Last August."

"What did he die of? What happened to the house?"

"Burned down."

"There was a fire?"

"Yes. Whole place went up. Lucky it didn't take the rest of the street."

Annie's mind raced. "Did you see it? The fire?"

"No. Gerald and me were in Spain. Go every summer. When we got back it was all over. Just a ruin."

"What caused it?"

"I don't know all the details, love. You'll have to ask the firemen."

"Did Mr. Masefield live alone?"

"Yes. He was a bachelor."

"Did he have any visitors?"

"Not that I saw. Bit of a dark horse. Reclusive."

"What did he look like?"

"About six foot, maybe a bit more. Stooped from bending over all those textbooks at university, I wouldn't be surprised. Going a bit gray."

"What university?"

"He was a lecturer at Warwick."

"What subject?"

"Physics, I think. Or chemistry. Some sort of science, anyway."

"How old was he?"

"Hard to say, really. Early-to-mid-forties, at a guess. Look, why do you want to know all this?"

"Just a case we're working on up north," said Annie. "Thanks, anyway. You've been a great help."

The woman stood there for a moment, until she seemed to realize she'd been dismissed, then she turned, sniffed, and walked back to her house.

"Well," said Annie, looking at Winsome. "I think we'd better get cracking and ask a few questions while we're down here, don't you?"

"Yes, Guv," said Winsome.

Banks wondered what the hell he was doing sitting on a park bench in Camden Town on a gray January afternoon. Nothing but a small triangle of grass, a few scrappy trees, swings and a roundabout and a couple of damp green benches. On the face of it, he was trying to pluck up the courage to visit Sandra, whose house he could see through the bare branches across the street. But why he wanted to see her was beyond him. Yes, Maria Phillips had told him that Sandra had talked to Thomas McMahon often, but it was unlikely she would be able to tell him anything useful about the dead artist. Banks hadn't seen Sandra in over a year, not since she told him she wanted a divorce, in a café not far from the spot where he was sitting. So why now? Was it the baby? Morbid curiosity? And why was it so hard to pluck up the courage?

He stood up and walked toward the gates. This was stupid, he told himself; he might as well head for King's Cross and catch the next train home. He could even phone Michelle. Maybe they could manage a bit more than a quick kiss through the train window. It would be easy to get off at Peterborough if she happened to have the evening free. There was nothing for him here.

Just as he turned the corner toward the tube station, he saw a woman walking toward him, pushing a pram. It was Sandra, no doubt about it. She was still wearing the same artsy granny glasses and short, layered haircut as the last time he saw her, blond hair and black eyebrows. She also wore a long beige raincoat and had a black wool scarf wrapped around her neck.

When she saw him, she stopped. "Alan. What . . . ?"

"I just wanted a word," said Banks, surprised the words came out so easily, with his heart stuck in his throat the way it was.

"I've just been to the shops," Sandra said. Then she leaned forward and adjusted the blanket in the pram. Banks was still facing her and couldn't see inside. She looked up at him again, her expression unreadable, except he sensed some sort of protection, something primal, unconscious, in the way she tended to the child. It was almost, Banks felt, as if he were perceived as a *threat,* as if he were the *enemy*. He felt like saying, "There's nothing to be afraid of. It's only me," but he didn't. Instead, Sandra spoke. Glancing over at the park, she said, "Walk?"

"Fine," said Banks. He stepped aside as she started walking again and fell in beside her. They paused to check the traffic carefully before crossing the road, and Banks sneaked his first glance at baby Sinéad. He almost breathed a sigh of relief to discover that she looked pretty much the same as any other month-old child did: like Winston Churchill. Sandra caught him looking, and he noticed her redden before she pushed the pram forward across the street.

"What is it?" she asked.

"What?"

"You wanted to talk to me."

"Oh, yes. It's nothing, really. Just a case I'm working on. Remember an artist called Thomas McMahon?"

"Tom? Yes, of course. Why?"

"He's dead."

"Dead?"

"Yes, killed in a fire. He was squatting on a barge down on the canal."

"I take it he was murdered, or you wouldn't be here?"

"Looks that way," said Banks.

"Poor Tom. He was harmless. He wouldn't hurt a soul."

"Well, someone hurt him."

"A fire, you said?"

"Yes. Arson. He was unconscious at the time. He wouldn't have . . . you know."

Sandra nodded. Her small, pale nose was a little red at the tip, he noticed, as if she had a cold. "I haven't seen him in five years or more," she said. "I don't know how I can help you."

"I don't know, either," said Banks, sticking his hands in his overcoat pockets. "I'm sorry. Perhaps I shouldn't have come."

They came to a bench and Sandra sat, wheeling the pram close and locking the brake with her foot. Banks sat beside her. He craved a cigarette. It wasn't a sharp, fast, overwhelming urge as he usually felt, but a simple, deep, gnawing need. He tried to ignore it.

"You smell of beer," Sandra said.

"I'm not pissed."

"I didn't say you were."

Banks paused. He'd had a couple of pints with Burgess, true enough. But that was all. And he certainly wasn't going to mention Dirty Dick to Sandra. Red rag to a bull. "Maria Phillips was asking after you," he said.

Sandra shot him an amused glance. "Between trying to get her hands down the front of your trousers."

"How did you guess?"

"She never was a subtle one, was Maria."

"She's rather sweet, really."

Sandra rolled her eyes. "To each his own."

"I didn't mean it like that," Banks rushed on. "I think she's just very insecure underneath it all."

"Oh, please."

"She said you spent a lot of time with Tom."

"And you think she was hinting at an affair?"

"I didn't say that."

"It's obvious in your tone. For your information, not that it matters anymore, but I didn't have any affairs while we were together. Not one."

Sinéad stirred and made a gurgling sound. Sandra leaned forward and did something with the blanket again, then she put her hand to the side of the baby's face, stroked it and smiled, murmuring nonsense words. It was a gesture Banks remembered her making with both Brian and Tracy when they were very young, and it cut him to the quick. He had forgotten all about it, and there it was, a simple maternal gesture with the power to hurt him so. What the hell was going on? he wondered, breath tight in his chest. This baby was nothing to do with him. If anything, it was an insult to the relationship he thought he had with Sandra. It wasn't even a particularly beautiful baby. So why did he feel so excluded, so alone? Why did he care?

"So what can you tell me about McMahon?" Banks asked.

"Tom had a lively mind, wandering hands and low self-esteem," Sandra said.

"Why the low self-esteem?"

"I don't know. Some people are just like that, aren't they?" She rocked the pram gently as she spoke. "Even when he was moderately successful, getting the odd exhibition and managing to sell a painting or two—and I don't mean just the tourist stuff—he still couldn't seem to believe in himself. You know, he once told me he felt more himself imitating other artists than he did doing his own work."

"Oh," said Banks. "Who did he imitate?"

"Just about anyone." Sandra laughed. "He once dashed off a Picasso sketch for me. It took him about five seconds. I don't know if you could have got it by a team of experts but it would have fooled me. Why are you so interested?"

"What about Turner?"

"What about him?"

"Do you think McMahon could have forged Turner sketches and watercolors?"

Sandra swept her hand over her hair. "Do I think he had the talent for it? Yes. Did I ever see him imitate or even hear him mention Turner? No."

"Just a thought," said Banks. "Some have turned up."

"Is this connected with his death?"

"It could be," said Banks.

Sandra shivered and adjusted her scarf.

"Is there anything else?" Banks asked.

"Not that I can think of."

"You didn't know his circle of friends?"

"Didn't know he had one. I only saw him at the gallery. Sometimes we'd have a coffee there together. That's all." Sinéad gurgled again and Sandra leaned over.

"She's a lovely child," Banks said.

Sandra didn't look at him. "Yes."

"Well behaved."

"Yes." Sandra glanced over at her house. "Look, I'd better go," she said. "It's nearly Sinéad's feeding time and . . ." She held her hand out. "I think it's starting to rain."

Banks nodded. "Good-bye, then."

Sandra stood up. "Good bye," she said. "And take care of yourself, Alan."

Banks watched her push the pram down the path as it started to drizzle. She didn't look back.

Chapter 13

"Well, Mark," said Banks, leaning back in his chair and linking his hands behind his head. "Why did you run?"

"How was I to know they were plainclothes coppers? You told me I was in danger, to watch out. That's what I did."

"And what do you have to say about it all now?"

"Just the same as I told those bastards in Scarborough yesterday. The bloke attacked me. I defended myself. What was I supposed to do, let him put his hands all over me?"

Banks scratched the scar beside his right eye. "I still don't know what you're talking about, Mark," he said. "What bloke is this? Who attacked you? Where?"

Mark stared at him. He'd been held overnight at Scarborough for resisting arrest and delivered to Western Area Headquarters that morning. The arresting officer had mentioned some gibberish about an attack and self-defense, but he had no idea what Mark was talking about, either. Nor did he want to know. Enough paperwork on his plate already without picking up Eastvale's leftovers. One thing that did bother Banks was the black eye, split lip and bruising on Mark's cheek. He wondered how "necessary" the force was that the two DCs who arrested him used. And had they announced that they were police officers first? Mark said not.

"You mean you don't know?" Mark asked.

"Know what?"

"The bloke. The poofter. He didn't report it?"

"Nobody reported anything, as far as I know. What are you talking about? Did you get into trouble hitching a lift?"

"Never mind," said Mark. "That's what I thought it was all about, when I found out they were coppers after me. It doesn't matter now. What am I here for this time, then?"

"Know anything about a fire in Jennings Field last Saturday night? Caravan?"

"I don't even know where Jennings Field is."

"You'd have passed close by there on your way east from your friend's house."

"I still don't know. Why are you asking me this?"

"Just seems too much of a coincidence, that's all. Two fires, and you pretty much on the scene of both of them."

"Look, you've already cleared me on the boat fire. Mandy told the truth about where I was, and your blokes tested my clothes. They didn't find anything."

"I know," said Banks. And he also knew that they couldn't test Mark's clothes for traces of accelerant this time because they'd been given to him by Banks himself. Even if the bloody things were soaked in petrol, that wouldn't make a scrap of difference to the Crown Prosecution Service. "But that doesn't let you out of the Jennings Field fire. Or out of killing Thomas McMahon."

"How do you work that out?"

"McMahon was unconscious before the fire. Maybe you drugged him. You certainly seem to be able to lay your hands on any drug you want."

"Why would I do that?"

"I don't know. Maybe he made a move on Tina. He was an artist. Maybe he offered to pay her for posing nude."

"He didn't."

"Only your word."

"He didn't. And I didn't touch him."

"Okay. Did you see anything when you passed Jennings Field on Saturday?"

Mark looked away, watching the workmen on the scaffolding around the church. "I thought I saw a fire," he said. "In the distance. But I wasn't anywhere near it. And I had other things on my mind."

"What time was this?"

"I don't remember. No watch." He turned to face Banks again. "Look, I'd nothing to do with it. You *know* that. Why don't you ask Dr. Patrick fucking Aspern where *he* was? Or is he beyond your reach? A *doctor*."

"Don't worry, Mark. We'll ask whoever we want. Anyway, what reason do you have to think Dr. Aspern had anything to do with the Jennings Field fire?"

"I don't know. But if you think it was the same person set both of them, then I'm saying you should have a good look at him, too."

"We will. Don't worry. Have you got any other suggestions?"

Mark shook his head and looked back out of the window. Banks wrote down a name, address and phone number on a sheet of paper and passed it to him.

"What's this?" Mark asked.

Banks nodded toward the window. "Name of the person in charge of the restoration crew out there," he said. "He's a friend of mine. Drop by the office or give him a call. Tell him I sent you."

Mark glanced back and forth from the men on the scaffolding to Banks. Finally, he folded the sheet of paper, and lacking a pocket in the red overalls he'd been issued, held on to it. "Thanks," he said.

"No problem. And your pal Lenny says it's all right to go back to his place, if you want."

"You talked to Lenny?"

"Yes, I talked to him. His wife is really sorry. She doesn't like surprises, that's all. They'd be glad to have you."

Banks could see doubt cloud Mark's features. He didn't blame the kid. He'd be suspicious himself. Things hadn't worked out especially well for Mark so far this past week or so.

"Up to you," he said. "One more thing."

"What?"

Banks slid the photograph of Roland Gardiner that Annie had got from Alice Mowbray across the desk. "Recognize him?"

Mark studied the photo. "Dunno," he said finally. "It could be one of the blokes I saw visit Tom. He's got the right sort of nose. But . . ."

"Okay," said Banks. He described Leslie Whitaker. "That sound anything like the other bloke?"

Mark shrugged. "Could be," he said. "But again . . ."

"I know," said Banks. "It's vague." He thought he should perhaps organize an identity parade, see if Mark could pick out Whitaker from a group of people who looked a bit like him.

"Can I go now?" Mark asked.

"As far as I'm concerned. Where will you be if I need you?"

"Need me? For what?"

"More questions. There's still a chance you can help us find Tina's killer."

"I'll be at Lenny's," Mark said.

"I take it you're not pressing charges?"

"What?"

"Police brutality."

Mark fingered his bruises and grinned. "The pavement was hard," he said. "I fell." He got up and walked to the door.

"There's a constable outside," said Banks. "He'll take you back down to the custody suite and get you sorted."

"Thanks."

"And, Mark?"

"Yes?"

"When you were arrested you had over two hundred pounds in your pocket, but when you first left here you only had about ten. Where did you get the rest?"

"Found it," said Mark, and nipped out of the door quickly.

There was more to it than that, Banks was convinced, but it didn't concern him now. No doubt there had been a problem with someone who had given him a lift, and Mark had probably nicked his wallet in the scuffle. That the theft hadn't been reported made Banks lean in favor of Mark's garbled explanation that he'd been assaulted by the man, who needed police attention like he needed a hole in the head. Call the two hundred "damages," then, and have done with it.

He watched the restorers at work for a few moments, thinking about the kind of life Mark had been living at home, in the squat and on the boat, and what the future might hold for him. It had to be better than the past. His phone rang.

"Alan, it's Ken Blackstone."

"Good to hear from you. Any news on the doctor?"

"Nothing you'd be interested in hearing, I'm afraid. Clean bill of health, even down to the scrupulously up-to-date shotgun certificate."

"He's got a shotgun?"

"Likes to shoot small winged creatures with like-minded people."

"It takes all sorts. No rumors, gossip?"

"No. Seems he's a capable doctor. Not much of a bedside manner. Some described him as a bit of a cold fish. There was just one little thing."

"What's that?" Banks asked.

"One of the neighbors saw a black woman coming out of his house carrying a plastic bag on Monday morning. She thought it might be drugs."

Banks laughed. "That would have been our very own DC

Winsome Jackman with Dr. Aspern's clothing for testing. Which came out negative, as expected, by the way."

"Well, at least he's been getting wind there's something going on," Blackstone said. "Already put a complaint in to Weetwood about harassment, and he gave one of his neighbors a right chewing out after he saw her talking to one of our men."

"Good," said Banks. "Let's hope it keeps him off balance."

"Have you thought, Alan, that maybe he hasn't actually done anything?"

"There's something there. Trust me."

"Instinct?"

"Call it what you will: body language, unspoken communication, but there's something there. The girl was screwed up, and why should she lie to Mark?"

"Junkies lie habitually. You know that as well as I do. And maybe the boyfriend has his own reasons for believing her."

"I've thought of that. We did a background check on him, and it's true he had it rough at home. I still think there's something going on, though. And if I get any proof, I'll have the bastard."

"The fires?"

"Possible. But I don't think so. He did something to Tina, though. I'm certain of it."

"Well, best of luck, mate. Want me to keep trying?"

"No, it's okay. Thanks, Ken."

"Cheers. And don't forget, if you're down in my neck of the woods, that sofa's always there for you."

"I won't forget."

Banks stood at his window after the phone call thinking and looking out at the people in raincoats down in the market square. He was certain that Dr. Patrick Aspern had sexually abused his stepdaughter, and that his wife knew about it. But he had no proof. Nor did he seem to have much hope of getting any now that Tina was dead. Her death was convenient for Aspern, but Banks was almost certain he hadn't started the fire on the boats. That had something to do with Thomas McMahon, he was convinced of it. Tina was incidental, maybe an unwanted witness. Which made the killer an especially nasty piece of work.

Thoughts of McMahon brought Banks back to Phil Keane and his little lie. He would have to contrive to have a chat with Phil without Annie around. He knew exactly how she would behave if she thought he was trying to dig up some dirt on her precious Phil. And maybe she would be right; maybe Maria Phillips's version was exaggerated or even untrue. But until he knew for certain one way or another, he would distance himself from Phil and Annie, do a bit of discreet digging and wait to hear from Dirty Dick.

It felt good to be wearing his own clothes again, Mark thought, as he headed out of Western Area Headquarters for the second time in a week. The old leather jacket felt like a second skin. And it was good to be free again. His face and body still ached from the beating the Scarborough cops had given him, for "resisting arrest," but, just as he had suspected, Clive hadn't reported the hitchhiking incident, and the police had no reason to keep him in custody.

And he still had over two hundred quid in his pocket.

Mark crossed the market square, anonymous among the crowd of shoppers and the occasional out-of-season tourist. He hadn't a clue where to go, but he knew he wasn't going back to Lenny's, no matter what he'd told Banks. That had been a mistake in the first place. Lenny was a decent bloke, but he had enough on his plate without bringing Mark home. Sure, maybe they did both feel all guilty right now after upsetting him, but that would soon wear off. He knew he wouldn't be able to bear Sal's silent resentment of his presence. And when he thought about it, he realized that, if it wasn't Clive, then it must have been Lenny who'd set the cops on him. He wouldn't have expected that from him, but there it was. Did Lenny believe he'd started the fires, too? No matter, he wouldn't be seeing Lenny or his bitch of a wife again.

Across the square, he turned left for a short way on York Road and went into the Swainsdale Centre. When he was at Eastvale Comprehensive and wanted to put off going home after school, he had often hung around the center with his mates, not doing anything, just loitering and smoking, sometimes looking in Dixon's windows at the fancy computers and stereos he couldn't afford. Well, there had been an occasional bit of shoplifting, he remembered, but that was as bad as the gang got. Sometimes, too, he had spent the day there instead of going to school at all.

The center wasn't very busy; it never was on a Wednesday morning. Just a few young women pushing prams, and kids skiving off school, the way Mark had done. On the upper level, at the top of the escalator opposite HMV, was a food court, and Mark bought himself a Big Mac, fries and a Coke and sat at one of the Formica-topped tables to eat. There was something about a shopping center that numbed your brain, Mark thought. Something to do with the weird lighting and the barely audible music. Maybe it hypnotized you into buying things. Well, there was nothing Mark wanted, except maybe a new CD. He'd grown tired of *Ziggy Stardust* over the past few days, and it was the only one he had left. Maybe he'd get something by Beth Orton in memory of Tina. He'd probably need new batteries soon, so he might as well pick some up in Dixon's.

As he sat there munching on his Big Mac, lulled by the bland ambience of the Swainsdale Centre, watching the people who seemed to float around him as insubstantial as ghosts or shadows to the faint, pale music of an orchestral version of "Eleanor Rigby," Mark mulled over the past few days. The fire had occurred on Thursday night, and it was now the following Wednesday. Had it really only been such a short time since Tina had died and Mark had had his adventures on the road? He'd also been assaulted by a queer, been in and out of jail twice, beaten up by the police and spent the most luxurious evening of his life in a B and B in Helmsley. And there was still a chance that someone out there was after him, wanted him dead.

It was hard to think with his brain so numb, but there was something very wrong with the picture he was seeing. What did he think he was trying to achieve? Did he have any control over his life at all? He'd run away from Lenny's more because of echoes of his past than anything else, but had it all happened because he'd been trying to force himself in the wrong direction in the first place?

He had been thinking about putting his life back together. Getting back to work on the building site. Living with Lenny and Sal. Making things normal again. But could they ever be normal again? When he thought about it, he really didn't think so. And what on earth did he think he was up to, running off to Scarborough? It was the same thing, when you got right down to it. A new start. A job. A place to live. The normal life.

But with Tina gone, nothing could ever be normal again. He felt that as he sat there in the Swainsdale Centre staring into space.

And all the things he had been aiming for, trying to do—the job, Lenny's, Scarborough—they weren't *meant* to be. That was clear now. They weren't meant to be because there was somewhere he had to go before he could get his own life sorted. Something he had to do. For Tina.

In the Queen's Arms that lunchtime, Banks, Annie and Winsome managed to bag a corner table near the window. As usual, one or two heads turned at the sight of Winsome, but Banks could tell she was used to it. She had a model's carriage and managed to handle all the attention with mild amusement and disdain.

"Lunch is on me," Banks said.

Annie raised her eyebrows. "Last of the big spenders." She looked at Winsome, who smiled, but Banks sensed less humor in the remark than Winsome had. Annie was still pissed off with him over Phil, even though she'd got her way in the end.

Banks wasn't very hungry, but he ordered chicken in a basket anyway, while Annie went for a salad and Winsome for a beefburger and chips. That settled, drinks in front of them, they got down to business, and Annie first told Banks about the visit to "Captain" Kirk's garage and the trail leading to the mysterious William Masefield in Studley.

"And there's no doubt this Masefield is dead?" Banks asked, after he'd digested what she had told him.

Annie glanced at Winsome. "None at all," she said. "We checked with the pathologist who conducted the post-mortem. Getting hold of him was one of the reasons it took us so long down there. We had to stay over. He couldn't see us until early this morning. Anyway, Masefield had no living relatives, so DNA was useless, but he was identified by dental records."

"So someone stole his identity?"

"Looks that way," Annie said. "And whoever did it simply had Masefield's post redirected."

"Where to?"

"A post office box in central Birmingham."

"I see," said Banks. "And the credit card company had no way of knowing about this?"

Annie shook her head. "All they cared about was that the bills were paid on time. It's a common-enough form of identity fraud."

"He used a bank account in Masefield's name?"

"Yes. And he paid all his bills from Masefield's bank account over the Internet, so no signed checks. There'll be a trail, but these things are complicated."

"We'll get computers on it," said Banks. "Why did no one in the post office spot what was going on?"

"Why should they?" said Annie. "Whoever arranged for the redirected post went to a busy central office, presented the right sort of identification and signed the forms. Whoever it was must have resembled Masefield enough and been able to forge his signature. Easy. And all aboveboard, as far as the post office was concerned. I mean, they're careful, they have their precautions, but the whole thing's pretty routine. Most clerks probably don't even examine the documentation closely."

"Are we certain it's the same car?"

"Well," said Annie, "the tire impressions are identical to those found on the lay-by near the boats. The SOCOs also managed to find a few soil and gravel samples, and they've gone to the lab for further analysis."

"Good."

"But there is one small problem."

"Oh?"

"The petrol in the Cherokee's tank matches the petrol from the garage—it's Texaco, by the way—but *not* the petrol used to start the Gardiner fire. That's Esso."

"Interesting," said Banks. "Maybe he used his own car, for some reason?"

"I suppose that's possible," Annie agreed.

"Anyway, whatever the explanation, forensics can tie the Jeep Cherokee that this 'Masefield' rented to the scene of the boat fires, right?"

"Yes."

"Thank heaven for small mercies. We're still in business, then."

Jenna, the young girl who worked in the kitchen, brought their food. Winsome was the only one who ate with a vengeance. Banks glanced at her. "I hope you didn't run up your expenses too high in the hotel restaurant last night," he said.

"No, sir," said Winsome. "We ate at McDonald's."

Banks looked at Annie. "It's true," she said. "And you can imagine what delights they had for a vegetarian like me. I told you we were busy. All we had time for before bed was a couple of drinks in the hotel bar."

"And those two good-looking businessmen bought us the second round, didn't they, Guv?" Winsome added.

"Yes," said Annie. "Connor and Marcus. So you needn't worry about our expenses, skinflint." She picked at her salad.

"It's ACC McLaughlin gets his underpants in a knot over things like that," Banks said. "Not me. Did you find out anything else about Masefield while you were down there?"

Annie and Winsome exchanged glances and Annie said, "A few things. We asked around about him—neighbors, co-workers at the university—but nobody seemed to know very much."

"And the fire?"

"Chip pan. There was no accelerant and no reason to treat it as suspicious at the time. The only thing even remotely interesting was that one of the other lecturers at the university where Masefield worked said he'd recently lost some money in a bad investment. I also got the impression that he was in a bit of trouble at the university over his drinking, that he might have stood to lose his job. But you know what academics are like when it comes to giving out information."

"A bit like us," Banks said.

"Anyway, there was a lot of alcohol in his system. The general assumption in the fire investigator's office was that he'd passed out and left the chip pan on. It happens often enough, especially with alcoholics and drug addicts. You come home pissed or high, put the frying pan on, pop another couple of pills or take another stiff drink, and the next thing you know . . ."

"No traces of Rohypnol or Tuinal?"

"No. Just alcohol."

"So it could have been an accident?"

"Yes."

"And someone, a colleague, friend, whatever, could have taken advantage of Masefield's demise and stolen his identity?"

"Or helped him along a bit. I mean, nobody saw anyone, but that doesn't mean whoever did it didn't leave Masefield passed out on the sofa with the chip pan on full heat."

"True," Banks agreed. "Did anyone have any ideas at all about exactly who might have taken Masefield's identity?"

"Unfortunately not," said Annie. "Nobody knew who he hung around with, if anyone. Apparently, he wasn't the gregarious type. If he did have any friends, he kept them a secret from his colleagues and neighbors."

"What about this bad investment? Who did he make it with? Was he swindled?"

"Don't know, sir," said Winsome. "That was all his colleague could tell us."

Banks sighed. He knew they could get a forensic accountant to look into Masefield's finances and a computer expert to track down the Internet banking records, but that would all take time. There would no doubt be all kinds of false trails and blind alleys. As it stood right now, they still didn't have very much to go on. The first big lead, the rented Jeep Cherokee, had led them to a dead end. Or so it seemed at the moment.

"How did 'Masefield' get to Kirk's garage?" Banks asked.

"I assume he took a bus," said Annie. "They run in a constant loop from Askham Bar to the city center."

"So he traveled to York by train?"

"Or by bus."

"What if he didn't?" Winsome said.

"Didn't what?" Banks asked.

"Take a train or a bus, sir. Maybe he's local. What if he *drove* to the garage? I mean, if he only wanted to use a rental car so that his own car wasn't spotted by the canal, or by Jennings Field, for whatever reason, then he probably has a car of his own, too."

"Well," said Annie, "there are plenty of residential streets around there where he could leave a car for a few days without attracting too much attention."

"Except he might have got unlucky," Winsome said.

"The Son of Sam," Banks said.

Winsome smiled. "Yes, sir."

"A parking ticket?" Annie said. "Isn't that how the Son of Sam got caught?"

"Yes," said Winsome. "It's possible, isn't it, Guv?"

"It would certainly be a lucky break for us," Annie said.

"It'll probably take a day or two," Banks said, "but it's worth checking. Can you get the numbers of all cars ticketed in the area on the dates in question and feed them into HOLMES, see if anything comes up?"

"Can do," said Winsome. "We don't exactly have a lot of number plates to cross-reference on this one, but I'll see what I can do. There might be something on the CCTV cameras, too. They're all over the place these days."

"Good," said Banks. "Definitely worth checking." He finished his chicken and left the chips, then drank some beer and leaned back in his chair. "This still doesn't let Whitaker off the hook," he said. "Even though it seems now that it wasn't his Jeep Cherokee at the scene of the boat fires."

"We'll check the petrol in his car against the accelerant used at the Gardiner scene. That might tell us something. And if we can dig out any connection, however remote, between Whitaker and Masefield . . ."

"Maybe," said Banks. "Anything new on those Turners?" he asked Annie, as casually as he could manage.

Her tone hardened. Pure professional. "Phil couldn't say at first glance for certain whether they were forged or genuine," she said. "Not without a more comprehensive examination. But he did say they *looked* genuine, the style and the paper, that sort of thing."

"Which means they could be very good forgeries?"

"Yes," Annie agreed.

"I've heard that McMahon was a good copyist," Banks said. "Apparently he didn't have much original talent, but he did have a gift for reproducing the work of others."

"Where did you find this out?" Annie asked.

"From someone who knew him," Banks said.

"What next?"

"I'm going to Leeds."

"What for?"

"I want to visit Tina's grandparents. I rang them earlier, and they agreed to talk to me. They might be able to tell me something about Tina's relationship with Patrick Aspern."

"Surely you don't think they *knew* what was going on, and that even if they did they'll tell you?"

"Give me some credit. I'm not that stupid, Annie. I just want to sound out their feelings, that's all."

Annie shrugged.

"What?" said Banks.

"Nothing."

"Come on. Out with it."

"It's just that I'm not sure the girl has anything to do with all this."

"What do you mean by that?"

"Aspern's clothes came out clean, didn't they?"

"Yes," said Banks. "That's the problem. So did everybody else's."

"To be honest, Guv," Winsome said, "he could have given

me any old clothes. I don't know what he was wearing that night."

Annie gave Banks a hard look. "We don't have any evidence against Patrick Aspern at all," she said. "I think you're going off on some sort of personal crusade against the man."

"So all of a sudden you're SIO on this case, are you?" Banks shot back.

Annie's mouth closed to a tight, white line. Winsome looked away, embarrassed. Banks wondered if Annie had told her all about the row they'd had over Phil Keane's involvement in the case. Maybe after a couple of drinks in the hotel bar last night.

He immediately regretted his sarcastic remark, but it was too late to take it back. Instead, he bade Annie and Winsome a curt good-bye and left the pub.

One thing Banks hadn't told Annie was that he was intending to stop off at Phil Keane's cottage on his way to Leeds. Well, it wasn't exactly on his way, but he thought it was worth the diversion.

Puddles from yesterday's rain spread out from the gutters and sent up sheets of spray as Banks drove just a little too fast into Fortford. Still annoyed with himself for his outburst over lunch, he parked on the cobbles in front of the shops by the village green and headed toward the cottage. Maybe Annie was right and he *was* on some sort of personal crusade against Patrick Aspern. But so what? Someone had to bring the arrogant bastard down.

Across the street, on top of a grassy mound, stood the excavated ruins of a Roman fort. What a bitter, lonely and dangerous outpost it must have been back in Emperor Domitian's time, Banks thought. Wild country all around and enemies everywhere.

It was another mild day, vague haze in the air, and perhaps a hint of more rain to come. Banks had no idea whether Keane would be at home or not, but it was worth a try. The silver BMW parked in the narrow drive beside the cottage was a good sign. It was 51 registration, Banks noticed, which meant that it had been registered with the Driver and Vehicle Licensing Agency—the DVLA—between September 2001 and February 2002. A pretty recent model, then, and not inexpensive. How much exactly did an art researcher make?

Banks's knock on the front door was answered seconds later by Phil Keane himself, looking every inch the twenty-first-century country squire in faded Levi's and a rust-colored Swaledale sweater.

"Alan," he said, opening the door wide. "Good to see you. Come on in."

Banks entered. The ceilings were low and the walls rough-painted limestone with nooks and crannies here and there, each filled with delicate little statuettes and ivory carvings: elephants, human figures, cats.

"Nice," said Banks.

"Thank you. The place has been in my family for generations," Keane said. "Even though I only remember occasional visits to my grandparents here when I was a child—I grew up down south, for my sins—I couldn't bear the thought of losing it when they died. Most of the knickknacks were theirs. Do sit down. Can I get you a drink or anything?"

"Nothing, thank you," said Banks. "It's only a flying visit."

Keane sat on the arm of the sofa. "Yes? Is it about the Turners? If indeed they are by Turner."

"Indirectly," said Banks. "By the way, our fingerprints expert has finished with them, so you'll be able to carry out further testing."

"Excellent. Did he find anything?"

"Not much. Do you want to pick them up, or should I have them sent to your London office?"

"I'll pick them up at the police station tomorrow morning and take them down myself, if that's okay?"

"As long as you're not worried about being hijacked."

"Nobody but you and me would know what I was carrying, would they?"

"I suppose not," said Banks. "Look, in your opinion, would it be very difficult to forge such a work?"

"As I told Annie," Keane said, "the actual forging would be easy enough for an artist who had the talent for such things. Turner isn't easy to imitate—his brush strokes are difficult, for example—but he's not impossible, as long as the artist got hold of the correct paper and painting materials, which isn't too hard, if you know how. Tom Keating claimed to have dashed off twenty or so Turner watercolors. The problem is the provenance."

"And you can't fake that?"

"It can be done. A man called John Drewe did so a few years ago, caused quite a furor in the art world. You might have heard of him. He even got into the Tate archives and doctored catalogs. But they've tightened up a lot since then. The last owner is your real problem. I mean, it's easy enough to fake who owned paintings years ago—there's no one to question it, as they're dead. But the last owner is usually alive."

"I see," said Banks. "So you'd need an accomplice?"

"At least one."

"Anyway," Banks went on, "as I said, my visit is only indirectly related to the Turners. It's actually the artist himself, Thomas McMahon, I wanted to talk to you about."

"Oh?"

"You told me you didn't know him."

"No, I don't. Neither him nor his work."

"Yet someone told me you were seen in conversation with him at the Turner reception last July."

Keane frowned. "I talked to a number of people there. That's where I first met Annie, too, as a matter of fact."

"Yes, I know that," said Banks. "But what about McMahon?"

"I'm sorry. I still can't place him."

"Short, burly sort of fellow, didn't shave often, longish greasy brown hair. Bit of a scruff. He'd been drinking."

"Ah," said Keane. "You mean the chap with rather disagreeable BO?"

McMahon had smelled of burned flesh the only time Banks had been close to him. "Do I?" he said. "I can't say I ever smelled him. Not when he was alive."

"Artist. A bit pissed, if I remember right."

"So you did know him?"

"No. I hadn't a clue who he was." Keane spread his hands. "But if you say he was Thomas McMahon, then I'm sure you're right."

"But you talked to him?"

"Just the once, yes."

"What did you talk about?"

"He was a bit intense. I do recall that. I think we just chatted about some of the paintings on the walls. He thought they were pretty dreadful. I actually quite liked one or two of them. And—yes, now I remember—he made some disparaging remarks about Turner, said he could easily dash off the other missing Yorkshire watercolor."

"The one we've just been talking about?"

"The very same."

"And you've only just remembered this?"

"Yes. Well, since you jogged my memory. Why? Is it important?"

"It could be. So you had an argument with McMahon?"

Keane smiled, and a bit of an edge came into his tone. "I wouldn't exactly call it an argument, just an artistic disagreement. Look, what are you getting at? What is all this about?"

"Probably nothing, really," said Banks, standing and heading over to the door. "I'm sorry to waste your time."

Keane's tone softened again when he noticed Banks was leaving. "Oh, that's all right. I'm just sorry I can't help you. Look, are you sure you won't have one for the road? Or is that against police regulations?"

Banks laughed. "I can't say that's ever stopped me before, but not this time, thanks very much," he said. "I'll be on my way. If you do remember anything else about that conversation, you'll be sure to let me know, won't you?"

"Of course."

Banks paused at the open door. "Just one more thing."

"Yes?"

"We're putting together an identity parade, and you're the same general build and coloring as the suspect. Seeing as you're practically one of the team, would you consider helping us out and being an extra?"

"How exciting," said Keane. "I've never been in an identity parade before. Of course. I'd be only too happy to help."

"Good," said Banks. "Thank you. I'll be in touch. Bye for now, then."

Chapter 14

*B*anks pondered over Phil Keane's response to his visit and his questions as he drove down to Leeds that afternoon. Quite often, he knew, it wasn't so much what a person *said* that was revealing, it was what he didn't say, the way he said something, or the body language he was unconsciously displaying at the time he said it. No matter how often he ran over it in his mind, though, Banks couldn't fault Keane's performance. Even the hint of irritation at being questioned was reasonable, realistic. He'd have felt the same way himself.

But there was something that niggled away at him. It wasn't until the roundabout at the Leeds ring road that Banks realized what it was. Keane's performance had been just that: a *performance*. He was anxious to know if Burgess had been able to dig anything up, but decided he'd leave it until the morning. If he hadn't heard by then, he'd phone Scotland Yard.

For the moment, though, he had a rather difficult interview with Tina's grandparents, the Redferns, to concentrate on. He found their house easily enough, a large bay-window semi on a quiet, tree-lined Roundhay street, and parked outside.

"Mr. Banks," said the matronly woman who answered the

door, "we've been expecting you. Please come in. I'm Julia Redfern. Let me take your coat."

Banks gave her his car coat, which she put on a hanger in the hall cupboard. The house smelled of apples and cinnamon. Mrs. Redfern led him into the kitchen, where the smell was even stronger. "I hope you don't mind if we talk in here," she said. "The study and the sitting room are just too formal. I always think the kitchen is the real heart of a house, don't you?"

Banks agreed. Though he spent most of his time in his living room reading, watching television or listening to music, he loved his own kitchen. In fact, the kitchen was the main reason he had bought the cottage in the first place, having dreamed about it before he saw it. The Redferns' kitchen was much larger than his, though, done out in rustic style, with a heavy wood dining table and four hard-backed chairs. French doors, closed at the moment, led out to a small conservatory. Banks sat down.

"Besides," Mrs. Redfern went on, "the pie should be ready. I'll just take it out and let it cool a minute."

"I thought I could smell something good," said Banks.

"I always like to do something a bit special when we have company," Mrs. Redfern said, taking the apple pie out of the oven and setting it on a rack. The crust was golden and flaky. There was something surreal about the whole scene, Banks was beginning to feel: rustic kitchens, cooking smells, apple pie fresh from the oven. It was a far cry from Mark's and Tina's world. He wondered if Mrs. Redfern felt that she needed some sort of activity to take her mind off his impending visit, or to calm her nerves.

Dr. Redfern strode in. He looked fit and energetic despite being in his seventies, and he still had a full head of silver hair. His handshake was firm. Banks wondered if he had been a good doctor. "Maurice Redfern," he said. "Pleased to meet you." Then he sat opposite Banks.

"First of all," Banks said, "I just want you to know that I'm very sorry about what happened to your granddaughter, and that we're doing our best to find out who did it."

"I don't see how we can help you," said Dr. Redfern, "but we'll do as much as we can, of course."

His wife fussed over tea, then set the pot and three cups and saucers down on the table and cut them each a slice of apple pie. "Some cream with your pie?" she asked Banks. "Or a slice of Cheddar, perhaps?"

"No, thanks. It looks fine as it is."

"Milk and sugar?" she asked, tapping the teapot.

"Just as it comes, please," said Banks. She poured and sat down. She seemed on edge, Banks thought, unable to keep still. Perhaps it was just her nature. Banks sipped some tea. It was strong, the way he liked it. Sandra always used to say he could stand a spoon up in his tea. She preferred hers weak, with milk and two sugars. In his mind's eye, he saw her walking away from him in the rain, pushing the pram. "I'm just after some background, really," he said. "You'd be surprised how helpful little things can be, and you don't know what they are until you find them. Rather like a doctor's diagnosis, I suppose?"

"Indeed," said Maurice Redfern. "Very well. Go ahead, then."

"Were you close to your granddaughter?" Banks asked.

The Redferns exchanged glances. Finally, Maurice answered. "Christine lived here with us until she was five years old," he said slowly. "After that, she was a frequent visitor, and sometimes she even stayed with us for longer periods. We'd look after her if her parents took a short holiday, that sort of thing."

It was a very evasive answer, Banks thought. But maybe his question was too difficult, or too painful, for the Redferns to answer. "Did she confide in you about things?"

"She was a quiet child. A dreamer. I don't know that she ever confided in anyone."

"What about when she got older? Did you remain close?"

"Do you have any children of your own, Mr. Banks?" Julia Redfern asked.

"Two," Banks said. "A boy and a girl."

"Grandchildren?"

"Not yet."

"Of course not," she said. "You're far too young. But you'll know what I mean when I tell you how relationships change when children become teenagers."

"You didn't see as much of her?"

"Exactly. The last thing a teenage girl wants to do is come and visit old grandma and grandad."

"Boys, too," said Banks. "I was the same, myself." Banks's grandparents had all lived in London, so he hadn't seen them that often, but he remembered endless rainy train rides with his parents and his brother Roy, remembered the old Hornby clockwork train set his grandad Banks kept for him to play with in the spare room, the old war souvenirs in the attic—a tin hat, a shell casing and a gas mask—and the rabbit hutches in the big back garden of his grandad Peyton's house, facing the railway tracks, the long trains rumbling by in the night, through his sleep. All four grandparents were dead by the time he was seventeen, and he was sorry he hadn't had a chance to know them better. Both his grandfathers had fought in the First World War, and he wished he'd asked them about their experiences. But back when he was a kid, he hadn't cared so much. Now the subject interested him. He hoped that if Brian or Tracy had kids it wouldn't be so far in the future that he was a useless old man. "But you did see her on occasion, didn't you?" he asked.

"Oh, yes," Maurice Redfern answered. "But she was uncommunicative."

"Did you ever suspect there was anything wrong?"

The muscles on Maurice's face seemed to tighten. "Wrong? In what way?"

"Did you suspect drug use, for example? It's not uncommon among teenagers."

"I never saw any evidence of it."

"Was she happy?"

"What an odd question," Maurice said. "I suppose so. I mean she never said, either way. She was very much in her own world. I assumed it was a benign place. Now it appears that perhaps I was wrong."

"Oh? Why is that?"

"You'd hardly be here asking all these questions otherwise, would you?"

"Dr. Redfern, I'm sorry if I appear to be prying into private family history, but this is a murder investigation. If you know anything at all about your granddaughter's state of mind prior to her death, then you should realize it might be important information."

"We don't know anything," said Julia. "We were just a normal family."

"Let's go back a bit," said Banks. "How old was Christine's mother when she got pregnant?"

"Sixteen," said Maurice.

"Was she a wild child?"

He thought for a moment, fingertip touching his lips, then said, "No, I wouldn't say that, would you, dear?"

"Not at all," Julia agreed. "Just foolish. And ignorant. It only takes once, you know."

"And the father was an American student?"

"Apparently so," said Dr. Redfern. "He soon disappeared from the scene, whoever he was."

"What kind of a mother was Frances?"

"She did her best," said Julia. "It was difficult, her being so young and all, but she tried. She did love little Christine."

"Was Dr. Aspern on the scene then?"

"I've known Patrick Aspern for nearly thirty years," said Dr. Redfern. "He was my junior at the infirmary, and we even practiced together in Alwoodley for a period."

"So you were his mentor?"

"In a way. His friend, too, I hope."

"How did you feel about Dr. Aspern's interest in your daughter?"

"We were pleased for both of them."

"How early did you notice it?"

"What do you mean?"

"I assume Patrick Aspern was around the house a lot. Did he seem interested in Frances *before* she had Christine?"

"Don't be absurd," said Maurice. "She would have been under sixteen then. He knew her, of course, had done almost since the day she was born. But Frances was twenty-one when they got married, well above the age of consent. There was nothing untoward or unhealthy about it at all. Besides, an older man can bring a bit more stability and experience to raising a family. Frances needed that."

"So your daughter was grateful for Patrick Aspern's interest in her?"

"I wouldn't say 'grateful' is the right word to use," Maurice argued.

"But his interest was reciprocated?"

"Of course. What do you think it was, an arranged marriage? Do you think we forced Frances into it?"

"What are you getting at, Mr. Banks?" asked Julia. "What's this got to do with Christine's death?"

"How long were they courting?" Banks asked her. "These things don't happen overnight."

"You have to remember," Julia explained, "that there was Christine to think about. Always. It was hard for Frances to lead a normal life, make friends and go out with boys like other girls her age. She didn't get out very often, so she had no chance to meet boys. Patrick took her out a few times, while we looked after Christine. Just to the pictures, that sort of thing. More as a favor, really, to get her out of the house for a while. Sometimes he'd take the two of them to the country for a day out. Whitby, or Malham. Somewhere like that."

"Weren't you worried?"

"About what?"

"That they might be up to something."

"Why should we be?" said Maurice. "Patrick was my closest and dearest friend. I trusted him implicitly."

"But didn't it bother you, him being so much older than Frances? Weren't you concerned that he might take advantage of her?"

An edge of irritation entered Maurice Redfern's tone. "Not at all," he said. "Why would we be concerned? Frances was twenty and Patrick was in his thirties when they first started 'stepping out' together. She was a very attractive young woman, and he was a dashing, handsome, talented doctor with a great future. What could be wrong with that? Why should we object or feel concern? We'd almost despaired of Frances finding anyone, and then . . . this happened. It was perfect. A miracle. An occasion for joy. Two of the people I loved most in the world finding one another. I couldn't have wished for a better match."

So that was it, Banks realized. The reason for all the edginess and embarrassment he had sensed. The Redferns had wanted to get Frances married off, and baby Christine had been an impediment to that. They were the ones who were grateful for Patrick's interest in their daughter. After all, not many young men are willing to take on a young woman *and* a baby, especially if that baby isn't his own. When the good Dr. Aspern took both Frances and the child as well, it would have been easy for the Redferns to turn a blind eye to any number of things. Perhaps they had even encouraged him, left the two alone together, offered to baby-sit? But to what, exactly, had they turned a blind eye?

"What was their relationship like?" Banks asked.

"Perfectly aboveboard," said Julia Redfern. "There was no

hanky-panky. Not in this house. And, take my word for it, we'd have known."

"Were they affectionate? Demonstrative?"

"They weren't always touching and feeling each other like some of the kids today," said Julia. "It's disgusting, if you ask me. You should keep that sort of thing for private."

"And they didn't get much privacy?"

"I suppose not," she said. "It was difficult."

"We were just happy that Patrick took an interest in her," Maurice added. "He brought her out of her shell. It had been a difficult few years. Christine wasn't always the easiest child to deal with, and Frances was becoming withdrawn, old before her time."

"Christine was five when Patrick and Frances married?"

"Yes."

"How did he take to fatherhood?"

"He was very good with her, wasn't he, darling?" Julia said.

"Yes, very," Maurice agreed.

Well, what had Banks expected? That they'd suddenly come out and tell him that the pure and holy Patrick Aspern was a daughter-diddling pedophile? But the portrait of utter mind-numbing ordinariness that they were painting just didn't ring true. Had they suspected something and tried to ignore it? People did that often enough, Banks knew. Or were they really blissfully, willfully ignorant of Aspern's sexual interest in Tina? And when did that start? When she was six, seven, eight, nine, ten? Or before? Had he been interested in Frances when she was a child, too? He wished he could find out, but he couldn't think of a direct way of getting an answer to these questions. He would have to see if he could get there indirectly.

"Did the marriage have any effect on Christine?" he asked.

"Well, it gave her a father," said Maurice. "I'd say that's pretty important for a child, wouldn't you? No matter what some of these special interest groups say."

"Did she behave any differently after the marriage?"

"We weren't with her so much, so we wouldn't know. They had their own house by then, out Lawnswood way, not far from where they are now. I'm sure she had her problems adjusting to a new routine, though, as we all do."

"When they brought Christine to visit, did she seem the same as usual?"

"Yes," said Maurice. "Until . . ."

"Until when?"

"What I told you earlier. Until she became a teenager."

"Then she became uncommunicative?"

"Somewhat, yes. Rather quiet and brooding. Sullen. She could be quite snappy, too, if you pushed her on anything. Hormones."

Or Patrick Aspern, Banks thought. So he had his answer. It had started, in all likelihood, when she hit puberty. What's a cut-off point for some pedophiles is the starting point for others.

"Did you see her after she left home?"

The Redferns looked at each other, and Julia nodded. "She came here once," she said, close to tears. "Maurice was out. Oh, she looked terrible, Mr. Banks. My heart just . . ." She shook her head and grabbed a tissue from the box on the window ledge. "It just went out to her, I'm sorry," she said. "It was just so upsetting."

"In what way did she look terrible?"

"She was so thin and pale. Her nose was running constantly. Her face was spotty, her skin terrible. Dry and blotched. She used to be such a pretty young thing. And I hate to say it, but her clothes were filthy and . . . she *smelled*."

"When was this?"

"Shortly after she'd left. About a year ago."

When they were living in the Leeds squat, before the boat, perhaps even before Mark. "What did she come for?"

"She wanted money."

"Did you give her any?"

She looked at her husband. "Fifty pounds. It was all I had in my purse."

"Did she say anything?"

"Not much. I tried to persuade her to go back to Patrick and Frances. They were beside themselves with worry, of course."

"What did she say to that?"

"She said she wasn't going back. Not ever. She was quite emotional about it."

"Did she say why?"

"Why what?"

"Why she wasn't going back. Why she left."

"No, she just got very upset when I mentioned the subject and refused to talk about it."

"Why did you *think* she left?"

"I thought it must be something to do with a boy."

"A boy? Why? Did Patrick Aspern say that?"

"No . . . I . . . I just assumed. She was the same age as her mother was when she . . . I don't know. It's a difficult age for young girls. They want to be all grown up, but they don't have the experience. They lose their hearts to some no-good layabout, and the next thing you know, they're pregnant."

"Like Frances?"

"Yes."

"So you saw history repeating itself?"

"I suppose so."

"Did you ask your daughter or her husband why Christine left home at sixteen?" Banks persisted.

Julia put her hands to her ears. "Please stop! Make him stop, Maurice."

"It's all right, Mrs. Redfern," said Banks. "I'm not here to badger you. I'll slow down. Let's all just take a minute and relax. Take a deep breath." He finished his tea. It was lukewarm.

"As you can see, Mr. Banks," Maurice said, "this is all very upsetting, and I can't see what any of it has to do with Christine's unfortunate death. Perhaps you'd better leave."

"Murder's an upsetting business, Dr. Redfern, and I haven't finished yet."

"But my wife . . ."

"Your wife is emotional, I can see that. What I'd really like to know is why."

"I'd have thought that was quite obvious."

"Not to me it isn't."

"You coming here and—"

"I don't believe that's the reason, and I don't think you do, either."

"What are you getting at, man?"

Banks took a deep breath. Here goes, he thought. "There have been serious allegations that Patrick Aspern had been sexually abusing his stepdaughter, probably since puberty."

Maurice Redfern shot to his feet. "Are you insane? Patrick? What allegations? Who made them?"

"Christine told her boyfriend, Mark Siddons, that that was partly why she started using drugs, drugs she got from her stepfather's surgery, to escape the shame and the pain. He also suggested that Patrick Aspern later let her have the drugs in return for her silence, and perhaps for her sexual favors."

"I don't believe it," said Maurice, sinking back into his chair, pale. "Not Patrick. I *won't* believe it."

"So that's what she meant," Julia Redfern said, in a voice hardly louder than a whisper.

"What?" said Banks. "What did she say?"

"Just that I was better off not knowing, that's all. And that I wouldn't believe her, never in a million years, she said, even if she told me. And that *look* on her face." She turned to her husband, tears welling up in her eyes again. "Oh, my God, Maurice, what have we done?"

"Get a grip on yourself, Julia," said Maurice. "It's all lies. Lies made up by some drug-addled boy. We've done nothing to be ashamed of. Our daughter married a good man, and now someone's trying to blacken his character. That's all. We'll deal with this through our solicitor." He stood up. "I'd prefer it if you left now, Mr. Banks. Unless you're going to arrest us or something, we don't want to talk to you anymore."

Banks had nothing more to ask, anyway. He already had his answers. He nodded, got up and left, the apple pie still untouched on its plate.

It was well after dark when Mark got off the number one bus outside the Lawnswood Arms, just past the Leeds Crematorium. His journey had taken so long because there weren't that many buses from Eastvale to Leeds, and he had to change in Harrogate. Then he had to buy a street map at W.H. Smith's to find out how to get to Adel. He had never visited Tina's parents before—never had any reason to—but the address was on the inside cover of some of the books she had kept with her in the squat and on the boat, and he remembered it. He also knew the security code you had to punch in to stop the burglar alarm from going off. Tina had made him memorize it. A month or so ago, Danny Boy had suffered a brief disruption in distribution, and to keep Tina sane, Mark had pretended to go along with a half-baked scheme to break into her father's surgery and steal some morphine. Luckily, Danny Boy had come through before things really got out of hand.

There was nothing but fields across the main road, and beyond them, down the hill, Mark could see the clustered lights of Adel village. Still unsure of exactly what he was going to say or do, Mark was drawn by the lights of the Lawnswood Arms and went inside. He hadn't eaten any lunch, so he was hungry, for one thing, and maybe a few drinks would give him some Dutch courage.

The Lawnswood Arms seemed more of a family pub than a

local watering hole, though at eight o'clock that evening there were hardly any families in evidence. Mark went to the bar and ordered a pint of Tetley's cask and looked at the menu. Steak and chips would do just fine, he decided. The first pint went down so fast the barman gave him a dirty look when he ordered a second. He'd seen that look before: "I've got my eye on you, mate. I know trouble when I see it." Well, maybe he *was* going to be trouble, but not for the bartender.

He got two pints down before his food was ready and ordered a third to wash down the steak. He wasn't showing any signs of drunkenness, so they had no reason to refuse to serve him, and they didn't. He just sat quietly in his corner, smoking and thinking. If they knew his thoughts, then maybe they'd call the police, but they didn't. The more he drank, the darker his thoughts became. Surges of emotion, sometimes anger, shot with red, black and gray.

He'd been wandering aimlessly, he realized now, with nowhere to go and nobody to talk to, nobody to share his grief with, nobody to hold him when he cried. But he never had had anyone. He had always been alone. Just him and his imagination, and his wits. The only difference was that he was even more adrift than ever now that Tina, his anchor, his burden, his reason for being, was gone.

He thought about Crazy Nick lying bleeding on the floor; he thought about his mother, how she'd never wanted him because he got in the way of her good times, though when he heard she was dead he had felt oddly alone in the world. But most of all he thought about Tina. He had never seen her body, he realized, so her parents must have identified her. The thought of Aspern gloating over her, touching her, made his flesh crawl. His last memory of her, the one he would carry forever, was the frail figure huddled in the sleeping bag, needle barely out of her arm, giving a little sigh of pleasure, and Beth Orton playing quietly on the CD. Not "Stolen Car" but a more recent one, a song about being on a train in Paris, as he snuffed out the candle and left her to sneak off to the welcoming arms of Mandy. If only he'd stayed with her, the way he'd promised, the way he had always done before . . .

"You all right?"

The voice sounded far away, and when he looked up, Mark noticed it was one of the bar staff collecting glasses, a young girl, perhaps not much older than Tina, though he knew she had to be over eighteen to work in a pub. She had a short spiky haircut and a gold stud through her lower lip, just like Tina, and in a way she reminded him of her, the way she could be when she held the darkness at bay.

"Yeah," he said. "Fine. Just thinking."

She stared at him, an assessing look in her eye. "Not good thoughts, by the looks of you."

"You could say that."

She lowered her voice. "Only, old misery-guts over there has been giving you the evil eye all night. One wrong move and you're cut off. You weren't thinking of making any wrong moves, were you?"

"No," said Mark. "Not here, at any rate."

"Well, that's all right, then." She smiled. "I've not seen you here before."

"That's because I've never been here before."

"Not from around these parts?"

"No."

"Cathy!"

The new voice came from the bar. "Oops," she said, grimacing. "Got to go. Old misery's calling. Remember, tread carefully."

"I will," said Mark.

The brief conversation had brought him back to a world of normality, at least for a few moments, and he wondered if his life could ever be good again. The girl might not have been trying to pick him up, but she was definitely flirting with him, and he could tell she fancied him. If his world were normal he'd have pursued the matter and maybe gone home with her, if she had her own flat. She probably did, he thought. Looked like a student, and the university wasn't far down the road. The bus had passed it on the way out of town. But after what happened to Tina, and him being with Mandy at the time, somehow made it so he just couldn't contemplate anything like that, even though this girl Cathy reminded him of Tina.

The barman gave him the evil eye again when he ordered his next pint, his fifth, he thought, though he was still steady on his feet, and his speech wasn't slurred. The look told him, "This is your last one, mate. After that you're on your bike." Fine, he didn't want any more. It was nearly closing time anyway.

Mark lit another cigarette, the last in his packet, and tried to work out exactly what he wanted to do or say when he got to Aspern's house. The way he felt whenever he thought about Patrick Aspern, he thought he'd probably do what he did to Crazy Nick, or worse. He didn't know about Tina's mother. He'd nothing against her and didn't want to hurt her, but she hadn't been there for her daughter any more than his mother had been there for him. True, he'd never been sexually molested by any of her men friends, but more than one of them had beaten him up, and more often than not they just used him to fetch and carry for them and clean up their messes. Mothers ought to be there for their kids—they were supposed to love them and nurture them—and Tina's had failed in that as much as his own mother had, no matter how far apart they were in social status. When it came right down to it, a doctor's wife could be just as useless a mother as a whore, because that was what his mother had been; he had no illusions about that.

A bell rang and someone called out time. Mark had about half a pint left in his glass. He'd had five, and he still didn't feel in the least bit pissed. He fiddled for change in his pocket and bought another packet of cigarettes from the machine. When he'd finished his drink, he stuck a cigarette in his mouth, lit it and headed for the door.

"Good night," a voice called out behind him.

It was the girl, Cathy. She was closer than he thought, a cloth in her hand, wiping down the tables.

"Good night," he said.

"Maybe I'll see you again?"

Was that a note of hope in her voice? he wondered. He managed a smile for her. "Maybe," he said. "You never know."

Then he walked out into the chilly night air.

"Have you thought any more about New York?" Phil asked Annie as they lingered over café noir and crème brûlée in Le Select, Eastvale's prestigious French bistro. Already well sated with several glasses of fine claret, Annie was feeling warm and relaxed, and the idea of a weekend away with Phil held immense appeal. Especially New York.

"I can't go, Phil, really I can't," she said. "I'd love to, honestly. Maybe some other time?"

"If it's a matter of money . . ."

"It's only *partly* a matter of money," Annie chipped in. "I mean, you might be able to go swanning off to America on a whim, but I *do* have to think about the expense."

"I told you I'd get your ticket. Security consultant."

"That's very sweet of you, but it doesn't seem right," Annie said. "Besides, if I went with you to New York, I certainly wouldn't want to go as your employee."

Phil laughed. "But that would only be on paper."

"I don't care."

The waiter came over with the bill and Phil picked it up.

"See what I mean?" Annie said. "You're always paying."

"I'll split it with you, then?"

"Fine," said Annie, reaching for her handbag. The Visa wasn't maxed out, she was certain. How embarrassing it would be, after all her bravado about paying her own way, if that obsequious waiter with the phony French accent trotted back and told her her card had been rejected.

"You don't know what you're missing," Phil went on. "We could stay at the Plaza. A carriage ride in Central Park, top of the Empire State Building, Tavern on the Green, Saks Fifth Avenue, Bloomingdale's, Tiffany's—"

"Oh, stop it!" Annie said, slapping his arm and putting her hands over her ears. "I don't want to know, okay?"

Phil held his hands up in mock surrender. "Okay. Okay. I'll stop."

"Besides," Annie said, "we've still got a major crime investigation on the go."

"Still stumped?"

"We don't have a lot to go on. Even the rented car turned out to be a dead end. Literally. The man who rented it died six months ago."

"Oh," said Phil. "Then how . . . ?"

"Don't ask. All I know is it's a real bloody headache, and it's nice to take my mind off it even for a few hours. Christ, I even had to spend last night in a motel outside Redditch fighting off the attentions of two traveling salesmen from Solihull."

Phil laughed. "Successfully, I hope."

"Yes. I had Winsome with me. She can be quite fearsome when she wants." Annie smiled. "Fearsome Winsome."

The waiter returned with their credit card receipts to sign. Annie breathed a sigh of relief. When they had finished, they picked up their coats from the rack by the table and walked out into the cobbled alley off King Street, at the back of the police station.

"Ooh," said Annie, when the cold night air hit her. "I feel

dizzy. I think I've had a bit too much wine." She linked arms with Phil.

"Come on," Phil said. "My car's just around the corner. Where did you park?"

Annie was wearing high heels, and it was difficult walking on the cobbles, especially with the effects of the wine and the patches of ice that were forming as the temperature dropped. "Police station car park," she said.

"Leave it there, then. I'm perfectly okay to drive."

And he was, Annie knew. She had never seen Phil drunk, never known him to drink more than one glass of wine with dinner. "But what . . . ?"

"Look," he said, "I'll take you home, if you like. Or, if you want . . ."

Annie looked up at him. "What?"

"Well, you could come back to my place, if you like."

"But how will I get to work in the morning?"

"Maybe you won't. Maybe I'll keep you there. My love slave."

Annie laughed and pushed him.

"Seriously," he said. "I'll drop you off there in the morning. I have to pick up the Turners to take them to London, anyway."

"You're going back down?"

"Have to."

"Pity."

"Work goes on. Anyway, how about it?"

"You'll bring me back in the morning? You'll do that?"

"Of course. Unless I decide to keep you prisoner."

"Go on, then."

"But I'm warning you. I know you've had a bit too much to drink, and I might take advantage of you."

Annie felt better than she had in a long while about that prospect, but she was damned if she was going to let Phil know it. "I'm not *that* drunk," she said. "And I'm definitely not that easy."

"Well, I'm sure we'll find some way of keeping your mind off your work for a few hours more, at least."

Annie tightened her arm around his and they turned the corner onto King Street.

"Dad? I'm sorry to ring so late, but I just got back in."

Banks glanced at his watch. Almost midnight. "Where've you been?"

"The pictures. With Jane and Ravi."

"What did you see?"

"The new *Lord of the Rings*."

"Was it good?"

"Brilliant. But very long. Look, Dad . . ."

Banks turned down the old Jesse Winchester CD he was playing and settled back in the armchair with his glass of Laphroaig, his used paperback copy of Ambler's *The Mask of Dimitrius* open facedown beside him. The peat fire crackled and filled the small living room with its warmth, the acrid smell harmonizing with the taste of whiskey. He didn't like the ominous tone of his daughter's "Look, Dad." "What?" he asked.

"I was talking to Mum earlier today," Tracy went on.

"And?"

"She said she saw you. In London."

"That's right. I was down there on business."

"She said she thought you were watching her. Stalking her."

"I was doing no such thing."

"Well, she says you were hanging around her house. In the rain."

"It wasn't raining. That started later."

"Dad, she's worried about you."

"I don't see why."

"She thinks you're becoming weird."

"Weird?"

"Yes. Hanging around her house and all. It *is* pretty weird. You must admit."

"I had a few questions I wanted to ask her."

"About a case?"

"As it happens, yes. About an artist she once knew when she worked at the community center. It's part of a case I'm working on."

"The burning boats. Yes, I've read about it in the paper." Tracy paused. "She didn't tell me that."

"Well, it's true. What? Don't you believe me? Do *you* think I'm getting weird in my old age?"

"Nobody said anything about old age."

"Still . . . my own daughter grilling me."

"I'm not grilling you. Can't you see, she still cares about you?"

"She's got a funny way of showing it."

"You scare her, Dad. She just can't cope with you. You always seem so angry with her. She thinks you hate her. All she can manage is to go cold when the two of you talk to one another."

Banks remembered that from their marriage. Whenever Sandra couldn't deal with a situation emotionally, she would just sort of turn off. Sometimes she would even fall asleep in the middle of an argument. It used to infuriate him. "I don't hate her," he said.

"Well, that's how she feels."

"It's a funny turn of events, isn't it, my own daughter giving me advice on marital relationships?"

"I don't have any advice to give. And you're not married anymore. That's the problem. How's your girlfriend?"

"Michelle? She's fine."

"Seen her lately?"

"No. We've both been too busy."

"There you go, then."

"And what's that supposed to mean?"

"Dad, you've got to make time to have a life. Stop and smell the roses. You can't just . . . Oh, I don't know. What's the point?"

"I stopped to smell the roses last summer," Banks said. "But it didn't last." He remembered the two weeks of bliss he had spent on a Greek island, the sun, the light on white and blue planes of the houses straggling down the hill, scents of lavender, thyme, oregano, a whiff of dead fish and salt spray. He also remembered how restless he had felt and how, though it seemed a great wrench at the time, he was secretly pleased to feel himself being called back home to a case. And to the lovely Michelle Hart. How he wished she were with him tonight, but he wasn't going to let his daughter in on his longings.

"That was because you came running back to get involved in another case," Tracy said.

"Tracy, Graham Marshall was an old friend of mine. How could I—"

"Oh, I know. I'm not saying you shouldn't have come back. Of course I'm not. But remember the time before, when we were supposed to be going to Paris for the weekend, and you went off searching for Jimmy Riddle's runaway daughter instead? There's always something. Always will be. You just have to . . . I mean, you can't solve the world's problems single-handedly. You're not the only detective in the country, you know. Sometimes I think you just use your job to hide yourself from yourself. And from everybody else."

"What's that supposed to mean?"

"Oh, it's too complicated to go into right now."

"Quite the philosopher you've become. And here's me thinking you were a history student."

"You know what Socrates said: 'The unexamined life is not worth living.' "

"Well, I wouldn't examine it *too* closely, if I were you. You never know what you might find."

"Oh, Dad. You're just playing word games now."

Banks felt the urge for a cigarette peak and wane. He took another sip of whiskey. "Look," he said, "I'm sorry for being facetious. It's just been a long day. A long week, as a matter of fact. I haven't had much sleep, and I've got a lot on my mind."

"When was it ever any different?"

"Tell your mother I don't hate her."

"Tell her yourself. Good night, Dad."

And Tracy hung up.

Banks held the phone in his hand for a few moments and listened to the buzzing sound. He'd been about to tell Tracy that seeing the baby for the first time had been a shock, that he hadn't been prepared for the way it made him feel. But she'd hung up on him.

He put the phone down and went into the kitchen to top up his glass. As he stood there pouring the Laphroaig, he felt an overwhelming sense of melancholy envelop him. But it came from the *outside,* not the inside. Though he didn't generally believe in the supernatural, he had long believed that the kitchen contained some sort of spirit. It usually gave him a strong sense of well-being, and he had never felt its sadness before.

Banks shuddered and went back to the living room, turned up Jesse Winchester singing "The Brand New Tennessee Waltz" and settled down gloomily to get drunk. He knew he shouldn't, knew that tomorrow would be just as busy as today, and that the hangovers only got worse as he got older. But his daughter had hung up on him. He thought of phoning her back, but decided against it. He didn't feel he had the emotional energy to deal with the sort of discussion Tracy seemed to have in mind tonight. Best wait till they'd both slept on it. He was sure she would ring him again tomorrow and patch things up. Still, it was a sour note to go to bed on, which was why he had refilled his glass.

He wanted to talk to Michelle. The way things had turned

out, he hadn't called her from London, hadn't spent the evening in Peterborough. It was after one o'clock, but he would ring her anyway, he decided, reaching for the phone. But before he could pick it up, it rang. He thought it might be Tracy ringing back to apologize, so he answered it.

"Alan?"

"Yes?"

"Ken Blackstone here. Sorry to bother you at this hour, but I thought you might be interested. I just got a call from Weetwood."

Banks sat up. "What is it?"

"Another fire. Adel. Patrick Aspern's house."

Banks put his glass down. "I'll be there as soon as I can," he said.

"I'll be waiting."

Banks took stock of the shape he was in. Luckily, he had only taken a sip or two of his second drink, and he knew he wasn't over the limit. He put the kettle on and poured plenty of fine-ground coffee into a filter. While the water was coming to a boil, he stuck his head under the tap and ran cold water over it for a couple of minutes. Then he poured the boiling water into the filter and watched it drip through, filled it once again and brushed his teeth and sucked on a breath mint. Just before he left, he filled a travel mug with hot black coffee and carried it out to the car. The night was cold and hoarfrost had formed on the trees and drystone walls, giving them a ghostly white outline in the night. The sky was studded with stars.

There was no time for Jesse Winchester's bittersweet musings now. Banks flipped through the CDs he carried in the car and went for The Clash's *London Calling*. If that and the hot, strong coffee didn't keep him awake all the way to Adel, nothing would.

Chapter 15

*T*he fire engines were gone when Banks arrived at Patrick Aspern's house shortly after two in the morning, and two police patrol cars were parked diagonally across the street, blocking it to all traffic. He hadn't known what to expect in terms of damage, but from the outside, at least, the house seemed intact. The local police had sealed off the path, and a line of blue-and-white tape barred the gateway, where a young constable, who looked to be freezing his bollocks off, even in his overcoat, was logging everyone who came and went. Banks went up to him and asked for DI Ken Blackstone.

The PC wrote something on his clipboard and gestured with his thumb. "Inside, sir," he said with a wistful tone.

Banks walked down the path. The front door was closed, but not locked, and there were signs of forced entry. The firefighters, or someone else?

Banks found Ken Blackstone and the local DI from Weetwood, Gary Bridges, in the living room. DI Bridges presented quite a contrast to Banks and the elegant, dapper Blackstone. In some ways he resembled DS Hatchley, though he was in far better shape. He was a big man in a baggy creased suit, an ex–rugby forward with arms and legs like steel cables, a head of thick sandy hair and piercing green eyes. The traces of his Belfast accent were still in his voice, even though he'd spent most of his life in England.

Banks looked around the room. There was no trace, or even smell, of fire or smoke damage anywhere. Sitting on the sofa, where he cut a slight and lonely figure indeed, was Mark Siddons. The room was warm, but Mark had a blanket wrapped around his shoulders and was trembling slightly. He looked over when Banks walked in, then quickly averted his eyes. What looked like streaks of dirt, or blood, stained his face and the hands gripping the blanket. There was also blood on the side of his head.

"What's going on?" Banks asked, after greeting Blackstone and Bridges. "Where's the fire?"

"Gary here rang me at home as soon as he heard the location," said Blackstone. "His lads had been helping us check up on Aspern, so he knew I had an interest."

"It started in Dr. Aspern's surgery," Bridges said. "At the back. An addition, really. The damage isn't serious, and it's pretty well contained." He gestured toward Mark. "Seems this lad here snapped into action with the extinguisher real sharpish."

Banks looked at Mark. "That right?" he asked.

Mark nodded.

"Was it you who broke in?"

Mark said nothing.

"Sure you didn't start the fire yourself?" Banks went on.

"I didn't start it."

"I warned you to stay away."

"I didn't do it."

"What makes you think he did?" Bridges asked. "What's going on here? DI Blackstone said Dr. Aspern was involved in a case you're working on, but that's about all I know. Do you think this might be related?"

"The personnel's the same," said Banks, then he explained about the other fires and Mark's problems with Patrick Aspern. Mark said nothing. He seemed to be lost in his own world, still trembling.

"So what happened?" Banks asked.

"We're still not clear yet," Blackstone said. "But the fire's not the main problem." He looked at Mark. "And the leading firefighter told me the front door was already open when they got here. Do you want a look at the scene?"

Banks nodded. Blackstone glanced at Bridges. It was a courtesy to seek his permission because they were on his patch. "It's okay," Bridges said. "Looks like we'll be working together on this one, anyway. I'll take the lad here down to the station."

"Why are you arresting me?" Mark asked. "I haven't done anything."

"Where else would you go at this hour?" Banks asked.

Mark just shrugged.

Bridges looked over at Banks. "Breaking and entering?"

"That'll do for starters. And see if you can get a doctor to have a look at him, would you? We'll talk to him tomorrow."

"Okay," said Bridges. "Be careful in there. The doc's been and gone, but the photographer's not finished yet, I think, and the SOCOs haven't done their stuff. Can't seem to get the idle buggers out of bed."

"It's pretty grim," Blackstone said as he and Banks walked down the plush-carpeted hall to the back of the house.

Banks remembered the scene on the boats and in Gardiner's caravan. He didn't imagine it could be much worse than either of those. And it certainly couldn't be worse than what he had witnessed in that tall, narrow terraced house all those years ago.

"There's just one connecting door through from the main house," Blackstone said, turning the handle. "And there's a separate entrance from the outside into a small waiting room for the patients. They're mostly private, and I expect they pay a little bit extra for the olde worlde charm. I'll bet the doctor paid house calls, too."

There wasn't much olde worlde charm in evidence when Blackstone opened the door to Aspern's surgery, but whatever damage had been done there hadn't been done by fire. Even with the slight charring and spray of foam from the extinguisher, it was plain to see that the walls and floor were covered in blood, and that the blood came from the body of Patrick Aspern, well beyond the help of any doctor now, spread-eagled on the floor, the entire front of his body ripped open in a glistening tapestry of tissue, organ, sinew and bone.

Banks glanced at Blackstone, who was looking distinctly peaky. "Shotgun?" he said. "Close range? Both barrels?"

"Exactly. Gary's bagged it and tagged it."

"Jesus Christ," Banks said under his breath. In such a small room, the impact must have been tremendous. Even now he could still smell the powder mingled with burned rubber, surgical spirit and blood. Banks could only imagine the deafening noise and the spray of arterial blood, the gobbets of flesh blown clean off the bone, leaving dark slimy trails on the walls. Even the eye chart was splattered with blood, and so was the hypodermic syringe on the floor by the chair.

"Who did it?" Banks asked.

"Looks like the wife," said Blackstone. "But she's not talking yet."

"Frances?" Banks said. "Where is she?"

"Station."

"And the boy was in the room, too? Mark?"

"Yes."

"What does he have to say for himself?"

"Nothing. You saw for yourself. I think he's still in shock. We'll have to wait awhile before we get anything out of him."

Banks kept silent for a few moments, looking around the room. A shambles, in the original meaning of the word. He noticed several strands of cord on the floor by the doctor's chair. "What's that?" he asked.

"We think the boy must have been tied to the chair."

"Why?"

"Don't know yet. But Mrs. Aspern must have cut him free."

"And the fire?"

"Hardly got started before the kid turned the extinguisher on it. As you can see."

He pointed to a burned patch on the carpet, which had spread as far as the cubbyhole used to store patient files and singed the crisp white sheets on the examination table.

"Who set it?"

"Again, it looks like the wife."

Frances Aspern. Well, maybe she had reached a snapping point, Banks thought. If what he suspected had been going on, and if she had known, then he could only guess at the power of the emotions she had suppressed, or how warped and dangerous they had become under the pressure of the years. But something must have happened to make her snap. A trigger of some sort. Maybe they would get something out of her or Mark later.

The outside door opened, letting in a draft of icy night air. "Sorry, lads," said the photographer, tapping his Pentax. "I finished the video, then I had to go back to the car for this."

The young photographer didn't seem at all fazed by the scene of carnage in front of him. Banks had seen the same lack of reaction before. He knew that photographers often managed to distance themselves through their lenses. To them, the scene was only another photo, an image, a composition, not real human blood and guts spilled there. It was their way of coping.

Banks wondered what his way of coping was and realized he didn't really have one. He looked upon these scenes as exactly what they were—outbursts of anger, hate, greed, lust or passion, which left one human being mangled and split open, the fragile bag of blood burst, and he didn't have any way of distancing himself. But still he slept at night, still he didn't faint or puke his guts up over someone's shoes. What did that say about him? Oh, he remembered them all, of course, all the victims, young and old, and sometimes his sleep was disturbed by dreams, or he couldn't get to sleep for the images that assaulted his mind, but still he lived with it. What did that make him?

"Alan?"

Banks turned to see Ken Blackstone frowning at him.

"All right?"

"Fine, thanks."

"My sofa?"

"Why not," said Banks, with a sigh. "It's a bloody long way home, and I'm knackered. Got any decent whiskey?"

"I think I could rustle up a dram or two of Bell's."

"That'll do nicely," said Banks. "Let's leave it to DI Bridges and go. We'll sort this mess out tomorrow."

Annie was in the office early, despite a mild hangover and a mostly sleepless night. Phil had picked up the Turners and set off for London after dropping her at the front doors of Western Area Headquarters. She made a pot of strong coffee in the squad room and settled down to some much neglected paperwork. She was just starting to enjoy the relative early-morning peace and quiet when the place started springing to life. DC Rickerd was first in, followed by Winsome. Then Kevin Templeton and the others came and went, attending to the varied tasks and minutiae of a major investigation. Annie felt embarrassed to be wearing the same clothes she'd gone to dinner in the previous evening, but nobody noticed, or at least nobody said anything. Banks wasn't there, anyway. She could only imagine the kind of look she'd get from him.

Sometimes she felt as if he could smell the sex on her, no matter how long she had showered.

It wasn't long after nine when an excited DC Templeton came up to her waving a sheet of paper. "I've got it!" he said. "I've got it."

"Alleluia," said Annie. "What have you got?"

"McMahon and Gardiner. The connection."

Annie felt the excitement of a big break spread around the squad room like the first breath of spring. Everyone put in hard and long hours on a case, and something like this was payday for them all, whether they'd worked that particular angle or not.

"Come on, then, Kev," she said. "Give."

"They were at university together," said Templeton. "Well, it wasn't actually a university back then, but it is now."

"Kev, slow down," said Annie. "Give me the details so they make sense."

Templeton ran his hand over his wavy brown hair. He had some sort of gel on it, Annie noticed, which made it look wet, as if he'd just walked out of the shower. He always did fancy himself a bit, did Kevin Templeton, she thought, and he was a good-looking, trim, fit lad who probably did really well with the girls. He had a touch of the Hugh Grant boyish charm about him, too, the sort of quality that called out for a bit of mothering, but just enough to make it an attractive proposition for the right type of woman. Not Annie. She wasn't the mothering kind.

"Okay," he went on, reading from the sheet. "Between 1978 and 1981, both Thomas McMahon and Roland Gardiner attended the former Leeds Polytechnic, since 1992 known as Leeds Metropolitan University. Back then it was made up of the Art College, the College of Commerce, the College of Technology and the Cookery School. Thomas McMahon attended the Art College, obviously, and Roland Gardiner went to the College of Commerce."

"Did they know one another?"

Templeton scratched his forehead. "Can't tell you that, ma'am. Only that they were both there at the same time."

Winsome shot Annie a glance. Annie smiled at her. One day she'd get Kevin Templeton out of the habit of calling her "ma'am," too. Coming from a handsome young lad like him, it really did make her feel like an old maid.

"In my experience," Annie said, "it's pretty unlikely that art and commerce students shared the same interests. I doubt they'd ever mix."

"Not the same subjects, maybe," said Templeton, "but that's only a part of what college is all about, isn't it? There's the pub, student politics, the music scene. Leeds Poly always had great bands. They could have met through something like that."

" 'Could have' isn't good enough, Kev. If we're to make any sort of link, we need to know for certain. And we need to know who else they hung out with. There's a fair chance that whoever killed them met them back then, was someone who was maybe part of the same scene. I certainly don't believe it's a coincidence that two men who were murdered so close together and in much the same way just *happened* to go to the same poly at the same time. But we need a definite connection, if one exists. And there's the late William Masefield to consider, too. How was he linked with the others, if he was?"

"Well," said Templeton, "I could always get on to the authorities in Leeds. I'm sure their records go back that far."

"And what do we do then? Check up on every student who attended Leeds Poly from 1978 to 1981? It'd be like looking for the proverbial needle in a haystack."

"Can you think of any other way?"

"I've got an idea," said Winsome.

Annie and Templeton looked at her. "Go on," Annie said.

"Friends Reunited dot com. I'm a member. I've used it before to locate people. I admit it's a short cut, but it might help narrow things down a bit. Of course, you've only got the people who have taken the trouble to register on the site, but there's a chance one of them might remember McMahon or Gardiner. We can send out an e-mail to everyone on the list who left Leeds Poly in 1981, asking if they knew a Thomas McMahon and a Roland Gardiner, and see what kind of response we get back. Plenty of people are constantly online these days, so if we're lucky we might even get a speedy reply."

"It's worth a try," said Annie, getting to her feet. "Come on, let's do it."

The interview room was the same as just about every interview room Banks had ever been in: small, high window covered by a grille, bare bulb similarly covered, metal table bolted to the floor. The institutional green paint looked fresh, though, and Banks fancied he could still smell traces of it in the stale air. Either that or the Scotch he had drunk with Ken Blackstone the previous night was giving him a headache. He massaged his temples.

Frances Aspern sat opposite Banks and DI Gary Bridges, who was not only wearing the same suit as he had last night, but looked as if he'd slept in it, too. Dressed in disposable navy overalls, Frances Aspern seemed listless and distant, and much older than she had when Banks first saw her. The dark circles under her eyes testified that she hadn't slept, and she was fidgeting with a ring. Not her wedding ring, Banks noticed. That was gone.

"Are you ready to talk to us?" Bridges asked, when he had issued the caution and set the tape machine rolling.

Frances nodded, a faraway look in her eyes.

"Can you speak your answers out loud, please?" Bridges asked.

"Yes," she said, in a small voice. "Sorry."

"What happened last night?"

Frances paused so long before answering that Banks was beginning to think she hadn't heard DI Bridges's question. But eventually she began to speak. "We were asleep. Patrick heard a noise downstairs. He took his gun out of the cabinet and went down." Her voice was a monotone, disconnected from her feelings, as if the things she was saying were of no interest to her.

"What happened then?"

"I waited. A long time. I don't know how long. Then I went downstairs. He was going to hurt the boy. I picked up his gun and shot him, then I cut the boy free and told him to go."

"What about the fire?" DI Bridges asked.

"Fire cleanses," she said. "I wanted to purify the house."

"What did you use to start it?"

"Rubbing alcohol. It was on the table."

"What happened?"

"The boy came back and put it out. I told him not to, but he didn't listen. Then he made me sit down and he rang the police. I just felt so tired I didn't care what happened, but I couldn't sleep."

"I'm trying to understand all this, Frances," Bridges said. "Why did you kill your husband?"

Frances looked at Banks, not at Bridges, her eyes burning with tears now. "Because he was going to hurt the boy."

"He was going to hurt Mark?" It was DI Bridges who spoke, but Frances continued to look at Banks.

"Yes," she said. "Patrick is a cruel man. You must know that. He was going to hurt the boy. He was tied to the chair."

"But why did he want to hurt Mark?" Bridges asked.

Slowly, Frances turned to face him, still fiddling with her ring. "Because of Christine," she said. "The boy took Christine from him. Patrick couldn't bear to lose."

Banks felt a chill ripple up his spine. Bridges turned to him, looking confused. "DCI Banks," he said, "you're familiar with the background to this case. Is there anything you'd like to ask?"

Banks turned to Frances Aspern. "You're saying that your husband was going to harm Mark because Mark lived with Christine on the boat, is that right?"

"Yes."

"Did Patrick go to the boat last Thursday evening? Did he start the fire?"

Frances looked up sharply, surprised. "No," she said. "No, we were at home. That much is true."

"But was your husband sexually abusing Christine?"

The tears spilled over from Frances's eyes and rolled down her cheeks, but she didn't sob or wail. "Yes," she said.

"For how long?"

"Since she was twelve. When she . . . you know, when she started to develop. He couldn't stop touching her."

"Why didn't she stop him? She must have known what was happening, that it was wrong? She could have gone to the authorities."

Frances wiped the tears from her eyes and cheeks with the sleeve of her overalls and gave Banks a what-do-you-know look. "He was the only father she had ever known," she said. "He was strict with her when she was growing up. Always. She was terrified of him. She never dared disobey his demands."

"And you knew about the sexual abuse from the start?"

"Yes. From very early on, at any rate."

"How did you find out?"

"It's not hard to recognize the signs, when you're around all the time. Besides . . ."

"It happened with you, too?"

"How do you know?"

"I'm just guessing."

She looked away. "I tried to tell Daddy, but I couldn't. He wouldn't have believed me, anyway, and if he had, it would have broken his heart."

"So you did nothing about Christine, either?"

"How could I? I was terrified of him."

"Even so, after your experiences, your own daughter . . ."

She slapped the table with her palm. "You've no idea how cruel Patrick could be. No idea."

"Why? Did he hit you? Did he hit Christine?"

She shook her head. "No. What he did . . . it was worse than that, much worse. Cold, calculated."

"What did he do?"

Frances looked away again, at a spot on the wall above Banks's head, her eyes unfocused. "He . . . he knew chemicals." She gave a harsh laugh. "Of course he did, he was a doctor, after all, wasn't he?"

"What do you mean, Frances?"

She looked directly at Banks, her expression unfathomable. "Patrick knew drugs. Not illegal drugs. Prescriptions. What made you sleep. What made you stay awake. What made your heart beat like a frightened bird inside your chest. What made you sick. What made you have to go to the toilet all the time. What made your skin burn and your mouth dry."

Banks understood. And wished he didn't. He looked at Bridges, who seemed to have turned a shade paler. Just when he thought he'd seen and heard it all, dug about as deep as anyone can into the darkness of the human soul and remained sane, something else came along and knocked all his assumptions out of the window.

"Now you understand," Frances Aspern said, a note of shrill triumph in her voice. "But even that wasn't it. I could have stood the pain, the cruelty."

"What was it, Frances?" Banks asked.

"My father. He worshiped Patrick. You know he did. You've talked to him. He rang us after you left. How could I tell him? It was like before, like I told you. Even if I could have made him believe, it would have broken his heart."

"So for the sake of your father's trust in Patrick Aspern

you let your husband abuse both you and your daughter? Is that what you're saying?"

"What else could I do? Surely you understand? If it came out what kind of man Patrick was, what he *did,* it would have destroyed my father. He's not a strong man."

He had looked healthy enough the other day, Banks thought, though appearances could be deceptive. But there was no point in pursuing this line of questioning. Whatever her reasons, Frances Aspern knew the enormity of what she had done, and she knew she had to live with the consequences.

"What about Paul Ryder?" Banks asked.

"Who?"

"Paul Ryder. Christine's birth father, remember? We haven't been able to find him."

Frances looked down at the scarred tabletop and ran her fingertips over its rough surface.

"There was no Paul Ryder, was there?" Banks said.

She responded with a barely perceptible shake of the head.

"Patrick was Christine's real father, wasn't he?"

"Yes," she said, still looking down at the table.

"Remember when we first met, when Patrick wanted to drive you to Eastvale to identify the body?"

Frances just looked at him.

"You said, 'She's *my* daughter.' I took it to imply that you were putting him in his place, reminding him that he was only Christine's stepfather, but that wasn't it, was it?"

"When you live a lie for long enough," Frances said, in little more than a whisper, "you come to believe it."

Banks let the silence stretch, with only the hiss of the tape and muffled sounds from the station in the background, then he looked at Bridges, who shook his head slowly. "Let's suspend this interview for now," Banks said. Bridges nodded and turned off the tape machine.

* * *

"Alan out again, is he?" asked DS Stefan Nowak, popping his head around the squad room door close to lunchtime that day.

"Another fire," Annie said. "In Leeds, this time. I've just been on the phone with him, and it seems that Mrs. Aspern, the doctor's wife, has killed her husband and tried to set fire to the body."

Stefan whistled between his teeth.

"Indeed," said Annie. "Have you got anything new for us?"

"I might have." Stefan walked into the room and sat down opposite Annie. He looked as handsome and regal as ever, and just as remote and unreadable. Not for the first time, Annie wondered what sort of private life he had. Did he have friends outside the force? Family? Was he gay? She didn't sense that in him, but she had been wrong before.

Stefan opened the folder he had brought with him. "What do you want first," he asked, "the good news or the bad news?"

"I don't care," Annie said.

"Well," Stefan went on, "apart from the soil and gravel samples, which do match samples from the lay-by, we drew a blank with the Jeep Cherokee. The car rental company had done a bloody good job of cleaning it, inside and out. We did find some hair, fibers and a partial print under the front seat, but it's not much more than a smudge. We might be able to do some computer enhancement, but don't expect too much."

"That's pretty well what I figured," said Annie. "I wouldn't be surprised if our killer gave it a good going over, too. He seems to be the meticulous type."

"And we checked a sample of petrol from the fuel tank of Leslie Whitaker's Jeep Cherokee with the accelerant from the Gardiner fire."

"And?"

"It doesn't match."

"Shit," said Annie.

"We do have the Nike trainer impression, though. That's

pretty distinctive. If he hasn't ditched them, we can match them when we find a suspect."

"Was that the good news or the bad news?"

Stefan smiled. "It might be nothing, but one of our lads found traces of candle wax puddled near the point of origin in Roland Gardiner's caravan."

"You mean he'd been having a romantic evening?"

"No," said Stefan, "that's not what comes to mind. Not my mind, anyway. Call me a cynic, but I see it in a different light altogether."

"Joke," said Annie. "Never mind. Wasn't there also a candle beside the girl who died on the boat?"

"Yes," said Stefan, "but that's different. The fire didn't originate on the boat, and it was pretty clear she'd used the candle to prepare the heroin she'd injected. Also, the boyfriend said in his statement that he made sure the candle was out before he left."

"Mark Siddons? I can't understand why everybody is so quick to believe anything he says. He could easily have been lying."

"No, this is something else."

"I think I know what you're getting at," said Annie.

"Yes. It looks as if it was used as some sort of primitive time-delay ignition device. It's not unusual in arson cases."

"So the killer makes sure Gardiner's fast asleep, pours out the petrol, then lights the candle and leaves?"

"And an hour, or two hours later, the candle burns down, meets the petrol, and *puff!* Up it goes."

"Can you estimate how long?"

"If we can discover exactly what make and length of candle it was, and if we assume it hadn't been used previously, was still whole, then yes. But don't hold your breath. We don't have a lot to go on."

"An estimate?"

"Well, an ordinary household candle is seven-eighths of

an inch in diameter, and it burns one inch every fifty-seven minutes in a draft-free environment."

"The caravan could hardly have been a draft-free environment, could it?"

"Agreed," said Stefan. "But there was hardly any wind that night. Anyway, let's say you've got a six-inch candle, that gives you nearly six hours of burn time before ignition, all factors being equal."

"How could the killer rely on Gardiner's remaining unconscious for that long?"

"He couldn't. Look, Annie, it could have been just a candle stub. Half an inch, an inch. Half an hour, or an hour at the most."

"Or it could have been two hours, or three?"

"Afraid so. It could even have been one of those fancy thick candles, which would burn much more slowly. We're doing what tests we can on the wax, but as I said, don't get your hopes up."

"What about Thomas McMahon's barge? Anything there?"

"No signs of candle wax. It looks as if that fire was set directly."

"But not the Gardiner fire?"

"No."

"Isn't using a candle like that unreliable?"

"Extremely. Very crude and unpredictable. Not to mention dangerous. Any number of things can, and do, go wrong. You could accidentally ignite the accelerant when you're lighting the candle, for example. Or you light it and leave and a draft blows it out. Or it topples over and sets the accelerant off sooner than you'd hoped. It's amateur, but it can also be very effective, if it works. I'm sorry it's not very much to go on," Stefan apologized, "but it does tell us one thing, doesn't it?"

"Yes," said Annie, already turning over the implications in her mind. "It tells us that whoever set the second fire needed time, most likely time to arrange for an alibi. And which of our suspects seems to have a watertight alibi?"

Stefan thought for a moment, then answered. "Leslie Whitaker?"

"Exactly."

"But what about the petrol?"

"He must have been bright enough to siphon some from someone else's car. Maybe he knew there was a chance we'd be able to trace it. Don't you see, Stefan? It makes sense. Whitaker said he went out for an eight-o'clock dinner in Harrogate with nine other booksellers. They all vouched for him. We already know that he supplied Thomas McMahon with the special paper he needed to produce his forgeries. They were in it together. He practically admitted as much. One reason we almost ruled Whitaker out was that he's got an alibi for the Jennings Field fire, but not the one on the barges."

"But this timing device puts paid to his alibi?"

"Yes," said Annie. "If he was in Harrogate for that dinner at eight o'clock, then he must have left Eastvale, or Lyndgarth, where he lives, at about seven. But surely it would have been possible for him to use a two- or three-inch candle and gain a couple of hours or more burn time before the accelerant ignited?"

"Easily, assuming it all went according to plan."

"This time it did," said Annie. "We'll have him in, Stefan. And then we'll have him."

After the interview with Frances Aspern, Banks picked up a coffee in the canteen and remembered that he had intended to ring Dirty Dick Burgess. He found an empty office and took out his mobile.

"At last," said Dirty Dick. "I've been leaving messages for you in Eastvale all bloody morning."

"Bit of a crisis up here," said Banks, giving a brief explanation of his night and morning. "Anyway, what have you got?"

"Not much, I'm afraid. Business aboveboard. Solo operation. No partner. No employees. Philip Keane is a well-respected and popular member of the art community. Judgment valued, pals with all the movers and shakers, dealers, collectors, gallery owners, that sort of thing. Not exactly Anthony Blunt, but you get the picture."

"Blunt?" said Banks. "Why mention him? Wasn't he a spy, along with Philby, Burgess and MacLean? The fourth man?"

"Yes," said Burgess, "but he was also surveyor of the Queen's Pictures and director of the Courtauld Institute."

"Of course," said Banks. "Yes, I remember. Interesting. A master of the art of deception. Anything else?"

"Nothing. Philip Keane has lived a completely blameless life. At least for the past four years."

"Four years? And before that?"

"There's the glitch. Before that, there's nothing. Nada. Zilch. Bupkis."

"What do you mean?"

"I mean that he appeared fully formed on the scene four years ago, like Athena from the head of Zeus. And if you're thinking of teasing me about classical analogies, Banksy, don't. I got a first in classics at Oxford."

"Bollocks," said Banks. "Go on, though. You've got me interested."

"Like I said, there's nothing else to tell. The trail stops there. It's as if Keane didn't exist until four years ago."

"He must have been born, for a start."

"Oh, well, if you'd like me to send a team down to Saint Catherine's House . . . Or perhaps I should go myself? Shouldn't take long. Let me see, unusual name that, Philip Keane. I suppose you've got the details of his date and place of birth?"

"All right," said Banks. "I get the point. Give it a rest.

Maybe Keane studied and worked in museums and galleries abroad. Maybe that's where he was before."

"Maybe he did, and we can certainly check that, too, given time and resources. How official do you want this to be?"

Banks thought for a moment. He didn't want it to be official at all just yet. Not unless he got something more concrete to go on. On a whim, he asked, "Can you check if anyone called Philip Keane was connected in any way with a fire four years ago, and if he was ever associated with someone called William Masefield?"

"Fire? Where?"

"I don't know," said Banks, explaining about William Masefield's stolen identity. "It's a long shot. But if it *is* him, it could be an MO. He might have done it before."

"So you want me to keep digging?"

"If you can. But still discreetly. This case is confusing enough already. It just keeps shifting in the wind. It'd be nice to get some good solid information for a change."

"I do have one practical suggestion to make," offered Burgess.

"Oh, and what's that?"

"You could talk to his wife."

Chapter 16

"Mark," said Banks, "we must stop meeting like this."
Mark Siddons grunted and sat down.

"How are you feeling?" Banks asked.

"I'm all right. A bit tired. And my head feels like it's stuffed full of wet cotton wool."

"Must be the tranquilizer the doctor gave you last night. Are you ready to talk?" Banks and Bridges had already agreed that Banks would do most of the questioning, as he had interviewed Mark before and knew the terrain.

"If you like. Can I have some water first?"

Banks asked the constable waiting outside the door, who brought in a jug and three glasses. Mark filled his, but Bridges took nothing and Banks stuck with coffee.

"Are you going to charge me?" Mark asked.

"What with?"

"Breaking and entering."

Banks looked at DI Bridges. "That depends," Bridges said.

"What on?"

"On how cooperative you are."

"Look, Mark," Banks said, "we know it was you who put out the fire and you who rang the police and the fire brigade and waited with Mrs. Aspern until they arrived. All that will work in your favor. You're not being charged with anything just at the moment, but you'd better tell us exactly what went on. Okay?"

"Can I have a smoke?"

Smoking wasn't allowed in the police station anymore, but Bridges took out a packet of Silk Cut and offered Mark one. He also lit one himself. Banks felt no craving at all, just a slight wave of nausea when he smelled the smoke. Mostly, he was trying to put what he had just heard from Dirty Dick Burgess out of his mind. And its implications for Annie. For the time being, at any rate. He had got the London address of Keane and his wife, Helen, and checked train times from Leeds. After he'd finished with Mark, he'd head straight down to London on an early-afternoon train and talk to her, get things sorted. But until then, he had Mark Siddons and Frances Aspern to occupy his mind.

"There is one question I'd like answered before we start," Bridges asked.

"What?" said Mark.

"The burglar alarm. How did you disable it?"

Mark told them about the scheme Tina had come up with, and how he had memorized the code.

"All right," said Bridges, looking over at Banks. "Your turn."

"What time did you get to the Asperns' house?" Banks asked.

"I don't know. It was late, though. After closing time. I came out of the pub and put it off for a while, just walking around, then I went there."

"Put what off?"

"I don't know. All I know is that I was going the wrong way, and it didn't make sense anymore."

"What do you mean?"

"Scarborough and all that. That was why all those things happened. The bloke in the car. Those plainclothes cops on the seafront. Because I was going the wrong way. It was Adel

I had to go to, not Scarborough. I couldn't get on with my life until I'd faced them."

"What happened with the bloke in the car?" Banks asked.

"Nothing," said Mark. "He . . . you know, he tried to proposition me. I said, like, no way, and he just stopped the car and made me get out."

Banks didn't believe him. There was the matter of the mysterious two hundred pounds, for a start, but he let it go. Either Mark had capitulated and earned the money with his body, or he had stolen it. Either way, no accusations had been made against anyone, as far as he knew, so best let it lie. "What were you going to do in Adel?" he asked.

"I don't know. I didn't have a plan."

"So what *did* you do?"

"I had a bit too much to drink in that big pub on the main road, to get my bottle up, I suppose. Anyway, like I said, I just got into the house. They were in bed. I walked around a bit, wondering what the hell I was going to do now I was there. I mean, was I supposed to go upstairs and strangle the bastard, or what? I found a bottle of something, brandy, I think, and I took a few swigs of that, just sitting in the kitchen in the dark, thinking. Or trying to. I didn't even hear him coming."

"What happened next?"

"I don't know. I felt this sharp pain on the side of my head and everything went black."

"And when you came round?"

Mark paused and stubbed out his cigarette. He looked over at DI Bridges, who sighed and pushed the packet toward him. Mark fidgeted with the packet but didn't open it immediately. "I was in the surgery, wasn't I? All the lights were on, and *he* was there, standing over me with that evil fucking smile on his face."

"Patrick Aspern?"

"Who else?"

"What was he doing?"

"Filling a syringe with morphine. He had me tied to the chair so I couldn't move my arms, and he'd shoved some sort of cotton-wool gag in my mouth so I couldn't scream out."

"How do you know it was morphine?"

"He told me. That was all part of the fun for him. He wanted me to know what was going to happen to me, to be scared thinking about it for as long as he could draw it out."

"What else did he say?"

"He said he was soon going to inject me with a fatal dose of morphine, that it was more than a piece of scum like me deserved, because it was quick and merciful, and if he had his way he'd make me suffer for much longer." Mark glanced at Banks. "He was enjoying himself, you know. The power. Enjoying every minute of it."

"I believe you, Mark."

"He said the thought of me in bed with his daughter disgusted him, that she was a no-good ungrateful slut who deserved to die for betraying him like that, and now I was going to die, too."

"He referred to Tina as his daughter?"

"Yes."

"Did he say anything about being responsible for her death?"

"He didn't say he killed her, if that's what you mean."

"Did he mention his wife?"

"No."

"All right. Go on."

"He said nobody would shed any tears about a piece of junkie filth like me being found dead of an overdose in a back alley somewhere, which is exactly where he was going to dump me."

"What happened next?"

Mark lit his second cigarette and looked away. His voice became quieter. "I could see her standing behind him, in the doorway. Just standing there. Watching. Listening. He didn't know she was there, but I could see her."

"Mrs. Aspern?"

"Yes. At least, I guessed that's who it was."

"You'd never seen her before?"

"No, never."

"Not around the boat or anything? She'd never come to visit Tina?"

"No. I'm not even sure she knew where the boat was."

"Carry on."

Mark swallowed, took a sip of water and went on. "He said . . . he started talking about the things he did to her, to Tina, you know, and how much she loved it when he touched her and put himself inside her and all the things she did to him. He was making me crazy, but I couldn't break free. I couldn't yell out and make him stop. And I could see her behind him all the time, her face just going paler and paler. It was sickening, what he said. I mean, I know Tina told me he'd abused her, but she . . . I mean, the details. He had to go into every little detail. She never told me all that . . . all that stuff he said, what he did. I wanted to shut my ears, but you can't, can you? And all the time he was doing it, he had this strange sort of distant smile on his face, and he was fiddling with the syringe, giving a little squirt, like they do on television."

"What did Mrs. Aspern do?"

"The next thing I knew, she was holding the shotgun—he'd left it in the doorway—and she told him to leave me alone, that I hadn't done anything."

"What did he say to that?"

"He turned to her and he laughed. He just laughed."

"Is that when she fired?"

"No. He started telling her to put the gun down, the way you'd talk to a child, said that she hadn't the courage to pull the trigger, just like she hadn't had the courage to stand up for her daughter, that she was weak and cowardly. Then he started moving toward her with his hands out, like he expected her to hand him the gun. Then it just exploded."

"She fired?"

"It was deafening. My ears are still ringing, but I was tied up, so there was no way I could have covered them up." He shook his head and rubbed his face with his hands. "It was . . . I was covered in stuff, blood and stuff . . . I don't know . . . It was just like he'd burst open, you know, a bagful of blood, like those water balloons you burst, and it went all over the place, all over me. The smell was awful. I closed my eyes, but I couldn't close my nose any more than I could my ears. Gunpowder. And his insides. Shit and stuff. I had bits of him all over me. Slimy bits." Mark shuddered and finished his water. He refilled his glass with a shaking hand.

"What happened next, Mark?"

Mark took a deep drag on his cigarette. "She cut me free with some scissors or something and just told me to leave."

"She didn't say anything else?"

"No. Just to leave. Then she took that stuff they put on you before they stick the needle in. You know what I mean. He had it on his desk, though I don't think he was going to use it on me." Mark gave a harsh laugh. "I mean, what would it matter if I got an infection when he was going to kill me anyway? I was backing out of the room, and she was pouring the stuff on the floor. You could smell that, too, some sort of surgical spirit, along with everything else. I was feeling pretty sick by then. Anyway, I saw a small fire extinguisher in the hall and I took it. She'd already started the fire by the time I got back, but it wasn't a very big one. Just a small patch where she'd poured the spirits. It was easy to put out."

"What was Mrs. Aspern doing while you put the fire out?"

"Nothing. She didn't even try to stop me, if that's what you mean. To be honest, she looked as if she'd had it, like she'd given up and didn't care anymore. When I was sure it was out, I took her into the other room and she went with me, quiet as a lamb, like she was in a trance or something. I rang nine-nine-nine."

Banks and Bridges said nothing for a while as Mark smoked and the tape recorder ran on. Finally, Banks asked, "Is there anything else?"

"No," said Mark.

Bridges turned off the tapes.

"What are you going to do now?" Banks asked Mark.

"Are you charging me?"

Banks looked at Bridges, who shook his head. "I don't think the CPS would find much of a case there," he said. "You're free to go. But you're an important witness, and the CPS will want to talk to you, as well as Mrs. Aspern's lawyers. Whatever you do, you need to stay close, stay available, make sure we know where you are."

Mark nodded. "I know. I've still got some money left. I suppose I can buy myself some new clothes and find a place to stay for a while."

"Why don't you come back to Eastvale? Give my contact on the restoration project a call? He's always looking for keen apprentices."

"Dunno. I might do. To be honest, right now, I just want a bit of space, some peace and quiet. I want to try and get all these horrible pictures out of my head."

Good luck, thought Banks, who hadn't succeeded in getting the nightmare images out of his own head after years of trying.

Leslie Whitaker seemed to have done a runner. His shop was closed, and he wasn't at his Lyndgarth home. Cursing herself for not keeping a closer eye on him, Annie set the wheels in motion to track him down.

They had at least been lucky with Friends Reunited, Annie thought, pulling up outside the small detached house with

Winsome late that afternoon. Elaine Hough lived on the out-skirts of Harrogate, where she worked as an executive chef in one of the spa's best restaurants. Elaine wasn't the only one to reply to Winsome's request, saying she remembered both Thomas McMahon and Roland Gardiner—two others out of the 115 alumni registered at the Friends Reunited Web site had also responded quickly and said they remembered the two—but she was by far the most easily accessible of the three—one being in Eastbourne and the other in Aberdeen—and she also said that Gardiner and McMahon had been good friends of hers.

Elaine Hough seemed a no-nonsense sort of woman with a brisk manner and short black hair streaked with gray. If she ate what she cooked, she didn't show it on her tall, lean frame.

"Come in," she said. Annie and Winsome followed her through to the sparsely decorated living room, all exposed beams and stone and heavy oak furniture.

"Nice," Annie said. But if truth be told, it wasn't her fa-vorite style of interior decoration.

"I'm glad you like it. It's more a reflection of my hus-band's taste, really. I spend most of the time in my little den when I'm at home."

"Not in the kitchen?"

Elaine laughed. "Well, it's true, I still *do* love cooking, and I don't get much of a chance to do any at the restaurant any-more. It's the old, old story, isn't it? You work your way up in an area you love, and then you find you're so successful you spend all your time running the business side, and you don't have time to do what you love best anymore." She laughed. "But I can't complain. And I don't. I know how lucky I am. Would you like tea or coffee or something?"

"Coffee would be nice," said Annie. Winsome nodded in agreement.

"Come through to the kitchen, then. We can talk there."

They followed her into a modern kitchen with stainless steel oven and fridge, copper pots and pans hanging from a rail over the central granite-topped island, and a wood-block of expensive-looking chef's knives. Annie had sometimes thought that she would like such a well-stocked and attractive kitchen herself, but her cooking skills extended about as far as vegetarian pasta and ordering an Indian take-away, so most of the fancy equipment would be wasted on her.

Elaine put the kettle on, and while it boiled, she ground coffee beans and dropped them in a cafetière. The aroma was delicious. All her movements were economical and deft, Annie noticed, betraying her occupation and her training. Even something as simple as making coffee got her full attention. She probably even knew how to chop up a string of onions quickly, and without crying, too.

They sat on stools around the island while the coffee brewed and Annie went through her mental list of questions.

"You said you knew both Thomas McMahon *and* Roland Gardiner at Leeds Poly?" she started.

"Yes."

"Did you know them together, or separately?"

"Both, actually. Look, I was in the School of Cookery—surprise, surprise—but four evenings a week I worked behind the bar in the student pub. My parents weren't well off and my grant wasn't exactly huge. At least we still got grants back then, not loans, like today. Anyway, that's where I first met Tommy and Rolo. That's what we called them back then. I was so sorry to read about what happened, but I couldn't see how it could be at all relevant to me until your e-mail. Otherwise, I'd have come forward sooner."

"That's all right," said Annie. "How were you to know what we were looking for? Anyway, we're here now."

"Yes." Elaine poured the coffee. Winsome asked for milk

and sugar while Annie and Elaine took theirs black. "Actually," she said, "I went out with Rolo a few times. Just casual, like. Nothing too heavy."

"What was he like?"

"Rolo? Well, I heard he was living alone in a caravan when he died—very sad—but back then he seemed ambitious, bright, ready to take on the world. I remember we all used to get into a lot of arguments because Rolo was a Thatcherite and the rest of us were wishy-washy liberals." She laughed. "But he was fun, and intelligent. What can I say? We got along fine."

"Even after you split up?"

"We remained friends. It wasn't a serious relationship. You know what it's like when you're a student. You experiment, go out with different people."

"Did you go out with Thomas McMahon, too?"

"Tommy? No. Not that he wasn't attractive, or that he had any shortage of admirers. We just . . . I don't know, we just didn't hit it off on that level. Besides," she added, "you may have noticed I'm a bit taller than the average woman, and Tommy was short. Not that I've got anything against short men, you understand, but it's always been, well . . . just that little bit awkward. Even Rolo was only just about the same height as me."

"I understand what you mean," said Winsome, looking up from her notebook and smiling.

"Yes, I'll bet you do," Elaine said.

Annie sipped her coffee. It was still hot enough to burn her tongue, but it tasted as wonderful as the ground beans had smelled. "So Tommy and Rolo were good friends?" she went on.

"Yes. They met in the pub, liked the same music, and even though he was studying business, Rolo was no slouch when it came to the arts. I think he liked hanging around with the artsy crowd. He said more than once that most of his fellow business students were boring. I remember, he used to write. Stories, poetry . . . His poems were quite good. What he showed me, anyway. Not your usual adolescent rubbish. Thoughtful. Some of them even rhymed. And he was well-read."

"So they weren't such odd bedfellows?"

"No, not at all."

"Did you ever know anyone back then by the name of Masefield? William Masefield?"

"No. I can't say I did. Why?"

"Doesn't matter. What about a Leslie Whitaker?"

"Can't say that rings a bell, either."

"Was there anyone else?"

"What do you mean?"

"Was it just the two of them hung out together, or were they part of a larger group?"

"Oh, I see what you mean. Well, there used to be quite a few of them sat in the back corner. Mostly art students, and a few guests from outside. But it was the three of them stuck together most of all."

"Three of them?"

"Yes. Rolo, Tommy and Giles."

"Who was Giles?"

Elaine smiled and, to Annie's eyes, even seemed to blush a little at the memory. "Giles was my boyfriend. My real boyfriend. For the second year, at any rate."

"And he was a friend of Tommy's and Rolo's?"

"Yes. Thick as thieves, they were."

"This Giles, what college was he attached to?"

"He wasn't. Giles went to the uni, Leeds University."

"To study what?"

"Art history."

That was interesting, Annie thought. "He wasn't a painter or a sculptor?"

"No." Elaine laughed. "He said he had no talent for it, but he loved it. The same with music. He liked to listen—classical mostly, but he did often come to see bands with us—although he couldn't play an instrument."

"How did he know Rolo and Tommy?"

"I don't know. They probably got talking in one of those pubs on Woodhouse Lane near the campus. The three of them just came as a package."

"And you say you went out with Giles?"

"For a year, yes. My second year."

"Serious?"

Elaine looked down into her coffee cup. "Yes, I suppose so. For me. At least, that was what I thought at the time. Young love. It's all so long ago. It feels strange to be thinking back after all this time, all that's happened since."

"What happened to Giles?"

"He vanished."

"Vanished?"

"Just like that. I don't mean he was abducted or anything. At least I don't think he was. He just disappeared as quickly as he'd arrived on the scene."

"Had he finished his degree?"

"No, that was the funny thing. It was only the end of his second year. He never came back."

"What did you do?"

"I tried to find out about him from the department, but they wouldn't tell me anything, of course."

"Did you have a row or something?"

"No. Honestly. He just . . . One day he was there, and everything was fine, but the next day he was gone. Maybe not quite like that. I mean, we were all away for the holidays, but he just didn't come back. Not a trace. It was sad . . . I mean, I don't know if you've ever experienced this, but he was one of those people who leaves a big hole in your life when he goes." She laughed. "Listen to me. Aren't I being silly? Anyway, I suppose what I'm saying is that I was a little bit in love with him."

"Can you tell me anything more about him?"

"Not really. He was a bit of a dark horse. That's probably one of the other things that was so exciting about him. The mysterious quality. But he was great fun to be around. And generous. He always seemed to have plenty of money."

"Do you know where he got it from?"

"His parents were wealthy. His father had something to do with defense work, government contracts. Knew Maggie Thatcher personally, apparently. If you ask me, I think he was an arms dealer. Come to think of it, Giles was a lot closer to Rolo in his political ideas than any of the rest of us. And his mother was related to the Duke of Devonshire. Only distantly, mind. Anyway, they had a big old family mansion house outside King's Lynn."

"Did you ever go there?"

"No. Not inside, at any rate. Giles drove me past it once, perhaps because I nagged him about it so much. But we didn't go in. He said his parents were away in Italy and the place was locked up. Very *Brideshead Revisited*."

"He didn't have a key?"

"Apparently not. They had to give him money, he said—it was some sort of inheritance or trust fund, and it belonged to him—but they didn't actually get on. They weren't on speaking terms."

"Did you ever try to get in touch with them after he'd disappeared?"

"No. After a while I just gave up and got on with life. You know what it's like when you're young. A broken heart feels like it'll never mend for at least a couple of weeks. You pull out all your sad, romantic records and indulge in a bit of tearful melancholy for a while, maybe go out, get rat-arsed and fuck a stranger, then you move on. Pardon my language."

"I remember. Neil Trethowan."

"Sorry?"

"The one who first broke my heart. Neil Trethowan was his name."

"Yes. Well, Giles . . . It was so long ago, but now you've got me talking about it, it seems just like yesterday. Some of it, anyway."

"Did you ever see him or hear from him again?"

"No."

"Do you know if Tommy and Rolo kept in touch with him?"

"If they did, they didn't tell me. We all lost touch when we graduated, of course, as you do, though we had every good intention."

"What was his last name?"

"Moore. Giles Moore."

With the name and some of the details Elaine had given them, they would be able to dig a little deeper into the background of this enigmatic Giles Moore, Annie thought, perhaps even locate him. Of course, he might have had nothing to do with recent events, but at least he sounded a promising start. They were looking for someone who was linked with both Thomas McMahon and Roland Gardiner when they were at Leeds Polytechnic, and it looked as if they'd found that someone.

"Do you have any photographs?" Annie asked.

"No. They disappeared after one of my many moves."

"Pity," said Annie. "This might sound like a strange question, but was there ever any connection between Giles or the rest of you and a fire?"

Elaine frowned. "A fire? No, not that I remember. I mean, I'm sure there were fires in the city, but none of them concerned us. Surely you can't think Giles had anything to do with what happened to Tommy and Rolo? Not after all this time."

"I'm not saying he did," said Annie. "But don't you think it's a big coincidence that two men living about ten miles from one another, both killed in suspicious fires only days apart, happened to be at Leeds Polytechnic at the same time? I do. Not only that, but since we've talked to you, we now also know that they were close friends over twenty years ago. And then there's this mysterious third: Giles Moore."

"But Giles wouldn't hurt anyone. Why would he do that?"

"Is there anything else you can tell us about him that might help us find him?"

"No," said Elaine. Annie could sense her closing down. She didn't like the idea of her old lover being in the frame for a double murder. Annie didn't blame her; she wouldn't feel too good about it, either.

"What did he look like?"

"He was very good-looking. A bit taller than me, slim. Wavy hair, a bit long. Chestnut. But that was years ago."

"How old was he at the time?"

"Twenty-one, a couple of years older than the rest of us."

"Any distinguishing marks?"

"What do you mean?"

"Like birthmarks, scars, that sort of thing."

"No," said Elaine. "His skin was smooth, without a blemish." She blushed at the memory. "Apart from an appendectomy scar."

"Any regional accent?"

"No. A bit posh, maybe, but not too much. Educated, upper-class. Just like you'd expect, coming from the background he did."

"Smoker? Drinker?"

"He smoked. We all did back then. I mean, it's not as if we didn't know what it did to you—it was 1980, after all—but we were young, we felt invulnerable. I stopped ten years ago. As for the drinking, we all did."

"To excess?"

"Giles? Not really, no."

"Was there anyone else on the scene you think we might be able to locate and talk to?"

"It was so long ago. I've lost touch with all of them. Can't even remember most of their names. You do lose touch, don't you? Move away, get married, have kids or concentrate on your career."

Annie realized that even though she was younger than Elaine, and not so distant from her past, she didn't know a soul she went to school or university with, hadn't kept in touch at all. Still, given the police life, the frequent relocations, the unreasonable hours, it was hardly surprising. Apart from Phil, the only friends she had were colleagues from work, the only social life an occasional drink with Banks or someone else in the Queen's Arms. "Do you have any ideas who might have done this to Tommy and Rolo?"

"Me? Good Lord, no. I just don't believe Giles had anything to do with it."

Annie gestured to Winsome, who put away her notebook. She hoped Elaine was right, though perhaps a part of her also hoped that they could track down this Giles Moore and prove that he *was* the one who did it. At least then the case would be solved and a murderer would be off the streets. In the meantime, it was time to see if any progress had been made on tracking down Leslie Whitaker.

As Banks walked out of the underground station on to Holland Park Avenue, he was grateful for yet another mild evening after the previous night's cold snap, and thankful that he had been in Leeds when he got Burgess's message. He was also lucky that both the trains and the tube were running on time that day. As a result, it was a little over two and a half hours since his train had pulled out of Leeds City Station, and now he was heading for Helen Keane's flat—the one she shared with her art researcher husband, Phil (now short for "philanderer" in Banks's mind) Keane—in one of the residential streets across the main road, overlooking the park itself. Maybe it wasn't Mayfair or Belgravia, but you didn't live around here if you couldn't afford the high rents.

Banks didn't know what to expect when he pressed the buzzer. For obvious reasons, he hadn't rung ahead, so he didn't even know if Keane himself would be there. He hoped not, but it didn't really matter. He needed to know what the hell was going on. It wasn't just a question of Annie's feelings being hurt, but of someone being not exactly the sort of person he presented himself as. It probably meant nothing, but coming hot on the heels of the lie about not knowing McMahon, Banks wanted some answers.

A cautious voice came over the intercom. "Yes?"

Banks introduced himself and said he wanted to speak to Helen Keane. Naturally, she was suspicious and nervous— people always are when the police come to call—but he managed to convince her that it was information he wanted, nothing more. She agreed to let him in but said she would keep her chain on until she had seen his identification. Fair enough, Banks thought, climbing the plushly carpeted stairs. Foyers, halls and stairs said a lot about the quality, and cost, of the place you were visiting, Banks always thought, the way bath towels and toilet paper said a lot about the hotel you were staying in.

As promised, she kept the chain on while she examined his warrant card, then she let him in.

The flat was an interior designer's paradise, all sharp angles and reflective surfaces, colors named after rare plants and southwest American states. There was no clutter. The stereo was state-of-the-art, brushed steel, hanging on the wall next to the large plasma wide-screen TV, and if the Keanes owned any books or CDs, they were stored elsewhere or hidden well out of sight. A couple of artfully placed art and design magazines were the only reading materials in plain view. At the far end of the high-ceilinged room stood a narrow black chair with a fan-shaped back. When he looked more closely, Banks couldn't be sure whether it was a chair or a work of art. At any rate, he wouldn't want to try sitting on it.

The woman who came with the flat was every bit as much of an expensive package and a designer's wet dream—beautiful, chic, petite, dark-haired, thirty at most, with intense blue eyes and a pale, flawless complexion. She was wearing ivory silk combats, high-heeled sandals and a delicate lace top that didn't quite obscure her skimpy black bra.

She bade Banks sit on the modular sofa and sat opposite, on a matching armchair, the color of which Banks couldn't name. Pink, or coral, came closest, but even they were a long way off.

"It's all right, Mrs. Keane," said Banks. "There's no need to be nervous. As far as I know, nobody's done anything criminal. I'd just like a bit of background information, if you don't mind."

"About what?"

"Your husband."

She seemed to relax a bit at that. "Philip? What about him? I'm afraid I don't know where he is right now."

Banks noticed a trace of an accent. It sounded vaguely Eastern European to his untrained ear. "How long have you been married?" he asked.

"Three years now."

"How did you meet?"

"At a club."

"Where?"

"In the West End. I was working there. It was a gambling club. A casino. Philip used to come there to play cards. We talked once . . . he asked me to dinner . . . you know . . ."

"Where are you from?" Banks asked.

"Where from?"

"Yes. Your accent."

"Ah. Kosovo," she said. "But everything is legal."

"Because of the marriage?"

"Yes. I have a British passport now. Everything is legal. Philip did that for me."

"But when you met?"

She smiled. "You know . . . I was Jelena Pavelich then, just another poor refugee from a war-torn country trying to make a simple living." She gestured around the room. "Now I am Helen Keane."

"It's a nice flat," Banks said.

"Thank you. I designed it myself."

"Is that what you did? In Kosovo?"

"No. I studied at university there. Languages. To be a translator. Then the fighting came. My parents were killed. I had to leave."

"How did you escape?"

"People helped me. It was a long journey. One I want to forget. I saw many terrible things. I had to do many bad things. But you said you wanted to know about Philip?"

"Yes," said Banks. "Do you know what he was doing before you met?"

"He said he was working abroad. In galleries and museums, in Italy, Spain, Russia, America. Philip is very clever. He has traveled all over the world."

"Yes, I know that," said Banks.

Helen's eyes narrowed as she studied him. "Has he taken your girlfriend? Is that why you want to ask me about him?"

Banks felt himself blush. "Why do you say that?"

She smiled the way women do when they think they've gained the upper edge, put their finger on your weakness. "Because Philip is a very attractive man, no?"

"I suppose so," said Banks. "But what makes you think he would have another woman? Has he been unfaithful before?"

She laughed. It was a deep, hoarse, almost crude kind of laugh, not at all the sort of sound he would have expected from such an exquisitely petite woman, but more like the way you'd laugh at a dirty joke in a smoky pub. Banks liked it. It made her seem more human to him, less of an ethereal beauty. "Philip always has other women," she said.

"And it doesn't bother you?"

She made a little moue, then answered, "Ours is not that kind of marriage. We do what we want."

"Why stay together, then?"

"Because we like one another. We are friends. And because, well . . ."

"Go on."

She looked around the flat and ran her hand over her lace top, all the way down over the rise and fall of her small breasts. "I like nice things. Do you not think I'm pretty?"

"Very."

"I think for Philip I am a business asset also, no? He likes to be seen with his pretty young wife on his arm. All his friends and colleagues envy him. They all want to go to bed with me. I can tell by the way they look at me."

"And Philip enjoys that?"

"Yes. We go to openings and dinners and galas together. All sorts of official functions with many important people. And all of them look at me the same way. Young men. Old men. Some wives. It is good to be married when you have a business, yes?"

Banks agreed that it was. For some reason, marriage gave the semblance of both conservatism and stability that people require from a business. Potential clients were much more inclined to be suspicious of a bachelor of Phil's or Banks's age than they were of a married man. And the fact that his wife was a mysterious Eastern European beauty would certainly do no harm in the circles he moved in. If anything, it might make him seem a little more daring than most. Not too much, but just enough of a risk-taker to be worth running with.

Yes, if Phil Keane wanted everyone to think he was a traditional, solid and dependable sort of fellow, he could do a lot worse than step out with Helen on his arm. And for her part, she had already indicated that she loved the trappings of wealth, the opulent lifestyle. Perhaps she had lovers, too? It seemed to be an open sort of marriage, according to what she had said, so no doubt she had plenty of freedom. Banks felt a little uncomfortable now as his eyes strayed to the outline of her skimpy bra under the lace top, and the exposed black strap against her pale shoulder. He found himself wondering just how much Phil Keane's lifestyle cost him, and whether ArtSearch made enough to support it.

"Did your husband ever mention a man called Thomas McMahon, an artist he knew?"

"No."

"You never met anyone called Thomas McMahon?"

"No."

"What about William Masefield?"

"No."

"Leslie Whitaker?"

"I haven't heard the name. But Philip never talks about his friends. If he's not here, then I have no idea where he is or what he's doing."

"Does he have many close friends?"

"Close friends? I don't think so. Mostly it is work."

"You mean colleagues he's met through work, in the art field?"

"Yes."

"Does he have any partners, anyone he works closely with?"

"No. He says he doesn't trust other people. They only mess things up. If he wants to do something, he does it himself."

"Does Philip ever take you to the family cottage in Fortford?"

"What family cottage?"

"Apparently it belonged to his grandparents. In Yorkshire. He inherited it."

"I know nothing about any grandparents. All Philip told me about his family is that his father was a diplomat and they were always moving from one country to another when he was young. Where did you hear about these grandparents? Who told you?"

"It doesn't matter," said Banks. "Did you ever meet his parents?"

"They're dead. They were killed in a plane crash ten years ago, before we met."

"And he never said anything about owning property in Yorkshire?"

"Never. Whenever we go away we go to California or the Bahamas. But never to Yorkshire." She hugged herself and gave a little shiver. "It is cold there, no?"

"Sometimes," Banks said.

"I love the sun."

"Helen," said Banks, mostly out of exasperation, "do you know *anything* about your husband?"

She laughed again, that deep, throaty sound, then spread her hands as if to display her body. "I know he likes the good things in life," she said, without a hint of false modesty.

Banks realized there was nothing more to be learned from her, so he said his good-byes and made a speedy exit, more confused than when he had first arrived.

Chapter 17

*A*fter a good night's sleep and a morning spent catching up with the previous day's developments—especially Elaine Hough's statement and the candle wax found in Roland Gardiner's caravan—Banks asked Annie if she fancied a cup of tea and a toasted tea cake at the Golden Grill, just across from the station. He needed to build a few bridges if they were to continue working together.

He'd been struggling with the dilemma that Helen Keane posed all the way home on the train from London the previous evening, and all that morning, and he still hadn't come to any firm decision. Maybe he'd probe Annie a bit, find out how she really felt about Phil. It wasn't fair to charge right in, he realized, and tell her outright. Especially as Keane's marriage was definitely the unusual kind. On the other hand, he was concerned about her feelings, and he didn't want her getting in too deep with Keane before she found out he was married. Still, he could only imagine how his news would be received, especially as their relationship was hardly on firm ground at the moment.

The bell over the door pinged as they entered. The place was half empty and they had their pick of tables. Banks immediately headed for the most isolated. As soon as they were settled with a pot of tea and tea cakes, Banks stirred his tea, though there was nothing added to it, and said, "Look, Annie, I'd just like to say that I'm sorry. I was out of line the other day. About bringing Phil in. Of course it made sense. I was just . . ."

"Jealous?"

"Not in the real sense of the word, no. It just feels awkward, that's all."

"He thinks you don't like him."

"Can't say I have an opinion one way or another. I've only met him a couple of times."

"Oh, come on, Alan."

"Really. He seems fine. But when it comes down to it, how much do you know about him?"

"What do you mean?"

"I mean about his background, his past, his family. Has he ever been married, for example?"

"Not that he's mentioned to me. And I don't think he has. That's one of the refreshing things about him."

The remark stung Banks, as he thought it was intended to. His failed marriage and the baggage thereof had been a constant bone of contention in his relationship with Annie. The wise thing to do would be to move on, not to retaliate with what he had learned from Dirty Dick Burgess. He teetered on the brink for a moment, then asked, "Anything new this morning?"

"Not a lot," said Annie. "Winsome's been looking into William Masefield's background and come up with one piece of interesting information: He attended Leeds University, and he was there at the same time as McMahon and Gardiner were enrolled at the Poly. From 1978 to 1981. There's no evidence that they knew one another, however, and Elaine Hough says she'd never heard of him."

"Pity," said Banks. "Still, it does give us a tenuous link. Wasn't Giles Moore at the university?"

"That's another thing. I checked with the university this

morning, and they say there's no record of him ever being there."

"Interesting," said Banks. "Maybe he didn't get accepted, felt he needed to impress people."

"Even so," said Annie. "It's a pretty odd thing to do, isn't it?"

"He sounds like an odd person altogether," Banks agreed. "Which gives us all the more reason to be interested in him. He's got to be somewhere. He can't just have vanished into thin air."

"We're looking," said Annie. "The only problem is that we're running out of places to look. As far as we can tell so far, there aren't any Moores living in mansions near King's Lynn. We haven't actually asked Maggie Thatcher or the Duke of Devonshire whether they knew a Giles Moore yet, but it may come to that."

Banks laughed. "So he's a liar, then?"

"So it would seem."

"What we need to do," Banks said, "is have the Hough woman look at a photograph of Whitaker. I know it was a long time ago, but she may still recognize something about him." And a photo of Phil Keane, too, if he could get his hands on one, Banks added to himself. "I seem to remember there was a framed photo on the desk in the bookshop. As he's missing, and people have been dying, I suppose it's reasonable for us to enter the premises, wouldn't you say? I mean, he could be lying dead in the back room soaked in petrol, with a six-hour candle slowly burning down beside him, for all we know."

"Good idea," said Annie. "I'll get on to it. What's going to happen with the Aspern woman?"

"Frances?" Banks shook his head. "I don't know. From what Mark Siddons told us, she might have a damn good case for pleading provocation."

"What about diminished responsibility?"

"I'd leave that one to the experts. She needs psychiatric

help, no doubt about it. She's not clinically insane—at least not in my layman's opinion—but she's confused and disturbed. I think she just couldn't accept that her husband was sexually abusing his own daughter the same way he'd sexually abused her. It was easier in her mind to embrace the lie they'd lived right from the start—from when he first got her pregnant—that this fictitious American, Paul Ryder, was the father, and that Patrick was Tina's stepfather. Maybe sometimes she actually believed it. It's a thin line."

"It certainly is," Annie agreed. "I suppose this knocks both her and her husband off the list of suspects?"

"Yes," said Banks.

"And how seriously are we taking Andrew Hurst and Mark Siddons?"

"Not very. Hurst's weird. I mean, if it turns out that the art forgery angle's a blind alley and the fires were set by some nutter who just likes to set fires, then I'd look closely at him again. But he's got no connection with McMahon, Gardiner and the rest. Neither does Mark Siddons, except that he happened to be a neighbor of McMahon's. Mark has his problems, but I don't think arson is one of them. Besides, he has a good alibi. You said so yourself."

"I could talk to Mandy Patterson again. Go in a bit harder."

"No," said Banks. "What could she possibly gain by giving Mark Siddons an alibi for murder? If Mark had wanted rid of Tina, there were far easier and more reliable ways of doing it than fixing himself up with a dodgy alibi and setting fire to Thomas McMahon's boat."

"Which brings us back to Leslie Whitaker," said Annie.

"What's his educational background?"

"He attended Strathclyde University from 1980 to 1983. Unfortunately, there's no evidence that links him to either Gardiner or Masefield, but we're still looking. And the way he's taken off certainly makes him seem more suspicious. That and some of his recent financial idiosyncrasies. According to the auditor, his business books are a bit of a mess, to say the least."

"I suppose if he was involved in some sort of scam with McMahon, he had to hide the profits somehow. Tell me your thoughts, Annie."

"McMahon was known to be a good imitator, and he gained access to period materials through Whitaker's bookshop, and no doubt from other sources. Maybe Whitaker, Moore, or whoever set it up, enlisted his old buddies to help him in a forgery scam and they fell out?"

"Okay," said Banks. "That makes sense up to a point. But what parts did Gardiner and Masefield play?"

"Masefield provided the identity for the killer to remain anonymous in his dealings with McMahon," said Annie. "Whenever they met, he hired a Jeep Cherokee in Masefield's name, no doubt so we wouldn't be able to trace him. Remember, when Masefield died, or was killed, our man had his post redirected to a post office box, used his bank accounts, paid his bills. Assumed his identity."

"What about Gardiner?"

"I don't know yet. But he must have played some part in it all. Don't forget the Turners and the money we found in his safe. They can't be just coincidence."

"No. I haven't forgotten them. But none of this gets us any closer to who that person actually *is*," said Banks. "Even if it *is* Giles bloody Moore, he's not going by that name now, and that name probably won't lead us to him. He's slippery. We're dealing with a chameleon, Annie. A damn clever one, too. Did you find out anything else about Moore? Anything at all that might help us?"

"No," said Annie. "Not yet. It's a lot of legwork. And legwork takes time, and more legs than we've got right now."

"I can talk to Red Ron about manpower."

"Thanks," said Annie. "I could do with a couple more good researchers, at least. But for the moment, my money's still on Leslie Whitaker. Just because we haven't been able to find a past connection between him and Gardiner doesn't mean one doesn't exist, or even that we need one. I mean, maybe McMahon himself is the link. Maybe Whitaker put the idea to McMahon and McMahon recruited Gardiner."

"Maybe," said Banks. "We'll have to ask him when we find him." He finished his tea and let the silence stretch a moment before asking, "How are you and Phil getting along, by the way?"

"Fine," Annie said. "Why do you ask?"

"No reason. Where is he, anyway? I haven't seen him for a couple of days."

"He's down in London dealing with the Turners. You know that. Why the sudden interest?"

"Nothing. Just wondering, that's all."

Annie looked him in the eye. "Phil's right, isn't he? What I said earlier. You denied it at the time, but you didn't like him right from the start, did you? I mean, you never really gave him a chance, did you?"

"I told you, I've got nothing against him," Banks said. But if truth be told, he had a very uneasy feeling about Phil Keane, like an itch he couldn't quite scratch, and though he wouldn't tell Annie this, he was going to keep on digging into the man's background until he was satisfied one way or another. "I don't want to start another argument, Annie," Banks said. "I just asked you how you two were getting along."

"Yes, but it's not as simple as that, is it? It never is with you. I can tell from your tone of voice. There's always another agenda. What is it? What do you know? What are you getting at?"

Banks spread his hands. "I don't know what you mean."

"Is it jealousy? Is that what it is, Alan? Because, honestly, if it's that, if that's what it is, I'll just get a fucking transfer out of here."

Banks didn't remember ever hearing Annie swear before,

and it shocked him. "Look," he said, "it's not jealousy. Okay? I just don't want to see you get hurt, that's all."

"Why should I get hurt? And who do you think you are? My big brother? I can take care of myself, thank you very much."

And with that, Annie tossed her serviette on the remains of her toasted tea cake and strode out of the café. Was it Banks's imagination, or did the bell ping just that little more loudly when she left?

Annie spent the rest of the day avoiding Banks. It wasn't difficult; she had plenty more paperwork to hide behind, and she took Winsome along to Whitaker's shop, which they entered through the backdoor, leaving no sign that they had been there, and borrowed the photograph. A quick trip to Harrogate didn't provide the conclusive answers she had hoped for. It was over twenty years ago, after all, said Elaine Hough, and Whitaker's chin and eyes were wrong. Even so, that didn't let Whitaker off the hook for the fires as far as Annie was concerned.

Had she overreacted to Banks in the Golden Grill? She didn't know. There had just been something about the way he kept on bringing up the subject of Phil that irritated her. Perhaps she should have let it go; after all, that would have been easy enough. But if she was going to carry on seeing Phil and working with Banks, then something would have to change, and it wasn't going to be Annie.

Banks clearly had something on his mind, and she wished she knew what it was. Had he been investigating Phil behind her back? Had he found out something? If so, what? Annie dismissed her fears as absurd. If Banks had found any dirt on Phil, he would have made sure she was the first to know. Otherwise, what was the point? Except to hurt her. Lash out because of his jealousy.

But the suspicion and anxiety persisted throughout the day and made it hard for her to concentrate. Late in the afternoon, by which time Annie already knew she was going to be working late into the evening, the phone rang.

"Annie, it's Phil here."

"Well, hello. It's nice to hear from you, stranger."

"I just thought I'd let you know that the consensus of opinion is that the Turner sketches and watercolor are forgeries."

If Annie was a bit disappointed that Phil was calling her on business, she tried not to let it show in her voice.

"Oh. Why's that?" she asked.

"It's nothing specific. Just a number of things adding up, or not adding up. Some of the scientific tests indicated the paper used was slightly later than the dates of the sketches. Then there's the style. Little details. I told you Turner was hard to fake. When you add to that the lack of provenance, the loose sketches and the coincidence of these pieces turning up so quickly after the major find, then . . ."

"What about fingerprints? In the paint, I mean."

"There were none. So no help there."

"Would there have been if the painting were genuine?"

"Not necessarily."

"Okay, Phil. Thanks," said Annie. "Does this cast doubt on the other watercolor?"

"Not at all. We've got some provenance there, and the same tests didn't turn out negative. I think that one was a genuine find. It must have given someone the idea of forging the other missing piece."

"McMahon?"

"I've no idea who did it, but if you found it at the site of the caravan fire, and you've managed to link the two victims, yes, I'd say you're probably on the right track. They must have hatched some harebrained get-rich-quick scheme. It's quite possible to be a fine artist and pretty useless at almost everything else."

"Tell me about it," said Annie, thinking of her father. She had grown up surrounded by beards and endless arguments on Impressionism versus Cubism, Van Gogh versus Gauguin and the like. While Ray seemed reasonably well equipped to handle the real world, he could lose himself in his work for days on end and forget about petty irritations like bills and housecleaning.

"Anyway, that's all I've got to say, for better or worse. I'll get them packed and have them couriered back up to you. They're worthless, but I suppose you might still need them as evidence?"

"Thanks," said Annie.

"How are things up there?"

"Fine, I suppose."

"Closing in for the kill?"

"Maybe," Annie said. "Whitaker—you know, the bloke who supplied McMahon with the paper—he's disappeared."

"As in been killed?"

"No. As in legged it."

"Oh, I see. Best of luck then."

"Thanks."

"What's wrong? You sound a bit glum."

"Oh, it's nothing. I had a bit of a barney with Alan, DCI Banks, this morning. It's left rather a bad taste in my mouth."

"What about?"

"Nothing. That's it. Just me being oversensitive. I wish the two of you could get on better."

"Why, what's he said about me?"

"Nothing. It's just . . . I don't know, Phil. It's me. Don't pay any attention."

"Did he say anything about me?"

"No. He just asked about you, that's all. See what I mean about being oversensitive?"

"I shouldn't worry about it, then," said Phil. "I've got nothing against him. I've only met the man the once, and you were there."

"Like I said, Phil, it's just me. Where are you? Will you be up tonight?"

"Afraid not. I'm still down in London. I'll try to make it to-morrow or the next day, all right?"

"Okay. See you later, then."

"See you."

Annie put the phone down and looked at the piles of ac-tions and statements on her desk. Well, at least it would keep her from thinking about Banks. And about Phil.

But before she could even pick up her pen, DC Templeton dashed into the squad room. "We've got him," he said. "We've got Whitaker. He's downstairs."

"Well, Leslie," said Banks. "It's quite a merry dance you've led us, isn't it?"

"I had no idea you'd been looking for me," said Whitaker. "How could I?"

They were in the same interview room as last time, only today Whitaker was already wearing the disposable red over-alls. He hadn't been charged, but he had been arrested and read his rights, and the tape recorders were running. The duty solicitor, Gareth Bowen, sat beside him. Banks could still sense some tension between Annie and himself, but he knew that they were both professional enough to do their jobs, es-pecially now they seemed close to the end. If they could break Whitaker, it would be drinks all around in the Queen's Arms, and there was a good chance Banks would get to see Michelle this weekend.

"Where were you?" Banks asked.

"I needed to get away. I went to visit a friend in Newcastle."

"Rather an opportune time to go away, wasn't it?"

"As I said, I had no idea you would want to talk to me again."

"Oh, I think you did, Leslie," said Banks. "In fact, I'm sure you did."

"Why don't you tell us about it?" Annie said. "You'll feel better if you do."

Whitaker curled his lip. "Tell you about what?"

"About Thomas McMahon. Tommy. And about Roland Gardiner. Rolo. How long have you known them?"

"I don't know what you're talking about. I've already told you I saw Thomas McMahon in the shop from time to time, but I don't know the other person you're talking about."

Banks sighed. "All right, we'll do it the hard way."

"Lay a finger on me and I'll sue you." Whitaker looked over to Bowen, who just rolled his eyes.

"What I meant," said Banks, "is that I'm tired, DI Cabbot's tired, and I'm sure you and Mr. Bowen are tired, too. But we'll stay here as long as it takes to get the truth." He glanced at Bowen. "With all requisite meal breaks and rest periods, as required by the Police and Criminal Evidence Act, of course."

"I don't have to tell you anything," said Whitaker.

"No, you don't," Banks agreed. "In fact, if you remember that bit in the caution about later relying in court on something you *didn't* say when we first asked you, you'll understand exactly what it means not to have to tell us anything. But let me lay my cards on the table, Leslie. At the moment, you're our main suspect in the murders of Thomas McMahon and Roland Gardiner."

"But I told you, I was in Harrogate, at a dinner party. Surely you must have checked?"

"We checked."

"And?"

"Everyone we talked to corroborates your statement. You were there."

Whitaker folded his arms. "I told you so."

"I wouldn't look so smug if I were you, Leslie," Banks went on. "We now have evidence to suggest that a timing device was used in Roland Gardiner's caravan."

"A timing device?"

"Yes. A candle. Crude but effective. It allowed the arsonist to prepare the fire scene but leave before the blaze started. A good couple of hours before. Easily. Wouldn't you agree, DI Cabbot?"

"Yes," said Annie, turning the pages of Stefan Nowak's report. "Easily."

"But do you have any evidence specifically to connect Mr. Whitaker to the scene?" Bowen asked. "All you're saying is that *anyone* could have set that fire."

"Have you ever heard of a man called William Masefield?" Banks asked Whitaker.

"No. Never."

"All right. We'll leave that for the moment. Did you or did you not supply period paper to Thomas McMahon?"

"He bought books and prints from me. It's my business. It's what I sell."

"But did you sell them to him for the purpose of forging works of art?"

"Chief Inspector Banks," Bowen cut in. "Mr. Whitaker can hardly be held responsible for what a client did *after* a purchase, or even know what he intended to do."

"Perhaps in this case, he can," said Banks. "If money was involved."

Whitaker looked sheepish.

"Leslie?" Banks went on. "What's it to be?"

"I told you," Whitaker repeated. "I sold him what he wanted. It's what you do when you're in business."

"You own a Jeep Cherokee, am I right?" said Banks.

"You know I do. Your men have been taking it apart since we last spoke."

"And," Bowen added, "might I say that they have come up with nothing to connect my client's car with either crime scene."

"Not yet," said Banks.

"In fact," Bowen went on, "I understand that a Jeep Cherokee *has* been connected with the Thomas McMahon fire, and that it was rented to this mysterious, and late, Mr. William Masefield by a garage outside York. Are you now saying that my client is this Mr. Masefield?"

"I'm saying that it might be the case that your client has taken Mr. Masefield's identity," Banks went on.

"Have you any proof of this?" Bowen asked.

"The investigation is ongoing."

"In other words, you haven't?"

"This is ridiculous," said Whitaker. "I've already got a Jeep Cherokee. Why would I rent one?"

"To avoid exactly the kind of situation you're in," said Banks.

"But I'm in it anyway, aren't I?"

"There are several counts against you. First, you're a minor art dealer and one of the victims was a forger you supplied with paper. Secondly, you drive a Jeep Cherokee and such a car, or one very much like it, was spotted at the scene of the Thomas McMahon fire."

"But you've already found—" Bowen started.

Banks cut him off. "That doesn't mean Mr. Whitaker's Jeep was *never* there." He went on. "Add to this that you have no alibi for either murder, and that you lied to us in your previous interview, I'd say it adds up to a pretty strong case against you."

"Circumstantial," said Bowen. "You've no proof my client had ever heard of, let alone knew, Roland Gardiner; the car in the lay-by spotted near the scene has been identified; the accelerant used did not come from Mr. Whitaker's fuel tank; and there's no connection between Mr. Whitaker and the man whose credit card was used to rent the car. I'd say that adds up to nothing."

"Except," said Annie Cabbot, "that Mr. Whitaker's business has been reporting a loss for two years in a row now, yet he has recently made several rather expensive purchases. For cash." Annie opened a file folder. "To wit, a thirty-two-inch widescreen television and a home theater system, a state-of-the-art Dell desktop computer system, and he's had his house repainted and added a new conservatory. Do you deny these purchases?"

Whitaker looked at Annie. "I . . . er . . . no."

"Where did you get the money?"

"I won it. The horses."

"You don't bet on the horses."

"How do you know?"

"Do you think we overlook the bookies when we're investigating someone's financial status, Leslie?" Annie said. "Do you really think we're *that* stupid?"

"It was a gift. A friend gave it to me."

"Which friend?"

"He wants to remain anonymous. A tax thing. You understand."

Banks was shaking his head, and even Gareth Bowen looked anxious.

"Where did you get the money, Leslie?" Annie repeated.

"You don't have to answer," said Bowen.

"Right," said Banks, standing up. "I've had enough of this. Interview terminated at six thirty-five P.M. I'm going home and the suspect is going back to his cell."

"You can't—"

Bowen touched Whitaker's sleeve. "Yes, they can, Leslie," he said. "For twenty-four hours. But don't worry. I'll be working for you."

Whitaker glared at the solicitor. "Well," he said, "you've no idea how bloody confident that makes me feel."

*   *   *

Annie munched on a salad sandwich Winsome had brought her from the bakery across Market Street and started reading through the statements again. Andrew Hurst. Mark Siddons. Jack Mellor. Leslie Whitaker. Elaine Hough. There had to be something there to link Whitaker more closely to the killings, but if there was, she was damned if she could find it. It didn't help that she was having trouble concentrating, partly because she still couldn't stop herself wondering what Banks was up to, and partly because of something else, something she couldn't quite put her finger on. It would come, she knew, if she let her mind drift.

Phil had suggested that McMahon and Gardiner were involved in some art forgery scam, an ill-advised and ill-timed attempt to come up with a Turner watercolor that had been lost for over a century. Annie agreed. But if that was the case, her question remained: Who killed them, and why? Leslie Whitaker still seemed the most logical culprit, despite the Jeep Cherokee rented under William Mase-field's name. Perhaps that was a red herring, another issue entirely?

Annie ruled out the Siddons-Aspern angle, as she had done almost from the start, despite her mistrust of the boy. Tina's death was an unfortunate but irrelevant distraction; she had died because she was at the wrong place at the wrong time and in the wrong state of mind. In other words, she wasn't the intended victim. Thomas McMahon was. And in Gardiner's case, there was no question. He lived alone, and in isolation. The two knew each other from their time at Leeds Polytechnic, and they had also once been close to a mysterious character named Giles Moore, who had misled all his friends about being a university student.

Why? What possible reason could he have had, unless lying was an essential part of his character? If it was, it could easily be put to criminal purposes. This Giles Moore had claimed to be studying art history, and according to Elaine

Hough, had seemed to know plenty about the subject, whether he learned it at university or not. Was this, then, the person who had assumed William Masefield's identity when hiring cars for meetings with McMahon? Meetings about their scam. Because she was certain it was he, not McMahon or Gardiner, who was the brains behind it. And was this person Whitaker?

But again the question remained: Why had Moore-Masefield-Whitaker, or whoever he was, killed the goose that laid the golden eggs—McMahon? Unless. . . . unless, she thought, the Turners weren't part of his master plan, and he believed they would ruin everything and expose him. Phil had said that any forger worth his salt goes for lower-level stuff, artists who fetch a decent price but don't draw too much attention to themselves, like Turner or Van Gogh. And Phil should know. He was in the business. An expert. Dead artists were a better bet, too, especially if they'd been dead so long that nobody living had known them, because the provenance was easier to forge. So who was it?

Winsome walked by with a handful of papers she had been keying into HOLMES.

"Anything?" Annie asked.

"My fingertips are bleeding," said Winsome. "I don't know if that counts as anything." She dropped the papers on Annie's desk. "The list of parking tickets from the Askham Bar area. You'd think with all those vehicle numbers something would jump out, wouldn't you?"

"Son of Sam?"

"Like that, yes."

"Fancy a drink?"

Winsome grinned. "You're talking my language."

Annie glanced over the list of car numbers that had been given parking tickets in the area around Kirk's Garage, where "William Masefield" had rented his Jeep Cherokee and she saw one that immediately jumped out at her. It couldn't be right, she thought. It wasn't possible. She looked again. Maybe she'd remembered the numbers wrong. But she knew she hadn't. She never did.

Banks felt irritable when he got back to his cottage that evening. It was because of his argument with Annie, he knew. He didn't think he'd been too heavy-handed, so maybe she had simply overreacted. Love can make you feel that way sometimes. Was Annie in love with Keane? The thought didn't make Banks feel any better, so he poured himself a generous Laphroaig, cask strength, and put some Schubert string quartets on the CD player. Should he have told her about Helen? Probably not. What he should do, he realized, was talk to Keane again and suggest he tell Annie himself. After all, if it was such an open marriage, what had he got to hide? Annie wouldn't like it, would no doubt promptly end the relationship, but that was Keane's problem, not his.

He was trying to decide whether to get back to his Eric Ambler or watch a European cup match on TV when someone knocked on his door. Too late for traveling salesmen, not that there were many around these days, and a friend would most likely have rung first. Puzzled, he put his glass aside and answered it.

Banks was surprised, and more than a little put out, to see Phil Keane standing there, a smile on his face, a bottle clutched in his hand. He'd wanted to talk to Keane again, but not in his own home, and not now, when he was in need of solitude and relaxation, and the healing balm of Schubert. Still, sometimes you just had to take what you were offered when you were offered it.

"May I come in?" Keane asked.

Banks stood aside. Keane thrust the bottle toward him. "A little present," he said. "I heard you like a good single malt."

Banks looked at the label. Glenlivet. Not one of his favorites. "Thanks," he said, gesturing toward his glass. "I'll stick with this for now, if you don't mind." No matter how paranoid it seemed, he felt oddly disinclined to drink anything this man offered him until he knew once and for all that he was who and what he claimed to be. "Would you like some?" he asked. "It's an Islay, cask strength."

Keane took off his coat and laid it over the back of a chair, then he sat down in the armchair opposite Banks's sofa. "No, thanks," he said. "I don't like the peaty stuff, and cask strength is way too strong for me. I'm driving, after all." He tapped the bottle he'd brought. "I'll have a nip of this, though, if that's all right?"

"Fine with me." Banks brought a glass, topping up his own with Laphroaig while he was in the kitchen, and bringing the bottle with him. If he was going to have a heart-to-heart with Keane, he might need it.

"You know," said Keane, sipping the Glenlivet and relaxing into the armchair, "when it comes right down to it, we're a lot alike, you and me."

"How do you get that?" Banks asked.

Keane looked around the room, blue walls and a ceiling the color of ripe Brie, dimly lit by a shaded table lamp. "We both have a taste for the good things in life," he said. "Fine whiskey, Schubert, the English countryside. I wonder how you manage it all on a policeman's salary?"

"I do without the bad things in life."

Keane smiled. "I see. Very good. Anyway, however you work it, we have a lot in common. Beautiful women, too."

"I assume you mean Annie? Or Helen?"

"Annie told me about you and her. I didn't know I was poaching."

"You weren't."

"But you're not happy about it. I can see that. Are you going to tell her?"

"About Helen?"

"Yes. She told me about your little visit yesterday."

"Charming woman," Banks said.

"Are you?"

"Don't you think it would be better coming from you?"

"So you haven't told Annie yet?"

"No. I haven't told her anything. I've been trying to decide. Maybe you can help me."

"How?"

"Convince me you're not a lying, cheating bastard."

Keane laughed. "Well, I *am* a bastard, quite literally. I admit to that."

"You know what I mean."

"Look," Keane went on, "the relationship Helen and I have is more like that of friends. We're of use to one another. She doesn't mind if I have other women. Surely she told you that?"

"But you *are* married."

"Yes. We had to get married. I mean, she was an illegal immigrant. They'd have sent her back to Kosovo. I did it for her sake."

"That's big of you. You don't love her?"

"Love? What's that?"

"If you don't know, I can't explain it to you."

"It's not something I've ever experienced," Keane said, studying the whiskey in his glass. "All my life I've had to live by my wits, sink or swim. I haven't had time for love. Sure you won't have a drop of this?" He proffered the bottle.

Banks shook his head. He realized his glass was empty and poured a little more Laphroaig. He was already feeling its effects, he noticed when he moved, and decided to make this one his last, and to drink it slowly. "Anyway," he went on, "it's not a matter of whether Helen minds if you have other women or not; it's how *Annie* feels."

"Still her champion, are you? Her knight in shining armor?"

"Her friend." Banks felt as if he was slurring his words a bit now, but he hadn't drunk much more since he'd poured the third glass. There was also an irritating buzzing in his ears, and he was starting to feel really tired. He shook it off. Fatigue.

Keane's mobile played a tune.

"Aren't you going to answer it?" Banks asked.

"Probably work. Whoever it is, they can leave a message. Look, Alan, if it makes you feel any better, I'll explain the situation to Annie," said Keane. "She's broad-minded. I'm sure she'll understand."

"I wouldn't be too certain of that."

"Oh, why? Know something I don't?"

"I know Annie, and deep down she's a lot more traditional than you think. If she's got strong feelings for you, she's not going to play second fiddle to your wife, no matter how convenient the marriage, or how Platonic the relationship."

"Well, we'll just have to see, won't we?"

"When?"

"The next time I see her. I promise. How's the case going?"

Banks wasn't willing to talk about the case to Keane, even though he had assisted as a consultant on the art forgery side. He just shrugged. It felt as if he were hoisting the weight of the world on his shoulders. He took another sip of whiskey—the glass was heavy, too—and when he put it down on the arm of the sofa he felt himself sliding sideways, so he was lying on his side, and he couldn't raise himself to a sitting position again. He heard his own telephone ringing in the distance but couldn't for the life of him drag himself off the sofa to answer it.

"What about this identity parade you mentioned?" Keane said, his voice now sounding far away. "I've been looking forward to it."

Banks couldn't speak.

"It was very clever of you," Keane said. "You thought your witness would identify *me*, not Whitaker, didn't you?"

Banks still couldn't make his tongue move.

"What's the problem?" Keane asked. "A bit too much to drink?"

"Go now," Banks managed to say, though it probably sounded more like a grunt.

"I don't think so," said Keane. "You're just starting to feel the effects. See if you can stand up now. Just try it."

Banks tried. He couldn't move more than an inch or two. Too heavy.

"Eventually, you'll go to sleep," Keane said, his voice an echoing monotone now, like a hypnotist's. "And when you wake in the morning, you won't remember a thing. At least you wouldn't remember a thing if you *were* to wake up in the morning. But you won't be doing that. I'm really surprised you don't have more security in this place, you being a policeman and all. It was child's play to get in through the kitchen window just after dark and add a little flunitrazepam to your cask-strength malt. Plenty of strong taste to cover up any residual bitterness in the drug, too. Perfect. They call it the 'date rape' drug, you know, but don't worry, I'm not going to rape you."

"What's wrong, Guv?" Winsome asked, leaning over her.

"This number." Annie pointed. "I know it. It's Phil's BMW."

"Are you certain?"

"Yes. I don't know why. I just remember these things. There's no mistake. He got a parking ticket two streets away from Kirk's Garage on the seventeenth of September."

Winsome checked with her file. "That's one of the times Masefield rented the Jeep Cherokee," she said. "Look, it doesn't make sense. Maybe the bloke who wrote the ticket made a mistake?"

"Maybe," said Annie, as the thing that had been bothering her rose to the surface of her mind. Banks had said during their argument that morning that he had met Phil a *couple* of times, but later Phil had said he only met Banks *once*. The three of them had met the previous weekend, several days ago, but Banks had also said he hadn't seen Phil for a *couple* of days. Why was that? Had he been to see him since? And if so, what was it about? What were they keeping from her?

It might be nothing. An easy mistake to make. But now this. The BMW number. And it was true that Phil had only come onto the scene last summer, when both Roland Gardiner and Thomas McMahon had told people their fortunes were on the rise. Annie had only met him herself at the Turner reception, and he had phoned her a month or so later, determined not to take no for an answer.

Annie didn't like the direction in which her thoughts were turning, but even as she fought against the growing realization, she found herself remembering the night she was called away from her dinner at The Angel with Phil to the Jennings Field fire. Of course the accelerant didn't match the petrol from the Jeep Cherokee's fuel tank. Phil had been in his own car that evening, the BMW. He could hardly turn up for dinner in the rented Cherokee the police were all looking for, and he wouldn't have had time both to return it and to get cleaned up. Worth the risk for the alibi. Annie herself. A perfect alibi. And a source of information on the shape the investigation was taking. The horse's mouth. Horse's arse, more likely.

"There could be a simple explanation," Winsome suggested. "It was well before the murders, too. Maybe it's just coincidence?"

"I know that," said Annie, remembering that it was also around the time he had phoned and asked her out for the first time. "But we have to find out."

Her hand was shaking, but she dialed Phil's mobile number.

No answer. Just the voice mail.

She phoned Banks at home.

No answer. After a few rings she was patched through to the answering service. She didn't leave a message. She tried his mobile, too, but it was turned off.

That was odd. Banks had *said* he was going straight home. Of course, he could have gone somewhere else, or maybe he just wasn't answering the telephone. There were any number of explanations. But when Banks was on a case, especially one that seemed so near to its conclusion, he was always on call one way or another. She had never, in all the time they had worked together, been unable to get ahold of him at any hour of the day or night.

Annie felt confused and uneasy. She couldn't just sit there. This had to be settled one way or the other, and it had to be settled *now*.

"Winsome," she said. "Fancy a drive out in the country?"

Chapter 18

*I*t was a struggle just to cling to consciousness, Banks found. But the longer he stayed awake, the better his chances of staying alive. He could hardly move; his body felt like lead. He knew that he had to conserve whatever strength he had, if he had any, because when Keane set the fire, as he was certain to do, he was going to leave, and Banks might have just one slight opportunity to get out alive. *If* he was still conscious. If he could move. Neither McMahon nor Gardiner had got out alive, and the thought sapped his confidence, but he had to cling to what little hope he could dredge up.

"I'm doing this," Keane said, "because you're really the *only* one who suspects me. Annie doesn't. And she won't. I know you haven't shared your suspicions with her or anybody else. I'd have been able to tell from the tone of her voice. I'm not an official suspect. And I'm pretty certain I've covered my tracks well enough that with you out of the way, I'm in the clear."

Burgess, Banks found himself thinking, in his muddled, muddied way. *Dirty Dick Burgess*. Keane had no way of knowing that Banks had enlisted Burgess's help. He also knew that if anything happened to him, Dirty Dick would have a good idea who was behind it, and that he wouldn't rest until he'd tracked Keane down. But a fat lot of consolation that was to him if he was dead.

Banks felt himself slipping in and out of consciousness as Keane's words washed over him, some of them resonating, some not connecting at all. All he could think, if you could call it thinking, was that he was going to die soon. By fire. He remembered again the image of the little girl etched forever into his mind, sculpted by the fire into an attitude of prayer, kneeling by her bed, a charred angel. "Now I lay me down to sleep, I pray the Lord my soul to keep."

Banks heard the door open and felt a brief chill as the draft blew in. It revitalized him enough to make that one last attempt to move, but all he could manage was to roll off the sofa and bang his head on the sharp edge of the low coffee table. As he lay on the floor, the blood dripping in his eye, fast losing consciousness, he heard the door shut again and then the sloshing of petrol from the can. He could smell it now, the fumes overwhelming him, and all he wanted to do was hug the floor and fall asleep. The andante from "Death and the Maiden" was playing, and Banks's final thought was that this was the last piece of music he was ever going to hear.

Annie felt no real sense of urgency as they drove along the Dale to Banks's cottage. Only that she had to see Banks, to talk to him about what she had discovered and what she was beginning to suspect. But Winsome was behind the wheel, and whatever inner alarms were ringing in Annie seemed to have communicated themselves to her, and she was doing her best Damon Hill imitation.

She slowed down as they passed through Fortford. A few lights showed behind drawn curtains, and here and there Annie could make out the flickering of a television set. One bent old man was walking his collie toward the Rose and Crown. There was a long stretch of uninhabited road between there and Helmthorpe, nothing but dark hills silhouetted against the night sky, distant farm lights and the sleek shimmer of moonlight on the slow-flowing river.

There were a few people out on Helmthorpe High Street, mostly heading for folk night at the Dog and Gun, Annie guessed. The general store was still open and the fish-and-chip-shop queue was almost out into the street. Annie was still hungry, despite the salad sandwich. She thought of asking Winsome to stop. She didn't eat fish, but if the chips had been cooked in vegetable oil, then they might go down nicely with a pinch of salt and a dash of malt vinegar. But she held her hunger pangs at bay. Later.

Winsome turned sharp left, past the school, with only a slight screeching of rubber on Tarmac, and slipped smoothly down into second for the hill up to Gratly. Just before the village was a narrow laneway to the right, leading to Banks's cottage, and as they approached, a car came out and turned right, heading away from them. It wasn't Banks's Renault.

"That looks like Phil's car," Annie said.

"Are you sure?" Winsome asked.

"It can't be. He told me he was still in London."

Winsome stopped before turning into Banks's drive. "Shall I follow it?"

Annie thought for a moment. It would be good to know for certain. But if it was Phil, what on earth had he been doing visiting Banks? "No," she said. "No point in a car chase over the moors. Let's do what we came here for and see if Alan's in."

Winsome turned into Banks's drive, and ahead she and Annie could see the flames climbing up the curtains in the living room. *Christ, no!* Annie thought. No. Not after all this. She couldn't be too late. But they were flames, all right, and they were all over the front room.

"Call the fire brigade," Annie said, unbuckling her safety belt and jumping out before the car had even come to a full halt. "And tell them there's danger to life. A police officer's life." That might speed them up a bit, Annie thought. The local station was staffed by retained men, and it would take an extra five minutes for them to respond to their personal alerters and get to the station. Rural response time was eighteen minutes, and there'd be nothing left of the cottage by then.

Annie couldn't just stand there and watch the place burn. She knew that the worst thing you could do with a fire was open the door and supply more oxygen, but opening the door was the only chance she possibly had of getting Banks out alive. If he was still alive.

Annie pulled the wool blanket from the boot of the car. Luckily, the rain had left a few puddles in Banks's potholed drive, so she rolled it around quickly to soak it, then she wrapped it around herself, paying special attention to covering her hair and face.

Winsome had her car door open by now, mobile still in her hand. "What are you doing, Guv?" she yelled. "You can't go in there. You know you can't."

"Did you ring?"

"Yes. They're coming. But you—"

Annie went up to the door.

Locked.

"Guv!"

Rearing back, she kicked at the area around the lock. It took her three tries, and it hurt her foot like hell, but she succeeded in the end. The door flew open and the fire surged, as she had expected. She heard Winsome shouting behind her against the roar of the flames, but she couldn't stop now. She took a deep breath and rushed inside. She had only seconds, if that.

The smoke was thick and the petrol fumes seeped through the blanket she had wrapped around her mouth and nose. As soon as she was inside, Annie could feel the intense heat licking at her, the tongues of flame on her legs and ankles. She hadn't believed fire could make so much noise. She called out Banks's name, but she knew he wouldn't be able to answer. He would be drugged, just like the others. It was a small living room and Annie was fortunate to know her way around. She had been there often enough to know about the low coffee table between the sofa and armchairs, for example, so she wasn't going to trip over that.

The flames roared and smoke billowed. A painting fell off the wall and the glass smashed. Annie's eyes were stinging. She needed to breathe again. Her lungs felt as if they were exploding.

Then she saw him, just a leg, through the smoke down on the floor near the table. She rushed over to him. No time for subtleties, now, Annie, she told herself, as she threw the table over, grabbed Banks's legs with both hands and tugged. The limp body slid across the carpet. Annie's arms strained at her shoulder sockets.

Banks banged his head on the leg of the table as Annie pulled him around its edge. She couldn't see clearly, but she sensed that the open door was right behind her. All she had to do was keep on pulling him, moving backward. She thought she was going to keel over from the heat and smoke, but she kept dragging him, and soon she felt the chill of the outside piercing the blanket over her back. Almost there. A part of the ceiling fell down close to her, and flames singed her eyebrows. Annie couldn't go on. She felt her strength waning, her legs beginning to buckle under her. So close. Her vision shimmered. Her knees bent and she started toppling forward.

Then she felt herself bodily lifted and practically thrown across the lane. As she landed unceremoniously in the mud, she was able to rub her eyes and see Winsome finish the job, drag Banks's body out of the doorway to safety. Annie breathed the fresh air deeply and let herself fall back, hair and arms spread out in the mud, still wrapped in her damp blanket.

Winsome was outside the cottage now, and a few more feet would free Banks from the flames. His head bounced down the steps. Annie didn't know if he was dead or alive. She didn't even want to look at him for fear he would be grotesquely disfigured by the fire, or just lying with his eyes wide open.

Finally, Winsome set Banks down a few feet from the cottage and hurried over to Annie.

"You all right, Guv?"

"I'm fine," said Annie.

"That was a bloody stupid thing to do, if you don't mind my saying so."

"Alan . . . ?"

"I don't know, Guv. It took all I had to get the two of you out of there."

Annie flung off her blanket and took a deep breath. And another. The cold fresh air made her feel dizzy. The two of them went over and squatted beside Banks. His clothes were smoldering, so Annie put the damp blanket on him. His face was blackened by the smoke, and she really couldn't tell if he was badly burned or not. She didn't think so, hoped to God not.

Holding her own breath, Annie leaned forward and listened for his. She thought he was still breathing. She wished she had some oxygen, wished that the firefighters and the ambulances would hurry up. She didn't even know whether it would help to give him the kiss of life, or if it would only make things worse. *Live, you bastard, live*, she whispered, Winsome beside her, hand on her shoulder, and in the distance she heard the welcome sound of a fire engine.

It was the middle of the night when Annie finally got home from the hospital, exhausted beyond belief, leaving Detective Superintendent Gristhorpe to keep a bedside vigil. There was more paperwork to do, of course, always more paperwork, but that could wait until morning.

Banks wasn't out of danger yet. He still wasn't conscious, for a start. Annie told the doctor that he had most likely been drugged with Rohypnol, or something similar, probably mixed with alcohol. The flames had done *some* damage, mostly to his right leg and side, which had been closest in proximity to one of the seats of the fire, and to one side of his face. They were second-degree burns, with blistering, which would be extremely painful and cause some scarring. Banks's shallow breathing had prevented the high level of smoke inhalation that might have done more serious damage more quickly, and the bumps on his head from the table and steps were superficial.

Annie moved around like a zombie. She knew she should go to bed but she was certain she wouldn't be able to sleep. She needed a drink; she knew that much at least. She didn't often drink spirits, but tonight called for something stronger than wine, so she poured herself a stiff cognac and coughed when she first tasted the fiery liquor.

When she caught a glance of herself in the mirror, she was surprised at the muddy hair, sooty face and the frightened eyes that looked back at her. The doctor who had examined Annie and Winsome had been reluctant to let her go, but there was no real damage and no real reason to keep her. She had insisted she was fine. And she was, physically. Her muscles ached, and her foot was bruised and swollen from kicking the door in, but other than that she had been spared the ravages of fire and smoke. She had probably been in the burning cottage for no more than thirty seconds, she reckoned. Of course, the station officer had given her a bollocking for going in at all, but she sensed that he did so because it was expected of him, because it was his job, and that he secretly approved. He must have known, as Annie did, that there was nothing else she could have done to save Banks's life.

Phil. Phil Keane had done all this. He had enlisted his old polytechnic pals McMahon and Gardiner to help him with the art scam, and they had got together and turned on him. For that, he had killed them. It had to have happened that way. It was the only thing that made sense now. Philip Keane, not Leslie Whitaker, was Giles Moore. Philip Keane, not

Leslie Whitaker, had assumed William Masefield's identity, and perhaps even killed him, too.

Annie would never understand in a million years how she could have felt so close to someone capable of doing what he did, of thinking she was in love with him, of sharing his bed. The thought made her skin crawl.

She realized that Phil, or whatever his name really was, was one of those rare creatures indeed: part charming con man, part cold-blooded killer. Con men didn't usually kill, not unless they were cornered and could see no other way out. And that was what must have happened. The threat of exposure. Of ruin. Of prison.

Phil Keane made people feel special so that he could manipulate them. Chameleonlike, he metamorphosed from one identity to another, leaving chaos in his wake. And he did it for profit and self-protection. Annie shook her head in disbelief at her own blindness. How little we know even those closest to us, she thought. Phil Keane kept his true self locked in a dark, secret place nobody could ever penetrate. You saw what he wanted you to see, believed what he wanted you to believe.

And he made you feel special.

Annie tossed back the cognac and poured herself another large one. What the hell. She felt as if she had been raped all over again, and right now she didn't know if she hated Phil more for killing McMahon and Gardiner, and for almost killing Banks, or for deceiving her so completely. He had used her all along, of that she was certain. While he hadn't known he was going to kill McMahon and Gardiner, he had been in a criminal partnership with them by August, when he had pursued Annie, and he had no doubt thought it would be useful to get close to someone with inside knowledge of what the local police were thinking and doing.

And to cap it all, the bastard had got away.

There was a huge manhunt going on, even now, but Annie doubted they'd find him. After all, he *was* a chameleon. If it had been a television drama, of course, they would have hushed up Banks's survival, let the world believe he was dead, and Annie would have waited for Phil to get in touch, to come and offer his sympathy and condolences on the loss of her friend.

But the reporters were on the scene almost as quickly as the fire brigade. This was big news. Banks was a well-known local detective with a number of successful cases under his belt. In no time flat, the local news on TV and radio was informing the good citizens of Eastvale and, no doubt, the rest of England, that DCI Alan Banks had been pulled from his blazing cottage by his heroic DI Annie Cabbot and DC Winsome Jackman, and that he was now in Eastvale General Infirmary. There was no way Phil wouldn't hear that, and when he did, he would know the game was up. He would disappear and reemerge as yet someone else.

Annie smelled of smoke, and she wanted to go up and have a shower and get clean. She took her cognac to the bathroom with her. They would go over Keane's cottage with a fine-tooth comb, she thought. Meticulous and fastidious as Phil was—and she had no doubt that he would have cleaned up behind him—the odds were that they would find *something*. A hair. A fingerprint. *Something*.

She stripped her clothes off and dropped them in the laundry basket. Already, she noticed, her foot was turning yellow, black and blue. At least it wasn't broken. The doctor had told her that much.

Annie paused at the sink, gripping its edge, again looking at her black face. Like a soldier going into battle. She couldn't understand the expression in her eyes now, didn't know what she was feeling. Just before she turned to get in the hot shower, she noticed the toothbrush lying on the sink. It wasn't hers. She remembered when Phil had stayed a few nights ago she had given him it to use, and it looked as if he had. She knew she hadn't cleaned up the bathroom since.

Taking a plastic bag from the cupboard under the sink, she

dropped the toothbrush in it. You never knew. It could contain Phil Keane's DNA. Because one day they'd catch the bastard, and then they would need all the evidence they could get.

It was two days before Banks was allowed visitors at Eastvale General Infirmary, and Annie was the first to go in. Beyond the window, occasional shafts of sunlight shot through the cloud cover. Cut flowers brightened up the drab-olive room.

Banks lay propped up on his pillows, one side of his face bandaged and smeared with antibiotic salve, looking at the rain through his window. He looked spent, Annie thought, but there was still life in his eyes, life and something that had not been there before. She didn't know what it was.

He had lost everything. Banks's cottage didn't exist anymore. She had seen it with her own eyes reduced by fire to nothing more than a roofless shell. Everything he owned had gone up in flames: his CDs, clothes, furniture, stereo, all his memorabilia, family photographs, papers, letters, the lot. He had nothing left except his car and whatever personal effects he kept in his office. Did he know this? Surely someone must have told him.

"How are you doing?" she asked, laying her hand on his bare forearm, near the spot where the needle rested.

"Can't complain," Banks said. "If I did, no one would listen."

"Are they treating you well?"

"Fair to middling. Mostly I'm bored. Did you—"

Annie passed him the hip flask. "It's not Laphroaig," she said.

"Good," said Banks, slipping it in the drawer. "I'm not sure I could stomach that stuff again."

"What has the doctor said?"

"I should heal up okay," Banks said. "But there might be

some scarring. We'll have to wait and see. At least the headache's gone. Worst I ever had."

"Pain?"

"Pretty bad, but they keep me dosed up. Ever burned your finger?"

Annie nodded.

"Well, multiply the pain by a few thousand and you'll have some idea. Thing is, with second-degree burns the nerve endings stay intact. That's why it hurts. I didn't know that. The hair follicles and sweat glands, too. It's only the upper layers of skin that are burned. You know what the worst thing is, though?"

"What?"

"The memory loss. I can't remember a bloody thing, from the moment I answered the door to the moment I woke up here. Except for the taste of the whiskey. The doctor says it might come back or it might not. Which is a pretty bloody useless thing to say, if you ask me."

"Tracy's been by a couple of times," Annie said, "and she'll be back. Brian rang. He's in Amsterdam with the band. Wants to know if you need him."

"I shouldn't think so," said Banks. "I'll be home in a day or so."

Christ, thought Annie, the poor sod. He *didn't* know. "Alan," she said. "Look, I wouldn't . . . you know . . . the cottage, I mean. The fire caused quite a lot of damage."

Banks looked at her as if she was confirming what he already suspected, and nodded. "Well, I'll be out of *here*, at any rate," he said.

Annie handed him a gift-wrapped package. "Everyone in the squad room put together for this."

Banks opened it and inside found a new personal CD player and a copy of Mozart's *Don Giovanni*.

"We didn't know what you'd want," Annie said. "It was Kev's idea. I think it's the only opera he's ever heard of. There's batteries already in it."

"It's fine," said Banks. "Thank everyone for me."

"You can do it yourself soon."

Banks turned the CD player over in his hands for a few moments and looked away, as if the emotion were too much. "Have you caught him yet?" he asked.

"No," said Annie. "Not yet. But we will. It's just a matter of time."

"Tell me what you've found out."

Annie sat back in her chair. "Quite a bit, actually," she said. "Greater Manchester Police found his BMW parked at the airport, which means he could have gone anywhere. We're pursuing inquiries with the major airlines and at the railway stations, but nothing yet. And the cottage hadn't been in his family for generations. It was leased from a couple who live in south London. We've got fingerprints and DNA, but there are no matches with anything on record yet."

"So he's clean?"

"Not quite," said Annie. "Spectral analysis matched the petrol in the BMW's fuel tank with that used at the Gardiner scene and . . ."

"And?"

"And at your cottage."

"So he used his own car to visit Gardiner, too?"

"Had to," Annie said, looking away. "He was having dinner with me at The Angel when the fire started."

Banks said nothing for a moment. "Anything else?" he asked finally.

"His prints match a partial the SOCOs found on the rented Jeep Cherokee, which confirms what we already suspected."

"That the killer was using Masefield's identity?"

"Yes. The accountants digging into Masefield's investments have discovered that he was dealing with someone called Ian Lang of Olympus Holdings, registered in the British Virgin Islands, but they're not having a lot of luck tracing Mr. Lang or his company."

"They wouldn't have, would they?" said Banks. "Any more on Masefield?"

"All we know is that he was at university in Leeds at the right time, so I assume 'Giles Moore,' if that's who we're looking for, must have known him somehow and kept in touch. There's every chance that Keane had something to do with whatever lost Masefield all his money, and that he killed him. But we can't know for sure. Maybe it was just opportune. Maybe Masefield did commit suicide—everyone said he was depressed and drinking too much—and Keane found him dead, stole his identity and started the fire. But one way or another, he was involved in the death."

"Yes," said Banks. "And it would have been easy for him to pass himself off as Masefield if the two of them had a passing resemblance. It's amazing what you can do with a pair of glasses, a different hairstyle or coloring, maybe a slight stoop and a little paunch."

"Anyway," Annie went on, "I talked to Elaine Hough again, and she reluctantly dug out a couple of old letters Giles Moore had written to her. She said she hadn't wanted anyone else to read them. No detectable prints, unfortunately, but we do have samples of Keane's handwriting, and our expert cautiously admits they might match. But they're years apart, so it's hard to be certain. Nothing that would stand up in court, at any rate."

"It's a start," said Banks. "Can you show her Keane's picture?"

"We don't have a picture," Annie said. "Another problem is that we can't seem to dig up any background on Giles Moore. He definitely existed for Elaine Hough, and for McMahon, Gardiner and Masefield, and whoever else he hung around with in Leeds, but outside that, we have no record of him. You do realize we might never find out?"

"Someone like him," Banks said, "is bound to be clever. Keane and Moore are probably only two of his identities.

Maybe he's Ian Lang, too. God knows who he is now, or where, but if I read him right, he'd have an escape route—and a new identity—all set up for an eventuality like this. I'll bet he's overseas already. He's been at this all his life, Annie. Conning people, stealing identities. Maybe this is the first time he's killed, maybe not. But he's been at the game for a long time. Look how he conned *us*."

Annie produced a cheap pocket-sized notebook bound in stiff cardboard covers and tapped it with her forefinger. "We found this at the cottage," she said. "One of the SOCOs discovered a false ceiling in the wardrobe. The measurements didn't agree. In it we found the notebook, a passport in the name of Ewan Collins, and about twenty thousand quid in fives and tens."

"So he didn't have time to get back there and pick them up," said Banks. "Which means maybe he doesn't have a passport—not one he can use, at any rate."

"Which means he may well be still in the country."

Banks looked at the notebook. "What's that?" he asked.

"Roland Gardiner's journal. It looks as if he started keeping it when Keane first came to visit, and it stops on the evening of his death. It's quite touching, really. Elaine Hough told us Gardiner fancied himself as a bit of a writer when he was at the Poly."

"Does it tell us anything?"

"Not really," Annie said. "It's more of a personal, poetic record than anything else. Gardiner was taken in by the excitement and romance Keane offered. It does help explain why they had to die, though. It was mostly McMahon's fault. Not only did he get greedy, he also intended to try to pass off the Turner as genuine. According to Gardiner, he was embittered. He wanted revenge on the art world for failing to recognize his great talent, and he thought the best way to get it was to put one over on them. A big one."

"And Keane?"

"Ever the pragmatist," said Annie. "McMahon tried to blackmail him into helping authenticate the Turner. Said if he didn't he'd pass on the names of all the fakes he'd channeled through Keane to the press, the police, the galleries, the dealers. It would have ruined Keane, and he'd probably have ended up in jail. McMahon could have claimed that all he did was paint them, not try to pass them off as genuine. Keane obviously realized what trouble McMahon could cause him, so the artist became more of a liability than an asset. And Gardiner was a loose end."

"Why did Keane hang on to the notebook? Why not burn it?"

"Vanity," said Annie. "It never names him, but it's all about him."

"What was Gardiner's role?"

"Forger of provenance, letters, old catalogs, bills of sale. That sort of thing. Go-between for nonexistent owners, dealers and auction houses. McMahon could dash off the paintings, but that's as far as his contribution went."

"As we thought," said Banks.

"Yes." Annie paused. "We've also talked to Keane's wife, who was less than useful, and we've been having a close look at his business. It was clever," Annie went on. "Very clever. He chose lesser-known artists. Eighteenth-century English landscape painters. Dutch minimalists. Minor Impressionists. And McMahon churned them out in quantity. Sketches. Small watercolors. Nothing big enough to draw too much attention to itself. Ten thousand quid here, fifty thousand there, twenty, five. It all adds up to a tidy sum."

"Christ," said Banks. "Keane *told* us all this, you know. He told us everything we needed to know. He was toying with us. We just weren't listening."

Annie said nothing.

"Anything more from Whitaker?"

"I've talked to him again. He admitted supplying the paper and canvas for a small cut, most likely from McMahon's take. He knows nothing about the real magnitude of what was going on, knew nothing about Keane, but he *did* know why McMahon wanted the materials and what he did with them. He also confirmed what Gardiner wrote, that McMahon was bitter and bragged about 'showing them all.'"

"Are we charging Whitaker?"

"What with? Being an arsehole?"

Banks managed a weak smile, but Annie could tell it hurt. "Have you seen or heard anything of Mark Siddons?" he asked.

"No," said Annie. "We've no unfinished business with him, have we?"

"No," said Banks. "I was just wondering, that's all." He glanced toward the window again, and Annie could see he was looking at the scaffolding around the church tower.

Annie tapped the notebook again. "It really is odd," she said, "the way Gardiner seemed to look up to Keane, hero-worship him, as if their scam was all that made life bearable, and when it was over . . ." She dropped the notebook on the bedsheet. "Well, you can read it for yourself."

"Keane made him feel special?" Banks suggested.

"Yes. He made him feel special." Annie leaned forward. "Look, Alan . . ."

Banks touched her hand. "Later," he said.

Then the door opened and Michelle Hart popped her head in. "Not interrupting anything, am I?"

Banks looked over at her. "Well," he said, "you're a sight for sore eyes."

Annie left the room.

18th JANUARY

*H*e'll be coming for me soon. Today, tomorrow, or the next day. I can feel his dark mind reaching out to me. It doesn't matter. I'm tired now. I'm the cancer patient who lives longer than the doctors have given him, the sad father who outlives all his children, the condemned man who receives a stay of execution. But now it's time. Soon he will come.

In my weak and foolish moments, I dream we go away together, start anew, embark on another escapade, but in the cold, dark reality of my caravan, I know he likes to travel light, and I know he doesn't like loose ends. I don't think he enjoys killing. Yes, there is a coldness at the core of his being, and I doubt that he's overly troubled by conscience. But I don't think he actually enjoys it. My murder will be dispassionate, calculated, a necessary end.

The irony is, of course, that I would never betray him. I'm not like Tommy, the fool, who let his greed and his pride ruin everything. Why did he have to spoil it all? These past few months have been a great adventure, full of camaraderie, romance and the thrill of the game, but Tommy had to let his ego ruin it for everyone. So we weren't getting enough money. I could have lived with that easily, so long as he still came to visit me in the caravan and we had our long talks into the night with the rain tapping against my flimsy roof.

I can hear him coming up the rickety steps. Now he's knocking at my door. When I open it, he will be standing there with a smile on his face and a bottle in his hand. Quick. I must stop now. Another drink, another pill, Beethoven's *Pastorale*. We have come full circle.

Acknowledgments

*F*irst of all, I would like to give special thanks to Fire Investigation Officer Terry Calpin and to the firefighters of Pontefract Station, White Watch: Sub Officer Peter Lavine, Leading Firefighter Barry Collinson, and Firefighters Gary Dixon, Andy Rees, Richard Beaumont, Dave Newsome and Arran Huskins. Thanks for your time, and an extra thank-you to Gary for setting it all up. Also for their professional help, I would like to thank Detective Inspector Claire Stevens of the Thames Valley Police and Commander Philip Gormley of the Metropolitan Police. As usual, any technical mistakes are entirely my own and are usually made for the benefit of the story.

Thanks also to those who read and commented on the manuscript: Dominick Abel, Dinah Forbes, Trish Grader, Sheila Halladay, Maria Rejt and Sarah Turner. Your help is invaluable when I can't see the woods for the trees.

Coming in 2005

STRANGE AFFAIR

by Peter Robinson

Was she being followed? It was hard to tell at that time of night on the motorway. There was plenty of traffic, lorries for the most part, and people driving home from the pub just a little too carefully, red BMWs coasting up the fast lane, doing a hundred or more, businessmen in a hurry to get home from late meetings. She was beyond Newport Pagnell now, and the muggy night air blurred the red tail lights of the cars ahead and the oncoming headlights across the divide. She began to feel nervous as she checked her rear-view mirror and saw that the dark Mondeo was still behind her.

She pulled over to the outside lane and slowed down. The Mondeo overtook her. It was too dark to glimpse faces, but she thought there was just one person in the front and another in the back. It didn't have a taxi light on top, so she guessed it was probably a private hire car. Some rich git being ferried to a nightclub in Leeds, most likely. She overtook the Mondeo a little farther up the motorway and didn't give it a second glance. The late night radio was playing Old Blue Eyes singing "Summer Wind." Her kind of music, no matter how old-fashioned people told her it was. Talent and good music never went out of fashion as far as she was concerned.

When she got to the Watford Gap rest stop, she realized she felt tired and hungry, and she still had a long way to go,

so she decided to stop for a short break. She didn't even notice the Mondeo pull in two cars behind her. A few seedy-
looking people hung around the entrance; a couple of kids
who didn't look old enough to drive stood smoking and playing the machines, giving her the eye as she walked past, staring at her breasts.

She went first to the ladies' room, then to the café, where
she bought a ham and tomato sandwich and sat alone to eat,
washing it down with a Diet Coke. At the table opposite, a
man with a long face and dandruff on the collar of his dark
jacket gave her the eye over the top of his glasses, pretending
to read his newspaper and eat a sausage roll.

Was he just a garden variety perv, or was there something
more sinister in his interest? she wondered. In the end, she decided he was just a perv. Sometimes it seemed as if the world
was full of them, that she could hardly walk down the street or
go for a drink on her own without some sad pillock who
thought he was God's gift eyeing her up, coming over and laying a line on her. Still, she told herself, what else could you
expect at this time of the night in a motorway service station?
A couple of other men came in and went to the counter, but
they looked respectable enough, burly, like security guards.

She finished half the sandwich, dumped the rest and got
her travel mug filled with coffee for the road. When she
walked back to her car she made sure that there were people
around—a family with two young kids up way past their bedtime, noisy and hyperactive—and that no one was following
her.

The tank was only a quarter full, so she filled it up at the
petrol station, using her credit card right there, at the pump.
While it filled, she took out her mobile and dialed. Not home.
Dammit. Where could he be? When the answering machine
came on, she left a brief message, just to let him know she
was doing what he'd asked her to, then she put the phone
away. The perv from the café pulled in at the pump opposite,

but she ignored him, and he didn't bother her, just stared. She could see the night manager in his office, watching through the window, and that made her feel more safe.

Tank full, she turned on to the entrance ramp and slid in between two trucks. It was hot in the car, so she opened both windows and enjoyed the play of breeze they created. It helped keep her awake, along with the hot black coffee. The clock on the dashboard said 11:31 P.M. Only about two and a half hours to go, then it would be all over. She didn't notice the dark Mondeo on her tail again.

Penny Cartwright was singing Richard Thompson's "Strange Affair" when Banks walked into The Dog and Gun, her low, husky voice milking the song's stark melancholy for all it was worth. Banks stood by the door, transfixed. *Penny Cartwright*. He hadn't seen her in over ten years, though he had thought of her often, even seen her name in *Mojo* and *Q* magazine from time to time. The years had been kind. Her figure still looked good in blue jeans and a tight white T-shirt tucked in at the waist. The long, raven's-wing hair he remembered was now cut short, but looked just as glossy as ever in the stage lights, with a few threads of gray here and there. She looked a little more gaunt than before, a little more sad around the eyes, perhaps, but it suited her, and Banks liked the contrast between her pale skin and dark hair.

When the song ended, Banks took advantage of the applause to walk over to the bar, order a pint and light a cigarette. He wasn't particularly happy with himself for having started smoking again after six months or more on the wagon, but there it was. He tried to avoid smoking in the flat, and he would stop again as soon as he'd got himself back together. But for the moment, it was a crutch, an old friend come back to visit during a time of need.

There wasn't a seat left in the entire lounge. Banks could

feel the sweat prickling on his temples and at the back of his neck. He leaned against the bar and let her voice transport him as she launched into "Blackwater Side." She had two accompanists, one on guitar and the other on stand-up bass, and they wove a dense tapestry of sound against which her lyric lines soared.

The next round of applause marked the end of the set, and she walked through the crowd, which parted like the Red Sea for her, smiling and nodding hello as she went, and stood next to him at the bar. She lit a cigarette, inhaled, made a circle of her mouth and blew out a smoke ring toward the lights.

"That was an excellent set," Banks said.

"Thanks," she said without turning to face him. "Gin and tonic, please, Kath," she said to the barmaid. "Make it a large one."

Banks could tell by her clipped tone that she thought he was just another besotted fan, maybe a weirdo, a possible stalker, and she'd move away as soon as she got her drink. "You don't remember me, do you?" he asked.

She sighed and turned to look at him, ready to deliver the final putdown. Then he saw recognition slowly dawn on her, and she seemed flustered, embarrassed, and unsure what to say. "Oh. . . . Yes. It's Detective Chief Inspector Burke, isn't it?" she managed finally. "Or have you been promoted?"

"Afraid not," he said. "And it's Banks, but Alan will do. It's been a long time."

"Yes. What happened to you?" She raised a hand as if to touch his cheek but stopped short.

Banks touched it himself, felt the familiar small patch of rough, ribbed skin. "Just a little accident," he said.

Penny got her gin and tonic and raised it to Banks, who clinked it gently with his pint glass. "Slainte," he said.

"Slainte."

"I didn't know you were back in Helmthorpe."

"Well, nobody put on a major advertising campaign."

Banks looked around the dim lounge. "I don't know. You seem to have a devoted following."

"Word of mouth, mostly. What brought you here?"

"I heard the music as I was passing," Banks said. "Recognized your voice. What have you been up to lately?"

A hint of mischief came into her eyes. "Now that would be a very long story indeed, and I'm not sure it would be any of your business."

"Maybe you could tell me over dinner some evening?"

Penny faced him and frowned, her brows knit together, searching him with those sharp blue eyes, and before she spoke, she gave a little shake of her head. "I can't possibly do that," she whispered.

"Why not? It's only a dinner invitation."

She was backing away from him as she spoke. "I just can't, that's all. How can you even ask me?"

"Look, if you're worried about being seen with a married man, that ended a couple of years back. I'm divorced now."

Penny looked at him as if he'd missed the point by a hundred miles, shook her head and melted back into the crowd. Banks felt perplexed. He couldn't interpret the signals, decode the look of absolute horror he thought he'd seen on her face at the idea of dinner with him. He wasn't that repulsive, even with the new scar. A simple dinner invitation. What the hell was wrong with her?

Banks gulped down the rest of his pint and headed for the door as Penny took the stage again, and he caught her eyes briefly across the crowded room. Her expression was one of puzzlement, mostly, and of confusion. She had clearly been unsettled by his request. Well, he thought, as he turned his back and left, face burning, at least she didn't still look so horrified.

The night was dark now, the sky moonless but filled with stars, and Helmthorpe High Street was deserted, the streetlights smudgy in the haze. Banks heard Penny start up again back inside The Dog and Gun. Another Richard Thompson song: "Never Again." The haunting melody and desolate lyrics drifted after him across the street, fading slowly as he walked down the cobbled snicket past the old bookshop, through the graveyard and on to the footpath that would take him home, or to what passed for home these days.

The air smelled of manure and warm hay. To his right was a drystone wall beside the graveyard, and to his left a slope, terraced with lynchets, led down, step by step, to Gratly Beck, which he could hear below him. The narrow path had no lights, but Banks knew every inch of it by heart. The worst that could happen was that he might step into a pile of sheep shit. Close by he could hear the high-pitched whining of winged insects.

As he walked, he continued to think about Penny Cartwright's mysterious reaction to his dinner invitation. She always had been a strange one, he remembered, always a bit sharp with her tongue and too ready with the sarcasm. But this had been different, not sarcasm, not sharp, but . . . horror, shock, repulsion. Was it because of their age difference? He had just turned fifty, after all, and Penny was about ten years younger. But even that didn't explain the intensity of her reaction. She could have just smiled and said she was washing her hair. Banks liked to think he would have got the message.

The path ended at a double-barreled stile about halfway up Gratly Hill. Banks slipped through sideways and walked past the new houses to the cluster of old cottages over the bridge. Since his own house was at the mercy of the builders, he had been renting a flat in one of the holiday properties on the lane to the left.

The locals had been good to him, as it turned out, and he'd got a fairly spacious one-bedroom flat, upper floor, with private entrance, for a very decent rent. The irony was, he realized, that it used to be the Steadman house, long ago converted into holiday flats, and it was during the Steadman case that he had first met Penny Cartwright.

Banks's living-room window had a magnificent view over the dale, north past Helmthorpe, folded in the valley bottom, up to the rich green fields, dotted with sheep, and the sere, pale grass of the higher pastures, then the bare limestone outcrop of Crow Scar and the wild moors beyond. But his bedroom window looked out to the west over a small disused Sandemanian graveyard and its tiny chapel. Some of the tombstones, so old that you could scarcely read the names anymore, leaned against the wall of the house.

The Sandemanian sect, Banks had read somewhere, had been founded in the eighteenth century, separating itself from the Scottish Presbyterian Church. Its members took holy communion, embraced communal property ownership, practiced vegetarianism, and engaged in "love feasts," which Banks thought made them sound rather like eighteenth-century hippies.

Banks was a little pissed, he realized as he fiddled with his key in the downstairs lock. The Dog and Gun hadn't been his first port of call that evening. First he'd had dinner alone in The Hare and Hounds, then a couple of pints in The Bridge. Still, what the hell, he was on holiday for another week, and he wasn't driving. Maybe he'd even have a glass of wine or two. He was still off the whiskey, especially Laphroaig. Its distinctive taste was the only thing he could remember about the night his life nearly ended, and even at a distance, the smell made him nauseated.

Could the drinking have been what put Penny off? he wondered. Had she thought he was drunk when he asked her to dinner? But Banks doubted it. He didn't slur his words or wobble when he walked. There was nothing in his manner that suggested he'd had too much. No, it had to be something else.

He finally opened the door, walked up the stairs, and unlocked the inside door, then switched on the hall light. The place felt hot and stuffy, so he went into the living room and opened the window, which didn't help much. After he had poured himself a healthy glass of Aussie Shiraz, he walked over to the telephone. A red light was flashing, indicating messages on the answering service.

As it turned out, there was only one message, and a surprising one at that: his brother Roy. Banks wasn't even aware that Roy knew his telephone number, and he was also certain that the card and flowers he had received from his brother in the hospital had come, in fact, from his mother.

"Alan . . . shit . . . you're not there and I don't have your mobile number. If you've got one, that is. You never were much of a one for technology, I remember. Anyway, look, this is fairly important, at least I think it might be a bit urgent. If I'm right, I could be in serious trouble. I've been . . . Look, damn it, I can't really talk about this to your answering service. I'll try again later, but can you ring me back as soon as possible? I'm sending someone up. Take care of her. She'll explain what she can, but she doesn't know everything. I really need to talk to you. Please." Banks heard a buzzing noise in the background. "Someone's at the door. I'll have to go now. Please call." Roy left his number, and that was that.

Puzzled, Banks listened to the message again. He was going to listen a third time, but he realized there was no point. He hated it when people in movies kept playing the same message over and over again, and how they always seemed to manage to get the tape in exactly the right spot every time. Instead, he replaced the receiver and took a sip of wine. He'd heard all he needed. Roy sounded worried, and perhaps a little scared. The call was timed by his answering service at 10:03 P.M., about an hour ago, when Banks had been listening to Penny Cartwright in The Dog and Gun.

Roy's phone rang several times before an answering machine picked up: Roy's voice in a curt, no-nonsense invitation to leave a message. Banks did so, said he'd try again later, and hung up. There was nothing else he could do. If Roy had a mobile, which he almost certainly did, Banks didn't have the number. He could find out—call his parents for example—but it was too late to do that tonight without waking them. Maybe Roy would ring back later, as he had said he would. And then there was this mysterious person he was sending. Who was she? When would she arrive?

Often, Banks would spend an hour or so perched on the window seat in his bedroom looking down on the graveyard, especially on moonlit nights. He didn't know what he was looking for—a ghost perhaps—but the utter stillness of the tombstones and the wind soughing through the long grass seemed to give him some sort of feeling of tranquillity. But not tonight. No moon. No breeze.

The baby downstairs started crying, the way it did every night around this time. Banks turned on the TV. There wasn't much to choose from: films, a chat show, or news. He picked *The Spy Who Came in from the Cold*, which had started half an hour ago. That didn't matter; he'd seen it many times before, and he knew the plot by heart. But he couldn't concentrate. As he watched Richard Burton's edgy, intense performance and tried to pick up the threads, he found his mind wandering back to Penny Cartwright and to Roy, felt himself waiting for the phone to ring, for a knock on the door. There was nothing he could do about any of it right now, but he resolved to confront Penny Cartwright again as soon as possible, and if he couldn't get in touch with Roy by morning, he would head down to London himself and find out just what the hell was going on.